TIN QUEEN

Courtney
Live to ride! Wander free.
Devney Perry

USA TODAY BESTSELLING AUTHOR
DEVNEY PERRY

TIN QUEEN

Editing & Proofreading:

Elizabeth Nover, Razor Sharp Editing

www.razorsharpediting.com

Julie Deaton, Deaton Author Services

www.facebook.com/jdproofs

Karen Lawson, The Proof is in the Reading

Judy Zweifel, Judy's Proofreading

www.judysproofreading.com

Cover:

Hang Le

http://www.byhangle.com

OTHER TITLES

Jamison Valley Series

The Coppersmith Farmhouse

The Clover Chapel

The Lucky Heart

The Outpost

The Bitterroot Inn

The Candle Palace

Maysen Jar Series

The Birthday List

Letters to Molly

Lark Cove Series

Tattered

Timid

Tragic

Tinsel

Tin Gypsy Series

Gypsy King

Riven Knight

Stone Princess

Noble Prince

Fallen Jester

Tin Queen

Runaway Series

Runaway Road

Wild Highway

Quarter Miles

Forsaken Trail

Dotted Lines

The Edens Series

Christmas in Quincy - Prequel

Indigo Ridge

Calamity Montana Series

Writing as Willa Nash

The Bribe

The Bluff

The Brazen

CONTENTS

PROLOGUE

"Nova, don't touch that." Shelby smacked my hand before my fingertips could skim over the gleaming chrome on Daddy's motorcycle.

"What?" I shot her a glare and touched the metal anyway, feeling its warmth from the afternoon sun.

She rolled her eyes as the screen door smacked closed and Dad walked out of the house with TJ on his hip.

TJ was eight and too big to be carried around. I was ten and Mom said I was growing like a weed. But no matter how big TJ or I got, Daddy still picked us up. Except Shelby. She was thirteen and I think Daddy would have tried but she didn't like it anymore.

She didn't like *him* anymore.

Mom sniffled as she followed Dad down the driveway and my heart sank.

She always cried when he left. We all did.

Except Shelby.

"Be good for your mom." Dad set TJ on his bare feet,

then knelt in front of my brother and leaned in, whispering something in his ear.

TJ nodded and puffed up his chest. "Yes, sir."

"Good boy." Dad stood and ruffled TJ's dark hair, then walked over to Shelby and me standing beside his bike. He held out his arms to my sister. "Got a hug goodbye?"

She shot him a glare.

"Come on, Shelby. Don't be like that."

"My *name* is May." She took a step away from him and crossed her arms.

I rolled my eyes. Daddy called us by our middle names but lately she only wanted to go by her first name, May. Even when I called her Shelby, she'd get mad at me and pinch my arm.

My sister was a brat. That's what TJ and I called her.

Daddy rubbed at the whiskers on his face, the hair scratching against his palm. Then he took one long step to Shelby and pulled her into a hug. She might say she didn't want one, but it wasn't like she tried to push him away either.

He let her go and came to me, arms wide open.

I fell into his embrace, burying my face in his shirt and squeezing my eyes shut as I hugged his waist as tight as I could. Maybe if I hugged him hard enough, he'd stay a little longer. "Do you have to go already? You just got here."

We hadn't seen him in three months and this visit had only been two days. Normally he would stay for a week. Sometimes ten days. Those were the best visits. Those were the days when Mom smiled and TJ laughed and I hugged Dad every chance I got.

"Yeah, Nova. I gotta go."

Mom would be sad now. TJ would pout for the rest of the

2

day and probably most of tomorrow. Shelby would be grumpy and lock herself in her room. And I'd go back to waiting, marking my calendar and wondering when we'd see him again.

I hugged him tighter. His black leather cut was soft against my skin. He wore it everywhere, other than in the house. Beneath the fabric, I felt the straps of his holster and the sharp metal of the gun tucked against his ribs.

Daddy always carried a gun so that if the bad guys came, he could keep us safe.

"When are you coming back?" I asked.

"I don't know. Soon, I hope."

Soon was never soon enough.

He peeled my arms away and knelt in front of me like he had with TJ. "Help your mom with the chores."

"Okay."

"Study hard."

I nodded. "I will."

"Remember to keep your secrets. Can I count on you?"

"Yes." He could always count on me.

"Do you trust me?"

"Yes."

"That's my good girl." He kissed my cheek, his goatee tickling my chin, then he stood and took a pair of sunglasses from the collar of his shirt. He slid them over his dark eyes and turned, walking to Mom.

She fell into him, much like I had, holding tight like maybe she could make him stay.

He whispered something to her that made her arms fall away. Then, like TJ, she nodded and lifted her chin.

She wouldn't cry until he was gone because Daddy didn't like weakness.

He took a step away from her, but Mom's hand shot out, brushing his elbow.

"We love you, Tucker."

"I love you too. Be careful."

"Always." She went to TJ, pulling him against her leg.

Daddy climbed on his bike, his legs straddling the machine. He looked to Shelby, waiting for something, but she kept her arms crossed. She stared at a mailbox, at the blocky white painted letters on its side that read *JOHNSON*.

She'd painted our last name on it five days ago. The mailman knew exactly who lived here, we'd lived here our entire lives, so it wasn't like the name was necessary. Shelby wouldn't admit it, but I think she'd done that to irritate Daddy because Johnson wasn't his last name.

It wasn't really ours either.

It was Talbot. Legally, it was Johnson, but in our hearts, we were Talbots—that's how Mom had explained it.

With one last look at Mom, Dad started the engine of his Harley and the roar forced me back a step, the rumble vibrating the sidewalk beneath my feet. Then he was gone, a streak of black down the road that disappeared too soon around the corner.

We all stood there until the echo from his bike disappeared.

Mom didn't say a word as she turned and retreated into the house, the screen door smacking closed.

"Great, now she's going to cry all day." Shelby kicked at a pebble on the sidewalk. "I wish he'd just stop coming back."

"Shelby," I hissed.

"May."

"Whatever," I muttered. "Why are you so mean to Daddy?"

"He doesn't love us, June."

"That's not my name."

"Yeah, it is. Sooner or later, you're going to need to get used to it."

"Shut up, Shelby."

"May," she corrected again.

"Daddy does too love us."

"He loves his club more."

I opened my mouth to argue but stopped because she was right. Daddy loved the Arrowhead Warriors.

But was that such a bad thing? That club was the reason we had such a nice house. It was the reason we always had new shoes and new clothes and Mom didn't have to work. Being in his club was his job. It wasn't that different from our neighbor three houses down whose dad was in the Army and he was gone all the time too.

"I hate his club," Shelby spat.

"Well, I don't."

TJ marched over and slipped his hand into mine. "I don't either."

"Because you two are stupid." Shelby huffed and before I could think of a comeback, she walked away.

Her best friend lived two blocks away. She'd go there and jump on their trampoline and they'd talk about boys. Shelby would pretend she didn't care that Dad was gone and that it didn't hurt her when he left.

Shelby was the best at pretending. But she'd had more years to practice.

"What did Daddy say to you?" I asked TJ when Shelby was far enough away she wouldn't hear.

5

"It's a secret."

Daddy always told TJ the secrets, and TJ never told me what they were. It was because TJ was a boy.

"I'll give you five bucks if you tell me."

TJ pondered it for a minute, then he shook his head. "Nope."

Figures. Why couldn't I know the secrets? I was good at keeping them. We all were.

Because our lives depended on it. That's what Dad said.

CHAPTER ONE

NOVA

"Hey," I answered my sister's call.

"Hey, where are you?"

Prison. "Just running some errands over lunch," I lied as I crossed the parking lot for my car. Behind me, the state penitentiary loomed behind a twelve-foot chain-link fence topped with rows of razor wire.

"Oh, good. Can you swing by for like five minutes? I need to get this cake loaded into the van, but I can't lift it by myself. I was stupid and didn't think ahead. I should have done it in two parts and assembled it at the bank. Jack is stuck in a meeting until three and Mom isn't answering her phone. I need to have it delivered by two for this guy's retirement party."

"Um . . ." *Shit.* "I can't."

"Why not?"

"Because I need to get back to work. I'm swamped."

"You're already out running errands. Five minutes. Pretty, pretty please? You know I wouldn't ask if I wasn't desperate. I even went to Mrs. Frank next door, but she was gone. I promise to give you a cupcake when you come over."

Shelby had just started her own business making custom cakes. She was baking out of her house, but it had taken off faster than she'd expected thanks to a string of satisfied brides who'd hired her to decorate their wedding cakes. Missoula was one of the larger towns in Montana, but word of mouth still traveled fast through the right circles.

Her orders had exploded, and she was hesitant to turn away business, so while she searched for the right assistant and commercial bakery, we'd all promised to pitch in and help through the growing pains.

She paid me in cupcakes, so I didn't mind. And if I were actually in Missoula, I'd drop everything to help her in a heartbeat. She was going to be pissed when she found out where I actually was.

I braced and stopped walking. "When I say I'm running errands . . . I actually mean I'm out of town."

My confession was met with silence. A long, drawn-out silence that meant when the intercom turned on in the background and a loud buzzer filled the air, she most definitely heard the announcement that the inmates currently in the yard were to line up and return inside.

Damn.

"You went to see him again, didn't you?" she asked.

The air rushed out of my mouth and my shoulders slumped. "Yes."

"What are you thinking, June?"

"Don't call me that." My words were as short as the click of my stiletto heels on the pavement.

"It's. Your. Name."

8

"You know that's not my name." Maybe it was to the rest of the world, but to my family, to the people who knew the truth, I was Nova.

She scoffed. "You're thirty-two years old and still haven't figured it out. He's manipulating you. This is all a sick and twisted game to get what *he* wants."

I bit my tongue, not wanting to have this fight. Again.

My sister and I agreed on almost everything. Almond cake was better than vanilla. Buying designer heels was money well spent. Her son, Christian, was an angel on earth. The list went on forever, but the one topic where we never shared common ground was our father.

"I don't want to get into a fight about this." I reached my car and set my briefcase on the trunk. "I'm sorry I'm not there to help."

And after the meeting I'd just had with our father, my absence from Missoula was going to extend well past a single afternoon trip to the prison. Something I'd tell her later. Maybe.

"What are you doing?" she asked, her voice no more than a whisper.

"What needs to be done."

"Don't get mixed up in his bullshit. Please. Let it go. Let *him* go."

"I can't."

"You can. Walk away. Live your life."

She'd never tried to understand Dad's loyalty to his club. Maybe because she'd been kept in the dark. I had too, until recently. But the blinders were gone now and there were things that needed to be done.

People who needed to pay.

"Can you just . . . trust me?" I asked.

She groaned. "Now you sound like him."

"He's counting on me, Shelby."

"My name is May." And with that, she hung up.

"Goddamn it." I frowned at my phone, then put it into my purse.

May. When it was just the two of us, I always called her Shelby, just like Dad. Just like he'd always called me Nova. But she'd been relentless about her name again lately. Even Mom had stopped calling her Shelby.

I'd assumed it was because Mom spent a lot of her time babysitting Christian and now that he was two and starting to talk, they didn't want to confuse him with names. But maybe that had nothing to do with it. Maybe since Dad's arrest and conviction, she wanted to completely erase him from her life.

Her husband didn't even know that her name—her intended name—was Shelby. Jack thought it was her middle name and he always gave me a curious stare when I slipped and used it.

Legally, she was May Shelby Johnson-Barnes. But her real name was Shelby Talbot.

Mine was Nova Talbot. My driver's license read June Nova Johnson, but that was all part of the ruse. The secrets that kept us safe.

Not even Jack knew who we were. Because the best way to ruin a secret was to tell people.

And we told no one. Dad had taught us all that lesson young and I'd had thirty-two years to perfect the illusion. Shelby—May—was content with the façade. She wanted to be May, while I loathed being June.

Maybe once my task was complete, I'd be Nova. I'd let go of the ruse and just be me, for myself and for the world.

I turned and stared at the prison grounds, leaning against the warm metal of my car. The facility sat isolated on a wide expanse of land. In the distance, indigo mountains broke through the green and gold fields. But those mountains were miles away and if an inmate did manage an escape, there was only space to run, not hide.

There were numerous buildings within the fenced enclosure, each one a shade of beige or gray with slits in the walls they considered windows. Dad was held in the building closest to where I'd parked.

He was trapped inside. This was where he'd spend the rest of his days. This was where he'd die, not surrounded by his family, but alone in a cell.

Maybe if Shelby came here to see him, she'd feel the same rage that coursed through my veins, though it was doubtful. She said this was what he deserved. That it was his choices that had landed him here with three consecutive life sentences.

She wasn't wrong.

Dad had made numerous mistakes. He'd lived his life on the wrong side of the law, and his crimes had caught up to him. But if he was going to spend his life in prison for his sins, it was only fair that the men who'd put him here, the men who were just as guilty, were in cells too.

The Tin Gypsies.

My father was a tall, powerful and strong man who would wither away behind the prison's concrete walls. He'd never again take a free breath. He'd never again ride his bike under the summer sun. He'd never again hold my mother in his arms.

The same was true for my brother.

All because of those bastards in Clifton Forge.

If Dad couldn't take his revenge personally, then I'd take it for him. He was counting on me.

I shoved off the trunk and picked up my purse and briefcase, tossing them in the passenger seat as I slid behind the wheel. I shrugged off my blazer and let the heat of the leather seat soak through my ivory lace top and black slacks.

I'd worn my favorite suit today. Mom always teased that I wore my blazers like a coat of arms, and she was right. I wore them like Dad had worn his cut before they'd ripped it off his back.

I needed this suit because today, I was going to war.

I hadn't expected Dad to give me his nod of approval today. I'd thought it would take more than one trip to convince him that his revenge didn't lie with a distant relative or a young Warrior prospect. If he wanted revenge, he could count on me to see it through.

But he'd given me his blessing. He'd given me his trust. And I wouldn't let him down.

Tucker Talbot would have his vengeance by my hands.

Starting now.

Turning the key in the ignition, I let the purr of the engine seep into my bones. I let its rumble slide over my skin like the touch of a lover in the dark of night. I ran my fingertips around the wheel, taking one last moment to breathe before I dove in.

The drive home to Missoula would take a little over an hour. But in the other direction, the highway would take me to Clifton Forge.

I wasn't going home.

My 1969 Chevy Nova Coupe soared over the road as I left the prison in my rearview mirror. The car had been a gift from my father on my twenty-first birthday and if ever there was a place where I felt most like myself, it was behind the wheel of this car.

The machine was loud and fast. It was sexy and sleek. Dad always said that the Nova was a little badass and a whole lot cool. It was the reason he'd named me Nova. It was his second favorite car—the first being the Shelby Mustang.

The whirl of the tires on the asphalt soothed my nerves and with the sun shining, the sky above me was as clear as an azure jewel. The fields streaked past in a blur of green and gold.

Dad couldn't enjoy the open Montana road, but I'd do it for him.

I rolled down the windows, pulling off the blond wig I'd donned for my visit to the prison. It got tossed into the passenger seat along with my fake, black-framed glasses. Then I let the rush of wind whip my long hair out of its twist. The fresh air filled my lungs, and I drew it in, holding it for a long moment as I reminded myself why I was doing this.

For Dad.

For TJ.

I might not be a member of the Arrowhead Warriors, but that didn't mean the club hadn't been a part of my entire life. Sure, not a single living member of the Warriors knew I existed. But that didn't mean I hadn't been told their secrets.

I was not a Warrior.

But I was a warrior.

It was time to put my plan into action.

Dad had asked me for the specifics during my visit today, but I'd kept them to myself. The prison's meeting rooms where lawyers could meet with clients were allegedly private. It was illegal to record conversations between a lawyer and her client, but I also knew that the FBI was ruthlessly pursuing the Warriors.

I didn't trust the feds not to bend the rules and create a convenient loophole.

Besides, discussing how I was planning to seduce my way into the Tin Gypsy fold wasn't exactly something I wanted to delve into with my dad. A bonus of him missing out on most major life events had been the absence of those awkward father-daughter discussions regarding sex and boyfriends.

I wasn't sure exactly how he'd feel about me sleeping with the enemy. I wasn't exactly sure how I felt about it either, but this plan of mine had been spinning around in my head for months. There was no other way to infiltrate their circle.

My body was the price I was willing to pay.

The drive to Clifton Forge passed in a blur. As my tires rolled, so did my plan, over and over in my mind until it felt as solid as the road beneath my wheels. Really, it was simple —infiltrate and discover.

My father had been a master of secrets, but even he hadn't been able to protect them all. I doubted the Tin Gypsies had guarded theirs perfectly either. They were criminals, or they had been before disbanding their club.

All I had to do was find the truth.

I'd be lying through my teeth to pull this off. But lying was something I'd been doing my entire life. My very existence was a secret and not once had I slipped, not even after TJ had died and I'd been devastated by his death.

I reached for the five dice resting in the car's ashtray and plucked one out, holding it in a fist. TJ used to carry these dice around with him. Years ago, when we were kids, Dad had taught us how to play liar's dice and from that moment on, TJ had declared it *his* game. After he'd died, Dad had brought me these dice. They were the five TJ had always kept in a pocket.

"Wish me luck, little brother."

A ray of sunshine streamed through the window, warming my face. I hoped TJ, from wherever he was watching, knew how much we missed him. Me. Mom. Even Shelby, in her own way. They'd had a falling out the day he'd joined the Arrowhead Warriors, and he'd died before they'd spoken again.

The day we'd found out that TJ had died, Shelby had held me while I'd cried. She'd been . . . numb. When I'd asked her where she was hiding her tears, she'd told me that she'd already shed them the day TJ had joined Dad's club.

She blamed the Warriors.

I blamed the Tin Gypsies. They were the ones who'd pulled the trigger.

A speed limit sign approached, and I slowed the Nova, my pulse racing as I passed a green sign.

Welcome to Clifton Forge.

Central Avenue was lined with businesses and offices. I passed a coffee shop and a diner. Then came a small movie theater and a hardware store.

Clifton Forge served as the hub for this county and was large enough to support a number of businesses as well as the farmers and ranchers who tended the land sprawling past the town limits. There was a hospital and a handful of banks. Like most small Montana towns, there were an equal number of bars and churches.

Unlike Missoula and the larger cities in Montana, this was a community. A place where neighbors were friends and new faces didn't go unnoticed. I'd have to remember that and be careful where I spent my time.

I lingered on the roads as I drove in circles, getting my bearings and a layout of the town. I found the high school and grocery store. The Dairy Queen and the Burger King. I passed the police station that sat on the banks of the Missouri River and a park where a woman tossed a frisbee for her labradoodle.

Clifton Forge was surprisingly charming. Quaint, even. I'd expected a rural, rough-around-the-edges town, which it was, especially when compared to a college town like Missoula. But it had a Western vibe and a wholesome flair that welcomed its visitors.

Montana was irresistible in the summer and Missoula had been flocked with out-of-state tourists lately, but as I drove, most of the license plates were Montanan. That was how I'd explain my being here. I was in Clifton Forge for the rest of the summer to escape the bustle and growing popularity of Missoula.

The afternoon was nearly over. The clock on the car's dash showed four thirty, which meant my time exploring for today was over. I needed to scope out the Clifton Forge Garage before they closed. With the route punched into my phone, it didn't take me long to make my way across town.

To the heart of the Tin Gypsy Motorcycle Club.

My heart was hammering as the garage came into view. Before I got too close, I eased the Nova off the road and parked next to the sidewalk. My car was all flash and given that the Clifton Forge Garage was renowned for their work on restoring classics, there was no way it would go unnoticed.

Today was about stealth, like driving down a dark highway with no headlights.

Tonight, I'd flip on the brights.

I climbed out of the car, shoving my sunglasses into the dark strands of my hair. I tucked my keys into a pocket of my slacks and then I walked, my Louboutins loud on the concrete.

The garage sprawled on the long and wide lot. The property itself was bordered by a tall chain-link fence that reminded me of the one at the prison. A row of Harleys sat adjacent to the fence and each one included custom modifications like those on Dad's and TJ's bikes—I'd expected nothing less.

At the end of the long parking lot was a dark building tucked beside a grove of trees. The windows had been boarded up. A thick chain, complete with a heavy-duty padlock, hung from the front door's handle.

The Tin Gypsy clubhouse.

Was that where they kept their secrets? I guess I'd find out.

Under the hot August sun, the steel siding of the garage radiated heat waves that floated into the sky. The office sat closest to the street and above its door a large mural had been painted in place of a sign. The words *Clifton Forge Garage* had been airbrushed onto the building's face with perfect strokes of red, black, yellow and green.

All four of the garage's bay doors were open and the

sounds of tools clinking and music playing drifted in my direction.

A man with dark hair appeared in a center bay. He strolled around the hood of a car—a Camaro, if my guess was correct. He leaned against the gray, unpainted, raw metal and smiled, stretching out his long legs.

Dash Slater. Owner of the garage. Former president of the Tin Gypsy club. Son of Draven Slater, one of the club's founders.

A blond man emerged from the same bay and walked across the lot for a bike painted orange and red. He had a similar build to Dash. The same cocky swagger. He raised a hand to wave as he straddled his bike, then he was gone, a streak on the road flying in the opposite direction without so much as a glance my way.

But why would he look? Leo Winter was probably racing home to his young wife and their baby girl. He'd pay no attention to a woman strolling along the sidewalk, her face shielded by a drape of dark hair and her attention fixed on her phone.

I waited until he was out of sight to look up and take another step closer.

Then there he was, my target, striding toward Dash.

Emmett Stone.

His legs were covered in denim-blue coveralls. The cuffs pooled at his thick-soled boots. The coveralls were tied at his waist, revealing a white T-shirt marred with a few grease streaks. His chocolate-brown hair was tied into a knot at the crown of his head. His face was covered in a short beard.

Emmett's tattooed biceps strained at the sleeves of his tee as the cotton stretched over his broad chest. He was bulkier than I'd expected. Taller too. The pictures of him on the garage's website didn't do his build justice. And he was more attractive than I'd let myself hope.

Good. A handsome face would make this easier.

Because Emmett Stone would be the key to the Tin Gypsies' downfall. Oh, I'd ruin Dash and Leo too. But it would start with Emmett.

I unlocked my phone and pulled up my boss's number.

"Hi, June," Brendon answered on the second ring.

I'd graduated from law school and immediately gone to work for Brendon's firm. We specialized in probate, estate, banking and real estate law. Mostly, my clients were families and local businesses. It was easy. Boring. But I cranked through a lot of work because I hated sitting idle, and though I didn't mind, Brendon was under the impression I was reaching maximum burnout.

An impression I'd purposefully let him assume.

"I didn't expect to hear from you today," he said. "Most people don't call their boss on a vacation day."

"Noted." I laughed. "Got a minute?"

"For you, I've got fifteen."

"I've been considering what we talked about last week, and if the offer still stands, I'd love to take you up on it and work remotely for a couple of months."

"Absolutely."

I smiled. "I think you're right. Some time away from the office, where I can catch up and have a little space, will do my stress levels good."

"Whatever you need. You're an asset to our team and we just want you to be happy."

"I appreciate it." I wouldn't exactly be working from *home*, but those were just semantics. "Thanks, Brendon. I'll check in later this week."

"Talk soon."

I tucked the phone into my pocket and stared at the garage, watching Emmett and Dash talk over the car.

Emmett smiled. It came easy. It was entirely sexy. And I liked that he could smile.

I also liked that one day, I'd be the woman to wipe that fucking smile off his face.

CHAPTER TWO

EMMETT

"Another beer?" Paul asked.

"One more. Then go ahead and close out my tab."

He nodded and walked the length of the bar for the register.

The Betsy was busier tonight than I'd thought it would be for a Monday. Normally it wasn't this crowded.

I'd come down after work to have a beer and play a game of pool with the regulars—a group of guys in their seventies who'd come down daily to reminisce about the old days. Each had his own stool and heaven help any man who dared to encroach.

Part of the reason I liked to come down and bullshit with the regulars was because a lot of times their reminiscing involved memories of my father. If he were alive, he'd have been one of the regulars. I'd have been coming to The Betsy for a drink with my old man.

Instead, I came down to be with those who missed him too. It was comforting to know I wasn't the only person who remembered him.

The regulars were gone now, most of them leaving before six to go home. They all preferred The Betsy before it got busy. Now their stools were occupied by others who'd come down for an evening drink.

August in Montana meant long days. People capitalized on their social time while the weather was warm and the sun shined until well after nine each night. Not that you could see a glimpse of sunshine from inside The Betsy.

The few windows were tinted and obscured with neon signs. More of those signs cluttered the walls next to various beer paraphernalia. The jukebox glowed on the far side of the room, its lights synchronized to the beat of the Aerosmith song someone had chosen.

The tables in the center of the room were full of men who'd discarded their suit jackets and rolled up their starched shirtsleeves. Along the bar, clusters of people stood to laugh and talk. The pool tables, which had been empty when I'd walked in the door, were now overrun and a long line of quarters was piled on its edge.

I'd had a good run at pool tonight, winning straight for the past three hours. But part of the fun in playing pool was who you played against, and during my last game, when the guys who'd been up next had only wanted to talk about rumors of my former motorcycle club, I'd taken it as a sign it was time to go home.

Paul came over with my bottle of Corona, leaving the top on and setting a lime wedge on a napkin. Then he set down my credit card and receipt with a pen. "Thanks, Emmett."

"Have a good night, Paul." I nodded and twisted the top off my beer.

About six months ago, a woman had slipped drugs into my friend's drink. Dash, Leo and I had been here for a night

22

of fun, taking tequila shots and hanging out. Dash had eventually gone home to his wife, Bryce. I'd left with a hookup. And Leo had been on his way home to his woman, Cass.

Except before Leo had made it out the door, he'd had one last shot. A shot that had been drugged, causing him to black out. The woman who'd done it had been paid by an enemy. A man connected to the Arrowhead Warriors.

The Warriors had been a rival club back in the days of the Tin Gypsies. Now, they seemed intent on ruining our lives, even though most of them were in prison.

The man who'd drugged Leo was the nephew of the Warriors' president. Both the nephew and his uncle were now behind bars, but that didn't mean we weren't still at risk.

So we didn't let other people touch our drinks. Paul let us open our own beers and if we were drinking liquor, we kept a careful watch with every shot poured.

I tipped the bottle to my lips and scanned the room for familiar faces. Not all that long ago, Leo would have been here by my side. He used to come to The Betsy nearly every night, but now that he had married Cass and they'd had a baby daughter, he had a better place to be. *Home*. All of the guys from the shop had a better place to be.

Because the scene at The Betsy was wearing thin.

This had once been Clifton Forge's dive bar, filled with bikers and men who weren't afraid of a rough life. This had been the Tin Gypsy bar.

Now the place was packed with locals who wouldn't have dared set foot inside ten years ago. The bar fights were fewer and fewer, something Paul was no doubt glad about. He'd just bought The Betsy from the original owner and was making it his own. It was cleaner now than it had ever been too.

The room was still dark, but the cobwebs were missing from the glass shelves behind the bar. The rack of pool cues that used to be loose and close to falling off the wall had been reattached. And Paul frowned upon couples using the storage room for a quick fuck.

The Betsy had changed.

We all had.

I took a long swallow of my beer, not feeling like finishing it, then quickly scribbled my name on the receipt, leaving Paul a decent tip. I tossed the pen down, ready to head for the door and ride home, when a glimpse of white lace molded around delicious curves caught my eye.

She sat on the opposite end of the bar, facing me, her shoulders straight and her posture perfect. Her black jacket rested on the bar in the empty place beside hers. On it sat a crocodile leather handbag.

Another suit.

But this one . . . this one I liked.

Her dark hair framed her face, spilling over her shoulders and down her spine. That lacey top was glued to her breasts and waist, leaving nothing to the imagination. The straps were so thin I could cut them with my teeth.

My cock twitched and my mouth went dry. I finished my beer after all, draining it in two gulps. Then I adjusted my hardening arousal before crossing the room, weaving around people and not once taking my eyes off her.

She sat perched on her stool, her eyes assessing the room. Her lips had a natural pout that she'd accentuated with a rosy lipstick. Her nude fingernails tapped on the martini glass in front of her.

Both seats beside hers were empty and nothing about the lazy way she took in the room showed she was waiting on a date or a colleague to join her. There was no ring on her left hand either.

Conversation and music drifted around me. Someone called my name but I ignored it, this woman stealing my entire focus.

Damn, but she was a stunner. She had to be new around town because that face was unforgettable.

Standing a head taller than most people in the bar had its advantages and when she lifted her cocktail to those lips, I had the perfect view of her tongue darting out to touch the rim before she took a sip. She swallowed and set the glass on its napkin, then looked around again. The moment she spotted me, her eyes traveled up my chest, landing on my face. Then she held my gaze, her own unwavering, as I rounded the corner and leaned on the bar beside her seat. She looked me up and down, only her eyes moving.

Her perusal wasn't subtle.

Neither was mine.

At thirty-eight years old, I was done playing games when it came to women. When I wanted one, she knew it. I didn't hide my intentions or pretend I wanted more than a casual hookup. What was the point? My friends might have settled down, but that wasn't in my cards.

So I lived for the good times while they lasted. And if this beauty wanted a good time, I'd show her one.

Her perfume hit my nose, the rich, floral scent complicated and expensive. It chased away the smell of beer and people.

My gaze drifted to the pressed crease of her black slacks, down the line to the sexiest heels I'd seen in years. The strappy sandals were black and sleek. Her toes were painted fire-engine red, a color that matched the soles peeking out.

That red meant those shoes were expensive. Classy shoes for a classy woman.

What the hell was she doing at The Betsy?

"Nice shoes," I said, meeting her gaze. Her irises were the color of coffee, so dark they were nearly black. Framed with long lashes and lined with a charcoal shadow, her eyes would bring a weaker man to his knees.

"Thanks." Her voice was like a curl of smoke, swirling around us and blocking out the noise.

I held out my hand. "What's your name?"

She looked at my fingers, then back up at my face. "You don't really want it."

I chuckled. No, I didn't need her name. "Not really."

"Good. I don't need yours either. I like what I see. That's enough."

Well, fuck. I think I'd just met the female version of myself. I dropped my hand and twisted, leaning both fore-arms on the bar. I was close enough that my arm brushed against hers. "You good to drive?"

"Yes." She slid off her stool and stood, taller than most women. Those six-inch heels had to help. Then she plucked up her purse and jacket. "Shall we?"

"Follow me."

The crowd parted in my wake and every click of her heels was like a jolt of adrenaline through my veins and a blast of heat to my groin. My body was thrumming with anticipation as we walked outside and into the yellow evening glow. Going straight for my bike parked beside the door, I swung a leg over and straddled the seat.

She kept walking, straight across the parking lot to a car nearly as sexy as the woman herself. A '69 Nova. Damn. That was a car I'd drool over later. At the moment I was too busy staring at the perfect shape of her ass as she walked.

This woman . . . damn, she had a way. Her hips swayed in a slow sashay. Her legs looked a mile long with those slacks and heels. My hands burned to grip those toned thighs and skate across the swell of her breasts.

I started the engine of the bike as she slid behind the wheel of her car. Even from behind the glass, I caught the smirk on her lips and the lust in her gaze.

Fuck, I was glad I'd come to the bar tonight.

I rolled out of the parking lot, resisting the urge to rev the bike's engine. I didn't want to lose her as we navigated through town. But the minute I hit the quiet county road that led toward the mountain foothills, I cut myself loose.

If she drove that hot-as-fuck car like a mouse, I'd be disappointed.

But she hit the gas and hugged the road's curves, never once letting me out of her sight. Every mile was an aphrodisiac. Every second part of the build. I hoped she was ready for a long night because I hadn't felt like this in a long damn time.

The wind whipped past my face as I pushed us both faster, wanting off my bike and inside her body. The turnoff to my place came into view and I flashed her my brake light, slowing onto the narrow private lane.

Part of the reason I'd bought this property was for the trees. Where other properties around Clifton Forge were situated in the middle of the sprawling range, my home was tucked into an outcrop of the forest that led straight up into the mountains.

The hills were covered in green, the forest luring us forward until we reached my clearing a half mile later.

My house was centered on thirty acres, tucked away from the world. The log exterior blended into the natural surroundings. Some of the trees had needed to be taken down—I didn't need a windstorm coming through and toppling one onto my roof.

Built into the side of a small slope, the main floor was level with one side and on the opposite, the basement opened to a wide, sprawling yard that extended to the tree line. A wrap-around porch extended the length of the front and on the rear I had a wide, covered deck. My three-stall garage had plenty of space for tools and a place to park my truck in the summer and my bike during the winter.

This home, this property, was my sanctuary. It was the place I came to escape the world and get some air.

Rarely did I bring a woman here, preferring to keep my hookups away from my private space. But this woman I wanted in my bed. I wanted that exotic, sultry perfume on my sheets. I wanted that silky hair spread across my pillows.

I parked my bike in the driveway in front of a garage door, not bothering to pull it inside. I was in too much of a hurry. The low rumble of the Nova's engine stopped at my side as she killed the engine.

I was off my bike and at her door, holding it open as she glided out. She moved with grace and confidence, and damn was I anxious to ruffle her perfect composure. To make her come undone.

"Sure about this, baby?" I asked, taking her hand in mine.

She arched her eyebrows. "Are you?"

I led her to the door.

The drive had taken us about thirty minutes and the sun was sinking beyond the horizon. The trees blocked out most of its fading light, making the house dark and empty. Unlocking the door and punching in the alarm code, I crossed the threshold. She followed behind me.

Then I was on her, my lips slamming onto hers. God, she tasted good. As sweet as warm honey and better than I'd imagined on the ride home. But her tongue was as wicked as the devil himself, licking and tangling and dueling with my own.

I sank into her, bending low as she rose to me. Her hands roved up my abs as mine dug into the soft flesh at her hips while I eased her back and against the wall of the entryway.

I went to work on the belt of her slacks, managing to get it free and unhooking the clasp of her pants. Then I dove inside, searching for the hem of that lace top to guide my hands underneath.

The minute my calloused grip skated up the smooth skin of her torso, she gasped. Then her teeth nipped at my lower lip.

I ripped my mouth from hers, dropping my lips to the long line of her neck. I sucked hard on her skin, hard enough to leave a mark, before trailing my tongue lower and dragging it across her collarbone.

She leaned into the wall at her back, baring her throat for my tasting pleasure. Her hands dove into my hair and freed it from the tie that had kept it out of my face. Some women didn't like my shoulder-length hair. I didn't give a fuck because haircuts were a pain in my ass.

Then there were the women who'd thread their fingers through the strands and hold on for the ride.

This woman . . . thank fuck she was the latter. Her fingernails grazed my scalp. The sting made me want her that much more.

My cock throbbed behind my zipper as I worshiped her skin, my hands splayed wide across the tight skin at her ribs.

"More," she whispered, tugging at my hair.

I pulled my hands out of her shirt and went straight for her thighs, hoisting her up and pressing my erection into her center.

Our gazes locked, her coffee gaze boring into mine.

There was doubt in her eyes. Like she didn't think I'd deliver.

Proving her wrong was going to be a blast.

I took the strap of her top, pulling it away from her shoulder. Inch by inch it stretched until it snapped. Her eyes flared as it broke away. Then I peeled down the lace and set her breast free. No bra. *Fuck.*

Her nipple was a pebbled ruby, a perfect size for the pad of my thumb. I tweaked it twice before tearing at the other strap, breaking it free and ripping it away.

Her chest rose, her back pressing against the wall as she arched into my touch and lifted her legs to wrap around my waist. Her luscious breasts filled my palms as I took them in my grip, bracing her against the wall with my hips.

She rolled her head, giving me the delicious column of her throat once more. I sucked on her pulse, feeling it quicken beneath my touch until I was so painfully hard that it was time to move away from the goddamn front door and get her into my bed.

I set her on her feet, annoyed at myself that she didn't sway. I wanted her to be as dizzy as I felt. With a hand clamped around her wrist, I tugged her through the house, past the living room and down the hallway toward the master. The whole time, those heels clicked to the rhythm of my racing heart.

The moment my feet pressed into the plush carpet, I let her go and reached behind my head to yank off my T-shirt. Then I went for my own belt, loosening the buckle and flicking open the button on my jeans.

Her hands skimmed the skin of my back, snaking up my spine, her fingertips digging deep to mark their trail. Then she dropped her hands and walked past me, straight for the bed.

That lacey top was in tatters as she peeled it off her body, her hair splaying with the movement. Naked from the belly button up, she kept her eyes glued to mine as she unzipped her slacks, shoving them and the black panties beneath to the floor.

"Heels stay on," I said when she bent to slip one from her foot.

She gave me a nod as she stood tall, her shoulders back and those tits begging for my mouth.

A mouth that had once again gone dry, this time at the sight of her bare body.

Christ, this had to be a dream. Her body was tall and lithe, rounded in the right places and made for a man my size.

I let myself study her, taking in every inch as she stood naked but for her heels. If my perusal intimidated her, it didn't show. There wasn't a hint of hesitation on her face.

This was my home, this was my room, but she was in control.

I'd take it back soon enough.

I shoved my jeans away, not having bothered with boxers this morning, and my throbbing shaft bobbed free. I took it in a fist and stepped to her, stroking it twice as I drank her in.

Her eyes dropped and she stared. I was a big guy and

instead of a hint of fear at how I'd feel inside her, she looked . . . hungry.

I was ravenous.

I moved to the nightstand for a condom. The packet got tossed to the bed where it would stay until I was ready. Then I picked her up, moving so fast it caught her by surprise. Her breath hitched as I twisted us both, crashing us onto the mattress.

Dark hair over my pillow. Her smooth, satin skin and scent on my sheets.

Her legs parted to cradle my hips as I kissed her again, hard and wet, until my lips were swollen and I felt the slickness of her folds coating my cock.

She panted.

I ached.

Leaning away, I gave her one last look as I took the condom and tore it from the wrapper to sheath myself. "Ready?"

She smirked. "Are you?"

I chuckled and dragged myself through her wetness. Then I lined up at the entrance and with one fast thrust, I drove deep.

She cried out, the sound sheer pleasure as she stretched around me. Her back arched off the bed.

"Fuck, that feels good." She was tight and hot and so damn perfect. I gave her a moment to adjust but when her fingernails dug into my shoulder, I took it as permission to get on with it. So I slid out and slammed in again, this time earning a mewl.

She might not know my name, but I'd make her scream regardless.

I shifted, getting to my knees and taking her legs in my

hands. Then I started slamming inside her, loving the bounce and sway of her breasts with each thrust.

Her eyes held mine, that silent dare still hanging in the air as the room filled with the scent of sex and sin. Maybe she didn't think I could make her come.

"Hold on, baby."

She smirked and raised her arms, pressing them against the wooden headboard. "I'm not that easy."

"We'll see."

Maybe some men wouldn't care. They'd take their pleasure and fail this test. I wasn't most men and if I was coming, so was she.

I rolled my hips, earning a hiss. Then I pressed in deep, as deep as she could take me, and felt the flutter of her inner walls.

"Look at us." I dropped my gaze to where we were connected. When I slid in again, it was purposefully slow, watching as I disappeared into her body inch by inch.

When I glanced at her face, her eyes were locked on where she stretched around me. I found her clit, touching it with the pad of my middle finger. I circled it, slowly at first, until her legs began to tremble.

"Watch," I ordered when her eyes drifted closed.

She snapped them open and shot me a glare for ordering her around.

I grinned and pressed in on her clit harder, savoring the flush that spread across her chest.

But her mouth was set in a firm line, her jaw clenched.

Why was she fighting it? Whatever the reason, I wouldn't lose, not tonight. Her body was mine to play with and she could resist all she wanted, but it responded to my touch. It was mine to command.

Stroke after stroke, I plunged deep. I alternated the pressure on her clit, hard to soft, fast to slow. She tried to twist and shift but I kept a firm grip on her legs, holding her exactly where I wanted her. Exactly where I could hit that spot inside.

She panted, her chest rising and falling, as her body shook until finally there was no resistance left. Her eyes slammed closed as her body arched, the orgasm coming over her like a tidal wave. Pulse after pulse she squeezed until the pressure built so tight in my spine I let go, losing myself too.

White spots broke across my vision and I tipped my head back, letting the release tear through my body like a freight train. A groan escaped my lips as I came long and hard. When the orgasm finally loosened its grip, I cracked my eyes open. My mystery woman lay limp and sated on the bed, her arms draped over her face.

I lifted them away, taking her chin and turning it to me as her lashes flickered open.

"Got anywhere to be?" I asked.

"No."

"Good. Now that we took the edge off, let's have some fun."

Those dark eyes laughed, and she leaned up on an elbow, brushing her lips against mine. "Do your worst. And I'll do mine."

"You're on."

———

HOURS LATER, I walked her to the door. The ruined straps of her top hung at her sides. Her slacks were wrinkled from their time on the floor. I'd finally taken her shoes off during the third round, but not before they'd left welts in the small of my back.

She didn't speak as she crossed the threshold, that sway of her hips making me wish I had stopped her when she'd started getting dressed.

I leaned against the door's frame, naked, and soaked her in as she strolled to the driver's side of her Nova.

She opened the door but didn't get inside. Instead she stared over the car's roof, studying me. Then she threw her head back to the midnight sky and laughed, her smile as white and blinding as the stars themselves.

Maybe she laughed because I'd surprised her. Maybe because tonight had been a fucking blast. Whatever the reason, I chuckled too, waiting until she climbed into the car and drove down the road.

Then I retreated inside and shook my head, a lazy grin on my face. I'd given her my number before she'd left. Maybe she'd call it. Maybe she wouldn't.

I chuckled again. "Damn, what a woman."

And I didn't even know her name.

CHAPTER THREE

NOVA

"Hey, Mama." I hugged her as she came into my condo.

"Hi, honey. How's my pretty girl?" She kissed my cheek, sweeping into the kitchen and setting her purse on the counter beside a vase of white roses.

Picking up those flowers and meeting with Mom were the last items on my massive to-do list. It had been two days since my trip to Clifton Forge and the hours had become a blur of rushing from one task to the next, all so I could leave Missoula today and carry on with my plan.

"I'm good. Thanks for doing this."

She touched the silky tip of a rose. "Would you like to explain why I'm housesitting for two months?"

"Do you really want to know?" I asked, knowing her answer.

"Probably not." She leaned in and drew in the fragrant scent of the bouquet.

Mom had always kept her distance from Dad's business with the Warriors.

They'd met at one of the club's ruckus parties. Mom had

36

been young and had gone to Ashton with a friend, the two of them somehow finding themselves at the clubhouse. But that had been the one and only time Mom had been around the Warriors. Once had been enough.

She'd gotten pregnant with Shelby that night and Dad had insisted that Mom and his unborn child be completely removed from the club scene. Mom had always gone along with Dad's wishes because she would do anything to keep us kids safe, even if that meant loving him in secret.

Mom didn't talk about Dad with her friends, just like we didn't discuss our father. She still lived in my childhood home and if our neighbors had asked questions about the man who visited infrequently, she hadn't answered.

Their marriage had been by vow only. Their love had been confined to the walls of her home.

I suspected the reason she turned a blind eye to Dad's club wasn't just to protect her children, but also to guard her heart.

If she'd talked about the Warriors with Dad, it had never been in my presence. I was sure she knew more than she let on but she didn't push for every detail. She trusted Dad.

We'd all trusted Dad, even Shelby.

Besides, Mom had no need for questions, because she had the life she wanted. Not once had she complained about raising three children on her own. She ran the show. She'd been the captain of our ship. Yes, she'd missed Dad and had cried whenever he'd left after his short visits, but the sad days had never lasted.

Until TJ.

After his death, Mom had changed. There was a bone-deep pain in her eyes now and that ghost showed no signs of disappearing.

I wouldn't burden her with more worry. She didn't need to know I was tangling with the very men who'd killed her child. I would make the Tin Gypsies pay for his death, and maybe then, with vengeance delivered, would I share.

"I spoke to your sister." She kept her gaze locked on the roses. "Did you see him?"

"Yes."

"And how is he?"

"He's okay." As best he could be in prison. "I gave him your letter."

I was the conduit for their communication because even though he was spending his life in prison, he still didn't want Mom making contact. He didn't want to risk his enemies discovering her identity, especially now that he would be helpless to protect her.

So she wrote letters and when I made my infrequent visits, I passed them along.

"You gave him the pictures of Christian?" she asked.

"Yes, the letter and the pictures of Christian."

It wasn't Shelby who made sure that Dad knew what his grandson looked like, it was Mom. With each of my visits, I'd bring a letter of Mom's for Dad to read. She'd always tuck in a picture or two of Christian that she'd taken on one of their many grandmother-grandson playdates.

The letters never stayed with Dad, but he'd keep the pictures. Those photos and my visits were his only connection to his family. Even I only visited with an expensive wig, reading glasses and a false identity.

Maybe once the Tin Gypsies were gone, maybe after enough time had passed that Dad's other enemies had forgotten about an old man living in a cell, she'd be able to visit. Maybe we could drop this ruse and be a family.

No more hiding.

"Where are you going?" she asked.

It would be easier to lie and tell her Bozeman or Billings, but if something happened to me, which was a real possibility, I wanted her to know where I was. "Clifton Forge."

Her face whipped to mine, her eyes widening. "Nova."

I loved my name. Even spoken in Mom's stern mom voice, I loved my name. But she called me June more often than not.

And I just wanted to be Nova.

"Trust me," I whispered.

She closed her eyes and shook her head.

"I know what I'm doing."

"Do you?"

"You just said that you didn't want to know."

She scowled. "Now I've changed my mind."

And yet I still wouldn't tell her the whole truth. Mom didn't need to know the lengths I was going to or that I'd spent the night in a Tin Gypsy's bed. She didn't need to know that her youngest daughter was fucking the enemy—literally and figuratively.

Or that it had been . . . unexpected. Even after two days, I hadn't quite figured out how I felt about my night with Emmett. Not that it mattered. I'd have years to dwell on it once this was over.

"Trust me, Mom."

"I can't visit another grave, Nova."

"You won't have to."

She looked to me, her eyes pleading. "You're playing with fire. I know who lives in Clifton Forge."

"They have to pay." And my revenge would be the lasting kind.

39

The three remaining Tin Gypsies deserved a lifetime in prison. If my father was destined to live his days without freedom, those men deserved it too.

Dash Slater.

Leo Winter.

Emmett Stone.

According to Dad, he'd brokered a truce with the Tin Gypsies long ago, a truce to save the lives of men in both clubs. Dad had honored that truce for years, and he'd ensured that the members of his club had honored it too.

When the Tin Gypsy club had disbanded, Dad had believed their rivalry was truly over. But those snakes had been biding their time. For years they'd waited to strike.

I hated that they'd won.

But I would balance the scales. I wouldn't rest until they'd lost everything. Until their wives had divorced them and their children had forgotten their names.

Maybe Mom thought I was seeking death, but death was not the goal here.

Too much blood had already been spilled.

"Nova . . ." Mom sighed.

"Trust me." I could—*would*—do this.

Not just for Dad, but for me too. *I* craved vengeance.

After Dad's arrest, for the first time in my life, he'd confided in me about his club. He'd told me story after story about the Warriors. He'd told me story after story about the Tin Gypsies.

He'd told me how they'd murdered my brother.

We'd always known that TJ had died because of a rival club, but Dad had spared Mom, Shelby and me the details. Now that I had them, there was a newfound rage in my blood. A fury that wouldn't ebb until the Tin Gypsies suffered too.

Months ago, I'd asked Dad to let me go after the Tin Gypsies. He'd refused.

Except Dad was running out of options and people he could trust. Fifty-seven Warriors had been arrested in the FBI raid of their clubhouse in Ashton. Most were looking at a minimum of five years. Senior members, like Dad, would never walk free again.

As time went on, fewer and fewer people would remain loyal to Tucker Talbot. As it was, some of the video footage he'd kept from the clubhouse was the reason his members were facing prison sentences.

Dad's allies were dwindling and those still loyal were being closely watched.

So Dad had been forced to be creative in his quest for vengeance. He'd been forced to enlist outsiders, like my cousin Doug Hamilton.

A cousin who I'd never met—who had no idea I existed—but who I knew was an idiot. Doug had lacked both the brains and the motivation to wipe out the Tin Gypsies. He'd concocted a harebrained plan that had not only failed but landed him in a cell too.

Doug's failure was fresh, and I'd capitalized on it during my visit to the prison on Monday. This time when I'd asked Dad to let me have a chance, he'd agreed.

Revenge didn't have to be some complicated ordeal. The Tin Gypsies were far from innocent and all I had to do was find proof of their crimes. Their murders. All I had to do was earn one man's trust.

Emmett.

It had been so easy to get into his bed. His arrogance was astounding.

He'd walked up to me at the bar, held out his hand and expected me to drop my panties. Probably because countless women before me had done just that. He knew how to use that handsome face and sexy swagger. I'd been just another easy score.

I only hoped that by refusing to give him my name, by playing aloof, he'd be game for another round. Hell, he'd even brought me to his home. I'd thought it would take a few nights before he'd let me in to his bed. Either he had no intention of seeing me again or I'd snared his interest.

I guess I'd find out soon enough.

The Nova was packed with enough clothes to last me through the fall. Yesterday, I'd spent the day working at the office to finish a few tasks and touch base with Brendon before working remotely for two months. Then today, I'd cleaned my condo and made sure the fridge was empty before calling Mom to come over. Once she left, I was driving to Clifton Forge.

"Does May know where you're going?" Mom asked.

"No. She knows I'm leaving town for a couple of months but I told her it was a work assignment in Bozeman."

Mom frowned. She was okay with us lying about our identities, but she didn't like us lying to each other. I didn't like it either.

But I knew my sister, and Shelby would not understand. If she knew what I was actually doing, she'd flip out and I wouldn't put it past her to come to Clifton Forge and blow the whistle. So this morning, when I'd taken a latte over as a peace offering, I'd looked her in the face and lied.

Shelby had been testing a new cake recipe—strawberry

42

with buttercream frosting—and I'd shoved an entire cupcake in my mouth the moment after the lie had passed my lips. The cake had kept the truth from slipping out.

The guilt of lying to my sister was gnawing at me already. But I'd tell her the truth when this was over. Two months would go by in a flash, and if I was lucky, I'd find evidence against the Tin Gypsies even sooner.

"Where are you staying?" Mom asked.

"A vacation rental." It wasn't the fanciest place in the world, but it would do for now. All I really needed was a bed, a table where I could set up a temporary office and high-speed internet. I hadn't seen the place in person but based on the photos and description, it checked the required boxes.

I was meeting the host at six tonight. It was about time for me to head out if I was going to make it in time.

"I'd better get going," I said, motioning to the flowers. "These are for TJ."

She smiled and picked up the vase. "Thank you."

It was Wednesday. Mom went to his grave every Wednesday.

Maybe someday, when this was over, we could get a new tombstone made for TJ. One with his real name.

Tucker Talbot Junior. Though he'd always been TJ, it would be nice to include his real name.

"Please be careful." Mom closed the distance between us and wrapped her arms around me.

I was in heels today—every day—and they made me a few inches taller. Otherwise, we were the same five nine. We had the same rich, brown hair and coffee-colored eyes. TJ had taken after Mom too, with her high cheekbones, heart-shaped face and full lips. Only Shelby resembled our dad. A fact that made her resent him more.

"I love you, Mom." I hugged her tight.

"I love you too. If you go there again . . ." *To prison.* Mom struggled with that word.

"I'll tell him you love him."

"Thank you." Mom would always love Tucker Talbot. For better or worse, he was the love of her life.

Mom held me for a long moment, then let me go and picked up the vase of roses. She buried her nose in the blooms and smiled. "It's a pretty day to sit with your brother."

"It sure is." And it was a beautiful day to drive in Montana.

I walked her out, giving her one last hug before handing over the spare keys to my condo. Lingering beside the door, I waited until she reversed out of the driveway before hustling through the house for one last check that the lights were off and the doors were locked. Then I climbed in my car and hit the road.

The Nova soared down the interstate for the first half of my trip. I turned up the volume on the radio and let it soothe any fears that I was diving into the vipers' pit.

I could do this.

I had to do this.

For Dad. For TJ. For Shelby. For Mom.

For me.

They'd stolen my father before he'd had a chance to become my father. Dad had always promised Mom that when he quit the club, he'd move home. They'd live a simple life like normal retirees. Dad could be a grandfather to Christian. And we could get to know him. Finally, after only glimpses of him in our life, we could become a real family.

That had seemed even more important after we'd lost TJ. Especially for Mom.

But it was just another dream lost.

I hated the Tin Gypsies for stealing that future. Almost as much as I hated them for stealing my brother's life.

I could do this.

I had to do this.

For my family.

Halfway through my drive, I exited the interstate and navigated the two-lane highway that led to Clifton Forge. Once in town, my vacation rental host was waiting by the front door when I pulled into the driveway at six.

Assuming my role as June Johnson, the persona I'd perfected after thirty-two years, I smiled brightly and thanked him profusely for arranging the rental on such short notice.

I'd left Emmett's bed on Monday and driven straight through the night for Missoula. Adrenaline and a huge cup of coffee had fueled the trip home. I'd crashed for a few hours, then woken for work yesterday. After arriving at the office, my first task had been to book a rental online.

My host handed over the keys after a brief tour, then left me alone to settle in. Unloading the car took three trips and unpacking took just an hour. I killed the next ninety minutes by checking emails and social media on my phone. Finally, when the clock ticked past eight, I swiped on a fresh coat of lipstick, combed my hair and headed out the door.

The Nova purred as I rolled down the streets of Clifton Forge. It took exactly seven minutes to reach The Betsy. And a shiny black Harley was parked outside the bar's door.

Emmett's Harley.

I smiled. Finding him here was better than having to call his number.

I slid out of the car and smoothed down my dress. It was a favorite, the design simple. The straps were thicker than those Emmett had shredded from my lace top. It was the color of sunflowers in bloom and the fabric skimmed my curves. The square neckline plunged low to reveal a hint of cleavage—just enough to draw attention. And then there were my heels, a strappy pair I couldn't wait to sink into the dimples above Emmett's squeezable ass.

It had been surprisingly easy to sleep with him.

Some night, years from now, I'd take the time to dissect my plan and the ease with which I'd orgasmed beneath his touch. Some night, I'd let myself replay it from different angles and wonder if there had been a different way to gain entry into his life besides using my body. Some night, I'd likely feel guilty and ashamed that vengeance and cold, calculating anger had pushed me this far.

Those worries were for some other night.

Tonight, I was marching into the bar wearing my favorite pair of two-thousand-dollar heels.

The Betsy smelled like beer and sweat and a gallon of industrial cleaner that would never erase the stale scent of cigarettes. It was even busier than it had been on Monday night. The tables were full of people who'd come for one drink after work but had stayed for four or five.

A country hit blared from the jukebox. The thunk of balls sinking into pockets at the pool table cut through the music but I didn't glance in that direction. I walked straight to the bar, slow and steady, then slid into a stool dead center. I chose one with an empty seat at my side.

The bartender walked over, bracing his hands on the bar and giving me a lazy grin. "Martini, right?"

I touched my temple. "You remember."

"You're hard to forget." His eyes flicked over my shoulder and his grin faltered. I didn't need to turn to know who was standing behind me.

Emmett took the empty seat, his movements deliberate and fluid, especially for a man of his size. He stood at least six four. Maybe six five. I'd always had a thing for tall men. Add in the longer hair and short beard, he was rugged sex appeal with that bad-boy edge.

His body was honed for pleasure and sin. He exuded confidence and control. His ego didn't need the boost so I'd be keeping it to myself, but he was the only man who'd ever made me orgasm. I'd even tried to fight it. But Emmett had a talented cock and wicked fingers, both of which he knew how to use.

My vibrator was in Missoula, safely tucked into the drawer of my nightstand, because I wasn't going to need it in Clifton Forge.

He was the type of man I didn't let myself date because *June* went out with clean-cut businessmen. Men like those were seated throughout the room, the ones who'd shed their suit coats and tried their best not to blatantly stare at my ass as I'd crossed to the bar.

Emmett had most definitely been staring at my ass and he wasn't the kind of man to hide it. I liked that.

He leaned forward, elbows on the bar, jerking up his chin at the bartender in a silent command to get lost. I liked that too.

Maybe I liked the entire package just a little too much. But again, that was a worry for some other night.

"Why the queen, Ace?" I asked.

"Ace?" He looked over and the corner of his delicious mouth turned up.

I dragged a fingernail over the forearm that rested between us, pressing hard enough to leave a white streak in the ink on his skin.

The tattoo I touched was of two cards. A queen. And an ace.

There'd be no calling him Emmett, not only because he didn't know I knew his name but because names meant attachment. Names were personal. And for my own sanity, keeping some boundaries was necessary.

Ace was the perfect nickname. There was no way in hell I was calling him babe or sweetie or honey. Besides, Ace fit.

"Why the queen and not a king?" I asked again, raising my gaze.

His pretty brown eyes were waiting. They were lighter than mine, most people's were, the color of toffee and chocolate swirls. Maybe the prettiest eyes I'd ever seen.

"It's from something my father said."

His father. Neal Stone.

A murderer.

"He told me that a king was nothing without his queen. That the two most important cards in a deck were the ace and the queen. You want the ace up your sleeve. And you need the queen at your back because women fight dirty."

A smile stretched across my face and I couldn't help but laugh. I'd laughed on Monday night, too, after I'd forced myself out of his bed. It was a laugh that said he had no idea what he was getting into.

Maybe neither of us did.

"Did you want a drink?" Emmett asked, bending low

enough for me to catch a whiff of his spicy scent. "Or should we skip it?"

"Do you really think I came here for their cocktails?"

He grinned, then stood from his stool.

I did the same, following him to his house and smiling the entire way.

The ace and the queen.

Oh, yes. Women fought dirty, especially this one.

The queen who'd shove her knife into his back.

CHAPTER FOUR

EMMETT

"That should do it." With my wrench in hand, I slid out from beneath the sink at one of my rental properties.

"Thank you, Emmett," Tera said, tucking a lock of blond hair behind her ear.

"No problem." I stood and swiped my hands on my jeans.

The kitchen faucet had sprung a leak this evening. Tera had shut the water off and called a plumber, but since it was almost six, they would have charged her double for an after-hours call, so she'd decided to wait until the morning.

I wouldn't have even known about the leak had I not come over to Mom's for dinner. I'd parked my bike in Mom's driveway and the moment I'd cut the engine, Tera's daughter, Maggie, had rushed over from where she'd been playing in her yard next door. She'd been the one to tell me about the sink.

"You can always call me, Tera."

"I hate to bother you."

"It's no bother. It's my responsibility to fix things like this."

"Well . . . thank you. Sorry to interrupt your night."

I waved it off. "Don't apologize. Just call me."

"Okay." She nodded and the last bits of stress on her face disappeared.

Tera was a single mom who worked as a teacher at the elementary school. She was new in town, having moved here three months ago. Timing had been on my side because I'd just bought this place from the previous owners, an older couple who'd lived next door to Mom my entire life. Mr. and Mrs. Henderson had retired and relocated to New Mexico. When Mom had told me they were moving, I'd offered to buy this house before they'd put it on the market.

It was a nice house and the Hendersons had taken good care of it over the years. A smart and reasonable investment. But mostly I'd bought it to control who lived next door to Mom.

As far as renters and neighbors went, I couldn't have dreamed up better than Tera.

If she decided to buy a home in Clifton Forge, I'd prob-ably offer to sell her this house before letting her leave the neighborhood. Not only was it nice to have someone I trusted next door to my mother, but Mom had officially deemed Maggie her adopted granddaughter.

Since it was unlikely she'd ever get grandchildren from me, having Maggie filled that hole.

"I'd better go rescue your mom from Maggie," Tera said, leading the way to the front door.

"Think it's the other way around."

She smiled over her shoulder. The freckles dusting her nose and cheeks were darker than they had been at the beginning of the summer. Her blue eyes sparkled as we stepped outside and into the evening sun.

"Ready for the school year?" I asked as we crossed the driveway to Mom's.

"Yeah, I think so. I've got my classroom set up and the faculty has been wonderful. Everyone's been so welcoming."

"Kindergarten?"

She nodded. "Yep. Good memory."

Not really. Tera had only told me once that she was teaching kindergarten, but Mom mentioned it every time Tera's name came up. Along with any other fact about Tera that she thought might encourage me to ask Tera on a date.

Yeah, Tera was a beautiful woman and yeah, her kid was cute as a button. But Tera needed a man who was in it for the long haul. A man who'd step up to be Maggie's father. A man who'd make vows and give her more children.

I was not that man.

Maybe ten years ago I would have dived into the family lifestyle headfirst, but I was inching closer to forty and was content with life as it was.

We were in the middle of Mom's yard when her door opened and a little blond bolt streaked outside, racing toward Tera.

"Mommy!" Maggie crashed into Tera's legs. "Guess what?"

"What?"

"I asked Cherie if we could stay for dinner and she said *yes*."

"Oh, honey." Tera's eyes widened. "Remember what we talked about? You can't invite yourself."

"Oh, it's fine," Mom said as she came our way. "I was going to offer anyway. I made too much."

Mom always made too much. She'd send leftovers home with me even though she knew I could cook for myself.

"We, um . . ." Tera looked to me, clearly not wanting to intrude.

"Stay. Mom's chicken parm is the best in town."

"Yes, it is." Mom looped one arm with mine, then another with Tera's, sweeping us both inside.

The dining room table was set for four people. Mom had pulled out her nice dishes from the china cabinet. When I'd come in earlier, it had only been placed for two and she'd had her *everyday* plates. If I didn't know better, I'd say that Mom had snuck into Tera's place and ruined the kitchen faucet herself just to arrange for this little dinner.

"Emmett, will you open a bottle of wine?" Mom asked.

"Sure." I nodded, then turned to Tera. "Red or white?"

"I'm not picky."

"Okay." I looked down at Maggie. "Lemonade, orange pop or 7-Up?"

"Orange." She gave me the same cute, shy smile I got whenever I came over.

Maggie hadn't quite warmed up to me yet but we were making progress. Mostly I think it was my height and size that intimidated kids—and some adults.

"Orange it is." I winked at her and went to the garage fridge where Mom kept most of her beverages. I chose a bottle of chardonnay because it was Mom's favorite, then an orange pop for Maggie.

By the time I had glasses poured, Mom was bringing the food to the table. No surprise, she insisted I sit beside Tera. She took the place beside Maggie, said grace, then we dug in while it was hot.

"This is delicious, Cherie," Tera said.

I nodded. "Great meal."

"It's his favorite," Mom told Tera. "I have to make it at least once a month so that he comes to visit me."

I took another bite and swallowed a retort. I swung by Mom's place at least once a week, though if she had it her way, it would be daily.

"He's always so busy," Mom added.

"With your rental properties?" Tera asked.

"That and work. I'm a mechanic at the Clifton Forge Garage."

"More than a mechanic." Mom raised her fork. "He builds custom motorcycles and restores classic cars."

"Interesting," Tera said. "I was actually just thinking I needed to get my oil changed. I haven't had it done since we moved here. Does your garage do that?"

"We do. Bring it on down."

"And maybe you can give her a tour of the shop." The gleam in my mother's eyes was not subtle.

We'd have a conversation later tonight about matchmaking. "It's just a shop, but sure."

"Did you know that Maggie is starting kindergarten?" Mom asked.

"Kindergarten was my favorite," I said, earning a blush as Maggie chewed. She had Tera's freckles and blue eyes. I wasn't sure what the story was with her father, but I was sure that Mom would get it in due time.

The rest of the meal went much like the beginning, Mom telling Tera about me and me about Tera. Until finally she brought out a mud pie and sliced me a piece so large that I'd have to spend an extra hour in my home gym tomorrow morning.

That, or stop by The Betsy and see if I could find my mystery woman for a late-night workout.

Just the thought of her made my dick twitch so I shoved her face from my thoughts, focusing on the food, my mother and her guests.

"This was incredible," Tera said, standing from the table to clear the empty dishes.

"I'll get it." I stood too, taking her plate and Maggie's. After three trips, I had the dining room cleared and got to work stowing leftovers and handwashing the china.

Mom and I had an unspoken agreement about the dishes. When she cooked, I washed. It had been that way since I'd moved out after high school. Those days, she'd cooked for me on a fairly regular basis, mostly because the food at the clubhouse was hit or miss. Then after Dad had died, I'd come over under the guise of dinner but really it had been to check on her. And for her company.

With the dishes done, I returned to the dining room table with another bottle of wine, refilling Mom's glass.

"Tera?" I asked.

"No, thank you." She stood from her chair. "We'd better get going. Thank you again for dinner, Cherie."

"My pleasure."

"And thanks again for fixing the sink," Tera said.

"Happy to. Call if it starts leaking again."

"I will." Tera moved to Maggie, taking her hand.

Then Mom escorted them out of the house while I settled into my chair once more, filling my own wineglass.

I took a long drink of the dry, cool liquid, waiting for Mom and the inevitable lecture about my lonely life.

"That was lovely." She swept into the dining room and her chair. "That Tera sure is pretty, don't you think?"

"She is."

"And such a sweetheart. Maggie is the most precious thing."

I hummed. Maggie was cute but she had nothing on Leo's daughter, Seraphina, or Genevieve and Isaiah's daughter, Amelia. Though I was biased.

"Did you know that Tera teaches kindergarten?"

"You've mentioned it." No less than ten times.

"She made me chocolate chip cookies. Did I tell you that? Last weekend."

"Did she?"

"They were excellent. Maybe better than my own."

I took another sip of wine, fighting a grin.

Mom was nothing if not obvious. "She's new in town. Maybe you should ask her out to dinner."

And there it was. "I don't think so."

"Why?"

"She's my tenant."

"Pfft. Who cares?"

"Me."

Mom narrowed her gaze. "Is it because of Maggie?"

"No. Of course not." It wasn't that I didn't like kids. I just doubted I'd have any of my own at this point in my life. Besides, I was perfectly fine being Uncle Emmett to my friends' kids.

"Then what is it?" Mom asked.

"Tera is just not for me."

"She's too pretty and smart?"

No, Tera was too pure.

But that was not something I'd be sharing with my mother.

Being so new to town, I doubted Tera had heard much

about me or my past. But it was only a matter of time. Tera didn't seem the sort who'd get involved with a former member of a motorcycle club.

And even if that didn't bother her, she was not the woman in my head.

No, my mind was consumed with a pair of coffee-colored eyes and silky umber hair.

My mystery woman had been on my mind all week, and though telling Mom I'd met someone would get her off my back about Tera, this was not the type of relationship I'd share with my mother.

"Anything exciting happening?" I asked Mom, ready to change the subject.

She frowned but went along with it. "Yes, actually. I started cleaning out your father's side of the garage."

I blinked, replaying her statement to make sure I'd heard it right. "Oh."

"It's time, Emmett. It's time to put things away."

Time? Fifty years could pass and it still wouldn't be enough time. My throat tightened. "Do you, um . . . need help?" *Say no.*

She gave me a sad smile. "Only if you want to help."

No, I did not. Dinner churned in my stomach. I wasn't ready for this conversation. It had been years, over a decade since Dad had been murdered, but I still wasn't ready. And during all that time, I'd been sure Mom hadn't been ready either. Dad's things had been in the garage for that long, and to my knowledge, she hadn't touched them.

"Why now?"

She shrugged. "I'm not getting any younger, son. I don't want you to deal with this when we're both gone."

DEVNEY PERRY

I was out of my chair before she could finish her sentence. "I gotta go."

"Emmett—"

"I'll think on Dad's stuff." I spoke over my shoulder, already heading for the door. The walls were closing in on me, and I needed some air.

Mom followed, standing in the doorway as I straddled my bike, shoved a pair of sunglasses over my face and roared away.

I'd text her later but what I needed at the moment was the road.

Why would she spring this stuff about Dad on me tonight? What was going on with her? She wasn't that old. Was she sick?

Maybe I'd have answers if I hadn't raced out of her house.

Shit. She'd worry, so I rode to the closest gas station and pulled over to shoot her a quick text.

Sorry. Caught me off guard.

Her reply was instant. *It's okay. Love you.*

Love you too.

I tucked my phone away and filled up the bike since I was here. And when I returned to the road, the grip of panic had loosened its hold. The sun was warm and night still hours off, so I took advantage and rode around town.

My first route was past the garage, making sure that the thick chain around the gates was secured. For years, we'd left the lot open but after all the shit that had happened with Leo these past few months—that son of a bitch Tucker Talbot's nephew staging accidents in the hopes of taking Leo out—we'd started locking up.

There were cameras mounted on the exterior of the

58

building and I'd added motion sensors just about every-where. At least twice a week an animal set them off at night, but thanks to the cameras, I could check both the lot and inside of the shop from my phone.

We'd installed new floodlights that would flicker on after dark and if someone managed to break in, Dash and I would be alerted immediately.

If the Warriors or their family members were going to come after us, they'd have to be at the top of their game. Considering their major players were all in custody, I liked our odds.

We were being careful, making sure that the women and kids didn't go anywhere alone. And I made time to do what-ever sleuthing I could online. Sometimes all it took was checking a person's social media feed or text messages. Most loved to overshare.

Every morning I checked my alerts. Hacking had been a longtime hobby, another escape and a skill I'd put to use for the club. A skill I was still putting to use.

There were a few Warriors who were not in jail or already convicted and in prison. Some had been released on bond as they awaited their trial. Those members were mostly in Ashton, but I checked their bank accounts and credit cards daily to ensure there was no sign of a trip to Clifton Forge.

Beyond them, there were known relatives of the Warriors, though that list wasn't as accurate as I would have liked. Hell, we hadn't even considered Tucker Talbot's nephew a threat because he hadn't had any connection to his club.

But that hadn't stopped Doug Hamilton from trying to kill Leo.

So I watched family too, especially Tucker Talbot's ex-wife and two daughters. Thankfully, they were exactly where they should be—South Carolina.

The Arrowhead Warriors had been our enemies for what felt like my entire life. After an FBI raid at their club-house over a year ago, their gang had been shut down, but that didn't necessarily erase a threat.

Their president was a ruthless son of a bitch.

Tucker Talbot was currently serving three consecutive life sentences in prison but that didn't mean he didn't have ties to the outside world. And obviously he blamed us for his club's ultimate demise—even though the paranoid mother-fucker had kept video evidence on his members that was more useful to the FBI than any evidence the Tin Gypsies could have produced.

I wasn't going to try and make sense of that bastard's thoughts. All I could do was put up the best guard I could manage and pray to God no one slipped through the cracks.

That we didn't have another nephew come to Clifton Forge to exact Tucker's revenge.

On paper, Doug Hamilton hadn't appeared to have anything to do with his uncle. Still, he'd come after Leo. Doug had failed but Tucker would find another pawn.

Maybe if we held him off long enough, he'd run out of toadies. Hell, maybe one of his own brothers, a Warrior who Tucker had damned to prison with his video footage, would do the world a favor and shiv the fucker between the ribs.

A man could hope.

Until then, we prepared. Maybe Tucker's daughters would prove to be a threat. Maybe it would be another Warrior's family who came after us. All we could do was keep our eyes open and pray we saw the threat before it was too late.

Leaving the garage, I rode toward another one of my rentals across town. I didn't stop, only took it in from the outside to see that the lawn had been mowed.

It was a two-bedroom house occupied by an older bachelor who worked at the fire department. The windows were dark and his truck was missing from the driveway, probably because he was on a long shift at the station. Another dream renter who took care of the place like it was his own and never missed a rent check.

From there I rode to the office complex I'd bought two years ago. It had taken me a while to fill the space, but with the insurance agency, the nail salon, the nutritionist and the speech pathologist, I had four long-term leases locked, and barring a disaster, it would run on autopilot.

That was the goal. Eventually I wanted enough properties and local business investments that my money would go to work for me. I loved being a mechanic and working at the garage, but an early retirement was the dream.

While I was still able in body and mind, I wanted to cut myself loose of that daily grind. Maybe I'd spend months on the road. Maybe I'd head south during the winter. Without a wife or kids, I had nothing tying me down.

A lot would depend on Mom and what she needed as she aged, but I wasn't going to be trapped in a job my whole life. Not that I thought of work at the garage as a job. I was lucky to enjoy every minute I worked when most men couldn't say the same. Regardless, the day I hated my job was the day I walked. My investments were the key to my freedom to do so.

As of last month, every one of my property investments

was covering its mortgage through rent. I'd be paying off Tera's place first, owning it free and clear like I did my own home. Mom's place was paid for, something Dad had ensured long before he died.

He'd made sure she was taken care of, even after their divorce.

And after his death, he hadn't saddled her with much of a burden. She'd planned his funeral. She'd cleared out his place, bringing his things to her garage, where they'd stayed beneath tarps and canvas cloths for years.

And now she was clearing it out. She'd be putting him away.

I should help her do it. I should carry that weight.

Except I wasn't sure I was strong enough.

It had taken me years to get over Dad's death. Given the tightness in my chest, maybe I still had work to do.

But not tonight. Tonight, I rode. I breathed the summer air and let the rumble of my bike tune out the thoughts in my head. I rode to escape.

Sex was a decent alternative too.

My bike seemed to steer itself toward The Betsy, drawn by the possibility that my mystery woman was there. She'd left my house last week without a word. Whatever her reasons, she seemed to be good with casual sex. Maybe she was coming off a bad breakup—I hadn't asked.

If our night together last week was the last time, I'd be disappointed. But I also knew better than to get attached to a hookup.

It was that thought that turned me around. That sent me home instead of the bar.

I was all for uncomplicated sex. But women rarely let it stop there. No matter what they said, feelings always got involved. So I made sure to set boundaries and cut a girl loose before it would hurt.

That had been Dad's advice. Better to leave a woman wanting more than break her heart.

There'd never been a shortage of women at the club-house. Sex had been easy, especially with a Tin Gypsy patch on my back. Those days, all I'd wanted was to fuck, fight and ride. The money we'd made had been a bonus.

When the time came to disband, there were brothers who hadn't wanted to give up the life. Leo had been that way, even though he'd voted in favor of shutting down. But not me.

I wished I missed the club. Maybe I should. But with every passing day, I summoned less and less longing for the old days.

I missed my dad. I missed Draven.

But not the club.

Money still got earned. And sex was still easy to come by.

I slowed as the turnout to my place came into view. I lingered at the mouth of my driveway, contemplating a secu-rity gate. The house itself had alarms and motion sensors inside and in the garage, but the property was wide open. Vulnerable. Untamed.

Making a mental note to do some research, I continued on up the drive to home.

The end of August was hot and this year had been dry, but here on my property, with the towering trees, the air was cool once I slipped between their shade. I dragged in the earthy pine scent just as a flash of gleaming black caught my eye from the house.

The Nova.

I guess I wasn't the only one who wasn't quite ready to end this little fling.

After parking the bike in the garage, I hit the deck, walking the length of the house. There was no way she'd made it inside, not without tripping my security system.

I found her on my favorite chaise lounge overlooking the backyard. There was no way she'd missed the thud of my boots on the porch boards, but she kept staring at the forest as I approached and took the seat beside hers.

Finding any other woman on my deck would have freaked me out that I'd hooked a clinger, but not this woman. She hadn't even asked for my name or offered her own.

Her name wouldn't take much to discover. I'd memorized her license plate after the first night. A quick search and I'd know her address, phone number, bank account balance and shoe size.

But why spend that energy? This was a physical relationship, and for once in my damn life, I didn't want to have all the information.

Information meant saying goodbye to the mystery. Information would tarnish the allure. Information would only lead to questions, and at the moment, I didn't want answers.

Tonight, I just wanted to escape.

"Hey there, Ace."

"Hey, baby." Baby worked and she didn't seem to mind. I didn't mind Ace either, especially in that sultry voice.

"Are you going to ask me why I'm here?"

"Nope."

The corner of her mouth turned up.

"Are you going to sit there? Or get over here?" I motioned to my lap and the growing bulge behind my jeans.

That earned me a full-blown smile. Her dark eyes

sparkled and those pretty, rosy lips spread wide. One day soon, I'd like to see those lips spread around my cock.

Devil that she was, she made me wait. She made me sit there, my dick hardening each time I caught her floral scent. Then finally, she swung her legs over the edge of her seat, stood and straddled my lap.

Her hands dove into my hair and released it from its tie. It hung to my shoulders as she ran those manicured nails against my scalp.

Then she leaned in and brushed her mouth against mine, teasing for a few seconds, before the grip on my patience shredded and I took over.

I put a hand on the back of her head, pinning her mouth to mine as my tongue swept inside those sweet lips.

She moaned, sinking her center into my lap. We ground against one another until I needed more and stripped away her gray silk blouse. The matching slacks came down next. Her heels with those familiar red soles were kicked free as she worked the belt on my jeans.

The second I had a condom in place, she took me in.

There was nothing slow or gentle about how we fucked, out in the open with the wilderness as our witness.

We came together in a rush, a tangled mess of mouths and limbs and pants and cries. And when we were done, she stood off me so I could dispose of the condom. I slipped inside and disabled the alarm system.

She was dressed and on her way around the deck, headed for the Nova, by the time I returned outside.

"Where do you think you're going?" I asked, catching her by the front door.

She smirked and slid close, her hand palming my ass. "Don't worry. I'm not done with you yet."

I chuckled. "Got a phone number?"

"I do."

"Gonna give it to me?" I'd given her mine but she'd never called.

"Depends. Are you going to get clingy?"

Fuck, but she was perfect. "I don't need promises or expectations. Just sex."

She studied me for a moment, then rattled off her number.

I memorized it immediately.

"See you later, Ace."

"Drive safe, baby."

She laughed and then, tires spinning on the gravel, disappeared.

Her license plate was burned into my head, along with that phone number.

Yeah, I should probably look her up. But not this time.

Besides, I'd cut her loose soon enough.

CHAPTER FIVE

NOVA

"I don't like this," Dad said, his voice low. "I don't want you there."

"It's the only way."

He frowned. "I have other options."

"Like Doug?" I whispered.

Another frown, this one making the crease between his dark eyebrows deepen. Dad didn't like failure and Doug had failed spectacularly in his botched attempt at revenge.

Selfishness was the reason that Doug had failed. He'd gone after the Tin Gypsy he'd considered the easiest target—Leo Winter. But instead of owning it, Doug had tried to kill Leo by accident. Probably so Doug could walk away unscathed.

There was no such thing.

The news reports speculated that Doug had drugged Leo and tampered with a jack at the garage, as well as Leo's truck's brakes. None of that had been proved yet and if Dad knew the specifics, he hadn't shared.

Dad was fickle about exactly what he told me, but he promised whatever secrets he kept were for my own good.

And while I trusted him, it meant that I had to gather my own information at times. Most came from the news. That was how I'd learned that Doug had rigged a bomb at Leo Winter's garage.

The explosion had nearly killed Leo's then-fiancée, now-wife Cassandra. And it had been Doug's downfall.

The staged accidents were a weak attack. Anything could—and had—gone wrong. And Doug was no longer a free man. They'd caught him anyway and his life as a free man was over.

"Was he acting on orders? Or of his own volition?" I asked.

Dad didn't answer.

"Was he even a member?"

Dad gave me a noncommittal shrug.

Apparently, I wouldn't be leaving here with information on Doug today. Not that I needed it. Today's visit was simply to check in.

Dad ran a hand through his hair. There were more gray streaks through the dark strands than there had been during my last visit two weeks ago. The goatee that had once been black was nearly white. He was aging before my eyes, but the fight was still etched into the weathered lines of his face.

The day I came here and the fight had vanished from his face was the day I'd worry.

At Dad's insistence, I didn't visit often. But with things set in motion, I doubted I'd be able to come here again for a while. I wanted one last meeting with him before I dove deeper into Emmett's life in Clifton Forge.

It had been two days since Emmett's deck, and I could

still feel him between my legs. His taste was a whisper on my lips and his scent a ghost on my skin.

So far, I'd played this slowly, methodically, but I was about to level up, and once I started, I couldn't risk another visit to the prison.

"What's your next move?" Dad asked.

It was a risk to have told him what I was doing, especially in this room with the camera mounted in the corner and the guard beyond the steel door. I'd hoped to avoid sharing details of my plan with Dad, but when I'd come here today, he'd made an offhand comment about getting in touch with a man connected to the Warriors on the outside.

The last thing I needed was interference, so I'd explained to Dad my plan and asked him for time. Time to infiltrate Emmett Stone's life, time to find information that would send him, Dash Slater and Leo Winter to prison.

"There's information at Emmett's house. I'm sure of it. You told me he was into hacking, right?"

"Yes."

"Then that's where I'll start. Now that I'm in, I can dig deeper. But you need to trust me. Give me time."

He blew out a long breath and nodded.

"Thank you." I opened the manila folder I'd brought in and slid it across the metal table between us.

Dad leaned on his forearms, bracketing the page before he began to read. To anyone watching, it was just an attorney giving her client some paperwork to review. But shielded by his arms, on the second page, was another letter from Mom and a recent photo of Christian.

As he read it, I glanced around the room. We'd sat here, in these exact seats, countless times since his sentencing.

The room was gray and windowless. His bright orange jumpsuit assaulted my eyes.

But it was in this room that Dad had finally pulled me into his circle.

The first time he'd talked about the Warriors, I'd been sure it was a mistake. The only member of our family he'd trusted had been TJ. Dad had always kept Mom, me and Shelby in the dark. But visit after visit, while I pretended to be one of his attorneys, he'd confided more and more in me. The floodgates had opened.

To his past.

To my anger.

Because it was in this room that I'd learned the details of my brother's death. That it wasn't just a nameless rival club who'd murdered him, but the Tin Gypsies.

Dad might think he had options besides me, but I didn't trust anyone besides myself to see this through to the end.

He finished reading the letter and looked up. His expression was blank except for the sadness in his eyes. The longing for my mother.

He loved her as much as she loved him.

"I won't be back for a while." There'd be no more letters and no more photos.

He nodded, hesitating with the papers before sliding them over.

"She's thinking of you," I murmured.

"I'm thinking of her too."

"Maybe one day she can come to visit."

"No." His tone brooked no argument. "Never."

"But—"

"I don't want her to see me here. Not like this. We had our goodbyes. We had them every time I left her house."

I sighed. "Okay."

He gave me a sad smile, then nodded toward the door. Time was up.

I collected the papers, a templated prenuptial agreement I used at work, and tucked them away in the folder. Then I put it in my briefcase beside my fake ID.

Technically it was a real ID. I was posing as an associate who worked at Dad's lawyer's firm.

Nancy Lennox.

We had the same height and a similar build. Her face shape was different than mine, but with the blond wig to match her natural hair color and my thick glasses, no one had ever looked twice.

Being Nancy allowed me to come and go from here without question.

"Stay safe," he said.

"You too."

"I love you, Nova," he whispered.

I hadn't heard those words enough from my father, simply for the lack of opportunity. For his club that had kept us apart. "I love you too, Dad."

"Work fast."

Dad was worried that as years passed with him in prison, he'd lose his influence. It was a valid concern. People outside of these walls would return to their normal lives and though there were members of the Warriors who wouldn't spend decades here, they'd be less likely to help him in his battle against the Tin Gypsies in five years than they were now.

But at the moment, many of them were as angry as Dad. As angry as me. Right now, things were raw.

Time would dull that emotion. Time would make them forget.

If I failed, if I couldn't find evidence to lock the Gypsies away and throw away the key, Dad would call in favors. He'd explore those other options.

The clock was ticking.

"I'm counting on you, Nova."

"I know. And you can."

"That's my girl."

My chest swelled with pride. How long had I waited for his confidence? How many years had I longed for him to include me in his life? It was sad that his arrest had been the catalyst that brought us together. It broke my heart that being in this room was where I'd felt the closest to my father.

"I'll be back when it's done," I said, shoving to my feet.

"Drive careful." *Be careful.*

"Always." I walked to the door and knocked. The guard appeared in the window and unlatched the lock. Then, leaving my father behind, I was led through the maze of prison hallways to the checkout station. It wasn't a quick process coming here, but finally I stepped outside into the August sunshine.

The parking lot was nearly empty today. Fridays were normally quiet. But tomorrow, Saturday, would be busy, as it was a regular visiting day for family members.

I walked to the parking lot and slid into the Nova. The riskiest move I took coming here was driving my own car. It was the one object, besides my fingerprints, that could connect the fake Nancy Lennox to the real June Johnson.

Though with my fake license plates, it would take some effort.

Luckily, since I claimed to be Dad's lawyer, the administration hadn't put me through the full visitor protocol. They'd no doubt done a background check, but they were satisfied to let me in based on my ID alone. Probably because I hadn't started visiting Dad until after his conviction. The FBI and state prosecutor were busy with the other Warriors and their respective trials at the moment.

Posing as Nancy, I was simply bringing paperwork to a client to settle his estate. Not that he had many assets left.

This ruse couldn't go on forever. But I'd push it for as long as possible.

The FBI might discover that I was not exactly who I said I was, though without testing my DNA, they'd never know I was Dad's daughter. It wasn't really the FBI who concerned me at this point. The worst they could do was keep me from Dad.

No, my biggest concern was Emmett and his friends in Clifton Forge.

One of his buddies was Luke Rosen, the Clifton Forge chief of police. I was sure Luke, in conjunction with the FBI, was monitoring Dad's visitors. They'd find Nancy Lennox on the rosters, but if they chose to follow Nancy . . .

It was good today was the last visit for a while.

I climbed in my car, took one last look at the prison through my window, then drove away. Ten miles outside the prison, I stopped on the side of the highway and made sure there were no cars approaching. Then I got out and went to the trunk.

Mom had taught Shelby and me to always keep emergency supplies handy in case we ever got stranded. Cell service could be spotty in Montana and it was better not to count on a rescue. Women often had to rescue themselves.

I didn't go anywhere without the emergency kit. In a duffel bag, I had a first-aid kit and a butane lighter. Hand-warmer packets, a coat and gloves. I even had an extra gallon of gas. It was something I'd kept on hand for years, not for myself, but because TJ had been known to drive until the very last drop of fuel in his car or bike was burned.

As a teenager, he'd called me at least five times to ask if I could bring him some gas. Then he'd died and I hadn't been able to take out that plastic gas can. The gas itself was probably too old to be usable, but every time I thought about clearing it out, I couldn't bring myself to pull it from the trunk.

Maybe I would when this was over. Maybe then I could put TJ and his death behind me.

There was an empty backpack in the trunk, one I kept for my disguise. I dropped my Nancy Lennox ID into the bag, then tugged the wig from my head and stowed it along with my glasses. My fingers dove into my dark hair as I shook it out, a sigh of relief escaping my lips like it always did when the wig was gone. I wouldn't be needing Nancy for a while, so I zipped up the bag and put it into the hidden compartment in the trunk's floor. A special customization Dad had put in the Nova before he'd given me the car as a gift. That compartment also held my gun.

With my things stowed, I stripped off my blazer before climbing behind the wheel. It was always unnerving to lose the disguise and become me again this close to the prison. Even in my favorite sleeveless silk blouse, a gray pinstripe pencil skirt and patent heels, I was vulnerable.

There was no way anyone knew I was pretending to be one of Dad's lawyers. No way. If Emmett suspected anything, he wouldn't have had sex with me again, right?

"No one knows." I spoke the words like a wish I desperately needed to come true.

I'd covered my tracks. I'd been careful, so careful.

No one knew.

Except Dad.

What would have happened if he had been more careful? The thought was one I'd had many, many times since his arrest. It was definitely not a question I'd be asking, but I wondered.

If Dad hadn't kept video footage of the club, what would the FBI have had on him? I suspected there was more evidence, that even without the videos, they would have had a solid case. But the videos had been so damning.

I understood why he'd taken them. He'd been protecting himself from club traitors, using information to keep his members in line.

Dad trusted no one but those in his inner circle—a circle I'd just recently joined.

Still . . . the videos had been a mistake.

A mistake I wouldn't be making. I'd been keeping secrets my entire life. Soon we'd see if the Tin Gypsies were good at protecting theirs.

Dad was one of the smartest, most cunning men I'd ever met. I had to assume that if he'd kept information on his club members, then the Tin Gypsies had as well. It was unlikely they'd destroyed it, hoarding their secrets for a rainy day.

These assumptions of mine were a gamble but one I was willing to chance.

Worst case scenario, I failed my father. I failed my brother. Then Dad would take it upon himself again until he had what he craved.

Blood.

My stomach twisted at the thought. The idea of Emmett's death shouldn't have bothered me so much, but death wasn't what I wanted.

There'd been too much blood spilled, which meant I couldn't fail. Yes, I wanted to balance the scales. But death was not the goal.

I shoved the car in drive and raced to Clifton Forge. An hour into my trip, my phone rang. I groaned at Ira's name on the screen but answered with a flirty laugh. "Hey, you."

"Hey, sugar pie." *Gag.* I hated the nickname. But Ira was fifteen years my senior and thought I was some young, sweet thing. Poor, delusional Ira.

"How's your day going?" I asked.

"It's been a long one. I was just hoping to wrap up work early for the day. And wondering if I could take my girl out for dinner."

"I wish I could." *Lie.* "I had to head out of town for work. It was last minute, and I was going to call you tonight. I didn't want to interrupt you at work. You've been so busy lately."

"You can always call me. Unless I'm with a client or in trial, I'll always answer for you."

Ira Hug was Dad's lawyer. Ira was Nancy Lennox's boss. Ira was currently representing three senior members of the Arrowhead Warriors. Ira and I had been dating for two months. And Ira had no idea that I was Tucker Talbot's daughter or that I was using him for information.

Dad didn't need to know that either. These were my secrets, after all.

"How long will you be gone?" he asked.

"Hopefully not long. I'll call you the second I get home and we'll take a rain check on dinner."

"Looking forward to it." He blew a kiss into the phone.

My lip curled. "Bye, sweetie."

I tossed the phone aside and hit the gas.

Ira had been the Warriors' club lawyer for years. He was far from clean and he wasn't the type to have moral dilemmas about his clients' crimes. As long as the money came in, he'd fight tooth and nail to prove his criminals were innocent.

He was flashy and bold. He was a snake in an Armani suit. And I suspected Ira knew more than most about my father and his own secrets.

But that wasn't why I'd lured Ira into this little tête-à-tête. I wasn't using him to get information on Dad. No, I was using Ira to get information on the other Warriors.

It had been so easy to slip into Ira's life. I was the younger, beautiful woman he could whisk away to expensive restaurants on the weekends. The woman he could show off to his friends around Missoula. Ira loved arm candy.

And he loved his gin and tonics.

During our dates, I'd let him parade me around the most popular restaurants. He'd always pick a table in the center of the room where everyone could see us eat. Then once the meal was over, we'd return to his place for a night cap. I'd slip a sedative into his gin and tonic, let him kiss me for a while, and like clockwork, just before he could suggest we go to his bedroom, he'd pass out.

Leaving me free to explore his house.

Ira really should leave his clients' files at the office.

I hadn't found a file on Dad yet, not that I was surprised. His case was closed. And besides, I trusted Dad. If I needed a question answered, I'd ask him, not reference Ira's notes.

Otherwise, Ira's client files were quite handy. I knew the status of each arrest and each ongoing trial. I had a log of visitors who'd seen each of the Warriors in prison and a long list of family names.

It was all part of my arsenal. A way to protect myself from interference.

I had to ensure there were no ticking bombs that might explode in my face while I was in Clifton Forge.

Ira was just another piece of the game. The poor man didn't even know just how much he was being played, not only by me, but also Dad.

Per Dad's request and a hefty cash payment, Ira had arranged for a copy of Nancy's ID to find its way into the mail. I hadn't been a part of that discussion, but the ID had shown up at my doorstep with a note to use it to visit Tucker Talbot.

Ira would never know I possessed Nancy's ID. Just like he'd never be invited to my home.

On one of my first trips to the prison, I'd asked Dad how. I'd asked if Ira knew about me. He'd promised our father-daughter status was safe and that Ira believed I was just another player for the club. It was the truth, after all.

And I was sure that the real Nancy Lennox was being compensated handsomely for the use of her identity. Not a single lawyer in Ira's firm was what I'd consider ethical.

Least of all Ira himself.

It was nothing short of a miracle that he hadn't pushed harder with our dating relationship. I refused to have sex with him.

Maybe I was crossing every moral line with Emmett Stone but at least there was a magnetic attraction there. An attraction that was probably going to get me into trouble. There'd only been the three times with Emmett, but I craved more. My core pulsed at the thought of him on his deck this week. The man had a way of turning me inside out with one thrust of his glorious cock.

A shiver rolled down my spine.

I shouldn't want him this much. I shouldn't let myself get caught up in the pleasure.

"It's just sex." I'd say that as many times as I needed until it sank in.

The miles flew by as I sped to Clifton Forge, ready to settle in for a while. After today, there'd be no more trips and I was looking forward to sinking into the small community, even if it was temporary.

A smile pulled at my lips as I passed the sign welcoming me to town.

On a Friday night, I suspected I'd find Emmett at The Betsy.

Later, I'd go in and make sure he hadn't forgotten about me. That he didn't get ideas of replacing me with a skank from the bar. But my first stop in town was the grocery store. The rental's fridge was nearly empty and though eating out was easy, most of the time I preferred simple food I cooked at home.

I'd just collected a cart and was walking toward the produce section when a gravelly voice caught my ear.

"Hey, baby."

Gotta love small towns. I smiled and turned toward Emmett as he strode my way with a bottle of water in his hand. "Hey, Ace."

The corner of his mouth turned up and the urge to kiss him came over me so strongly that I clutched the handles of the shopping cart, holding on so I wouldn't go to him. So I wouldn't appear as desperate as I really was for a touch.

"What's going on?" he asked.

"Shopping. You?"

He held up his water. "Hitting the road for a ride."

"Ah." I nodded. So he wouldn't be at The Betsy. That would save me a trip to the bar.

"What do you say?"

"To what?"

"To coming along." There was a glint in his eyes, one that told me we wouldn't just be riding his bike.

I answered by abandoning my cart and strutting toward the doors.

Emmett was right behind me, his gaze leaving a scorching trail down my neck, over my shoulders and settling on my ass. Motives aside, it was heady to be wanted by a man like Emmett. To be craved as much as I craved. To be desired by a man I lusted for with every fiber in my being.

Maybe I liked our nights together too much.

Some other night, I'd sort that out in my head. But tonight, I wanted to ride.

We hit the parking lot and I walked to my car, stowing my purse in the backseat and plucking my sunglasses out of the cup holder.

Emmett was waiting on his bike when I locked the car's doors.

I went to him and hiked up my skirt.

He grinned as I put both hands on his shoulders and straddled the seat behind him. There wasn't much space but I held on tight, smashing our bodies together. My skirt rode up so high my thighs beside his were bare.

"That's hot, baby." He trailed a hand up my skin.

I wound my arms around his waist and pressed my palms against the snug cotton of his T-shirt, feeling the washboard abs beneath. "Pretty hot yourself, Ace."

"Hold on."

I nodded, molding my chest to the roped muscles of his back.

Emmett's masculine scent, spice and earth and leather, filled my nose and I rested my cheek against his shoulder, dragging it in.

I closed my eyes and for just a moment, I wasn't June Johnson. I wasn't Tucker Talbot's daughter. Emmett wasn't my enemy, and this wasn't all part of some grand scheme to get my revenge.

For just a moment, I was a woman who shared a primal attraction with this sexy man. This man who pushed me to shed my inhibitions and be free.

The vibration and noise of the engine snapped my eyes open. I tightened my hold before Emmett shot out of the parking lot and aimed us out of town to the highway.

The air whipped through my hair and the smile on my face was impossible to hold back.

How many times had I seen Dad ride off, wishing I could be with him? Wishing he would let me sit on his motorcycle, just once? But it had been as forbidden as my real name.

Not today. Today I got to ride. As we settled into an easy cruise, the road as warm beneath us as the sun was above, I straightened. I gripped Emmett with my thighs and let my arms loose. The moment my arms unwrapped from around him, he dropped one hand to hold my knee and keep me steady.

He gave me the freedom to let go.

I opened, stretching my fingers to tickle the wind. And I flew.

Tonight, I'd fly.

Tomorrow, I'd get back to business.

CHAPTER SIX

EMMETT

I'd forgotten how good it felt to have a woman curled against me on a ride.

My hand went to her thigh, gripping it tight as she let go of my waist and spread her arms wide.

I chuckled into the wind.

Not many would let themselves go on a first ride, but she was fearless. She had this fire, and damn it, that fire was making it hard for me to walk away.

I could have avoided her at the store easily enough. She hadn't spotted me, and I could have kept on walking. But this pull between us was irresistible. She was a lure and I was her willing catch.

"Hold on," I called over my shoulder, ready to give her another thrill.

She obeyed instantly, her arms clamping around my ribs. Then I gunned the engine, shooting us forward and reveling in the thunder of my bike on the road. She laughed in my ear, and that sweet sound went straight to my cock.

I was going to need a name for this one because calling her *baby* wasn't going to cut it for long. The smart thing to do here would be to end it before *baby* wore thin, but with every mile we rode, the more I didn't want to call it off. Not yet. As long as she didn't expect anything serious, why not have some fun?

We rode for an hour, taking a highway loop that I'd ridden a hundred times. When Clifton Forge came back into view, she sagged against me, the disappointment in her body matching my own.

"Got anywhere to be?" I asked over my shoulder as I pulled up to the first stoplight in town.

"No."

"Good." Straight would take us to The Betsy. We could have a couple drinks, then I'd take her back to her car at the grocery store. But right would take us to my place.

I turned right.

The clouds had come in while we'd been riding. They nearly blocked out the evening sun and with the deep gray overcast and plummeting temperature, rain wasn't far away. It came just as we turned off the highway and onto my private drive.

"Ahh!" She laughed as the first drops hit. Then she loosened her grip and tipped her face to the heavens, letting them coat her face.

I hit the opener and eased the bike into the dark garage, parking it beside my truck.

She climbed off first and I expected her to head for the inside door. Instead, she walked toward the rain, stepping outside as the clouds opened.

The click of her heels was lost as the deluge began. She

didn't so much as flinch. She opened her arms and let the water soak through her blouse and skirt.

She was mesmerizing. Sexy. Mysterious. I was a statue, my eyes aimed at her like my entire purpose in this life was to watch her.

When she finally tipped her chin down, she glanced over her shoulder and gave me that sly smile while she crooked her finger.

She beckoned. I followed.

I strode into the rain. I walked willingly into her storm.

Without hesitating, I went to her, gripped her by the hips and smashed my lips on hers, tasting the water and the sweetness of her lips. She opened for me, her arms looping around my shoulders as I swept my tongue inside.

Her breath hitched and I swallowed the gasp as I took her perfect ass in my palms and squeezed. Hard.

Then I hauled her up by her legs, hooking my hands behind her knees and pulling them around my hips so I could carry her inside. The moment we walked through the door into the house, we were a mess of wet clothes and sloppy kisses.

I keyed in the code on the alarm while she worked my belt free.

She kicked off her heels while I toed off my boots. Then we left a trail of wet clothes, each piece smacking the hardwood floors as we fumbled our way to the bedroom.

Her hair was soaked but by the time we were through, after a string of orgasms and more condoms than I'd ever used in a single night, most of the tendrils had dried on my pillow.

"That was quite a ride, Ace." She smiled into the sheets as we each panted, regaining our breath.

I grinned. "Aim to please."

Her dark eyes sparkled in the muted light. The storm outside hadn't calmed, the rain pattering on the roof and windows.

"I'd better get going." She moved to leave but I reached for her, wrapping my arm around her waist and hauling her closer before she could disappear.

"Just stay. I'm not taking the bike out in the rain."

"Does that fancy black truck of yours not work?"

"Not in the summer." Unless there was ice and snow on the roads or the temperature was too cold, I was on the bike. But my vehicle wasn't the reason I didn't want her to go. I was wiped out and she felt good right here.

"I'll call a cab."

I didn't respond. I just held her tight and buried my nose in her hair as I closed my eyes.

She tensed but stayed still. Then finally, she relaxed and snuggled closer.

I waited until her breaths evened out. Until she burrowed deeper into my bed.

Then I let myself fall asleep too.

———

THE GLASS DOOR slid open behind me.

"Morning, baby," I said, glancing up as she stepped onto the deck wearing nothing but my white T-shirt from last night.

In her hands, she clutched a steaming mug and gave me a sleepy smile. Then she went to the chaise beside mine, curling into the cushion and tucking her legs underneath her. "Morning, Ace."

It was still raining, a light drizzle compared to last night's downpour. The air smelled of grass and pine and water. This covered deck was my favorite part about the house. On mornings like this, being able to sit here and watch the forest grow was about all a man needed.

And maybe the rare chance to share it with a beautiful woman whose hair was mussed from a night of sex.

"Hungry?" I asked.

"Yes."

"Finish that cup and I'll make you breakfast."

She nodded and sipped from her mug, content to listen to the rain.

When both of our mugs were empty, I took her hand and led her inside. Then I refilled her cup and had her sit at the kitchen island while I went about making us an omelet.

"Want some help?" she asked.

"Nope."

She drank her second cup of coffee while I fried bacon and chopped peppers, mushrooms and an onion. Then while I was whisking the eggs, she disappeared.

I figured she'd gone in search of her clothes. They were in the laundry room, hanging to dry. Instead, she came out wearing a pair of my sweatpants, the waist rolled a few times so they'd fit.

She padded to the stove, running her hands up and down my bare back. I'd only bothered with sweatpants this morning. With a kiss dropped to my shoulder, she stole my mug to refill it along with her own.

Having her here was . . . comfortable. I couldn't think of the last time I'd cooked a woman breakfast. It had to be at least ten years ago and never once had it been in this house. It was uncommon for me to let anyone stay and if I made an exception, the visitor would be out the door first thing in the morning.

But instead of ushering her out, I was coming up with reasons to delay the return trip to town. Why her? What was so special about this woman? Christ, I didn't even know her name.

That should worry me more than it did.

Maybe the reason she was here was *because* of the anonymity. It was an invisible line in the sand and when crossed, maybe this good time would disappear.

"Where are your plates?" she asked.

I pointed to a cabinet and she took out two, setting them on the island.

"Silverware?"

"Drawer beside the fridge."

The clink of forks and knives echoed as the eggs sizzled in the pan.

We moved in tandem, her setting our places while I added cheese and fillings and spices to the meal. When it was done, I split the omelet in two and we sat down to eat.

Not once over breakfast did she ask to be taken to her car. Not once did I offer.

We ate and did the dishes. Then before she could ask for a ride to town, I took her hand and led her to the leather living room couch, where I pulled her onto my lap and snagged the remote from the coffee table.

"What do you feel like watching?" It was a test to see if she'd push me.

She gave me a sly grin, like she knew exactly what I was doing, then snatched the remote from my hand. "*The Last Kingdom*? I just got started on it but so far I'm hooked."

"It's good. Pick up wherever you left off."

"We can watch something you haven't seen yet."

"Nah." I shifted, stretching out on the couch and shifting her so she was lying on my side. "This is a good show."

We watched three episodes before she finally pushed up off the couch and shut the TV off.

Once again, I expected her to ask for her clothes, to mention it was time to leave. Instead, she reached for the hem of the shirt she was wearing—my shirt—and whipped it over her head, setting those glorious breasts free.

My cock jerked as she plucked a condom from the pocket of the sweats. She must have stolen it from the night-stand earlier.

We fucked on the couch. We took a shower. We fucked in bed. We dressed in the same sweats and returned to the kitchen for lunch. The afternoon passed a lot like the morning, TV and sex.

It was one of the best Saturdays I'd had in years.

When was the last time I'd lazed around like this? When was the last time I hadn't rushed out the door or into my office first thing in the morning? When was the last time I'd held a woman on the couch and let myself unwind?

Never.

I'd never done this before. Not even with the few girl-friends I'd had. I couldn't recall a time in my life when I'd spent the day with a woman, simply enjoying her company.

Maybe the reason this was working was because she wasn't my girlfriend. Because we were acquaintances and nothing more. Because her company was a short-lived phenomenon.

Eventually, this would end.

Everything did.

As the hours passed and the rain finally stopped outside, I asked the question that I'd been dreading all day. "Want me to take you back to your car?"

She twisted, looking up at me from where her head was resting on my lap. One of my arms was draped over the back of the couch while the other was toying with her hair. "Not really. I'm enjoying doing nothing today. I don't do it often enough. But . . ."

"But."

"I don't want a relationship. I don't want to make promises I know I'll break. I don't want expectations that I won't meet. That's why I don't want names."

"I'm not looking for anything serious."

"Then no, I don't want you to take me to my car."

A no-strings arrangement was fine by me. "Kiss me, Nova."

She jerked at the name, her eyes flashing panic. "W-what did you call me?"

"Listen, as much as I like calling you baby in the bedroom, that's not going to work for me all the time. You can call me Ace. I'm calling you Nova after that sweet-ass car you drive."

"Oh." Her frame relaxed and she shook her head. Then before I could ask why that had surprised her, she was up and straddling my lap, giving me the kiss I'd demanded.

I took her on the couch, and after we were spent, we went to the deck, where I cooked us burgers. We lazed on our respective chairs, watching the sun set behind the trees.

"Do you like whiskey?" I asked.

"Yes."

I stood and went inside, getting two tumblers from the

kitchen and pouring us each a drink. I found her exactly where I'd left her, completely content in a chaise.

It would be hard for me to see that lounge chair as anything but hers for a while. I might as well have bought it for her. It was the chaise that matched my own but the one I never sat in. After dinner, she'd stolen a hoodie from my closet. It billowed around her, draping past her fingertips and hanging to her thighs.

She looked perfect there, her face fresh and makeup-free. Her hair in loose waves from air-drying. Her delectable body covered in my clothes.

I sipped my whiskey, enjoying the chirp of birds in the evergreens.

"What's your favorite food?" she asked.

"I'm not picky."

She turned toward me. "That's not an answer."

"Tacos. Burgers. My mom's chicken parm."

"Favorite cocktail?"

"This whiskey." I swirled the amber liquid in my glass, the ice cubes rattling.

This whiskey had been Dad's favorite. It wasn't top shelf or imported. But on special occasions, when he wanted more than a beer, he'd have a glass on the rocks. Sometimes, Mom would have one with him too.

"What's yours?" I asked.

"Depends on my mood. When I'm home after work and cooking dinner, I usually go for red wine. When I'm at a restaurant or bar, a martini."

"And how about when you're barefoot, sitting on a deck, wearing my clothes?"

She raised her glass. "This whiskey."

"Good answer." I grinned and took another sip. "What's your favorite place you've ever traveled?"

"Cabo. I went with a couple of friends for my twenty-first birthday. I laid on the beach and drank the entire week away. You?"

"Alaska. Took a month-long trip up there. Drove through Canada. Camped and hiked along the way. Got there and considered staying for good."

"That sounds fun."

"Can't wear heels camping."

She giggled. "I own shoes without heels. I just prefer heels on a regular basis."

"Considering how sexy your heels are, I prefer them too."

She laughed again. "What's your favorite movie?"

"*Braveheart.*"

"Is that why you've got the long hair? Going for a Mel Gibson look?"

"Just too lazy to cut it all the time. It grows fast and it's easier this way." I hit the barber shop every three or four months, either that or have Mom cut it straight across the bottom. When I'd kept it short, I'd had to go in every two weeks.

"When's the last time it was short?"

"When I was in my early twenties."

She took a sip, a smile on her pretty mouth. "I like it. I've never been with a man who had long hair. Gives me something to hold on to. Sort of like you do with mine."

Because she had great fucking hair. Thick and soft. Silky, and there was so damn much. Every chance I got I buried my hands in those strands and held on tight.

The questions continued, questions about nothing and

everything. Questions that didn't get into our personal lives but were personal questions. We talked until our glasses were empty and the lingering ice cubes had melted.

"What's your favorite sexual position?" she asked.

"You riding me on this chair like you did the other day wasn't bad."

She stood and picked up our empty glasses, taking them inside.

I found her in the kitchen, rinsing them clean at the sink. Walking to her, I pressed my chest against her back and snaked my hands underneath her hoodie and T-shirt, finding her nipples pebbled and waiting. Then I dropped my lips to her neck. "What's your favorite sexual position?"

"You'll know when you find it." She leaned back, pressing her ass into my cock.

It took me three times to narrow down her favorite, but when I had her in my bed, pounding into her from behind, she came harder and faster than any time before.

"I changed my mind," I said, my head spinning and my body totally spent.

"About what?" she panted.

"That's my new favorite too."

She laughed and no sound had ever sounded so good in my bedroom.

Then she fell asleep in my arms. Despite my better judgment, I wasn't ready to let her go.

When I dropped her off at the grocery store the next morning, I kissed her slow and long, not giving a shit who saw us making out in the parking lot. If this was the last kiss, I wasn't going to hurry.

"Thanks for the fun weekend, Ace," she said after we broke apart.

"Welcome. Don't be a stranger, baby."

She flashed me that breathtaking smile. "Oh, I think you'll see me again."

I hoped so. Because for the first time, riding home alone and walking into a quiet house didn't give me the normal sense of peace.

CHAPTER SEVEN

NOVA

"Not tonight," I told myself. "I'm not going there tonight. No matter what."

I had to break this streak.

Four days. I'd gone to Emmett's house four days in a row because he was an addiction. An addiction I *had* to get under control before I lost my nerve.

Easier said than done. My willpower had been nonexistent and it had all started because of the weekend.

On Sunday when he'd dropped me at my car still at the grocery store, I'd gone to my rental house and replayed the weekend. I'd replayed it a thousand times since and I still couldn't pinpoint the moment when my willpower had vanished. Maybe it had been over the omelet. Maybe it had been the whiskey. Maybe it had been one of the many orgasms he'd given me.

Hell if I knew.

It was probably a combination of everything because since last weekend, I couldn't get Emmett off my mind. And I couldn't get our weekend out of my head.

Over and over I'd analyzed our time together. I'd obsessed over what I'd told him.

The truth.

For each question asked, I'd told him the truth. A lie required effort. The truth was simple. There'd been no need to lie. I'd told him about my favorites as he'd shared his own.

I'd been completely honest with him, about everything except my identity. Not that he'd asked.

Though when he'd called me Nova, I'd nearly had a heart attack.

The car. A nickname because of my car.

If only he knew how often I'd wanted someone outside my family to use my name.

Maybe that was the moment my walls had cracked.

I'd spent Sunday night in my bed, the scent of him clinging to my skin because I hadn't wanted to wash it away. I'd planned to stay away on Monday too, but after a long day of work, my body had moved on autopilot, climbing into my car and making my way to his secluded mountain paradise.

Pulling up to his house, I'd promised myself not to spend the night. That we'd have sex and I'd go home. To my own bed.

Except his smooth white sheets had proved another addiction.

Monday had repeated on Tuesday. Tuesday on Wednesday. Wednesday on Thursday. Now it was Friday and I had to stop. I had to break this streak.

I didn't want to go to his house. Because I wanted to go so badly.

Shit. I was in trouble.

What was wrong with me? It was only sex. This was just part of the plan. So why couldn't I detach from him?

Every moment spent with Emmett was infuriating because he was so goddamn perfect. He was not who he should have been. He was not the monster I'd expected.

Part of me wanted to blame my infatuation on the orgasms—the many, *many* orgasms. And while they surely had contributed to the muddling of my brain, this addiction was because Emmett was so . . . everything.

It was the way he constantly touched or pulled me close, like he couldn't bear even an inch between us. It was the way he'd held me pressed into his side when we'd watched TV. It was the way he'd pushed the lounge chairs on his deck together so that even though we kept our individual seats, his leg would cross over to mine.

He moved like a dream in the kitchen. It was ridiculously sexy to watch a man who liked to cook and who did it well. I'd only ever seen my mother in our childhood kitchen. With Dad's constant absence, she'd carried that burden alone. Even Shelby's husband, Jack, didn't cook.

Nope, just Emmett.

Why couldn't he have been the man I met after this charade?

I would not allow myself to fall for Emmett. He was a criminal. He was a Tin Gypsy. And they deserved to pay for their crimes.

It was time to reset. To remember why I was here. Remembering was the reason I stood across the street from the Clifton Forge Garage, hidden behind the corner of a beige building.

The Nova was parked three blocks away on a side street. I hadn't wanted to risk Emmett seeing it. I'd parked, then walked here, keeping to the alleyways as I skirted nondescript buildings until I had a decent view of the garage and its open shop doors.

Emmett was working on a bike in the third bay. While I'd been spying, the other mechanics had been doing oil changes and tire rotations. But Emmett had been working alone, spending his time welding on the motorcycle. A shield covered his handsome face but I'd recognize that messy bun of his anywhere.

He was the only mechanic I recognized today. The other two Tin Gypsies, Dash and Leo, were either not working or off to a long lunch. Maybe they were in the office, hidden from my spying.

It didn't matter. They could have been standing in the street waving pink and purple flags and my attention would still have been drawn to Emmett.

He'd pulled on a pair of coveralls over the jeans he'd had on this morning, tying them at the waist. The colorful tattoos on his arms were all on display, his white tank top showing off his muscled biceps.

I'd traced nearly every one of his tattoos with my tongue. All except the skull on his back.

As a little girl, I'd memorized Dad's club's patch. Maybe because it was the last thing I saw when he rode away, the emblem stitched into his black leather vest. The Arrowhead Warrior patch was simple in design. It was an arrowhead framed by the club's name and the year it had been founded. The stitching was white but Dad's had faded to a grayish cream over the years after so much wear.

I would never admit it to my father, but compared to the artful Tin Gypsy patch, the Warrior emblem was like a child's drawing. Though I'd never seen the Tin Gypsy patch on a cut, I'd seen the design on Emmett's skin. And though I couldn't always avoid touching it completely, I didn't worship it like I did his other ink.

My phone vibrated in my pocket and I pulled it out. The garage was too far for anyone to hear me, but still I kept my voice low as I answered my sister's call. "Hey."

"Why are you whispering? Is this a bad time?"

"No, I'm good. Working."

"I just wanted to call and say hi."

I smiled. "Hi."

So much of me wanted to tell her everything. About Dad. About the Warriors. About Emmett. If anyone could help me make sense of the mess in my head, it was my sister.

But I kept my secrets inside and my eyes on the object of my confusion.

Emmett flipped up the face shield, giving me a glimpse of that strong jaw covered by a beard that had tickled my thighs last night. I would never be able to kiss those soft lips enough. I'd never have enough time in his arms. If I ever fell apart, those arms had the strength to keep my broken pieces together.

Except when I fell apart, he wouldn't be there, would he?

And the only person I'd have to blame was myself.

"What are you doing this weekend?" I asked, needing a distraction and a familiar conversation.

"Oh, nothing much. I'm delivering a batch of cupcakes to a birthday party tomorrow morning. The little girl wanted a *Frozen* theme, so I did blue and white frosting with these pretty sugar snowflakes. Then I think we're going to take Christian on a hike while the weather is still nice."

Fall was approaching fast, the summer coming to a close. Though short, autumn in Montana was my favorite season.

The temperatures would cool soon. The trees would become a kaleidoscope of color at the base of the indigo mountains. And the fields would turn from green to gold. We were entering those vibrant, fleeting weeks before winter. The gift of beauty before snow blanketed the ground.

The end was near.

By winter, would the Tin Gypsies be in their own prison cells? They might be, but only if I managed to get these feelings for Emmett under control.

Not tonight. I was not going to his house tonight.

With one last look at him, I turned away from the garage and started down the alley toward the Nova. "That sounds like a nice weekend. How's Mom?"

"She's good. She's helping a friend run a booth at the farmer's market tomorrow. I baked a few small cakes for her to take and sell."

"How's Christian?"

"Napping at the moment. He's getting so big so fast. Jack and I . . . we've been talking about another baby."

"Yes. I completely support this idea."

Shelby laughed. "It's crazy. Babies are so much work but . . ."

"But you make such beautiful babies."

"I want Christian to have a sibling or two. I can't imagine growing up without you or TJ." There was a note of sadness in her voice when she spoke TJ's name. Shelby rarely spoke of our brother and normally it came with some anger. Anger at Dad for dragging TJ into the club life. Anger at TJ himself for following. Mostly I think Shelby was angry because of how she and TJ had ended on a sour note. He was gone and she'd never have a chance to make it right.

"I don't know." She sighed. "We'll see how it goes."

"I vote yes on another baby. I need a fix." Maybe I'd have children of my own one day. I hoped so. But if all I had was the chance to be the fun aunt, then I would be the best aunt in the world.

"You could have babies of your own, you know. That means you'd have to go on more than a first date with a guy. But it is possible."

"Ha ha," I deadpanned.

If only she knew how many times I'd been with Emmett. Shelby loved to tease me about my ability to fault a man over a single dinner. In the past ten years, I'd been on countless first dates. A second date was rare. I'd gone on more dates with Ira than any man in ages and Ira was fake.

Just like Emmett was fake.

Because I was fake.

My entire life there had always been fake.

"Uh-oh," Shelby said. "I hear Christian on the monitor. I'd better let you go."

"Love you," I said.

"Love you too. And, Nova?"

My heart twisted. She used my real name less and less these days. "Yeah?"

"I miss you."

"I miss you too." I smiled, then continued my trek to the car, getting inside and scrolling through my emails before starting the engine. There was a pile of work waiting for me but the last thing I wanted to do was go to my rental and stare at a laptop all day.

I'd only end up thinking about Emmett. And then I'd crumble and drive to his house.

What I needed wasn't work but to get the hell out of Clifton Forge for a while. So I started the car and hit the highway, heading toward Missoula. I didn't go to my home or to Shelby's or to Mom's.

I drove straight to the cemetery.

I drove to visit my brother.

My heels sank into the grass as I crossed the lawn to the plot where we'd laid TJ to rest. Mom must have been here because there was a fresh bundle of flowers on his grave.

"Hi." I dropped to my knees, the warmth from the earth sinking through my jeans. "How are you today?"

I always talked to TJ like he could answer. Maybe because I hoped that he would. Maybe if he heard my voice from wherever he was watching us, he'd hear me and know that I loved him. We all loved him.

"It's a pretty day." I tipped my head to the sunshine and let it warm my face. "I went for a ride on a motorcycle last weekend. And I'm sleeping with the enemy."

TJ always got my truths. The raw. The ugly. The real.

I shifted, sitting on my butt and leaning back on my arms. "This is harder than I thought it would be."

Because Emmett was . . . everything.

"He's sweet, actually. Smart too. And he's a fucking god in bed."

A gust of wind came out of nowhere, blowing a lock of hair in my face.

"Sorry." I laughed. "I'll keep those details to myself."

I settled onto my back, lying on the ground and looking up at the blue sky streaked with a few clusters of white, wispy clouds. "He'll hate me when this is over."

Just the thought made my chest ache.

But what choice did I have? For our family, I had to see this through. If it wasn't me, it would be someone else. And that someone wouldn't be satisfied with prison terms.

Dad would send someone for blood.

Their wives, their children, might get caught in the crossfire.

"I want them to pay for what they did to you and Dad." The conviction in my words was lacking.

I'd come here, to TJ's resting place, hoping for a renewed sense of fire. Instead, I felt this deep, unsettling loneliness.

"I miss you, TJ." Tears flooded my eyes, blurring the sky, but I blinked them away. "Why does it have to be so complicated?"

Our entire lives had been so complicated.

I splayed a hand over his grave, feeling the spiky grass blades poke between my fingers. A bird flew overhead, its wings spread wide as it swept from one tree to another and then out of sight.

"Tell me I'm doing the right thing," I whispered.

There was nothing. Not a breath of wind. Not the chirp of a bird or a rustle in the trees.

There were only doubts. Crippling, crushing doubts. I hadn't been prepared to combat them all, which was probably why I was losing miserably.

The doubts were Emmett's fault. He'd put them there with his gentle smile and rumbling laugh and intoxicating smell.

I shoved off the grass and twisted to a seat, reading TJ's tombstone.

He'd died at eighteen. That was too young. He hadn't even had a chance to live his life. He wouldn't get to spend his Saturdays with a woman, lazing away a weekend on a couch and having sex. He wouldn't get the chance to cook her breakfast or watch the rain fall.

And it wasn't fair.

None of this was fair.

"I'm going to keep going. I won't stop." *Not yet.*

I lay down again, staring up at the sky. TJ and I used to do this on our trampoline when we were kids. We'd find animals in the clouds. We'd make up stories about them and give them names, watching as they'd shift from an elephant to a dolphin to a dragon. We'd stay outside for hours, just the two of us.

I loved Shelby but she was my big sister. We'd fought as sisters do. We'd bickered and griped. But TJ and I had been friends. He'd been my constant companion.

If I'd tried harder to convince him to go to college, could I have kept him away from the Warriors?

No. It would be a fool's hope to think TJ would have lived any other life than by Dad's side. The Warriors had always been appealing to both of us. The minute Dad had pulled TJ into the inner circle, we'd lost him.

I'd been jealous then. So jealous. Because TJ and Dad had always had a connection while I'd been kept at arm's length.

Until now.

Dad was counting on me. TJ was counting on me.

I could do this.

I had to do this.

I shoved up off the lawn and stood, brushing a few pieces of grass from my jeans. Without another word, I returned to the car and hit the road.

The drive to Clifton Forge was spent securing my defenses, reminding myself that Emmett was the enemy. When I rolled past the welcome sign, I went straight to my rental.

The fridge was mostly empty. The few items I'd

purchased at the store earlier in the week were nearly gone. My prospects for dinner included Cheerios, without milk, or half of the ham and swiss sandwich I'd picked up at the local diner on Wednesday over lunch.

"Don't do it." I walked to my purse on the counter and dug out my phone to call for pizza.

My fingers found a different name in the call log.

Ace.

I tapped his name.

"Nova," he answered and the way he said my name in that deep, rugged voice was my undoing.

I broke.

It was just another night, right? I had to spend time with him to get information. One more night didn't need to mean anything.

"Hey, Ace. Are you home?"

"No. But I can be."

I was doomed. "I'll meet you there."

Butterflies tickled my insides as I hurried to the bathroom to freshen my makeup and brush my hair. My toothbrush was plucked from the holder where I'd returned it this morning and put back into the travel case that was becoming a regular resident of my handbag. Then I hurried outside to the car.

I broke every speed limit through town as I crossed Clifton Forge for the country road that led to Emmett's. And when I turned down his lane and into his driveway, he was standing outside the garage, his bike parked inside.

He met me at my door, holding it as I swung out.

I rose up on my toes for a kiss. The moment his lips brushed mine, his tongue dragging across my lower lip, the doubts I'd been pondering all day disappeared. When I was here, I shut it all out.

I sank into him, savoring the warmth of his chest and the strength of his arms. I inhaled his spicy scent, holding it in like a gift to myself.

He took his lips away too soon and looked me up and down, grinning when he got to my snakeskin Louboutin stilettos. "Nice shoes, baby."

"Thanks." My heels were my indulgence and Louboutin my favorite designer.

"Want to go for a ride?"

I shifted and closed the car door. "Sure."

"I was hoping you'd say that."

He took my hand and led me to his Harley. Then we set off onto the road, me clutching him tight until we hit the highway and I opened my arms wide to fly.

We rode for an hour before going back to his place, where I sat on the kitchen counter as he cooked me dinner. Then we retreated to the deck to watch the sunset and share a whiskey on the rocks.

When he picked me up and carried me to his bed, a single word echoed in my mind before he kissed me.

Tomorrow.

Tomorrow I'd put some distance between us. For my own sake.

But not tonight.

CHAPTER EIGHT

EMMETT

No texts. I swung off my bike and shoved my phone into my pocket. No texts from Nova, just like there hadn't been before I'd left the house. Just like there hadn't been last night. Just like there hadn't been for the past four days.

Maybe that was it. The end. Maybe it was for the best. But damn, I missed her. That expensive, seductive scent of hers was gone from my pillows.

I crossed the parking lot for the office, shoving my sunglasses into my hair as I opened the door. "Morning."

"Good morning." Presley raised her cup of coffee as a salute. Nico was in a swing behind her chair, kicking and smiling at the safari animal mobile spinning above him.

"Hi, Emmett." Cass smiled from her chair across from Presley's desk. Seraphina was in her arms, chugging a bottle.

"Hey." Leo came striding out of the waiting room with two cups of coffee in his hands. He brought one to Cass, setting it on the desk as he bent down and kissed her hair.

"Just you two today?" I asked.

"Bryce is coming down with Dash and the boys," Presley said. "Scarlett's staying home with Mary. Genevieve is going to work."

I nodded and went to the waiting room for my own cup of coffee. While it brewed, I took in the room. The changes. So much at the garage was different. This waiting room used to be Draven's office and there were days when I walked in and expected to see him behind his desk, cussing over a parts order.

After his death, neither Presley nor Dash had wanted to take his space. For all of us, this would always be Draven's office. Just like to me, the shop would always mean Dad. Sometimes I still looked for him beneath a car.

He wouldn't be there, but I still looked, expecting him to give me shit about how I always liked to do things my own way instead of his. Dad wasn't there to talk through projects and how best to tackle them.

He wasn't there. But he was there.

Just like Draven.

They lived in these walls. They lived in these rooms. They lived in our hearts and our minds.

"You okay?" Leo leaned against the doorframe.

"Yeah." I tore my eyes from the wall and grabbed my full coffee mug. "Full place today."

"Every day," he said, fondness on his face.

None of us minded that the office was packed with family members more often than not. It allowed Leo, Dash, Isaiah and me some peace of mind while we were working, that the women and kids were within shouting distance. Here, they were safe.

If Dash could have it his way, they'd all be here each and every day. But there was a balance, giving them their freedom and independence while still keeping a close watch.

If Genevieve was working at the law office today, I suspected Isaiah would check in often. If Scarlett was at home, she wouldn't be alone. Luke would likely send a deputy to his house to sit outside all day until he made it home from the station.

It had been a couple of months since the explosion at Leo's place but that had scared the shit out of us all. Cass could have been killed, but she'd gotten lucky. We all had.

Caution had become everyone's middle name. Considering it used to be Trouble, it was yet another change.

The garage had become the common hangout spot during the week. There was an apartment above the office. Genevieve and Isaiah had lived there right after they'd gotten married, but it had been vacant since they'd moved out. So we'd cleaned it top to bottom, giving the women and kids an added space to roam.

"You guys heading upstairs?" Leo asked his wife as we walked out of the waiting room.

"Yeah," Cass said. "I'm hoping she'll take a nap and I can write today."

"Good luck, babe. I'm here if you need anything."

Cass smiled up at Leo as he leaned down to kiss her and then run a thumb over his daughter's cheek.

"What do you need me to do this morning?" I asked Presley.

"Sawyer and Tyler will probably need help with everything on the job board. It's busy today."

" 'Kay." I nodded, then headed for the shop, Leo close behind me. Inside, Sawyer and Tyler were talking beside a workbench. A bench my dad had built years ago. *Stone* was written on the underside. "Morning."

"Hey," they said in unison.

Sawyer and Tyler had worked at the garage for a couple of years now. They were good guys and both hardworking. Decent mechanics for the routine jobs. But they weren't Gypsies. They hadn't asked questions—both of them knew we wouldn't answer if they did—but the crowded office hadn't gone unnoticed. They didn't venture inside much these days unless it was to ask Presley a question or pick up their paychecks.

"Sounds like we've got a busy day." I went to the line of hooks on the wall beside the storage room and grabbed my coveralls.

I didn't wear them every day, but I'd put on a pair of jeans today that I didn't want stained with grease. I set my coffee aside, then stepped into the coveralls and tied the top around my hips. The white T-shirt I wore wasn't anything special and I didn't care if it was wrecked.

Leo and I bullshitted with Sawyer and Tyler for a few minutes as the fresh September morning air drifted through the open bay doors. Across the parking lot, my bike was alone today. Isaiah's would likely join mine, but I remembered a time when the string of bikes stretched nearly the length of the lot.

On the nights when we'd have a party at the clubhouse, there'd be a mass of Harleys surrounding the garage.

Mine gleamed under the sun but it looked lonely.

Dash's truck eased into the lot and parked a ways down, leaving plenty of room for customers. A chorus of small voices sounded outside before Xander and Zeke came racing through the shop, headed straight for Leo and me.

I caught Xander as he barreled for my knees. Leo caught Zeke. Both boys sailed into the air as we tossed them while Dash and Bryce walked into the garage, hand in hand.

"Morning," I said, plopping Xander over a shoulder. He kicked and giggled and I swatted his butt, earning a flurry of tiny fists against my spine. I chuckled and set him down, crouching in front of him and holding up my hands. "Ready?"

He got in his fighting stance, his right leg forward. Then he let his fists fly, punching my open palms with a succession of jabs. He was only five but he'd inherited his father's speed.

Dash had been one hell of a fighter. Put him in a ring and he didn't often lose. I'd won a lot of cash betting on him at the fights we'd hosted at the clubhouse and other places around the county.

"Me too!" Zeke squirmed for Leo to set him down and then he took his brother's place, punching my hands.

"Ouch." I shook my wrists out, pretending that they hurt. "When did you guys get so strong?"

Both boys beamed.

I stood and ruffled their hair, then winked at Bryce.

"We had a meeting with Xander's teacher last night," she said. "We started talking and I guess you know her. She rents one of your properties."

"Tera?"

Bryce nodded. "She's really nice. Her daughter was there too. Maggie. But she's not in Xander's class."

Xander was starting kindergarten tomorrow. Zeke would be going to preschool.

Today was the last day the boys would be around the garage, and even though they always stayed in the office where it was safe and they were out of the way, I was going to miss the energy they brought with them.

Dash knelt in front of his sons, and though he had a smile, there was longing in his eyes too. I wasn't the only one who'd miss having them here. Somehow, we'd all blinked and the boys had become boys, not babies.

Xander looked more and more like Dash every day. Which meant he looked more and more like Draven.

"Be good for Mom today," he said.

"Can we work on something later?" Zeke asked.

Lately the boys had been interested in helping on the cars, so we'd find some old parts for them to bang on with wrenches and screwdrivers.

"Sure. We can this afternoon, but only if you're good." Dash gave them both hugs, then sent them with Bryce to the office.

As she walked away with the kids, I checked my phone again. Nothing. *Damn.*

"Something wrong?" Dash asked, studying my expression.

"Nah," I lied. Then I jerked my chin for him and Leo to follow me to the other side of the shop, away from Sawyer and Tyler. Once we were in Leo's paint booth, I tied up my hair so it would be out of my face while we worked today. "Heard back from that PI in South Carolina again."

"And?"

"He sent me another file I've got on my laptop at home. Mostly pictures he tracked down from when the girls were younger and lived in Montana. Summary of their routines. He's good to keep an eye on the daughters for a while, but he doesn't think it's necessary."

The PI I'd hired had been following Tucker Talbot's

daughters for three weeks. There was only so much we could do from here and given they were Tucker's daughters, we had no idea if they might be a threat. So far, there'd been no indication whatsoever that they were in contact with their father.

"And the ex?"

"Same as the daughters. Nothing new."

Dash nodded. "I think it's worth paying him for another month or so. Just to be certain."

"Agreed," Leo said. "No chances."

"I'll let him know," I said. "I spent some time last night digging through the visitor log from the prison that the FBI sent Luke." It wasn't like I'd had anything else to do.

"Find anything?"

I shook my head. "The VP's wife came to see him two Saturdays ago during regular visiting hours. Otherwise, it's only been lawyers. Tucker met with his again."

"What for?" Leo asked. "His trial is over."

"It was one of the junior partners at the lawyer's firm. Nancy something. I'm guessing it was estate stuff."

"The FBI seized his assets," Dash said.

"Maybe he's fighting for some of it back. Maybe he's updating his will. Whatever it was, I'll keep an eye out for any filings."

"Thanks," Dash said, running a hand over his face. "Think this will ever end?"

"I hope so," I muttered. Maybe if enough time passed, Tucker Talbot and the Warriors would forget about the former Tin Gypsy Motorcycle Club.

"We haven't talked about it, but maybe we need to get in touch with some contacts at the prison." It was something I thought of often these days. "Tucker gets caught in a brawl and doesn't survive it. It's extreme but . . ."

"Better than looking over our shoulders our entire lives," Leo said.

Dash sighed. "If they traced it back to us—"

"Me. It would have to be me." I had no family. No wife or kids to leave behind if I was arrested.

"Let's just . . ." Dash shook his head. "I don't want to go there yet. We might get lucky. Tucker's reach might have ended with his nephew. We're being vigilant. The prosecutors are working through the other Warrior cases. Maybe this goes away."

Maybe. Or maybe not. But the chances of this disappearing were far greater if Tucker Talbot was rotting in hell instead of a cell.

His men were loyal but I doubted they carried the same thirst for vengeance as their former leader. If cutting the head off of the snake was what we had to do, then we'd do it. Plenty of men died in prison and if I needed to facilitate that for Tucker, so be it.

"We've been on the defense this entire time," I said. "Since Draven. Maybe it's time we move to offense."

"Yeah." Dash raked a hand through his dark hair. "I don't like sitting around and waiting for the storm either. But there are too many eyes on the Warriors right now. It's too obvious."

"So we give it time," Leo said. "Then revisit."

I nodded. "Until then, we keep up the guard."

"Enough of this." Dash clapped me on the shoulder. "Let's get to work."

The three of us left the paint booth and joined Sawyer and Tyler in the shop. The day went by quickly since we were busy. That and with family in the office, we popped in and out to see what was going on, and as per usual, the office was a source of constant laughter.

"It reminds me of the old days, having them all here," I told Dash, nodding to the office.

"I was thinking the same yesterday."

When Dad and Draven had been alive, this place had been crawling with family members. I'd spent my childhood at this garage, coming down with Mom to bring Dad lunch. The same was true with Dash and his older brother, Nick.

This garage had been the gathering place. For our families. For the club.

Not all memories here had been good ones. A cloud had hung over us all after Dash's mother, Chrissy, had been murdered. That same cloud had come back after Dad. Then Draven.

But the good outweighed the bad. All we had to do was make sure that cloud didn't get any darker because the Warriors came after us again.

Presley had propped open the door between the office and the shop. We'd ordered lunch from the deli and the scent of onions was too strong for her. Draven had loved that Pres preferred the scent of motor oil and metal.

The women's laughter and the kids' chatter drifted our way. After lunch, none of them had returned to the apartment upstairs. Bryce was telling Pres and Cass a story that she was printing in the next newspaper about a teenager who'd tried to steal a package of Oreos from a convenience store on Central. When the boy had been caught, instead of handing over the package to the cashier, he'd torn the top open and licked all the cookies.

"Did they give him the Oreos?" Pres asked Bryce.

"Yes, after the kid's mother came down and paid for them. I guess she hauled him out of there by his ear, and he was shoving Oreos into his mouth as they walked. The cashier gave me a picture she took."

I chuckled as they all crowded around Bryce's phone to see the photo.

Nova would fit in here.

That thought came on so fast I jerked.

"What?" Dash asked.

"Nothing." I waved it away and turned to the job board.

For a woman who was supposed to be a fling, Nova crossed my mind more than I wanted to admit. And damn it, where was she? Who was she?

It would only take an hour to find out. All I had to do was open my laptop, key in her license plate and I'd know everything there was to know about her. Her real name. Her address. Her job. Her social security number and how much money she had in her retirement accounts.

But I didn't want that. Not with her. I wanted to learn those things from her, not steal them.

If our fling was over, it was over. We'd gone from meeting every night to nothing for four days. I could read the writing on the wall. Time to walk away with the beautiful, pure image of her asleep in my bed.

"What do you want to work on next?" I asked Dash.

"Sawyer and Tyler can tackle the rest of this. Let's spend the rest of the day on the Stingray."

"Fine by me."

Leo and Isaiah joined us and we spent the rest of the day working on the garage's latest restoration. The Stingray was a hot car, one Dad would have loved. Though he would have loved all of the cars we'd brought in lately.

The Firebird we'd fixed up, the car Leo had given to Cass as a wedding present, would have made Dad drool.

He'd taught me to love classic muscle cars and their sleek design. He'd taught me about working with my hands and how to break machines down, then build them up again. With every car and every bike we built, Dad might not be here, but he was a part of it. Every one.

At four, Dash's boys came clamoring out of the office, dragging Bryce with them. We put the work on the Stingray aside and spent the last hour of the day letting Xander and Zeke dink around.

I found an old gear for Zeke to hammer on. Xander and Dash tore into a broken carburetor. And Leo and Isaiah disappeared into the paint booth, where Leo was teaching Isaiah some airbrushing techniques.

At five o'clock, Shaw rolled into the parking lot to pick up Presley and Nico. Leo loaded Cass and Seraphina into their Firebird, leaving for home. Isaiah left to get Genevieve and his kids. Dash, Bryce and the boys headed out at the same time as Tyler and Sawyer, leaving me alone at the garage.

The quiet was a stark contrast to the noise from the day. The silence, something I normally enjoyed here and at home, was too loud. Too obvious.

I found myself alone more often these days. A year ago, it hadn't bothered me.

Today, I didn't want to be alone.

So I shut the bay doors to close down the garage, then double-checked the office was locked. I flipped on the security system, heading to my bike. I rode out of the lot, stopping to slide the gates together and secure the chain and padlock around them. If someone really wanted to get in, they could scale the fence or bust through the gates, but it was a deterrent.

Whatever we could do to keep safe.

Traffic through town was bustling, people coming and going home from work. I headed toward Mom's neighborhood, wanting to stop and say hello. I parked in her driveway just as Tera and Maggie parked next door.

"Hey." I raised a hand and waved as Tera climbed out of her SUV.

"Hi." She smiled and opened the back for Maggie to scramble out.

Maggie went to her mother's leg, leaning close as she stared up at me. She was still not quite easy with me.

"Heard you've got Xander in your class," I told Tera.

She nodded. "I do. And I have a feeling he's going to keep me on my toes."

"He's a Slater." I chuckled. "It won't be boring."

Tera smiled and put a hand on her daughter's head.

She was a beautiful woman. She was smart and kind. For the first time, I wished I had something more than friendly feelings toward her, not just because she was beautiful but because at least with her, I wouldn't be alone. But there was no spark. Maybe Tera and I could have some fun, but it wouldn't go anywhere. And I wasn't going to lead her on, not when there was Maggie to consider.

So I took a step back and left her alone. "Good luck tomorrow. Have fun at school, Maggie."

The girl blushed as I winked at her.

Tera waved.

And I turned and strode for Mom's house, calling out as I opened the door, "Mom."

"Emmett?"

"Who else calls you Mom?"

She laughed, shaking her head as I came into the living room, where she was reading a book. "What are you doing here?"

"Just wanted to say hi." I bent to kiss her cheek, then took a seat on the couch across from her, leaning into the back and crossing an ankle over my knee. "How's your week going?"

She shrugged. "It's only Tuesday. Come back and ask me Friday. I might even have dinner for you then. But you're out of luck tonight. I ate a late lunch, and I won't be hungry for hours."

"That's okay. I don't expect you to cook for me every time I visit."

"I know. But I like to."

I motioned to her book. "What are you reading?"

She smiled and closed the cover, holding it up for me to see. I recognized it from the bookshelves Dad had kept filled at his room at the clubhouse. "It was one of your dad's."

"I know."

"It was in a box in the garage with a whole pile of others. I decided to read them. And look." She slid out of her chair and joined me on the couch. Then she opened the book to a page she'd dog-eared.

There were notes in the margin in Dad's blocky script. I hadn't seen that handwriting in ages. Not since the last time I'd bent beneath the workbench at the garage and found *Stone* written on the wood.

"He's got notes through this whole book. His thoughts on the story."

I swallowed hard. It had been so long since we'd lost Dad, but just seeing those notes brought back the pain from his death. Didn't Mom feel it? She'd been content to leave his belongings tarped in the garage. Couldn't they have stayed hidden for another ten years?

"It's time, Emmett." She must have heard my thoughts because she put her hand on my leg. "It's time."

"Why?"

"Because when I'm gone, I don't want you to go through it all on your own."

"Don't talk like that." I shoved off the couch and went to the kitchen for some water.

Mom followed, watching as I chugged a glass dry. Then, thankfully, she didn't talk about Dad again. "I had Tera and Maggie over for dinner last night."

"I saw them as I came in."

"She's a good woman, Emmett."

"She is."

"Why not ask her out to—"

"I met someone." The words came out so fast it surprised us both.

"Oh," Mom said, her voice full of hope. "I didn't realize."

"It's not serious." *Fuck.* This thing with Nova was not serious and it was likely over. But I'd opened my mouth and now I'd be backtracking. Because the last thing I wanted was for my mother to get her hopes up of a daughter-in-law or grandchildren. The chance she'd have those was slim at best.

Her shoulders fell. "Okay."

"I'd better get home. I've got some work to do around the house."

"Thanks for coming over." She smiled as I walked over and pulled her into a hug. "Friday?"

"Friday." I let her go, giving a quick glance to Dad's book on the end table beside the couch as I walked for the door.

On the wall was one of the last photos the two of them had taken together, Mom sitting behind Dad on his bike, both wearing bandanas tied around their foreheads and wide smiles on their faces.

Mom was in love with Dad. She'd loved him her entire life, even though they'd divorced when I was in fifth grade.

Mom still wore her wedding rings. Dad had always worn his. Their wedding picture was on the nightstand in her bedroom. A copy had been on Dad's dresser at his place. Never once had Mom gone on a date and as far as I knew, Dad had never been with another woman. Because he'd loved Mom too. Even though their marriage had ended, and he'd lived at his own place.

At the time of their divorce, I'd been too young to demand or understand an explanation. But years later, when I'd been a new member of the club, I'd gotten drunk at a party and asked Dad why.

He'd told me that after Chrissy Slater had been murdered, it had spooked Mom. Rightly so. Chrissy had been innocent, but because of her husband's club, she'd been murdered outside of her own home.

A rival club, the Travelers, had been causing the Gypsies some trouble back then. Mostly skirmishes over some drug runs and disputed territory lines. Draven and the club had been aggressive about expanding in those days. They'd taken on more drug routes, trying to boost club income. The Travelers hadn't liked it and had sent threats. Draven had ignored them.

He shouldn't have ignored them.

The Travelers came to Clifton Forge and went straight to the Slater house.

Chrissy was outside planting flowers. They shot her in

the back of the head. Dash and Nick were the ones to find her body after coming home from school.

Dad helped Draven kill every member of the Travelers. Every. Single. One. Then he divorced Mom, hoping that Chrissy's fate wouldn't fall on her.

Mom would never have asked Dad to leave the club—she knew how much it had meant to both of us—but Dad had insisted on the divorce.

They hadn't been married. But they'd been married.

And when Dad had died, it had broken Mom's heart.

Mine too.

Outside, I sat on my bike and walked it backward out of the driveway, then I cast a glance at the house as I started the engine. Mom was standing in the living room window that overlooked the front yard. She had that book of Dad's pressed to her heart and a hand raised to wave goodbye.

I waved back, then roared down the street. My chest was too tight. Mom's expression, with that damn book, was stuck in my head.

What I needed tonight was a distraction. A hard fuck. Maybe a fight. I could probably find both at The Betsy but instead of going to the bar, I rode home. The bar would be there later if I changed my mind.

I turned down my lane and when I spotted a black car in the driveway, the tightness in my chest vanished.

Thank fuck.

She was here. Nova.

I parked beside her car and stood off my bike.

She was waiting beside the front door, leaning against the log exterior.

I walked up, shoving my sunglasses away.

"Hi, Ace."

I hated how glad I was to hear her voice. I hated how relieved I felt to see her. But damn it, I hadn't been ready to call it off. Not yet. There wasn't a single woman I wanted to see tonight but her. "Hi, baby."

There was a stiffness to her body as she stood straight, her eyes falling to her fingers clasped in front of her before she looked up. Maybe she hated being relieved too. "I'm sorry I haven't been around. I've been—"

I held up a hand. "No explanations, right?"

Her shoulders fell. "Right."

I took the key and slid it into the lock, then shoved the door open and keyed in the code to shut off the alarm.

Nova hesitated outside, her lower lip between her teeth.

"Coming in?"

She waited long enough that my heart jumped into my throat. Then she stepped inside, her heels clicking on the hardwood.

Damn, but I'd missed that noise too.

The second she was clear, I slammed the door behind her and swept her into my arms. "Bed or couch?"

Her legs wrapped around my hips and her lips came to mine. "Bed."

CHAPTER NINE

NOVA

What am I doing? I took a long look at myself in the bathroom mirror. Steam from the shower billowed above my head, fogging the glass's edges.

What was I doing?

In the past week, I'd asked myself that question countless times. Did that stop me from coming back to Emmett's? No. Here I was, staring at myself in his mirror while I let the walls drop for just a moment. While I let the doubts creep in and tangle a nasty knot in my stomach. They screamed at me, shouting so loud they were all I could hear.

The twisting of my insides felt permanent, and my only reprieve was with Emmett. His mouth, his hands, his body linked with mine was the only time I could shut out the noise in my head.

What am I doing?

"What has to be done," I whispered.

For Dad.

For TJ.

I swallowed hard and went to the shower, stepping inside and under the spray.

Emmett's shower was a sanctuary in itself and in the last week, I'd made sure to take a shower here at every opportunity.

There was no door, just a wide opening. Two large heads dropped water from the ceiling and standing beneath them was like being in a warm rainstorm. One wall was finished in rough, coarse brown stone. The rest was tiled in a smooth bone tile.

I tipped my head back and let the water cascade over my body.

My nose was stinging and there was a prick at my eyes, but I squeezed them tight because I didn't get to cry. This was my choice.

This was my plan.

Go slow. Methodical. Gain access to Emmett's life and home. Except my plan was beginning to fray.

I'd come to Clifton Forge thinking I could compartmentalize sex with Emmett and take my revenge. Maybe if it was another man, but there was no such thing as compartments where Emmett was concerned. He'd torn through them all.

The sinking in my heart hurt so much I wanted to curl into a ball and drown.

Emmett was a good man.

He wasn't supposed to be a good man.

Why couldn't he have been an asshole? How many jerks had I dated in my life? Why did the one I needed to keep at a distance have to be the one I genuinely liked?

How did I make these feelings go away?

Staying away from him wasn't an option. Not only because that wasn't the plan, but because I craved him. The four-day break I'd taken last week hadn't done anything but make me miss him that much more.

Temptation had won out and I'd given in. I'd come to his house, praying he hadn't found someone else already, and since then, I'd spent every night here over the past week.

We still hadn't shared any important personal details but tonight, I'd almost slipped. I'd had a shit day at work and when I'd come over, all I'd wanted to do was tell him that there were days when I didn't like being a lawyer.

I loathed clients who were arrogant and rude. I'd spent my day drafting business documents for a wealthy man in Missoula. He was expanding his empire and starting a new corporation. The man barked orders and the three times I'd met with him in person, he'd spoken to my breasts, not my face. Today he'd called me four times, each time to change his mind, forcing me to redo the work I'd already done.

It didn't bother me when clients changed their minds— more billable hours. What bothered me was this guy's superior attitude and snarky tone, like I wasn't competent enough to even breathe in his direction.

Maybe I should have referred him to Brendon and washed my hands of him, but that felt like quitting and damn it, I wasn't a quitter.

But as I'd driven here tonight, I'd been on the verge of tears. This was not my dream. And the hell of it was, I didn't even know what my dream was.

I'd never been given the chance to come up with my own.

Law school hadn't been my idea, but Dad's.

The conversation with my father was as clear today as it had been at seventeen. I'd been going through college flyers, narrowing down my options. Shelby had stayed in Missoula

125

for school, but I'd wanted to leave. I'd wanted to stretch my wings and explore the world.

My top choices had been in Georgia and West Virginia.

When I'd told Dad about them on one of his rare visits, I'd expected him to help me decide. Maybe offer to go on a trip to visit campuses. Instead, he'd told me that staying close to home was important. That he wouldn't be able to visit me if I lived so far away.

His veiled meaning had been crystal clear. If I moved, I would lose my father. When he asked me what I wanted to do, I'd shrugged. General studies had been calling my name. But Dad had suggested I go into political science. That I'd make a great lawyer because I was so smart. And that one day, maybe I could work with him if I was an attorney.

Desperate daughters made for happy fathers.

I hadn't hated school. I'd excelled and after getting a job with Brendon, my paycheck had soothed most of my complaints. And ultimately, I was glad that I'd been in Missoula for college.

I'd been close to Mom when TJ had died.

The Tin Gypsies had stolen my brother's dreams. That was why I was doing this, right? For TJ.

Maybe when it was over, I'd quit my job. I could sell my condo and get the hell away from Montana.

Because once this was over with Emmett and the Tin Gypsies, I wasn't sure I'd be able to live here and not think of him. Even after I left Clifton Forge, I'd never see a stretch of Montana highway and not think about the hours I'd spent on the back of Emmett's bike.

Every evening this week we'd gone for a ride. The season was changing, and fall was crisp in the air. We'd go out for an hour, taking in the colors—the county was teeming with gold and orange and red and green. Then we'd come back to his place and he'd cook me dinner before we'd retreat to his bedroom and spend the rest of the night naked.

He stripped me down completely.

Everything. My clothes. My shoes. My defenses.

Normally after a few orgasms, I'd pass out in his arms. But tonight, darkness had fallen and I hadn't been able to quiet the doubts. So I'd slipped out of his arms and escaped to the shower.

I breathed in the scent of his soap, spicy and male, tipping my face to the water. My hair would be a tangled mess in the morning without conditioner, but I couldn't bring myself to haul my toiletry case over from the rental.

Shampoo. Conditioner. Lotion. Face cream. Bringing those would feel too intimate. Tomorrow morning I'd rewash my hair and spend the time necessary to comb out the rat's nest. That would be my punishment for being so damn weak.

Lost in the water and the steam, I gasped when a pair of calloused hands came to my hips, sliding down my thighs.

The heat from Emmett's chest seeped into my skin and the instant crackle between us had me leaning back. The man was a magnet, and I was cheap metal, helpless against the tug.

He dropped his lips to my shoulder, the scrape of his beard leaving tingles as he dragged his mouth up my neck. There seemed to be no limit to how much I desired him.

The feeling was mutual because we were insatiable. No matter how many times we were together, it wasn't enough. Sex had moved beyond a physical coupling. There was a connection, a language we'd learned.

He was as in tune with my needs as I was his.

I placed my palms over his knuckles, lacing my fingers between his thicker ones. Emmett had great hands. They were large enough to cup my breasts in his palms and knead the curves of my ass.

I pulled his hands up, letting them drag on the skin of my stomach and up to my breasts. Then he squeezed, hard. The rough pad of his thumbs found my nipples and flicked them mercilessly, all while his mouth continued its journey across my shoulder blades.

What am I doing?

Emmett's arousal pressed into me and the doubts disappeared. In their place, the throb in my core became a pounding need. An ache that only he could ease.

"Ace," I moaned. "Inside."

"I'm out of condoms."

We'd used three tonight. Later, I'd chastise him for poor planning.

A hand slipped free of mine, leaving my breast to trail down my stomach. Then he curled into my sex, one finger sliding through my slick folds. Those large hands meant his palm could massage my clit as his finger stroked.

But it wasn't enough. "Need more." I reached behind me, finding his shaft and gripping it tight.

He hissed. "I'm clean."

That snapped my eyes open. Water clung to my lashes as he continued his delicious torture.

The condoms had been another barrier. Another defense. Another wall toppled by Emmett.

"I'm on the pill. I'm clean." I stepped out of his hold, taking in the sight of his body. All that muscle, glistening with water. The lust in his eyes likely matched my own. "If we do this, you're mine. Only mine."

Maybe he'd been with other women since we'd started this thing. The surge of jealousy made my stomach clench but if I asked him, it would give too much away. And maybe I didn't want to know the answer. Maybe it would hurt too much.

He reached for me, his mouth brushing mine. "Same goes. Only mine."

I gave him a nod and then he surged, picking me up, twisting us both so my back slammed against the smooth tile. My legs wrapped around his hips and he thrust inside me without any hesitation.

"Ace," I cried out, tipping my head back as he stretched me. I was sore from earlier. I'd been sore for a week. He was big and no matter how many times we were together, it was an adjustment. But it was an incredible stretch, one I reveled in every time.

It was the pain I'd take along with the pleasure from a man who'd hate me before long.

"Fuck, Nova." He pulled out and slammed back inside. "Christ, you feel good bare, baby."

We should have been doing this all along. He was perfection, velvet and hard. His hips were magic as he fucked me against the wall, the steam billowing around us like a cloud.

I clung to his broad shoulders, then tipped down to take his mouth. His taste was intoxicating, and I gave myself permission to remember this. When it was done and the destruction of my game finished, I would remember Emmett inside me.

He gripped my ass, holding me tight as he pounded, stroke after stroke until my orgasm broke and my mewls echoed off the walls.

"Fuck," he groaned as I pulsed around him. Then he clamped his mouth on my shoulder, his teeth firm on my skin. While my obsession was leaving nail tracks on his shoulders and chest, his was leaving teeth indentations.

We marked each other.

In the years to come, would I look in the mirror and see those marks? Part of me didn't want them to fade.

Emmett came on a roar, his body shuddering as he poured himself into me, long and hard. Then he dropped his forehead to mine, holding me as we both came down from the high.

As the stars cleared from my head, he set me down on unsteady feet and took my hand, bringing me under the water once more. We washed each other and when I stepped out of the shower and into the towel he held out for me, I smelled like his soap.

I dried my body, then stood naked in front of the mirror, towel drying my hair as he stood behind me, glorious in his own nudity.

"What's this one?" I dragged a fingertip over the tattoo on his wrist. It was a black bird, its wings spread wide.

He reached past me for the top center drawer and opened it, pulling out a wide-tooth comb. I figured he'd brush out his own hair, but instead, he took the ends of mine.

Tingles raced up my skin as he combed, his knuckles occasionally skimming my shoulder. I closed my eyes, a low hum of pleasure breaking free as he worked from the ends up to my scalp.

"My mom wanted to get matching tattoos, so on my eighteenth birthday, we went to the local shop and this was what she picked out. Surprised the hell out of me. I figured I'd walk out of there with a heart or butterfly or something dainty. But she liked this bird. She said it suited us both."

It did suit him. It was bold and assertive. But there was a feminine edge to it too. The delicate tips of the wings. The sweep of the bird's tail.

Emmett finished with my hair, then quickly combed out his own. Tossing the comb aside, he went to the walk-in closet off the bathroom, emerging with two pairs of sweat-pants, one T-shirt and one hoodie.

I got the bulk of the clothes while he only stepped into a pair of pants. Clothed and breathing in the clean scent of the hoodie, I followed him to the kitchen, where he snagged two beers from the fridge.

"Living room or deck?"

"Deck." No question. I loved to sit outside, even if it was cold and dark.

He opened the door and stepped outside, settling into his lounge chair. I opted to sit with him, between his open legs so I could lean into his chest.

There was a book on the floor beside us, one that hadn't been there yesterday. "What are you reading?"

"Just a book Mom gave me. It was my dad's. She thought I'd like it."

His father was dead. Something I shouldn't know because he hadn't told me. "Your dad is . . ."

"Died when I was twenty-six."

I stayed quiet. The normal reaction would be to say I was sorry, except I knew I'd choke on the words.

Emmett's father, Neal Stone—or Stone, the only name Dad had ever called him—had murdered TJ.

Dad had taken his revenge. The Warriors had ambushed Stone at The Betsy and killed him.

My heart began to race because I didn't want to talk about Stone. That was personal territory, and we weren't personal.

"Mom's been going through his stuff," he said. "She gave that to me on Friday last week."

Friday night he'd texted and told me that he'd be late coming home, that he'd text me when he was on his way. We'd met after nine and I hadn't left until Monday morning.

I'd locked myself away, shut out reality and pretended the clock wasn't ticking.

"Have you read it yet?" I asked, shifting to see his face.

"No, but she did. She liked it."

His mother would likely be devastated when Emmett went to prison. But that was the point, wasn't it? To hurt these people the way they'd hurt us?

Emmett looked down and stared at me for a moment. His gaze was nearly unreadable in the dark light. Could he see the guilt crawling beneath my skin? It was black and tangled with my veins, darker than any of his tattoos.

I broke first, turning to stare into the black trees. The half-moon shone above us in the cloudless sky and illuminated the tips of the tallest evergreens.

What am I doing?

That question crossed my mind and weakness spread through my bones. Dad would hate my weakness. Dad would hate that my weakness's name was Emmett Stone.

I gulped a long drink of my beer. If he had any idea I was having these doubts, he'd chastise me endlessly. He'd tell me to do better.

Actually, he'd replace me.

He'd arrange for someone else to come after the Tin Gypsies. Maybe he'd contact another club, one that would blaze into Clifton Forge and leave a trail of dead bodies in their wake.

The only thing keeping death at bay was me.

My heart was pounding so loudly Emmett might hear it, so I inhaled a long breath, giving him my weight, and when I emptied my lungs, I willed myself to a shaky calm.

His fingers found the ends of my damp hair, twirling a lock around one of his fingers as he brought his own beer bottle to his lips.

He'd hate me.

A month ago, I'd hoped for hate. I'd hoped he'd rot in a prison cell, cursing my name. And if everything had gone to plan, I'd be free, reveling in my victory.

What a fool I'd been.

"Nova."

"Yeah."

Emmett bent and kissed my temple. "What's going on in your head?"

"Nothing," I lied. "I had a shitty day at work. That's all."

"Want to talk it over?"

"That's not really us, is it?" It couldn't be us.

He dropped his bearded cheek to my hair. "No, I guess it's not."

We sat there until our beers were empty and my cheeks were rosy from the cold. Emmett led me inside, flipping off lights and setting the alarm system before we retreated to his bed, where he curled me into his side.

I relaxed my body but kept my mind alert. *Stay awake.* His breathing evened out. The hold he had on me loosened. And as he slumbered, I fought the weight in my eyelids.

It was time to move forward. It was time to act. Before

my father deemed me unworthy. Before I lost the nerve completely.

I shifted away from Emmett and lay perfectly still, and when I was sure he hadn't woken from my movement, I eased off the bed.

His room, like the rest of the house, was full of fine furniture. I passed a six-drawer chest, my feet sinking into the plush Aztec-style rug that covered most of the hardwood floor and disappeared beneath his massive king-sized bed.

My steps were slow, my breath held in my lungs, as I tiptoed out of the room and down the darkened hallway.

Emmett trusted me in his home. A mistake on his part. Another prickle of guilt on mine. I swallowed it down and hurried down the hallway and past the living room.

In my time here, I'd spent hours in the living room and kitchen. I'd eaten meals at the dining room table and there was nothing in Emmett's bedroom I hadn't seen. But the other side of the house was a mystery. Just like we weren't the couple to talk about our days, he also hadn't given me a house tour.

I snuck past the kitchen, casting one last look over my shoulder to make sure Emmett hadn't woken up. Then I poked my head into the first room I passed. It was a guest bedroom, its closet mostly empty. The bed was made and nothing was hidden beneath its frame. The drawers of the nightstand were also bare.

The laundry room was next. The cupboards above the washing machine and dryer were full of detergents and softeners. Emmett had an iron and a bottle of starch that I suspected got little use. There was a pack of light bulbs and a stash of cleaning supplies.

I hadn't expected to find anything in plain sight. Emmett

wouldn't keep incriminating evidence in the tall, narrow closet that held his vacuum. So I felt my way along the interior walls to make sure there wasn't a compartment or something hidden.

My father had kept the videos and recordings he'd made of the Warriors in a lockbox that he'd stowed beneath his refrigerator. I had to give the FBI credit. Their search of Dad's home had been nothing if not thorough.

I moved silently toward the next door in the hall, one that opened to a black staircase. I gripped the railing tight, using my toes to feel from one step to the next, too afraid to turn on the light.

When I finally reached the bottom, I breathed, glad it was a daylight basement because moonlight streamed in through the sliding glass door that opened to the yard. The space was huge, running the length and the width of the house.

Emmett had a pool table in the main room. I poked at the pockets and green felt, feeling my way along the edges for anything that might open up. I did the same with the foosball table against the wall. Then I scoured the large entertainment center and sectional positioned on the other end of the space.

He hadn't once brought me down here to watch TV, even though this was clearly the better couch and television. We'd always stayed upstairs and watched the TV above the living room fireplace. Why? Was there something down here he didn't want me to see?

Another room had been set up as a home gym. It was far enough from the windows that the room was dark, so I'd have to check it later. There was one more guest bedroom with an en suite bathroom. And the last door opened to a storage room. Its shelves were organized and crowded with plastic tubs.

I'd have to go through them later too. Tonight was simply about mapping where I needed to spend more time.

Closing the storage room door behind me, careful so it didn't make a thud, I darted up the stairs. At the landing, I went to the last room.

Bingo. The office. A wide executive desk sat in the center of the room, its surface crowded with laptops and monitors. A gun safe was in the corner beside a window and a bookshelf. I'd bet money it had more than guns inside.

Before I worried about how to crack it open, I'd start with the laptops. Emmett wouldn't leave anything about the Tin Gypsies in the open, but there might be something on one of those laptops to point me in the right direction.

Worrying I'd been gone too long, I backed away from the office and turned, only to run face-first into a wall of muscle.

I gasped as Emmett's hands came to my arms, steadying my feet. "Oh my God, you scared me."

"What are you doing?"

I dropped my forehead to his chest, my heart pounding in my ears. "I couldn't sleep and didn't want to bother you, so I came down the hall to find a quiet corner to read on my phone."

The lie tasted like acid on my tongue, but if Emmett suspected anything, he didn't let on. He simply wrapped me in his arms, running his hands up and down my spine.

"Why can't you sleep?"

"I don't know." I sighed, hoping my breaths would level out. "Sometimes I have a hard time shutting off my brain."

"Yeah, I get that sometimes too."

"I saw this"—I motioned toward the office behind me —"and started wondering what you did for work."

"I'm a mechanic," he said. "But I have some rental properties and investments around town."

"Ah. Hence the office."

He nodded, taking my hand and leading me toward the other end of the house. He pulled with enough insistence either he was exhausted and wanted to go back to sleep, or he didn't want me in his office.

"Why a mechanic?" I asked, hoping my curiosity wouldn't trigger any alarm bells.

"I like to build. I like to take things apart and put them back together. My dad was the same way. He taught me about cars and bikes when I was young."

We made it past the living room and his pace slowed. A yawn stretched his handsome face.

"Sorry I woke you up, Ace. I hope you don't mind that I went down the hall. I was going to leave but you set the alarm and I didn't want to open a door and have it go off."

"No worries. And I'm glad you didn't leave." He let go of my hand to put an arm around my shoulders, hauling me into his side as we returned to his bedroom.

I climbed into bed and curled into his arms. The dusting of chest hair over his sternum tickled my chin and I ran a hand up his stomach, letting my fingers thread through the coarse strands.

"Does it bother you that you don't know my name?" My question streamed past my lips before I could shove it aside. The moment it was out, I realized how desperately I wanted the answer. Because if I hadn't known his real name, it would have driven me insane.

"Yes."

"It's Nova," I whispered, tipping up my chin to meet his gaze.

"Seriously?"

I nodded. "Yeah."

He chuckled and kissed my hair.

It was safe for him to call me Nova because Nova Talbot didn't exist. June Johnson on the other hand . . . that was the identity he could never know existed. It was the reason my car had fake license plates.

Looking those up would lead to a dead end, but a dead end would raise suspicion. At this point, I was fairly sure Emmett hadn't run my plates. Otherwise he would act differently toward me, right?

Right. There was no way he knew I was June Johnson, daughter of January Johnson. June's father was unknown. But June Johnson had a younger brother, TJ Johnson.

And TJ, even for a brief time, years and years ago, had been an Arrowhead Warrior. That was the link. That was the fact he could never discover.

It was better to tell him my name was Nova. Maybe it would even help me keep his trust.

"Want to know my name?" he asked.

I shook my head, leaning up to press a kiss to his lips. "No. I like calling you Ace."

CHAPTER TEN

EMMETT

My own bed is boring.

I chuckled at Nova's text, quickly typing out a reply. *Told you that you should have stayed in mine.*

Her reply was instant. *Tonight. Six.*

I'll be waiting.

Last night she'd opted to stay at her own place because she'd had an early meeting this morning. What type of meeting? No clue. I'd shared some personal details about my life, but she was as closed off as ever.

And it was really starting to fucking bother me.

In the past two weeks, we'd gotten into a routine. She'd come over each night. We'd have dinner. Over the meal, we'd talk about nothing and everything, the conversation interesting and engaging.

I was still reading the book of Dad's and last night I'd told Nova what it was about. The night before, we'd talked politics. The night before that, I'd told her about my businesses around town and why I'd chosen to invest locally.

Though I could probably make just as good of a return

putting my money in the stock market—I had a chunk there too—I liked being involved in Clifton Forge businesses. Nova had seemed impressed too.

I was a silent partner with a personal trainer who'd started his own gym. I went in once or twice a week to check in even though I mostly worked out at my home gym. A buddy of mine who owned a lawn service company had wanted to expand into landscape design, not just mowing and sprinklers, and rather than take a loan out from the bank, I'd bought into his business. Then there were my rentals.

Nova had peppered me with intelligent questions, wanting to know more and what I was going to invest in next and my capital strategy. The interest she took in my life was flattering. And it was a damn shame I couldn't show her the same.

Still, what we had was working for us. There was no drama. Dash, Isaiah, Leo, Shaw, Luke . . . my friends had all started their relationships with their women with a mess of drama. Not that Nova would be around long-term. She had no intention of starting a committed relationship and neither did I.

But I could admit to myself that the idea had some appeal. It was nice to have someone in my home, my bed, each night.

Too bad she didn't even want to know my name.

The anonymity had been fine at first. Now it was beginning to fester.

"Hey, man." Leo came up to my side. He'd been in the paint booth for hours this morning. "What's happening?"

"Nothing. Just reading a text from Mom," I lied, tucking my phone away.

Maybe someday I'd tell my friends about her. Maybe

not. If we weren't going anywhere, why share? The guys would only have questions. Their wives would too.

And despite the secrecy, Nova and I had a good thing going. I didn't need anyone butting in and screwing it up. That, and I'd feel like a damn fool if they asked a question—what does she do for a living, how old is she, where'd she grow up—and I couldn't give an answer.

I mean . . . I could. I'd just have to run her plates. It was as tempting as the woman herself.

"Want to take off for lunch today?" Leo asked. "Cass and I were thinking of heading to the diner with Seraphina in about an hour. Try to beat the lunch rush."

"I'm down. That'll give me time to put the new fender on the Stingray."

"Want some help? I'm done in the booth for today."

"That'd be great." The two of us returned to work and as soon as the fender was on, he went to the apartment upstairs to collect his wife and daughter while I washed up at the shop's sink.

Lunch with Leo, Cass and Seraphina would normally have been the highlight of my day, but as I sat across a booth from them and watched Leo with his family, a twinge of jealousy pricked at my skin.

Leo and Cass knew each other. Past, present and future. They trusted each other.

Nova's secrets shouldn't bother me, because we weren't headed in the same direction. But yeah, it was bothering me. Maybe it was time to start digging into Nova's life and figure out what kind of woman would want our kind of relationship.

I'd hacked countless people, but the idea of doing that to

Nova felt . . . wrong. Invasive. I'd betray her trust the minute I opened my laptop.

Every morning when I went to my office and checked through my alerts on Warriors and their families, I contemplated a quick search on Nova. So far I'd been able to resist. Except the longer she held out, the harder it became to leave the questions unanswered.

The afternoon dragged once we returned to the shop. The pit in my stomach made it hard to concentrate.

Was this temptation just because of my own trust issues? Dad had taught me early on to be wary of people. Probably from his experience with the club. He had only ever really trusted Mom and the Tin Gypsies.

I'd heeded that advice and kept my business private from anyone beyond my close circle. Relationships had never been a priority in my early twenties, and after Dad had died, after I'd seen the toll it had taken on Mom, I hadn't been in a place for a steady woman.

Sex was easy. There were always women at The Betsy and they knew the score when we hooked up. Casual worked for me. It fit into my lifestyle.

So why was this thing with Nova bothering me so much? I had the best of it all. An intelligent, witty woman who liked to fuck. We weren't in a relationship. This was mind-blowing, casual sex. That was it.

If she didn't need my name to let me inside her body, that was her choice.

"You okay?" Leo asked around five thirty as we finished up for the day.

"All good."

"You've seem distracted since lunch."

I waved it off. "It's nothing."

"Everything okay with your mom?"

"Yeah, man. She's good."

He gave me a nod. "I'm taking off. See you tomorrow."

"Bye."

Leo was the last to leave today. Dash had changed his work schedule since school had started so he and Bryce could both pick Xander up from kindergarten. He'd left around three. Isaiah was out before five to meet Genevieve at her law office. Presley had locked up the office after Sawyer and Tyler had clocked out at five.

Now there were no vehicles left in the lot. I locked up the garage and padlocked the gates behind me before heading out on my bike, doing my best to shake off the mood from the day. It would be better once Nova came over. We'd eat. We'd have sex. I'd take what I needed from her while she did the same from me.

And since tomorrow was Friday, maybe I'd tell her I was busy. I'd go to The Betsy and see what was happening. Not to pick up another woman, but because I hadn't been there in a month, not since the last time I'd seen Nova there. Maybe what I needed was a normal night at the bar and some distance from the woman tormenting my thoughts.

The fall air bit through my long-sleeved T-shirt as I rode for home. Nova and I hadn't been on a ride lately because it was getting colder. Maybe tomorrow I'd take a long ride before going to the bar. It would do me some good to hit the road for a few hours. Sooner rather than later, the bike would be in the garage, and I'd be driving my truck through the winter.

By the first snowfall, maybe Nova and I would have fizzled out too.

The rumble of my Harley echoed off the walls as I

pulled into my garage. I went inside, tossed my keys on the kitchen counter and headed for the office. I had a little time before Nova showed up and I wanted to check a few emails.

The PI in South Carolina had sent a follow-up while I'd been at the shop earlier. I'd glanced at his summary but hadn't dug in. I logged on to my laptop and spent thirty minutes reading his report and looking at photos.

Tucker Talbot's ex-wife was the main focus of his summary. She'd started dating a man since our PI had been tailing her. He'd been thorough, checking out the guy just in case it was a tie to Montana. But the boyfriend was clean, and besides a speeding ticket from three years ago, he was just a normal guy who had an ex-wife of his own and rented the occasional porno.

There was nothing new on either of Tucker's daughters. Both women had inherited their mother's chestnut hair, but they bore a marked resemblance to Tucker in the shape of their faces and the set of their noses and dark eyes.

The PI we'd hired wasn't cheap, but I shot him a note, asking him to stay with the ex and daughters. Peace of mind, priceless.

I logged off my laptop and shut it down completely, then went to the safe in the corner, opening it up and taking out some cash.

Back in the days of the club, cash had flowed like a mountain stream brimming with melting snow. Running protection runs on drug routes and betting thousands on underground fights weren't legal, but they had been lucrative. For the most part, I'd saved the majority of mine, whereas most of the brothers my age had blown through their envelopes of cash, spending it on booze and women and bikes. Sometimes drugs.

After Dad had died, I'd had my own dark days when I'd longed for any substance that might take the pain away. Alcohol had been my go-to. Weed an easy score. Cocaine on the worst days.

Not a proud time in my life, but I'd been lucky. Draven had seen me spiraling and he'd stepped in. He'd been heart-broken after Dad's death too, but he'd hit me with the truth—literally, he'd punched me and broken my nose—and told me Dad would have been ashamed. He'd reminded me that I had a mother who didn't need to watch her son lose himself to grief.

For Mom, I'd cut the drugs immediately, though the drinking had taken some time.

Even through all of that, I'd been flush with cash. What I hadn't spent, I'd saved, just like my father had taught me.

Dash and Leo had done the same. We were still living off the cash we'd earned from the club, though mine had dwindled since I'd been aggressive with my investments. Still, we didn't make lavish purchases. We didn't flaunt it. Food, clothes, gas. It all added up and allowed us to spend our salaries on other expenses.

Not only did I have my own stash here at home, but Mom had one in her basement—Dad's money.

I took out a thousand bucks and relocked the safe, heading upstairs and to the kitchen. I took out everything I'd need for dinner, chopping a tomato and a head of lettuce while a pound of ground beef simmered in the spices I'd added. The scents of cumin, chili pepper and paprika had filled the room when the front door opened and a familiar click of heels echoed down the hallway.

"Hi, Ace." Nova came up behind me at the counter, sliding her hands around my waist.

"Emmett. My name is Emmett."

Her hands stilled.

Maybe my mood from earlier wasn't as gone as I'd thought. But I wasn't going to apologize either. She could know my fucking name.

Her body stood as stiff as the knife in my hand hovering over the cutting board. Then, the tension in her body vanished. She leaned into me, whispering against my spine, "Emmett."

Fuck, I liked hearing my name from those lips.

I set the knife down and twisted, taking her mouth. I swept inside, savoring her taste, then broke away.

"What's for dinner?" she asked, her cheeks flushed from the kiss.

"Tacos," I answered.

"How was your day?" She moved to my side and hoisted herself up on the counter.

"Meh. You?"

"Fine."

"What did you do?"

"Worked."

"And what exactly did you work on?" Yeah, I was fishing for information and I might as well be obvious about it.

"Stuff." The corner of her mouth turned up.

I narrowed my eyes. "What stuff?"

"Boring stuff." She shrugged and plucked a piece of tomato off my cutting board, popping it into her mouth.

"You're not going to tell me."

"Why does it matter?" she asked.

I moved to her. She opened her knees, making space for me. "Because I want to know."

She reached over and picked up another piece of tomato, her eyebrows arching in a silent challenge as she chewed.

If it was a game she wanted, then we'd play. I trailed my fingers up her thigh, the roughness of my skin scratching against the denim of her jeans. A flash of lust crossed those beautiful brown eyes and her hands came to my shoulders.

I leaned in close as my hand caressed her hip. My lips brushed over hers, earning a small hitch in her breath, as I splayed my hand over her ribs.

Then tickled her mercilessly.

"Ace!" she squealed, squirming and swatting at me, but I kept at the torture until she was laughing so hard that she begged me to stop.

"Are you going to tell me?"

"Yes," she howled. "Yes!"

I let her go and grinned, dropping a kiss to her cheek as she swiped the tears from her eyes.

"You don't play fair."

"Fair is for losers." I went to the stove and checked on the meat.

"True. Very true." She hopped off the counter and went to my cutting board, taking over with the veggies. "I'm a lawyer."

"Now was that so hard?"

"Yes." She smirked with a laugh. "I spent my day drafting a will for a young couple. I hate doing them because it always makes me sad when I have to ask parents who will get their children if they die. After crying over it twice, I sent it to them to review. Then I drafted up LLC paperwork for a client who's starting a new business in Missoula."

A knot in my chest unraveled. A sigh of relief came out so loud I knew she'd heard it.

I put the lid back on the meat so it could simmer until we were ready, then went to Nova, propping a hip on the counter beside her as she chopped. "Missoula?"

She nodded. "That's where I live. I'm working remotely at the moment. I needed a break and change of scenery."

"Oh." That truth hit me like a sledgehammer to the chest and the pieces all clicked into place. She didn't live here. That was why I hadn't seen her in town before last month. Why she'd insisted this was casual.

She didn't fucking live here.

I swallowed hard. The end had always been inevitable. Now I knew why.

"Why Clifton Forge?" I asked, pretending curiosity to hide the fact that my head was spinning.

"It's close enough to Missoula that I can pop back if needed. One of the guys I work with at my firm comes hunting here every year. He's always saying how nice of a town it is and that it's not overrun with tourists like other areas. So I found a vacation rental and here I am."

A vacation rental. Son of a bitch. "How long are you staying?"

She kept her eyes on the cutting board. "I planned a couple of months. I need to be back in Missoula before the roads get bad."

If she was only staying for a couple of months, we'd burned through more than half already.

I regretted asking. Damn it. I should have kept my mouth shut.

Yeah, I would have figured it out eventually when she moved back to Missoula. But now all I'd be doing was watching the calendar as the days ticked by.

Nova looked over, her smile too bright as she set the

knife down, the tomato perfectly diced. Then she went back to the counter, hopping up to her seat. "Any other questions?"

A few, actually. Would she ever have told me that she was leaving? Would she have disappeared without a word? But I didn't ask because I didn't want the answers.

"What's your favorite color?" I asked, moving in between her legs again.

She lifted her hands, threading her fingertips through the hair at my temples. I'd tied it up earlier, knowing that she liked to take it down. "Your eyes."

"What's your favorite food?"

"Tacos."

I brushed a kiss to her lips, then went to the stove and turned it off. I was grateful for the task of setting out every-thing on the island for dinner. It gave the sting of her truth time to ease.

She was leaving.

I'd known this was a short-term thing and now I had the timeline. Another month at most. That was how much time we had.

"Where'd you learn to cook?" She hopped down and went to the silverware drawer.

"Mostly here, through trial and error. My mom tried to teach me a few things when I was in high school, but not much stuck until I was grown and fending for myself."

I hadn't gone to college or trade school. No professor could teach me more about cars than my own father and Draven could, so I'd joined the club and started working at the garage. Back then, I'd lived in the clubhouse. There'd always been food in the industrial fridge and usually a woman or two who'd cook for the brothers hanging around.

Sometimes it was a girlfriend or wife of a member. Other times it was a woman who thought cooking might land her the title of girlfriend—it rarely did.

It wasn't until I'd moved out of the clubhouse and into a townhouse of my own, wanting some privacy, that I'd learned how to cook.

"It was awful at first." I chuckled, taking plates out of the hickory cabinets. "Truly awful. But I'd always eat whatever I cooked. A punishment at first. Then it became a motivation to make something I'd actually enjoy."

I set the plates down on the island that sat in the center of my expansive, U-shaped kitchen. The cream granite was speckled with flecks of gray and burgundy stone. I ate at the island most nights, the dining room too big and lonely for one. Even with Nova here, we normally sat on the stools at the island, sitting side by side with my leg brushing against hers.

I'd miss that when she left. Her touch. Her company over a meal.

"I don't get fancy," I said, bringing everything to the island to assemble soft-shell tacos.

"I don't need fancy."

"You sure about that? I see your shoes."

She laughed. "In shoes, yes, I need fancy. In food, I prefer this. Normal food. As long as it doesn't have shrimp, I'm not very picky."

I sat beside her, each of us assembling our tacos. "You don't like shrimp."

"Nope. I also don't like sushi."

"Not a lot of sushi in Clifton Forge."

"Part of its appeal." She laughed, taking her first bite. Her eyes closed and she moaned as she chewed.

"I forgot drinks." I made a move to stand but she put a hand on my forearm, sliding off her stool first.

She went to the cabinet with glasses, taking out two. Then she filled them with ice and water from the fridge.

Just watching her move around my kitchen, comfortable in my space, made my chest ache. Nova was the closest I'd come to having a relationship in, well . . . ever. And she'd be gone soon. She'd go back to her life in Missoula.

She returned to our places, sliding my water into place.

"Tell me more," I said. "Tell me anything."

"I'm scared of spiders and snakes. I never say no to cookie dough ice cream. I think ballet flats are overrated. And . . ."

My food remained untouched. I couldn't tear my eyes away from her profile as her eyes turned sad. "And what?"

She looked over, pain etched on her beautiful face. "And I wish I had a better relationship with my father."

I reached for her, cupping her jaw with my hand.

Nova leaned in, forcing a small smile. "Your turn. Tell me anything."

"I hate shrimp too. And I'm glad you think ballet flats are overrated."

She giggled, turning to press her lips to my wrist.

Then we went back to our meals, talking and laughing through another night. The echo of her laugh rang through the house and I willed the walls to absorb it. So that maybe a part of her would remain long after she was gone.

CHAPTER ELEVEN

NOVA

"Did you make it back safely?" Mom asked.

"Yes." I smiled. No matter my age, Mom would always expect updates on my travel plans. Even though I'd texted her when I'd gotten back to Clifton Forge yesterday, she'd still called this morning.

"It was good to see you. I miss you."

"Miss you too, Mom."

The night before last, I'd driven to Missoula. I'd lied and told Emmett that the reason I was sleeping at my own place was because of an early meeting. In reality, I'd been in a different county.

Brendon had been great about me working remotely but he'd called for a bimonthly staff meeting and I'd wanted to attend in person. So I'd gone to Missoula for a night. Sleeping in my own bed had felt foreign and after the meeting at the firm and a quick visit to Mom's, I'd driven back to Clifton Forge.

"How much longer do you think you'll be gone?" Mom asked.

"I don't know." I sighed and sat down at the dining room table in my rental. There was a stack of mail beside my laptop, neither of which I wanted to open yet.

My morning had gotten off to a slow start. After waking early and taking a shower at Emmett's, I'd lingered at his place while he'd cooked us breakfast. Normally I'd head out as soon as I was dressed, but this morning I simply hadn't wanted to leave.

Something had changed last night over tacos. Something had shifted. And I wasn't sure exactly what to make of it yet.

"Give me a call later this week," she said.

"Okay. Love you."

"I love you too."

I ended the call and set my phone aside. It vibrated with an incoming email and though I knew there were plenty of tasks waiting for me, I had no motivation to jump into my day.

I was stalled.

When Emmett had asked me questions about work last night, I could tell by his tone that his patience for my silence and vague answers had worn thin. That should have been my cue to leave. Instead, I'd opened my damn mouth.

My answers had all been true. I was a lawyer. I lived in Missoula. I was in Clifton Forge temporarily. I hated shrimp and was terrified of both spiders and snakes.

He'd seemed satisfied and if I'd just left it at that, I probably wouldn't have felt so vulnerable. But then my stupid mouth had opened again and I'd told him I wished for a better relationship with my father.

Why? Why would I say that? I smacked my forehead with a palm. Would my epic stupidity ever end?

The confession had slipped out and revealed far too

153

much. There wasn't a person alive who I'd admitted that to before. Mom and Shelby could probably guess but I'd never spoken it aloud.

Until Emmett.

What was wrong with me? Why couldn't I have just stayed quiet? The man was slashing through my defenses one night at a time. The longer I stayed, the more it would hurt in the end. But I couldn't bring myself to leave.

Brendon seemed satisfied with the work I'd been doing remotely, and I had no doubt that if I asked, he'd let me continue for a while longer. Considering this revenge plan of mine had gone nowhere, I might need the extra time.

If I even had the guts to continue.

I'd only snooped around Emmett's house the one time. I should break into his safe. I should hack into his computers. I should do something, *anything*, but instead I'd stalled. Instead, I told myself that the dinners and the evenings on his deck and the nights in his bed were to earn his trust.

There was only so much more delaying I could manage. By telling Emmett I was in Clifton Forge temporarily, I'd put myself on the clock.

It was time to make a decision.

Either I acted. Or I walked away.

"Damn it," I groaned, slumping into my chair. What was I doing?

Maybe I should call it off. Maybe I should go and visit Dad, tell him that I couldn't find anything. If I swore that the Tin Gypsies weren't hiding anything, would he believe me? Would it matter?

Dad knew they were guilty of a plethora of crimes. My problem was evidence. I needed evidence for my plan. If there was none . . .

"He'll kill them," I whispered, my stomach sinking.

Dad would find a way to kill them, simply because he hated them that much. For a time, listening to Dad's stories, especially those about TJ's death, had made me hate them too. I'd hated them enough for revenge.

Until my thirst for vengeance had been quenched by a tall, ruggedly handsome mechanic who made me laugh. Who made me see stars. Who made me . . . happy.

Gah. Why couldn't Emmett have been an asshole? Why?

Only, he was not the man my father had made him out to be.

Dad had told me everything he knew about the Tin Gypsies. He'd gone back decades, explaining how their feud had started. He'd told me about the drug protection routes they'd fought over. He'd told me about the underground fights the Gypsies had organized around the state.

TJ had been murdered at one of those fights.

After the Tin Gypsies had disbanded, Dad and the Warriors had taken over their routes. They'd brought in a serious stream of cash and with no competition, the war between clubs had ended. They'd called a truce.

Until Draven Slater had been framed for murder by the former Clifton Forge chief of police, Marcus Wagner. Draven had reached out to Dad, wanting to know if the Warriors had been involved. Dad had told them the truth. They had all but forgotten about the Tin Gypsies.

It should have ended there.

It would have if the Tin Gypsies hadn't taken their retribution.

They'd gone to a secluded cabin in the mountains that they'd known was a Warrior hideaway. There'd been a Warrior inside, stationed there to protect the property. The

Gypsies had barricaded the man inside and burned the place down with him inside. They'd murdered one of Dad's brothers for no reason.

All because they hadn't trusted when Dad had told them the truth. They'd believed that the Warriors had framed Draven, so they'd killed a man.

They'd started a new war.

Draven had come after Dad again, forcing Dad's hand. Thankfully, Dad had come out the victor but only because he'd taken Draven's life.

Dad had promised me . . . he'd had to kill Draven. If he hadn't, Draven never would have stopped. Draven would have come after others and maybe even discovered Mom, Shelby or me.

When would the bloodshed end? When would enough lives be lost for this to stop?

Dad had staged Draven's death as a suicide. The authorities had no idea it had been Dad's rope that had hung Draven in his own home.

The state prosecutor hadn't included Draven's murder in the long list of charges against Dad. I guess for men like Dad who were skilled at taking lives, they were also good at covering up their crimes.

The same had happened with TJ.

After he'd been shot, they'd brought him to the hospital in Ashton, even though TJ had been dead on arrival. The guys TJ had been with that night had told the doctors it had been a hunting accident.

One of them had taken the blame. With two other Warriors to confirm the story, no one had thought to ask more questions. Or maybe people in Ashton knew better than to challenge a Warrior.

We'd always known that TJ had died from a gunshot wound. Dad had told Mom, Shelby and me that the hunting accident had been a lie. But he hadn't shared the gruesome details. When Dad had told me what had really happened to TJ, I'd gone into a rage. I'd wanted nothing more than to make the men who'd killed him pay.

Then one month with Emmett and everything was different.

I knew what I had to do. I knew my next steps. I was just struggling to take them.

Maybe a trip to visit Dad would inspire some action, except I didn't want to see him. How many years had I longed for just one more minute with Dad? One more day and one more conversation?

Now if he saw me, he'd see the truth on my face.

I was faltering. I was weak. If he knew, he'd send others to Clifton Forge.

The idea of Emmett's death made my stomach twist. I'd never wanted any of the Tin Gypsies dead. To spend their lives in prison? Yes. But never death.

My phone vibrated with another email but I ignored it, going for the stack of mail instead.

I discarded the credit card offers and insurance flyers. I opened and scanned my bank statement. I rifled through the plethora of clothing catalogs, only saving two that I'd go through later.

At the bottom of the stack there was a plain white envelope, my name and address written in a sloppy script. It didn't have a return address so I tore it open, unsure what it could be.

On a single piece of white paper was a phone number.

"What the hell?"

Curiosity won out and I picked up my phone, quickly dialing the number.

"Hello?" a man's sleepy voice answered after the third ring.

"Um . . . hi. My name is N-June. June Johnson. I got this piece of paper in the mail and—"

"Oh, yeah. He said you'd be calling."

"Who said?"

"A guy who knows a guy who knows Tucker Talbot."

My body tensed. "Who are you?"

"You can call me Hacker."

Hacker. "Okay," I drawled.

"Listen, I've got some stuff this morning but I'll come by about two. Cool?"

"Come by. How do you—"

He interrupted me by rattling off the address to my rental.

The blood in my veins turned to ice.

"Will you be there at two?" he asked.

"Sure," I muttered.

Then he ended the call and I sat, staring at the piece of paper, wondering what the fuck my father was up to.

A guy who knows a guy who knows Tucker Talbot.

Dad had covered his tracks. He'd clearly had someone else send this because the handwriting was not his.

My phone rang and I jumped, startled by the buzz.

I picked it up, swallowing hard, and answered the call from a client.

He prattled on about a change to the agreement I'd drafted and another few tweaks. I absently nodded, jotting it down on the back of an envelope because I knew I'd forget. My head was too busy replaying the call from Hacker.

His nickname—because nearly everyone in Dad's club went by something other than their actual name—was fairly indicative. But Dad had told me that the Warrior who'd done their hacking had been arrested. So who was this guy?

The clock on my phone showed it was only nine. Waiting five hours to meet with Hacker was going to send me into a spiral.

It did.

By the time I heard an engine pull into the driveway, I was jittery and sick to my stomach. I ran to the front door, whipping it open as a lanky man with a shaved head stalked my way from an old, blue Honda Civic.

"Hacker?"

He nodded. "Hey."

I moved aside, waving him in. He smelled like cheap aftershave and cigarettes. The smoke was so potent it was like he marinated in it each night. I grimaced as he passed by. "Um . . . come on in and have a seat."

Leading him to the living room, I dropped to the edge of a chair while he plopped into the couch, his long arms stretching across the back.

"Who are you?" I asked, cutting straight to the thick of it.

"I used to do some work with the Warriors. Got word that you might need some assistance."

"Assistance with what?"

He lifted a shoulder. "I dunno. You tell me."

"You're a hacker."

"They told me not to tell you my real name. I'm not creative with nicknames and shit so . . . whatever."

"Ah." I nodded. "How about you tell me exactly what *they* said?"

"Listen, lady. I drove a long way to get here."

"From?"

"They told me not to tell you that either."

I fought an eye roll. "What can you tell me?"

"I'm good with breaking into computers and hacking systems. I was paid some cash up front to do whatever you needed. They said you'd tell me what that was. I just had to wait for you to call. And after, you'd pay me too."

Christ. My father never did things normally.

I craved normal. Maybe that was why being with Emmett had been so refreshing. The moment I stepped into his home, life seemed normal.

"You don't know anything else?" I asked.

He shook his head. "Nope. So what do you have for me?"

"Nothing."

"Seriously? I drove all the way here."

"By your choice, not by my request. You could have told me this"—a whole lot of nothing—"over the phone."

He frowned and made a move to stand but I held up a hand.

"Wait." *Shit.*

I had the name of a hacker who I'd planned to contact once I found Emmett's laptops. Finding him hadn't been hard. I'd pulled records of criminal convictions, narrowed down the crime, and voila, a list of names of convicted hackers. I'd called three. The first two had been sure I was an undercover cop—both had hung up on me. But the third had agreed to meet me for coffee.

We'd gone to a trendy place in Missoula and I'd asked him a series of vague *what-if*s.

What if I gave you a name? Could you find information about that person?

160

What if I gave you a computer? Could you break in and tell me what was on it?

What if I asked you to forget we ever spoke? Could you do that?

He'd answered *yes* across the board.

But if Dad had sent Hacker here, it meant either he knew I was stalling or he thought I didn't have resources. My guess was the former. Dad might be in prison but he had his way of getting information. He had his influence. It was how he'd enlisted my cousin Doug to go after Leo Winter.

Exactly how Dad communicated to the outside world was a mystery. I suspected a lot passed through Ira. That, and through family members of the Warriors on Saturday visitations.

Whatever Dad knew, he clearly wasn't satisfied. And if he'd sent Hacker here, it would be best to utilize him. So I asked Hacker my same *what-if* questions.

"What if I brought you a computer? Could you break in and tell me what was on it? Maybe copy it for me to see?"

Hacker nodded. "No sweat."

"How long would it take?"

"Depends on what we're dealing with. What kind of laptop?"

"A Mac, I think. Two of them." Both Emmett's machines had been Macs, hadn't they? "But the owner has some hacking skill of his own. Can you break into those?"

"Maybe. Maybe not. Depends on his firewall and if he's encrypted the hard drive."

"Let's assume he has."

"You've got physical access, right?"

I nodded.

"Then like I said, no sweat. People are easier to hack

than machines. We'll just take physical control of his machines."

"I can't exactly steal them. They'll need to go back and he can't know they were missing."

"That's not what I mean." He waved it off. "Software hackers are always thinking about program weaknesses. Breaking past protections. I'm going to actually crack into the machine."

"Explain that to me in more detail."

"The machines themselves are easy to break into. All you really need is a screwdriver. Once I have the machine, I'll copy the hard drive. It'll be encrypted and unreadable until I get the password."

"I don't know the password." How was I supposed to glean that from Emmett?

"You don't need to. After I make the copy, I'll physically open the machine and splice in a tap on his webcam. It'll transmit whatever he types to a receiver over an unused radio frequency. He'll key in his password. We'll capture it on video. Then we can log right into the copied hard drive."

My head was beginning to spin. "Okay. So all I need to do is bring you the laptops."

"Yes. I'll take them and do my thing. Then you can put them right back along with the radio receiver. It's about as big as this." He drew out a little box in the air. "It needs to be placed within two hundred feet of his office. The widget in the laptop will send the video to the receiver. The receiver will transmit it to a function I have on my phone."

"And he won't notice that you made the copy or opened his laptop?"

"It's not foolproof. The widget I'll put into the machine steals power from the battery. If he notices the battery draining faster than normal, he might check. But the only way he'll know is if he physically opens the laptop casing too."

This seemed much too simple. "That's it?"

"There's no need to overthink this." Hacker shrugged. "I doubt he's expecting anyone to break into his house, right?"

"He's got a fairly sophisticated security system."

"Then there you go. You've got an in. Let's exploit it."

Exploit it. My stomach churned. "Is the number I called the best one to reach you?"

He nodded again. "Yeah. I don't live here so I just need time."

"If I call you and arrange a time to make the exchange, how long will it take you to get here?"

"Couple hours."

Which meant he probably lived in Bozeman.

"And how long would you need to break into the machines?"

"Couple hours. Tops."

"Okay." I stood. "I'll be in touch."

Without another word, he stood and walked out of the house.

I waited in the living room, listening for the sound of his car to disappear, then I sank into the chair and buried my face in my hands.

There was no way to stop this.

I couldn't stop.

Dad had boxed me into a corner. Either I did this, or someone else would.

"I can do this." There was no conviction in my voice. None.

How had it come to this? Just a month ago I'd been so

determined. I'd been so sure. Now . . . now I wanted to crawl in bed and hide under the covers. Emmett's bed, to be exact.

The rest of my afternoon passed with little engagement in my work. I went through the motions until six o'clock, and then I climbed into my car and headed for Emmett's.

I knocked on his door, not waiting for him to let me inside. "Hey."

"Hey, baby." He came striding toward the entryway wearing only a pair of athletic shorts. They were loose and the smooth black fabric clung to his bulky thighs with each of his long strides. The waistband sat low and my mouth watered at the delicious V of his hips. His washboard abs and strong arms glistened with sweat.

"Working out, Ace?"

"Yep." He bent low to brush a kiss to my lips. I loved that he was so tall. Even in my heels, he towered over me.

"Hope you saved some energy for me."

"I always have energy for you." He chuckled. "Want a glass of wine before dinner?"

"Sure." I kicked off my heels and padded down the hallway.

He went to the kitchen while I opened the door to the deck, escaping to my favorite spot in Montana.

I settled into my chair, curling my legs beneath me. Then I breathed and breathed, like I did almost every night.

I'd sit here, breathing in the clean air and scent of pine trees, and put the mental blocks in place. The ones that kept me from talking about my family and friends. The ones that might reveal my identity. Those blocks had slipped last night and maybe that was because I hadn't taken a moment like this to assume the role.

Emmett came outside carrying two glasses of red wine.

He handed one over, then sat in his own chair. He hadn't bothered finding a shirt and those glorious tattoos were on full display.

He shifted, setting his glass on the deck boards on his other side. The movement turned him enough that I had no choice but to stare at the skull decorating the space between his shoulder blades.

Their club patch.

It was his largest piece. Unlike the queen and ace tattoo or the bird on his wrist or the other inked artwork on his skin, that skull was one I hadn't asked about because I knew exactly what it was. My dad had something similar on his own back. TJ had too.

Emmett's skull was split in half. One side was decorated with a head wrap and bohemian embellishments. A gypsy. The intricate stitching around the eye and mouth was delicate. That half, feminine and beautiful.

The other half of the skull was devoid of all elegance. Its harshness was beautiful in its own right. The tattoo was silver, made to resemble metal. Tin. Behind it was a symphony of orange, yellow and red flames. Their tips traced the top of Emmett's shoulder and down over his ribs.

Then at the base of his spine, the club's motto.

Live to Ride

Wander Free

"I was in a motorcycle club."

I snapped my eyes to his face. He'd caught me staring. "Huh?"

He looked over his shoulder at the skull. "I was in a motorcycle club. This was our emblem. Our patch."

"You're in a motorcycle club?" I widened my eyes,

hoping I'd infused my voice with enough surprise. "Like *Sons of Anarchy*?"

"I hate that damn show." He shook his head. "But yes, I was. Not anymore. My club disbanded."

"Oh. Which club?"

"The Tin Gypsies."

I sipped from my glass, needing the wine tonight to help tell the lies. "I haven't heard of them. Should I have?"

"Probably not. We disbanded about seven years ago."

"What got you into it? Your Harley?"

"No, my dad." He took a sip of his wine, his gaze shifting to the trees beyond his house. "The Clifton Forge Motor-cycle Club was started ages ago by one of my best friends' grandfathers. It was tied to the garage where I work, also started by my buddy's grandfather. Back then, the club was small. Just a group of men, mostly veterans, who loved to ride on the weekends and escape their wives."

I took a drink, doing my best to keep my hands still and not let the wine slosh over the edges as they threatened to shake. He was confiding in me. Without prompting or digging, he was sharing about his club.

Emmett trusted me.

And it was a dagger to the heart.

"After high school, my dad went to California for a while. This was before he met my mom. He rode a lot and got hooked up with a big club. Didn't join them, but he saw enough. When he came home to Montana, he talked the guys in Clifton Forge into making some changes."

"What kind of changes?"

"The name for one. The Clifton Forge Motorcycle Club became the Tin Gypsy Motorcycle Club. Then they turned it into a functioning club. They expanded the membership.

Put some rules in place. Earned money. Did more than ride on the weekends."

"So it was like *Sons of Anarchy*."

The corner of Emmett's mouth turned up. "You're killin' me."

"Sorry." I laughed. "I won't bring them up again."

"Anyway, they became a stronger club. Dad was the vice president. I was too, at one point."

"Interesting. How big was your club?"

"About forty members at the peak."

"Wow. That's a lot." Not as many as the Warriors had grown to.

I wondered if Dad realized he'd let too many join his club. He hadn't trusted all of the members, hence the video footage to use for blackmail if one ever got out of line. Had the same happened to the Gypsies, or had they stayed small enough?

"I don't think my dad or the other leaders ever thought it would get so big," Emmett said. "But you know how things go. When it's good, other people want in. And for a while, things were really fucking good."

"Good how?"

He took a sip. "Money. Power. Brotherhood. Fun. It was a lot of fun."

"Then why did you disband it?"

"Circumstances changed. What was fun became danger- ous. People who weren't supposed to be involved got hurt. And my dad . . . he was murdered."

"Oh my God," I gasped. "Ace . . ." I still couldn't say I was sorry. For Emmett to lose his father, there was a twinge of sadness. But I wasn't sorry.

Emmett had a framed photo of Stone in the living room.

Every time I pictured that face, his bald head and thick white beard, I felt a surge of anger.

Because Stone had murdered my eighteen-year-old brother.

"He was killed by a rival club," Emmett said. "The motherfuckers hauled him out of a bar and shot him. Right between the eyes."

I flinched. Dad had ordered Stone killed—maybe he'd even pulled the trigger, I wasn't sure. But hearing the pain in Emmett's voice hurt more than I'd expected.

It was clear he'd loved his father.

Well, I loved mine too.

We were on opposites sides of a battle started by our parents.

"The guy behind it is rotting in prison. That's enough vengeance for me. The son of a bitch can die in a gray room, all alone. I wouldn't wish it any other way."

I took a huge gulp of my wine, unable to speak.

The irony was stifling.

Emmett's preferred vengeance against my father was the same vengeance I'd planned for him.

This was going to be a long night.

CHAPTER TWELVE

EMMETT

"My friends are having a barbeque today," I told Nova as we sat at the kitchen island, eating scrambled eggs and bacon. "Come with me."

Her fork froze midair. "Oh, I . . . can't. I have to work."

"It's a Saturday."

"I'm behind." She shoved the bite in her mouth, chewing longer than necessary.

I frowned and dove into my own food. The tension from last night hadn't eased in the slightest. If anything, it had only gotten worse.

Nova had been eyeing the door all morning. She'd nearly passed on breakfast but when she'd come out of the shower and seen that I'd already set her a plate, she'd stayed.

But the minute the dishes were in the dishwasher, I'd be watching her taillights streak down the lane.

What the fuck had I been thinking last night? Telling her about the club had freaked her out. Probably because she'd watched that fucking show. *Sons of Anarchy* and Jax Teller could rot in hell.

Not that the image they'd portrayed was significantly different than how the Tin Gypsies had lived. Maybe that was why it grated on me. That our lifestyle, something I'd cherished since birth, had been spun into sheer entertainment.

We'd been criminals. Murderers. We'd lived beyond the law and that had come with costs. Namely, my father's life. Draven's life.

When Nova had been staring at my tattoo last night, the story had just slipped out.

What a damn mistake.

If she ate any faster, she was going to choke.

After we'd sat on the deck, she'd been quiet. Too quiet. There'd been a distance in her gaze.

Even when we'd gone to bed and I'd stripped her out of her clothes and joined her, she hadn't cried out when she'd come. She'd had her bottom lip clenched between her teeth and her eyes squeezed shut as her inner walls had clenched me.

For only the briefest moment after I'd poured my release into her body did that withdrawn expression fade. But then she'd gone into the shower and when she'd climbed back into bed, her hair combed and wet, she'd turned her back on me. Normally she slept draped on my side, her head in the crook of my shoulder.

I'd pulled her back into my chest and though she hadn't squirmed free, her shoulders had been cold.

All because I couldn't keep my damn mouth shut. About the club. About Dad. I *wanted* her to know about me and my history. I wanted her to meet my friends. I wanted her to stop being a secret.

That wasn't happening today. Because she had to work.

Yeah, right.

Breakfast didn't taste appealing anymore so I stood from my stool, dumping the rest and rinsing my plate.

"Ace."

Emmett. Why the fuck couldn't she call me Emmett?

"I didn't think we were doing the friend thing," she said.

"Forget it," I clipped, not turning back to her as I opened the dishwasher with too much force.

"You're mad."

"Yeah." I was her fuck buddy and nothing more. She could sleep in my bed but not meet my friends. My family.

"I'm going to go." She brought her plate over to the sink, hovering at my side.

I snatched the dish from her hand, rinsing it too. Then I went to work on the skillet on the stove, scrubbing harder than necessary.

She sighed but didn't say a word as she walked to the front door, the click of her heels like a hammer to the chest as she left.

One of these days, I'd hear that click for the last time.

Maybe today was that day.

Maybe today needed to be that day.

I braced my hands on the counter, staring out the window over the sink and into the trees. They were the same trees we watched from the deck each night. In the distance, an engine rumbled, fading too fast.

"Fuck." I dragged a hand over my beard.

I was falling for her. I'd seen my friends do the same, watching from a distance. Leo hadn't even realized he was in love with Cass until I'd mentioned it.

There was no use denying it myself.

I was falling for Nova.

Maybe I already had. And she wouldn't use my fucking name.

The clock on the microwave showed it was only eight. The barbeque at Scarlett and Luke's place wouldn't happen until three. So I retreated to my home gym for a brutal workout, lifting weights for an hour before beating the hell out of a heavy bag. My knuckles were raw when I went to the shower, then hit the office to spend a few hours at my laptop.

The temptation to look into Nova's life was so overpowering that after a couple of hours, I had to leave the house, to get far away from my computers before I broke that trust. Granted, she'd never know, but I couldn't live with it. The curiosity was crippling, so I did what I always did when I was in a shit mood.

I went for a long, fast ride.

Forcing myself off the road took an effort, so much so that I was an hour late to Scarlett and Luke's place. Everyone was waiting for me on their sprawling deck. Scarlett and Luke had added it not long after they'd been married.

The women all smiled when I walked into the party. The guys stood, clapping me on the shoulder while Luke handed me a beer. Dash and Bryce's sons barreled into my legs, each of them wearing a Clifton Forge Garage sweatshirt to ward off the autumn chill. Then there were the babies, bundled and babbling.

Nova would fit here.

Bryce, Genevieve, Presley, Scarlett, Cass . . . they'd pull her into their circle and hold her tight.

Except she wasn't here. She'd never be here.

That wasn't what we were.

"You okay?" Dash asked, standing at my side as three different conversations carried on.

"No." I took a long chug of my beer. Lying to Dash, to any of my friends, made my skin crawl so I gave him the honest answer. And because we'd known one another for so long—fought, worked, killed side by side—he didn't ask for more.

Dash clinked the neck of his amber bottle against mine, a silent offer that if I did want to talk, he'd be there.

"Emmett, you're needed." Presley sat on one of the outdoor couches, nestled into Shaw's side as he kept one arm around her shoulders and the other cradling their son, Nico.

"Needed for what?"

She patted the seat beside her. "Birthday plans."

I groaned but went to sit beside her. Presley hated her own birthday and for years hadn't let us make a thing of it. Since Scarlett had come to Montana, that had changed. The twin sisters had planned a huge party for their last birthday and apparently the partying wasn't reserved for them alone.

Cass's birthday had been the most recent. And mine was up next.

"Do you want to have a party at your house?" Presley asked. "So you don't have to drive home?"

"Or we could just give him a ride," Shaw said.

"Yeah, but that's not the same."

"I think the better question is do you want to have the party at my house, Pres?"

She fought a smile. "We never do anything at your place and it's so nice."

"Fine by me." I waved a hand. "Go nuts. Just tell me when to show up."

"Yay." She clapped her hands together and looked to Cass, who had a similar smile on her face.

"They were going to have the party at your place

173

whether you agreed or not," Leo said from the armrest of Cass's chair. Seraphina was in her mother's lap, drooling over a plastic giraffe. "They've already planned the party too. Apparently thirty-nine is the new forty and they're going all out. Beware."

Cass's mouth fell open as she looked up at her husband. Then she poked him in the ribs and hissed, "Do you mind?"

Leo only chuckled, leaning down to brush his lips to hers.

"How big of a party are we talking?" I asked Pres.

She winked. "You'll see."

"It's going to be epic," Bryce said, coming up behind me. "Trust us. It'll be fun."

I did trust them. I trusted them with my life.

The barbeque should have soothed the tension and improved my mood. The fact that my friends had already planned a birthday party for me should have made me smile. But the entire afternoon and evening, none of my smiles came easy. No amount of laughter and time with my friends eased the pit in my gut.

Because what I really wanted to do for my birthday was have Nova around.

My birthday was next month and by then she'd be gone.

Maybe they sensed my mood, but when I excused myself not long after we'd finished eating our steaks, no one stopped me. Dash and Leo shared a look as I waved and strode through the door.

Then I was gone, riding through town.

Before Nova, I would have gone to The Betsy. I'd left the barbeque thinking of home, but fuck that. I turned left instead of right at the intersection past the grocery store and rolled down Central toward the bar.

If Nova had wanted to be with me, she could have come today. She could have met my friends and shared a meal with my family and heard them use my goddamn name. She'd made her choice and it was time to stop tailoring my actions to her own.

So I went to The Betsy, walked inside and drew in a long breath. Beer and sweat and heat. Smoking wasn't allowed anymore but the scent of cigarettes would never fade. It had infused the dark, neon-sign-covered walls.

"Emmett!" A guy at a table in the center of the room raised his beer bottle in a salute.

I waved on my way to the bar, shoving in between two stools.

"Hey." Paul appeared, reaching across the counter.

"Hey." I shook his hand, then surveyed the room. "Busy tonight."

"Saturday. What can I get you?"

"Just a beer."

He nodded, going to the cooler for my favorite. Behind him were rows of liquor bottles, shelved against a mirror that ran to the ceiling and made the bar feel bigger. When he returned with my beer, he slid it over. "Haven't seen you lately."

"Been busy too." I twisted off the top.

Another customer raised a hand to get his attention.

"Good to see you, Emmett," he said before disappearing to the same end of the bar where I'd met Nova.

I shoved her from my mind, left five dollars on the bar and walked to the pool tables, shaking hands with a few guys I recognized from the gym and around town.

The jukebox was playing rock tonight, an old song that had been one of Dad's favorites to blare at the garage while we worked. The noise was loud enough tonight that there wouldn't be a lot of conversation. People were practically shouting as they spoke, adding to the volume.

Loud was good. Loud meant no talking.

The clack of a cue hitting a ball rang through the air and the guys invited me to play a round. One turned into three, which turned into five and I made sure to supply the quarters because I wasn't giving up my spot at the table. Because when I left here, I'd go home and I wasn't ready to go home. I wasn't ready to know if Nova had shown or if she'd stayed away.

The noise in the bar ratcheted up and up until it was practically deafening by midnight. My beer was long gone but I hadn't felt like another. My mood was teetering on the edge as it was and getting drunk would only tip the scales. I was in that place where what I really wanted was to fuck or to fight.

A long, hard fuck. Or a violent, punishing fight.

In the corner beside the pool table, a man in his sixties wearing a cowboy hat occupied a stool.

Once, a long time ago, that stool had been Dad's favorite spot to sit. We'd come to The Betsy and he'd play one or two games of pool, then he'd take up his spot and spend the rest of the night bullshitting with whoever came close enough.

It was painful to look there and not see his face. To not see his shiny bald head and his long white beard braided down the center of his chest. Thank God I'd gotten Mom's thick hair. But I'd give up every strand for just one more day with my father.

A jolt of sadness came over me and suddenly I needed to get the hell out of this bar. Even if my house was empty, I didn't want to be here, in the place where he'd been killed.

It was like this. Either I'd come here and feel close to him. Or I'd come here and feel his absence like a gaping hole in my chest.

A room full of people and I was alone.

"Hey, Emmett." A familiar voice caught my ear and I turned. Tera was wading through the bodies surrounding the pool table.

"Hey, Tera." She wasn't who I'd expected to see. "How's it going?"

"Good." She smiled, her cheeks flushed. Then she turned and pointed to a cocktail table surrounded by four other women, only one I recognized. "I'm here with some of the other teachers. Girls' night. It's the first time I've been out since moving here and they told me that I had to check out The Betsy."

"Ah." I nodded. "Where's Maggie?"

"At your mom's, actually. I tried to get a babysitter, but she insisted."

"Sounds like Mom."

"She's not going to let me pay her, is she?"

I chuckled. "Nope."

Tera laughed and her eyes softened. "Well, I, um . . . just wanted to say hi."

"Glad you did."

"Have a good night, Emmett."

I opened my mouth, about to offer to buy her a drink, but clamped my mouth shut before the words could tumble out. And I let her turn away and retreat to the table with her friends.

If I bought Tera a drink, I'd feel like a complete bastard for leading her on. I couldn't—wouldn't—go there with her. Not when a pair of dark eyes haunted my every thought.

Even in the crush of the bar tonight, I could smell Nova's exquisite scent. I could hear her musical laugh and the way she moaned as she came around my cock.

For Nova, I'd consider the future. A wife. Kids.

If only she wanted that too. But she didn't. She wanted to use nicknames and keep her distance. The sooner I got my head wrapped around that, the better.

I gotta get out of here.

I put my pool stick away and waved goodbye to the guys I'd been playing with. Then I turned, ready to head for the door, and my eyes landed on a beautiful face.

I froze.

Nova sat at the bar, wedged in between two men who were facing the bar itself. But Nova was turned to the room. Her long legs were crossed. She had a martini in one hand. She raised it to her lips, taking a slow sip. Her eyes never breaking from mine.

How had I missed her coming in?

I changed direction, strode over and stopped one foot away. I stood there, not saying a word. What was there to say?

"Hi, Ace."

"Emmett."

"Emmett," she repeated.

"Why is it so hard for you to use my name?" My voice was barely audible above the noise, but she heard me because her eyes widened.

She reached behind her and set the martini aside, then stood and moved in close. "Because no good will come of me getting attached to you."

"Too late."

Her mouth parted on a gasp I couldn't hear.

I leaned in closer, bending so that my nose was barely touching hers. "Too fucking late."

She stared at me, her eyes searching, but I'd hit my mark. She was as attached to me as I was to her.

"Why'd you come here?"

"Because you weren't at home."

That pain in my chest, the one I'd been fighting all day, vanished. Poof. Gone. She'd come to find me and the relief was overpowering. My shoulders sagged. God, I was tired. Pretending not to care was exhausting. "What do you want from me, Nova?"

Her face fell, the same exhaustion I felt etched on her beautiful features. "The truth."

"When have I lied to you?"

"You haven't." She put her hand to my cheek, her nails sinking into my beard. Then her lips were on mine and the world melted away.

There was no music. No crowd. No drinks being served or drunk patrons laughing. It was just us, her tongue seeping against mine as I devoured her mouth, not caring about anything else.

This was all we'd have. Something in my mind clicked and the realization crept into my bones. This was all we'd have for one more month.

One more month.

Then I'd have to let her go.

CHAPTER THIRTEEN

NOVA

Moonlight cast Emmett's room in silvery blue. It muted the rust-colored shade of his sheets and quilt. The white walls practically glowed.

He was asleep beside me, his breaths slow and deep. Even sleeping, he held me in place, his chest to my back. The weight and heat of his body was better than any blanket.

The comfort of his embrace and the softness of his bed should have put me in dreamland, but I'd been awake for an hour. It had been that way for two weeks, ever since I'd tracked Emmett down at The Betsy. If I slept for three or four hours, that was a restful night.

Our routine hadn't changed. Each night I'd come over and we'd have dinner, then talk for a while before sex. After an orgasm or three, I'd crash, so exhausted that I'd fall asleep within seconds of closing my eyes. But then I'd pop wide awake around two or three and that was it. I was awake.

For two weeks, I'd been lying here, staring out his bedroom window, watching as the moonlight faded and sunrise took its place. One night, I'd snuck into his office and stared at the safe for an hour before finally working up the courage to try a few combinations. His birthday. His mom's birthday. His dad's birthday. Then each in reverse. Unsurprisingly, none had worked. Also unsurprisingly, I was glad none had worked.

Other than that failed attempt, my sleepless nights over the last two weeks had been spent right here in bed, wondering what the fuck I was doing.

As much as I knew I should slip away, disappear from his life forever, I couldn't bring myself to leave.

Two Saturdays ago, the day he'd invited me to his friends' barbeque, I'd raced to the rental and packed my things. My suitcases had been ready to load into the Nova, but the moment I'd opened the door to haul them outside, my feet had stuck to the floor.

I couldn't leave.

Why? Why couldn't I just vanish? This entire scheme of mine had fizzled the moment I'd let Emmett inside my body. Yes, it had taken me a few weeks to realize it, but I was incapable of hurting him.

Completely and utterly incapable.

What would Dad do when he found out I'd failed? What would he say? Did I even care?

My relationship with my father was complicated at best. I'd spent so long wanting his attention, his approval, and now that I truly had a chance to win both, was I really giving up?

Yes. What other option did I have?

Emmett wasn't the monster Dad had made him out to be. He was kind and generous. He was intelligent and too sexy for his own good.

He probably didn't even realize that the blond woman who'd approached him at The Betsy had been staring at him for an hour before she'd finally walked over to say hello. From my seat I'd seen the desire in her eyes. The blush of her cheeks and the way she'd tucked her hands into her jeans pockets to hide her nerves.

She was totally into him and if I was a better person, I'd walk. I'd give him a chance with a woman like that, sweet and smiley. Pure. Honest. She could give him a future.

But did I leave the bar? Nope. The moment he'd left the pool table and headed for the door, I'd turned, shifting away from the man I'd been hiding behind, so he could see me.

The blond was going to have to wait her turn. I wasn't done with him yet.

I doubted I'd ever be done. Even after I disappeared from his life, he would always linger in mine.

I was a coward. I wanted him too much. I wanted to keep him for myself, even if it was for just a short time more.

That night, he'd asked me what I wanted. *The truth.*

To learn it. To tell it. To live it.

When have I lied to you?

He hadn't and that was the problem.

The liar here was me.

Everything he'd told me had seemed honest. The only way to know for certain was to check. Over the past two weeks, I'd spent countless hours skipping work to do research.

I'd been attempting to cross-check each story he'd told me with an official report. Emmett had to be spinning his stories in his favor, right? Except the stories he'd told me hadn't been in the news.

First, I'd started with the online archives from various papers around the state. Murders and mayhem were uncommon in Montana and when something big enough happened, it made the papers in Missoula, Bozeman and Billings. When my searches there had turned up nothing, I'd switched to the *Clifton Forge Tribune*.

Their public online archive only went back five years, so I'd had to brave the newspaper office itself.

I'd made sure Bryce Slater was at the garage, where most of the wives seemed to congregate during the week. Then I'd gone down and met a very nice man named Art, who'd logged me on to their local electronic archive because I was a grad student writing my thesis about the evolution of small-town media outlets.

He'd offered to call Bryce and her father, Lane, into the office so I could interview them. I'd politely declined.

Sequestered away in a tiny room at the newspaper, I'd scoured every piece I could find on the Tin Gypsies. There hadn't been many.

Bryce Slater and her father were owners of the paper and as Dash's wife, I couldn't imagine she'd incriminate her husband.

Except, Bryce had moved to town after the Tin Gypsies had disbanded. The owners before her had had no connection to the club, at least not one I could find. And the tone of their articles from the time when the club had been fully functioning didn't suggest there was much love between the general Clifton Forge populace and the Tin Gypsies.

But people and businesses and reporters could be bought off—my father had most likely bribed the Ashton newspaper to keep the Arrowhead Warriors off the front page. The startling lack of news about my dad or the club, even after their arrests, was indication enough. Maybe the Tin Gypsies had done the same, because there wasn't much news about their club.

If there was mention about them in the archives, I'd read it. Nothing had screamed *Emmett Stone is a liar*.

I needed evidence to show that Emmett was fooling me. If I could just prove he was a monster, then I could shove these feelings aside and get back to my plan.

Police reports would do the trick, but it wasn't like I could pull them from the county courthouse. Requesting reports would be like shooting a flare into the midnight sky. It would call way too much attention to myself, especially given that Luke Rosen, Clifton Forge chief of police, was so deeply connected to the Tin Gypsies.

He'd probably been at the barbeque Emmett had invited me to.

My heart twisted and I closed my eyes, willing sleep to come. Willing the guilt to loosen its grip.

I knew what I had to do. The only way for me to move forward was with information. Facts that I could use to make a decision. So far, I was going solely off my father's opinions and while that had been good enough at the beginning, it wasn't enough now. Not now when I knew Emmett.

I'd been wrestling with my next step for weeks, trying to find a semblance of inner courage.

I knew what I had to do.

Starting tomorrow.

———

"HEY," I said when Emmett answered the call.

"Hey, baby."

"How's your Thursday morning going so far?"

"Good." There was the clank of metal in the background

and the thud of boots. He must be walking out of the garage for some privacy. "You?"

"Busy. The owner of the rental just called me and needs to come over to blow out the sprinklers. He said it's going to be loud for an hour or so and my afternoon is totally slammed with calls. I'd go to a coffee shop, but they can be loud too, and a couple of my clients can be really touchy. Would you mind if I went to your place?"

"No, not at all."

The air rushed from my lungs. He trusted me. I was betraying him, but he trusted me. Just that thought made my eyes flood with tears. "Are you sure?"

"Yeah. Just go through the garage." He rattled off the keycode to open the door, then the code to the alarm system.

"Thanks," I said through the lump in my throat.

He never should have trusted me.

"See you later?" he asked.

"I'll be there. Bye."

"Bye."

My heart was heavy, the phone a hundred-pound weight in my hand. My chest heaved as I tried to lift it from my side.

Do it, Nova.

I squeezed my eyes shut, gave myself three long breaths, then called Hacker.

"Are you on your way?" I'd called and woken him up while Emmett had been in the shower this morning.

"Yeah." He yawned. "About an hour out."

"Good. There's a Town Pump gas station on Central. I'll meet you there." I ended the call and forced myself to move.

I wanted information and it was time to collect. With my purse over a shoulder, I locked the rental up and climbed in the Nova. Then I raced to Emmett's, using the codes he'd given me to get into his house.

It smelled like him, wind and cedar and spice. I drew in a long breath as I marched down the hallway toward the office.

It was bigger in the daylight. There were no cameras inside that I could see, not like the exterior, where I'd noticed some mounted on the corners of the house and garage.

If he was taping the movements in his house, I'd have to risk it.

There were two laptops on his desk, both plugged in to display monitors and charging stations. I swept up both, casting one glance at the safe in the corner.

I paused, walking over and pulling the knob. Just in case he'd opened it this morning and hadn't closed it all the way.

Locked.

"Worth a try," I muttered, then hurried from the room and straight outside.

With a white-knuckled grip, I drove back into town to the gas station where Hacker was parked.

His window was open and a plume of smoke streamed out as I walked over, a cigarette pinched between his fingers.

"Here." I handed him the laptops.

He nodded, flicking his cigarette butt out. It landed beside my shoe. "Give me some time."

"You don't have much."

Emmett would be at work all day, but knowing I was at his house, he might decide to leave early.

"I'll hurry," Hacker promised, setting Emmett's laptops in the passenger seat. Then without another word, he reversed out of the parking lot and drove away.

I had no idea where he'd go to do whatever it was that he was going to do, but I couldn't stand in the gas station's parking lot all day, so I returned to Emmett's and waited for Hacker's call.

Work, for a change, saved my sanity. I didn't really enjoy it but being busy was better than fretting. I sat at the kitchen island, my body jittery for hours, until finally at two o'clock, Hacker's name flashed on my screen.

"Are you done?" I answered, already moving through the house for the door.

"Yeah."

"Meet you at the same gas station." I raced into town, finding Hacker parked in the same place.

The moment I approached his door, he had the laptops stuck out his window. I hauled them into my arms as he held out a simple black box. The receiver. "Put this within two hundred feet of the laptops."

"Okay. Anything else?"

"Nope. Just wait until he logs in."

"And when you get into the hard drive, what will that get me?"

"Emails. Files. Documents. I'll put it on a flash drive for you. Whatever that son of a bitch saved, you'll get."

I tensed at him calling Emmett a son of a bitch. "He won't know you opened these, right?"

"Probably not."

My heart dropped to the cigarette butt he'd tossed out earlier on the ground. " 'Probably not.' That's not giving me a lot of confidence."

"Look, like I told you before, this is mostly undetectable. But . . . there's always a chance. If I were you, I'd be thinking about my exit strategy."

No.

Just like that, my departure date had been set. My heart

broke. Right there, in the oil-stained parking lot of a gas station, my heart broke.

Time was up.

"You'll call me when you have the flash drive."

He nodded. "Yeah."

"And you'll make one and only one copy. Understood?"

"Understood."

I blew out a long breath, then reached into my purse for the envelope of cash I'd picked up at the bank this morning on my way home from Emmett's. "Three thousand. Per our agreement."

He snatched it from my hand and plucked a cigarette from its box. Then he rolled up his window and was gone.

I turned, hustling to my car. My hands were shaking as I started it up and pulled onto Central. Sweat beaded at my temples and I rolled the window down, gulping the early-October air, hoping it would cool me down before I got to Emmett's.

Please don't be home.

I broke every speed limit as I tore down the country road to his house. When I parked and keyed in the garage code, the door opened and the space was empty. *Thank God.* I ran to my car, my heels accentuating every rushed step, then swiped up the laptops and the receiver and scurried inside.

The rumble of an engine echoed from beyond the house the second I reached the office.

"Shit." I put the laptops in their places, reconnecting power cords and aligning them as best I could with how they'd been. Then I searched the room for a place to hide the receiver.

The safe caught my eye. There looked to be enough space to hide the box between it and the wall. I doubted

Emmett moved the heavy piece regularly. Flying across the room, I stretched an arm in the gap between the safe and the bookshelf beside it.

The box fit. "Thank God."

I wedged it in as best I could, wishing for more than a minute to make sure it was secure. But the sound of Emmett's Harley cut off and I was out of time.

There was no way I'd get to the living room before he came into the house and the closest door was to the basement, so I yanked my arm free and scrambled out of the office, bolting down the stairs. Emmett's bootsteps sounded on the floor above me.

"Nova," he called.

I hit the bottom step and ran for the couch, flinging myself over the back and plopping down. I whipped out my phone, holding it above my lap and doing my best to relax. "Down here!"

His footsteps grew louder as he thudded down the staircase.

My heart was pounding. I wiped at the sweat beaded at my temples. I sucked in a long breath and tried to calm my body.

Emmett rounded the corner too soon, a smile on his face. "Hey."

"Hey." I smiled through the sharp lance of guilt that slashed through my body. "I hope you don't mind I decided to take my calls down here. This couch is cozy."

"Not at all." He rounded the edge and sat down beside me, leaning in for a kiss.

My heart was still beating too hard but he didn't seem to notice. "Are you done working for the day?"

"Yeah. Since you were here, I left early."

"I'm done too." I set my phone on my lap. "I didn't get through all of my to-do list but what I didn't finish will have to wait until Monday."

"I need to run a lease renewal to one of my tenants. Want to come along?"

"Sure." I stood and started toward the stairwell, ready to get out of this basement. When we hit the main floor, I took a step toward the kitchen, but Emmett went the opposite direction, toward his office.

I held my breath, my body so still I could have given a marble statue a run for its money. Did I stay? Should I run now?

I inched toward the office door, watching as he went around his desk and took his seat. My knees buckled and I leaned on the frame to hold me up as he opened both laptops.

"I just need to print a few things off." His fingers flew over the keyboard in front of the monitor. Then he twisted to the other laptop, typing there too.

"Okay." Could he hear my entire body trembling? I held my breath, waiting for him to notice something wrong, but he simply printed off a document from one computer and a different document from the other.

Then he stood and swiped up the papers before striding my way. My breath exploded from my lungs as I turned, trying to hide the relief on my face as we retreated to the kitchen.

"You okay?" he asked, leading the way to the garage.

"Yeah." I let my shoulders fall. "Just a long day. A long week."

He threw an arm around my shoulders, hauling me close. Then he dropped a kiss to my hair. "We'll run this errand, then come back and chill. Eat dinner. Watch a movie or something."

"That sounds great."

Or it would except for this gnawing shame and the fact that I had to tell him I was leaving. Tomorrow.

I pulled in a long breath of his scent, feeling his warmth. How long would it take before I forgot both?

"Bike or truck?" he asked.

"Bike." If this was the end, I wanted one last ride.

He grinned, happy with my answer. I stole a jacket from the hooks on the wall, then we set off for town.

Never had I held him this close on a ride. Usually I'd let go and put my fingers to the wind, but not today. I hugged him tight through the whole ride, the sting of tears threatening the entire time.

We stopped in front of a charming steel-blue house with white shutters. The front door was painted a teal green. It stood out from the other homes on the street, the others a shade of taupe or gray.

"This is cute," I said as Emmett parked his bike and killed the engine.

"My renters wanted to paint it. They've been such great tenants that I didn't care what color they picked." He held out his hand and I handed over the papers that I'd kept in between us on the ride over. "Be right back."

I stayed in my seat, watching as he strode up the small sidewalk. Before he made it to the door, it flew open and a small boy with curly brown hair ran out, his mother close behind.

She smiled brightly at Emmett, standing on the small stoop with her hands on her pregnant belly.

He handed her the papers, spoke for just a moment, then

gave the boy a high five. The kid smacked Emmett's palm as hard as he could and Emmett pretended it hurt, shaking his hand out as the boy beamed.

I caught myself smiling at the scene.

Emmett was good with kids. It didn't surprise me in the least, because he was a good man.

How much more proof did I need?

My smile faltered. Apparently more because at that moment, my phone vibrated in my pocket. Hacker had texted.

That was fast. Got the passwords. I'll have the flash drive for you tomorrow.

I tucked the phone away and stared at Emmett.

How was I supposed to say goodbye? How was I supposed to look at that flash drive tomorrow? The moment I opened it, everything would change, of that I had no doubt.

Later.

It would all wait until later. If this was the last night, I wouldn't think about the flash drive until I was gone.

Emmett laughed at something, the sound echoing across the yard. He really was a good man.

But that didn't really matter anymore, did it?

Because my time with him was up.

CHAPTER FOURTEEN

EMMETT

"So . . ." Nova turned to face me from her seat on the chaise beside mine. The expression on her face made my stomach drop.

Damn. I'd known this was coming. I'd been waiting for it. "So."

It had been almost two months since we'd first met at The Betsy. Two months since we'd been having sex and sharing meals and spending time together. Two months, and dread of the end clung to the air like the autumn mist in the forest.

Nova had brought out a blanket tonight to ward off the chill. She had it pulled around her shoulders and her legs tucked beneath her. She'd stolen one of my hair ties to pile her tresses in a messy knot on her head. Her cheeks were rosy. The tip of her nose was a matching shade of pink.

Beautiful. Unforgettable.

I'd told her we could sit inside but she'd insisted on the deck. She seemed to love it out here as much as I did.

Hell, it was going to be lonely sitting out here without her.

"I have to go back to Missoula tomorrow."

Damn. Damn. Just because I'd known it was coming didn't make it easier to hear. It was on the tip of my tongue to ask her not to go, but the words would be wasted.

The past two weeks had been some of the best in my life, and I'd be a fool not to admit it was because of her. Ever since that night at The Betsy when she'd found me after the barbeque, we'd spent as much time together as possible.

Part of me knew it was because we'd been barreling toward the finish line. No amount of pumping the brakes would stop its fast approach.

And now we were here. The end.

"Okay." There wasn't anything else to say. Just . . . okay.

"I need to get my life back together there before Monday. Do laundry. All of that."

I nodded. God, I wanted to beg her to stay through tomorrow and the weekend. Tonight couldn't be our last night together. I wasn't ready to let her go yet.

"But I was thinking . . . maybe I could come back next weekend."

"Yes." No hesitation. "Come back. Except . . ."

"What?"

"My friends are throwing me a birthday party. Here."

"Oh." Her body sagged.

"Just think about it."

"Okay," she whispered, sadness in her gaze. She didn't want this to end either.

Not yet.

One more weekend wouldn't make it any harder. It

wouldn't make it any easier, but it wouldn't make it any harder, and I wasn't ready to say goodbye for good.

"Will you miss me this week?" she asked.

"Yes." Again, no hesitation.

"Good." A smile tugged at her mouth as she stood, shuffling to my chair and bringing the blanket along with her.

I shifted, making space for her to sit between my legs and lean against my chest.

The smell of her perfume enveloped me, sensual and deep and complicated, like the woman herself. I drew it in, holding it for a long breath, then wrapped my arms around her and held tight.

"Tell me something," she said.

"What?"

"Anything. I just want to hear your voice."

I kissed the top of her hair, then relaxed and stared off into the trees. The sun was setting earlier and earlier these days, but we sat out here regardless, staring into the trees as they were swallowed up by the night.

"We've got a Nova coming into the garage in a couple of weeks. Made me think of you."

She hummed. "What's your favorite part about working at the garage?"

"The people. Working with my brothers."

"From the club?"

"A couple of them, yeah. Everyone at the garage used to be part of the club, but after we disbanded, we hired others." Most of the brothers had scattered to the wind after we shut down the Tin Gypsies. First Presley had come along to act at the receptionist. Then Isaiah had been the first mechanic who hadn't been a member.

"Why did you disband?"

195

I blew out a deep breath, propping a knee up. The answer to her question was long and complicated. It was full of secrets that only a few people in Clifton Forge even knew.

Secrets I wouldn't—couldn't—tell her.

Maybe if we were going someplace, maybe if she was a lifelong companion and not leaving tomorrow, we'd get to a point where I'd share those secrets. But that wasn't our thing.

"I'm prying. Sorry," she said. "You don't have to tell me."

"No." I shook my head. "It's okay. I haven't talked much about it."

Maybe I should. Maybe I could air it out here, with her, without spilling the details I'd take with me to the grave.

"In a nutshell . . . the brothers decided to go their different ways. Some of the older guys retired, a couple settling here in town."

Big Louie still lived in town. He'd bought the bowling alley after leaving the Gypsies and we'd see him at The Betsy every now and then. Every time I saw him he wanted to talk about Dad—it wasn't always easy to bump into Big Louie.

"Others moved south for the weather." They'd wanted easier winters and the ability to ride their bikes year-round. "Some brothers moved to chase a woman. When they left, we didn't replace them with younger prospects."

Jet had moved to Vegas, following a girl. He had his own garage there now, and every couple of years, he'd call Dash out of the blue to bullshit. He'd texted me after Draven had died, asking if there was anything he could do.

Gunner had been my age. We'd prospected together. Like some of the older men, he'd gotten sick of the Montana winters and not being able to ride for months at a time, so he'd moved to Washington and bought a houseboat with the money he'd made from the club.

That was an explanation, but only a sliver of the whole story.

Most of those members would have stayed in Clifton Forge had the club not made the decision to pull out of all illegal activities—activities that meant the cash flow was going to recede.

There'd been members who hadn't wanted to give up the life, the money, the power. Most of them had left to join other clubs. Some had even joined the Warriors. It had been a slap in the face after those fuckers had killed Dad.

Those assholes had been hauled in with the FBI raid on the Warriors. I couldn't find it in me to feel bad that they'd been arrested. They'd made their choice when they'd put on the Arrowhead Warrior patch.

They'd made their choice when the Tin Gypsies had called for a vote. It just hadn't gone in their favor.

The decision had been the right one. The writing had been on the wall. If we had continued, there would have been prison sentences and early deaths.

Most members Dad's age had retired by means of the cemetery. When you put on the cut, you knew you were likely signing up for a shorter-than-average life expectancy. That hadn't mattered in the beginning. But after a while, after Dad's death . . .

"We all voted it was time to change," I said.

"Change from what?"

"Change from the men we'd been." Not the kind of men who'd have a woman like Nova in their arms.

"Oh," she muttered.

Yeah. *Oh.*

We'd fought easily and often. We'd used intimidation to get whatever the fuck we'd wanted. We'd lied, cheated and stolen. We'd killed when necessary. It had all been in the name of the brotherhood. And for most of my life, I'd bought that line.

Now, looking back, I saw it had really been for money.

The garage hauled in a damn good income stream now, but back then, we hadn't been known for our custom remodels and builds. The reason Draven had pushed so hard to expand the garage was to replace the money flowing in from the club. No way Draven would have been able to pay me then what Dash was paying me now. Except to get to this point, it had taken time and a lot of fucking work. Now that dream was realized.

Draven's dream.

Dad would have loved it too. As much as he had loved being a Tin Gypsy.

Since I was a kid, that was the life I'd known. The life I'd wanted. I'd never cared about the money. Living Dad's legacy had been more important.

Would Dad have voted to disband? I often wondered what side he would have taken. Though if not for his death, we probably wouldn't have called for a vote in the first place.

"There's more to the story," I said, not sure why I was even talking about this. Maybe because I needed to say it. Or I needed her to know what kind of man I was. To see a glimpse of the demons in my past. Maybe they'd scare her away and next weekend wouldn't happen.

"You don't have to tell me if you don't want to," she said.

I held her tighter. "The reason we put it to vote in the first place was because one of our rivals came after family. Shit got fucked up."

Nova listened, unmoving, waiting for me to continue.

"The president of the club, Draven, had two sons. Nick, who was never part of the club, and Dash. Dash runs the garage where I work. When I was VP of the club, he was president. We've been friends our whole lives. Grew up in the club together. We knew what we were getting into. When you signed up to be a member, you knew the risks. Families too."

"Risks like . . . death?"

I nodded. "Yeah."

"Oh."

"Nick wasn't in the club. He never joined. He left Clifton Forge and didn't look back. Got married and was living in Prescott. No connection other than his DNA. A rival club went after Nick's wife. She had nothing to do with the club. She was innocent."

"Is she . . . okay?"

"The Warriors tried to kidnap her. She got lucky. Local police stopped it. But it never should have happened in the first place." The Warriors who'd tried to kidnap her had allegedly been acting against Tucker Talbot's orders. At the time, the only reason we'd believed it hadn't been his idea was that he'd handed over those two members to the Tin Gypsies.

Their bodies were buried in the mountains, in a remote location where no one would ever find their bones.

But maybe Tucker had just been trying to get rid of two rogue members and he'd ordered the kidnapping himself. I wouldn't put it past the man to stab his own fucking brothers in the back.

"Then after that, the same rivals murdered my father. That was the catalyst. It was time to just . . . be done."

Timing had been on Draven's side when he'd asked for the vote. Dad had been beloved by all members and his death had rattled us to the core.

"Emmett, I'm . . ." Nova blew out a long breath. "I don't know what to say."

I held her tighter, taking the comfort of her in my arms while I could.

"Sounds like disbanding was for the best," she said.

"Yeah, it was."

The club's income had mostly come from drug protection routes. It was rare that we'd smuggle the goods ourselves. Draven preferred our members not touch the meth, cocaine, heroin and whatever else had been on the move.

Instead, we'd made sure the mules didn't have trouble along the way to their destination, either from rival cartels or from cops. I'd earned more than one reckless driving ticket for speeding past a cop who'd been too close to a drug shipment.

For the most part, we'd stayed to the routes where the police wouldn't be looking. The border between Canada and Montana was big and for many, many years, there hadn't been enough patrol officers to watch it all. Slipping through the mountains and onto the quieter highways had been an easy day's work.

Draven and Dad had both forged many of those routes.

Ambition had been Draven's greatest strength and his greatest weakness. The man's mind had been cunning and sharp. The Gypsies had been small in number compared to the infamous clubs in California, but Draven hadn't needed a massive membership to be effective. Though he'd always spoken about expanding across the Northwest.

Had my father not died, had Nick's family not been threatened, I think he would have done it. Instead, he'd pushed like hell in the other direction and shut it all down.

The drug routes. The local security jobs in town. The underground fights. Anything illegal.

It hadn't been worth putting our families in danger. Not anymore.

I'd voted with Draven and Dash simply because I'd been terrified that one day, an enemy would come after my mother like they had Dash's. I couldn't bury both parents, and quitting the club had seemed like the best alternative. To death and to prison.

Border patrol had gotten heavy during our last five years as a club. A handful of brothers had been busted and were serving time or had recently finished a stint.

We all might have been where the Warriors were sitting now, in ugly orange jumpsuits.

It had taken time to disband the club.

After the vote, we'd called a truce with the Warriors. They'd agreed to leave us alone in trade for our drug routes. That negotiation had taken time, getting the dealers on board. Then there'd been the task of shutting down the rest of the illegal activities. We'd pulled the fights. Stopped working protection rackets with businesses in town. Through that time, brothers had slowly moved away as they'd found other jobs.

In the end, it took nearly six years.

Then it was done. One day, I'd ridden around town with my Tin Gypsy cut on my back. The next, it had stayed home in a drawer.

We had peace.

We should have had peace for the rest of our lives.

Maybe we would have if Marcus Wagner hadn't framed Draven for murder and, in doing so, brought the Warriors back into our lives.

We'd been lucky that none of us had been hurt since Tucker Talbot had set his sights on Clifton Forge. Damn lucky.

It would tear our crew apart if something happened to any one of us. The idea alone made me tense.

"Hey." Nova nudged my leg. "You okay?"

"Yeah." I blinked myself out of the past and into the present. Shoved the worries away. If all I had was tonight, maybe next weekend, I didn't need to be dwelling on ancient history while Nova was here. "Sorry. It's not easy for me to talk about the club. There's a lot of history there. Not all of it good."

"What was a good thing?"

"The brothers." Easy answer. "We were brothers, not by blood, but by what counted. Two of my best friends were Gypsies with me. They work at the garage. They're my family. I love their wives like they were my sisters. I'd do anything for their kids."

"Uncle Emmett?"

I grinned. "Uncle Emmett."

Nova shifted so that the light from inside caught her face. It highlighted her cheekbones and the soft swell above her top lip. It caressed the soft pout of her mouth and made her dark eyes dance. She raised a hand to my collarbone, tracing a two-inch scar across my skin. "Where'd you get this?"

"A fight."

"Let me guess, you got into it at The Betsy with someone over a game of pool."

I chuckled. "No, I used to box a lot. The club organized a circuit of fights every year around the state. Not exactly legal, considering we gambled on the fights."

"My lips are sealed." She dragged a finger across her mouth.

"It was a way for us younger guys in the club to burn off some arrogant energy and make some extra cash. We'd fight. Get drunk afterward. There were always pretty women around."

"Let's skip that part."

I kissed her hair. "None were as pretty as you."

"Better. Continue."

"This one night, I was on a streak. Won all four of my fights and a good payout too. We were all standing around, drinking a beer afterward, bullshitting and icing black eyes. One of the guys I beat was a punk. He got drunk and pissed. Broke a beer bottle and threw it at me when I wasn't paying attention. Didn't hit my face but slashed me across the collarbone."

Nova winced. "Ouch."

"Meh." I shrugged. "It wasn't so bad that I couldn't give him his second beatdown of the night."

Maybe I was speaking too plainly, but Nova was tough. She deserved to know what kind of man she was sleeping with. Violence had been part of our lives. There were some things I'd regret for the rest of my life. Others, like kicking that punk's ass, I wouldn't feel sorry about.

"Do you miss it?"

"The fights? Sometimes." It was the one thing Dash and I had tried to convince Draven to continue even after the club shut down. "It's an adrenaline rush."

"And what about the club? Do you miss it?"

The answer should be yes. I should miss the club. I should miss it every single day. "No."

Maybe I'd missed it at first. Even with six years to come to terms with the end, there'd been a hole where the brotherhood had been. For a while, Dash, Leo and I had filled it with booze and women. Then Dash had met Bryce. Leo had found Cass.

And I'd worked my ass off to build a good life here. A legal life. Maybe I'd never have a family of my own, but if there was ever a woman to try it with, Nova would have been the one.

"Will you miss me?" Her question was so quiet that I barely heard it.

I held her tighter, burying my nose in her hair.

Easy answer. "Yes."

CHAPTER FIFTEEN

NOVA

Putting Clifton Forge in my rearview was harder than I'd expected. Maybe because it had been forced on me when I wasn't ready.

Would I ever have been ready?

With each mile on the highway, I fought a sting in my nose and the threat of tears. The Diet Coke I'd grabbed at the gas station churned in my stomach. The muscles in my body were strung tight like the wires on the barbed fences that bordered the pastures whipping past my window.

Forcing myself out of Emmett's bed this morning had taken every ounce of strength. I'd been on the verge of tears through breakfast and when he'd kissed me goodbye, I'd nearly broken. I'd been a second away from opening the seal and letting the truth spill free.

If I confessed and begged for a second chance, would he let us start again?

Probably not.

So I'd hugged him with all my might, then walked out

the door, not letting myself look back until I was inside the Nova.

Emmett had stood in his doorway, much like he had during our first nights together. This time, fully clothed. But he'd stayed there, watching me drive away.

His handsome face had been limned with sunlight. His hair had been loose, the tips brushing his shoulders. And his beautiful chocolate eyes had held as much longing as mine.

It had to be this way.

He would never trust me, not if he knew the truth. And I wasn't sure I could trust him.

After leaving his house, I'd driven to the rental and spent the rest of the morning packing my belongings, doing a sweep of the house to ensure I hadn't left anything behind.

I'd just finished loading up the Nova when Hacker had pulled in.

The flash drive he'd handed me was in the car's ashtray beside TJ's dice.

Hacker hadn't even gotten out of his car, just handed it over. When I'd told him that I'd left the receiver hidden at Emmett's, he'd simply nodded and disappeared. Then I'd waited for the owner to pop over and collect the keys. One quick stop at a gas station to fill up the Nova and grab a lunch of potato chips and a Snickers, I'd hit the road.

I'd left hours ago. The last mileage sign had shown Missoula only twenty-four miles away. Still, I wanted to turn back.

I wanted another night on the deck, listening to Emmett talk about the club. Sure, he'd glossed over details. No question about that. But he hadn't tried to camouflage the violence. He hadn't made it out to seem perfect or that he was infallible.

There'd been so much honesty in his voice and the entire time, all I could think was that there hadn't been the same in my father's as he'd told me about the Warriors.

I wouldn't have known the difference if not for having listened to Emmett.

Was that just my heart talking, wishing for my father's stories to be untrue? Or was I missing something? The nagging feeling in my stomach said the latter.

Maybe the flash drive would help me uncover the truth. If I could bring myself to open it. Every time I thought about it, I felt worse and worse for my actions. I was a coward. A liar. A bitch.

"I suck," I muttered.

Missoula had a few exits off the interstate, and I opted for the one that didn't lead to my house, but to my sister's. It was time to be honest with someone. If it couldn't be Emmett, then Shelby was the best bet. Next up, myself.

Maybe she could help me figure out what to do. Maybe I could give her the flash drive.

Everything would change when I opened it. I wasn't sure how I knew that, but I did.

Navigating through town, it didn't take me long to get to Shelby's place. I pulled into the driveway and hurried for the door.

I rang the doorbell, her footsteps echoed from inside, and then there was my big sister, dragging me into her arms.

"You've been gone forever."

I hugged her tight. "I know."

"Are you back now?"

"Yeah." I was back.

Because as much as I wished it weren't true, there was no

future for me in Clifton Forge. Not with my betrayal and deception.

It was unforgivable.

Shelby hauled me inside, where we spent an hour in the living room, me sitting on the floor playing with Christian while she told me about everything that she'd been baking lately. The wedding cakes and the birthday party cupcakes and the cake pops she'd tested just yesterday morning that she'd be doing for real on Halloween.

"You've been busy," I said before blowing a raspberry on Christian's tummy.

He giggled and squirmed out of my hold, then ran off to the couch, his arms raised. "Mama."

"Hi, baby." She picked him up and kissed his cheek.

"Where my snack?"

"Are you hungry? Here." She reached for a lidded cup on the end table, handing it over.

Christian dove inside the top, fitting his chubby fist between the plastic slots to yank out a few Cheerios and shove them in his mouth.

"I have news." Shelby ran a hand through her son's hair. "I'm pregnant."

"What?" I shot off the floor and went to the couch, wrapping my arms around her. "Congratulations. That's so exciting."

"We're pretty excited. It's really early, I just took the test a few days ago. I was going to call you but now that you're home, it's even better to tell you in person."

"How are you feeling?"

"Exhausted." She collapsed into the back of the couch. "Like I could sleep for hours."

"What can I do? Want me to take Christian for the night

so you can rest? Or I can come to babysit all weekend. Or I can make dinner."

"Dinner." She closed her eyes. "I would love you forever and ever if you made dinner. You can even call for pizza. I don't care as long as I don't have to stand in the kitchen."

"No pizza." I stood and picked up Christian, then whisked him away with me to the kitchen. As he sat on the floor, munching his cereal, I raided the fridge.

Cooking dinner took me longer than it normally would because I didn't know where everything was kept and Christian was my sous chef, but by the time Jack made it home at five thirty, the table was set and ready.

"This is amazing, June," he said after the first bite of a taco.

June. I was June here. Shelby hadn't called me by my name. Christian called me Auntie. But I was June again.

Besides missing Emmett, I was going to miss being Nova.

Even though my coworkers and clients called me June at work, over the past two months, on my own time in the bubble at Emmett's house, I'd been Nova.

Hearing my name, my real name, made him that much farther away. Even eating the same kind of tacos he'd made me, I was losing him, minute by minute.

One day, he'd be a dream I struggled to remember.

I got through the meal by entertaining Christian and conversing with Jack and my sister. Jack asked questions about the work trip I'd been on for months. I answered—*lied* —while dodging knowing looks from Shelby.

Either Mom had told her more about where I was going or she'd put it together before I'd even left. Both were probably true.

"I'll do the dishes," I said after we were all finished eating.

"No, you cooked." Shelby moved to clear, but I beat her to it, snatching her plate and taking it to the sink.

"Sit down and relax."

"Agreed." Jack stood and brought over his own plate. "I'll take care of Christian's bath."

He winked at me, then kissed his wife's cheek before taking their son out of his high chair and disappearing upstairs.

"Jack seems excited about the baby," I said, loading the dishwasher. Above us, rushing water rumbled into the bathtub.

"He is." Shelby smiled. "We both are."

"I'm happy for you guys."

Her smile faded, her eyes cast to the table.

"What's wrong?"

She blew out a long breath. "What are you up to, Nova?"

Now I was Nova. When things were serious, I was Nova.

I returned to the table, putting everything else away. Only when it was empty did I take the seat across from her. Shelby would only ask me if she knew Jack wasn't around, which meant we didn't have long.

Rather than avoid her questions and drag this out, I told her everything. I told her about my plan. About visiting Dad in prison. About Emmett. About how I'd gone to Clifton Forge for revenge and left in a mess of confusion.

"Shit." She closed her eyes. "What a cluster."

"I know," I whispered. "I don't know what is true and what's a lie. Everything Dad told me . . ."

"That's where the lies start."

I shot her a scowl. "He didn't lie to me."

"Everything about him is a lie, June. *Nova*. Our names should be enough of a clue. But you've always trusted him. You're like Mom."

"He's our father, Shelby."

"May," she corrected. "He's a criminal. And he's exactly where he needs to be."

My temper began to rise, my hands balling beneath the table. Shelby never gave Dad any credit and I probably gave him too much.

I uncurled my fingers, splaying my palms on my thighs. "I don't want to fight about Dad."

"Me neither." She sighed. "I just . . . I hate how he dictates your life."

So do I. Now, more than ever. "I don't know what to do about Emmett. I don't want to say goodbye."

Shelby gave me a sad smile. "You don't really have a choice. You lied to him. He doesn't know you. And when he finds out . . ."

"He'll despise me."

Shelby nodded.

I hated that she was right. I hated that this had gone too far.

There was no future with Emmett. And whether I liked it or not, I had to let him go.

"I fell for him," I whispered.

She reached over and put her hand on my shoulder. "I know you did."

"This is so fucked up."

"Completely fucked up." She huffed. "And it started the day we were born. The day Dad convinced Mom it would be safer for us to live his lies."

"It's who we are."

"No," she said quietly. "It was never who we were."

Maybe she was right. Maybe I should have listened to her from the start. "What about TJ?"

"He's gone. He died too young, but he's gone."

"I miss him," I whispered. "I miss how he'd always tease us. I miss that he'd come over and raid my pantry for chocolate. No matter where I put it, he found it. Even that time I stuffed a box of Dove bars into an empty cereal box."

My sister laughed. "Do you remember that time he told Mom she was going to be a grandmother?"

"How could I forget? Poor Mom." TJ had purposefully let us all believe that he'd gotten a girl pregnant. He'd been fourteen. Mom had launched into a string of questions about the girl and her name.

Beta. He'd told us her name was Beta.

And after an hour of stringing us along, of giving Mom gray hairs, he'd excused himself from the conversation only to come back a minute later with a betta fish.

"He was such a shit." I smiled. "But no one could make us laugh like he could."

It was like he'd seen how much of a burden Mom carried, always keeping our secrets and managing everything on her own, and he'd challenged himself to provide the levity. Even though Dad paid for our lives, he'd never been there to help with the cleaning or cooking or laundry. He hadn't been there to watch my track meets or high school graduation.

He hadn't been there.

It had always been Mom. And no person had made her smile like TJ. Even now, years after he'd passed, I hadn't seen that sort of joy on Mom's face.

It had been stolen with his life.

"It's not fair," I said.

"No, it's not. But this is how you honor him," she said. "Not by getting revenge. But by remembering him. Remembering how we loved him and how he loved us."

She was right. God, she was right.

And now that I realized it, it was too late.

There was giggling upstairs. Jack's laughter mixed with Christian's precious squeal. My sister looked to the ceiling and love shined in her brown eyes.

The ache of jealousy slashed deep. The only man I'd want this with, a simple life full of love, was one I'd never have. Those tears that had been plaguing me all day flooded my eyes. I ducked my chin, blinking them away, so that Shelby wouldn't see when she faced me again.

"What was on the flash drive?" she asked.

"I don't know."

"Are you going to look?"

I shrugged. "I have to."

"No, you don't."

Footsteps on the stairs meant our conversation was over for tonight. I had no doubt she'd want to talk more, to get the specifics I hadn't had the time to give. But as Jack and Christian returned to the dining room, we visited for a little while longer before I excused myself to go home.

My condo was dark and the air stale. I moved from the garage to the kitchen, flicking on lights as I walked. My heels were discarded by the fridge. Mom had neatly stacked all of my mail on the island.

I needed to unload my suitcases from the car. I needed to check my emails for what I'd missed today and call my mother to tell her I was home. Maybe she'd want to meet me for lunch tomorrow. But when I dug my phone from my purse, I hit a different name in the contacts.

Ace.

"Hey," he answered. The loud music in the background could only mean he was at The Betsy.

"Partying without me already?"

He chuckled. "It's too quiet at my place."

"Yeah, I know the feeling."

"Hold on. Let me go outside where I can hear you."

"Okay." I glanced around the condo.

I'd bought this place for its clean lines and modern vibe. The white cabinets were faced with frosted glass. Their slim, silver handles matched the smooth stainless appliances. The floors were a white-washed oak done in a herringbone pattern. The living room couch was the color of oatmeal splashed with too much milk. In my bedroom, it was more of the same scheme.

It suddenly seemed so cold. Outside it was dark, but in the morning the perfectly manicured lawn would glow neon green, and a few young trees would wave in the breeze, none taller than the roofs in this new development.

I missed Emmett's colorful, rustic home. I missed his spicy scent lingering in the air and the vibrant forest out every window.

The noise on the phone faded and Emmett blew out a long breath. "You still there?"

"I'm here."

"How was your drive? Roads okay?" His voice was like a smooth caress down my spine. How was I supposed to sleep tonight? It would be too cold without his body to keep me warm.

"They were fine." I pulled out a stool from the island and slid onto the seat.

"Hey." Emmett's voice was muffled as he greeted whoever was there with him. "Yeah. Be in after a sec."

He was busy. He was at the bar, having fun. I was at home with nothing to keep me company but a flash drive that I was leaving in the car tonight.

Maybe I should have been jealous that he was out, worried that he'd find someone else to warm his bed tonight. But I trusted him.

How had that happened? How had he gone from the enemy to the one man I trusted?

"Sorry, baby."

"It's okay. I'll let you go. I just wanted to say hi. Hear your voice."

"Talk soon?"

"Yeah." I sighed. Maybe. "Bye."

"Bye."

I set my phone on the white marble counter, staring at its dark face.

Two months and everything was different. Whatever plan I'd concocted in an effort to avenge my father had disintegrated like wet toilet paper.

Would I find answers on that flash drive? Maybe. If I could bring myself to open it.

There was no way I'd take that step tonight. It was a step in the wrong direction.

I needed to turn, to back up. To put everything in reverse. To unwind what I'd started.

"How . . ." I tapped my fingers on the counter. Thinking. Calculating. Planning.

The only way to end this would be to protect Emmett from my father. That was the answer.

Somehow, I had to make this stop.

Knowledge was key and at the moment, I was behind. Were the Warriors already regrouping, Dad having anticipated my failure? There was one person who would likely know. Or at least, he had information that might point me in the right direction.

It was time for an overdue date.

I picked up the phone and called a man who knew Dad arguably better than I did.

"Hello, stranger," Ira answered.

"Hello yourself," I purred, nearly making myself gag. "I was hoping to catch up. What are you doing for dinner tomorrow night?"

CHAPTER SIXTEEN

EMMETT

"Hey, man," Leo said after I answered his call. "Cass wants to know if you can come over for dinner tonight."

"Sure." I flipped on the light in my office. "What time?"

"Whenever. Might as well come early enough for a beer or two before we eat."

"Will do. Need me to bring anything?" I unplugged my laptop and carried it downstairs, planning on watching a game or something while I worked.

"Cass," Leo hollered, his mouth away from the phone. "What should Emmett bring?"

"Nothing," she called back.

"Nothing," he said.

I'd pick up some beers anyway. " 'Kay. See you later."

"Bye."

I settled on the downstairs couch, putting my phone on the coffee table. Then hit the power button on my Mac, scrubbing a hand over my face as it loaded up. Staying up late at The Betsy wasn't nearly as fun as staying up with

Nova in bed. I'd slept like shit after I'd come home from the bar, my bed too empty. The house this morning had been too quiet.

Goddamn, I'd missed her. Enough that I feared I'd do something stupid, like drive to Missoula and haul my woman home.

The temptation to do just that had been constant yesterday, since the moment she'd pulled out of the driveway. But I'd gone to work, pretended everything was fine, and immersed myself in a remodel project. I'd barely checked my phone, and after I'd left the shop for the night, I'd gone straight to The Betsy.

I'd stayed until they'd closed at two, then come home and crashed, burying my face in a pillow that still smelled like Nova. I'd tossed and turned until finally drifting off as the sun had come up.

Two hours in my home gym had burned through the rest of my morning. After a shower and a late lunch, I was here, ready to clear out my inbox and do some checking on the Warriors.

There'd been no trouble for months. There'd been no sign of them and according to the latest update Luke had received from the FBI, the trials were progressing—slowly, but progress was progress.

Two more of the senior members had been sentenced. One of them had been a Tin Gypsy who'd joined the Warriors and moved to Ashton not a week after we'd voted to shut down our club. He'd worked his way up the ranks with the Warriors. His fifty-year sentence was indication of his status.

If he made it out of prison at all, he'd be released as an old man.

Poor bastard.

My laptop dinged as the emails loaded. I flipped on the TV and let ESPN run in the background as I scanned my inbox. I sent a reply to my accountant, then paid my internet bill.

With my emails cleared, it was time to filter through my alerts, checking through a list of logs for anything that might show Tucker Talbot's known associates or estranged family members were coming to Clifton Forge. There was nothing to make me worry.

I was just about to shut down when a notification popped up on my screen.

"What the hell?" I muttered.

Last year, I'd added a program to all of my machines to monitor for abnormal battery usage. It was unlikely that anyone could get past my firewall, but if they did and managed to install malware, it would drain the battery faster than normal and throw up a red flag.

This red flag.

My heart raced as my fingers flew across the screen, checking my firewall and encryption. Nothing was out of place. And besides the programs I'd opened, there was no malware.

So why the flag?

I shut off the TV and took the laptop upstairs to the office, wanting more space to work. Was it the fan? This Mac wasn't that old, but sometimes the fans were faulty and ran too much.

Closing the lid, I ran my hands around the edges, turning the machine upside down and examining the screws. They all seemed fine—except one that looked to have been stripped. Turned too hard and too fast.

My stomach dropped. Mechanics were careful not to strip screws because then you'd never get them loose again. Dad had taught me that years ago.

Taking out a small screwdriver from my desk, I opened the casing and spotted the foreign device immediately.

"Oh, fuck." Someone had put a tap on my webcam.

Some motherfucker had messed with my machine.

No. *No fucking way.*

I'd spent years developing my security protocols. My firewall was impenetrable. The hard drive was encrypted. There was little to no chance of an online hack. How many years had I spent putting in those safeguards?

My protocols had been necessary because I couldn't exactly carry my laptops around with me. For years and years, I'd kept one locked up at the clubhouse. We'd boarded up the windows from the inside. The doors had been padlocked and only a few of us had the keys.

Except part of how Draven had been framed for murder was because the police had found his hunting knife at the scene of the crime. The bastard who'd framed him had broken into the clubhouse and stolen that very knife with Draven's fingerprints on it.

After that, we'd taken everything out of the clubhouse, anything that might be used against us, including my laptops.

They were currently in a waterproof container locked and sealed and buried five feet beneath a birch tree behind the clubhouse. With them were five guns, weapons that had killed men. Weapons that could be traced to unsolved murders and used to send Dash, Leo and me to prison for life.

Anything incriminating had gone in that box, buried and

forgotten. There was no way those would have been found. But someone had definitely opened this laptop. A computer that never left my home.

I quickly spun and picked up my other machine, flipping it over to open its casing too. The same goddamn device was there too.

Both machines. Physically cracked. I bet somewhere in my house I'd find a radio receiver that went along with the webcam tap.

There was only one person who had been in my house alone. Only one person would have had access to these machines.

Nova.

"No." My stomach pitched. My head was spinning and there was a very real chance my meal from earlier was going to come up.

Nova.

I'd trusted her. I'd . . . loved her?

No. It couldn't be her. She wouldn't do that to me. Someone else had to have come in.

Rationalizations aside, in my heart, I knew it was all bullshit. My security system was the best there was. If someone had broken into my house, I would have known, right?

Right.

"Fuck." I pushed my chair away from the desk, dropping my elbows to my thighs as I tried to breathe. The pain in my chest was like a gunshot wound seeping blood and death.

Why? Why would she do this?

The Warriors.

I gulped, a fresh wash of pain coming again. It squeezed so tight I could barely breathe.

"Fuck!" My voice echoed through the house.

She'd betrayed me. She'd fucking betrayed me.

The pain turned to anger in an instant. The anger morphed into blinding fury. I swiped up my phone and marched from the office, my strides quickening until I was jogging toward the garage.

I pulled on a pair of boots, then grabbed my wallet and keys. Then I was out of the house, passing my bike for the truck. Tearing away from my place, I seethed. The moment my tires hit the highway, I dialed Leo.

"Hey," he answered.

"Scratch dinner. I'm headed to Missoula."

"Uh . . ."

"Call Dash. Call Isaiah. Call Luke. Call Shaw."

"Why? What happened?"

"I've been seeing a woman."

"You have? Since when?"

"This summer. It was just a casual thing." Because that was how Nova had wanted it. She hadn't wanted names or commitment. And the stupid son of a bitch that I was, I'd let sex distract me. I'd been blind to her motives and now I felt like a fucking fool. "I don't know how yet. I don't know what is happening. But both of my laptops were tampered with. She's the only one who's been in my house. Had to have happened in the last couple of days."

Probably on Thursday, when she'd asked to work from my house because hers had been too loud.

How many lies had she told me? How many had I believed?

"The Warriors?" Leo asked.

"Who else? She's got to be connected to them somehow." And I'd been so caught up in falling for her that I'd pushed all common sense away. I hadn't insisted on getting her last

222

name. I hadn't pulled a background check. I hadn't run her license plates.

What the fuck had I been thinking?

"What are you going to do?" Leo asked.

I hit the gas pedal, my hands tight on the steering wheel. "Start by driving to Missoula and getting some goddamn answers." Maybe find out who the actual fuck she was.

"You know where she's at?"

"Yeah." I knew exactly where she was at.

Thursday night, when she'd told me she was leaving, I'd gotten worried. Because if someone from the Warriors was watching us, they would have seen Nova at my place. I hadn't wanted to send her home to Missoula without a way to find her in an emergency.

Bryce and Genevieve had been kidnapped once and it had only been luck we'd tracked them to the mountains before it was too late.

Ever since, Dash had had a location tracker on Bryce's phone. Isaiah had one for Genevieve. Shaw for Presley. Luke for Scarlett. And Leo for Cass.

I'd taken Nova's phone while she'd slept and added it too. Simple enough. I'd seen her enter her passcode enough times to capture the numbers. Unless she'd discovered it already and deleted it, I'd be able to track her down. Just in case.

Turns out my *just in case* would come in handy today.

"What can I do?" Leo asked.

"Call everyone. Tell them to keep alert."

"Want me to share specifics?"

"No." Right now I was guessing. What we needed were answers. For those, I needed time.

"Keep me posted."

"Will do." I ended the call and picked up the phone, driving with one hand while I navigated to the location tracker.

Nova was in Missoula. The location showed her in a residential neighborhood, most likely her home.

I set my phone aside and kept on driving, the hot rage from earlier ebbing, becoming a simmering burn beneath my skin.

How could she have done this to me? How was she connected to the Warriors? An hour into my trip, those questions pounded my mind like nails being hammered into my skull.

How could I have let this happen? I knew better than to trust anyone. I fucking knew better. But damn if she hadn't been a master manipulator. Damn if she hadn't used me. Damn if I hadn't let my cock lead the way.

She would give me answers. Either willingly, or I'd find them myself.

I swiped my phone and hit her name, the ring filling the truck's cab.

"Hey." Her voice was bright as she answered after the second ring. "I was hoping to hear from you today."

I swallowed a huff. Yeah, I bet she was. Probably to gauge whether I'd found her out or not. But I wasn't showing my hand yet and forced a steady voice. "My bed was too empty last night."

"It better have been empty, Ace."

God, that voice. There was affection there. Jealousy in that warning. She sounded like she would be heartbroken if I'd brought another woman home from the bar.

Was I wrong? Maybe she hadn't touched my laptops. Maybe I'd immediately jumped to the wrong conclusion because trust didn't come easy for me. Maybe she'd worked her way so easily into my life that I was terrified and finding every reason to shove her away.

Because she scared me.

This woman scared me to death. She had the power to break me, something I hadn't given to anyone. Ever.

"What are you doing today?" she asked.

"Errands."

"Yeah, me too. I need to get some groceries. The fridge is empty here. And I'm doing laundry. But I'm planning on staying in my sweats all day."

"Exciting Saturday."

"Yeah," she muttered. "I've been thinking about next weekend. About your birthday party."

"And?" I held my breath, waiting for whatever excuse was coming because I'd bet my left nut she'd never set foot in Clifton Forge again.

"And if the invitation still stands, I'd love to come and celebrate. Meet your friends."

What. The. Fuck?

She wanted to come to my birthday party. Why? Because she wanted intel on my friends. Or because she was innocent.

Christ, what was happening?

"Yeah," I managed to choke out as my mind raced. "That'd be great."

"Good. I have the perfect gift in mind."

I hummed. It was the only sound I could muster. My mind was reeling, my focus barely on the road as the truck flew across the pavement. "I'm just pulling up to the store," I lied. "Better let you go."

"Okay. Bye."

The line went dead and I pinched the bridge of my nose. What was going on? A guilty woman would have bolted and never looked back. A guilty woman wouldn't be coming to my birthday party.

Unless . . .

This was like being on a goddamn roller coaster, forced to go up and down and around and sideways. Nothing made sense. Nothing clicked.

Maybe the smart thing to do would be to turn around. Go home, examine my laptops again, and pull information on Nova. Information I should have pulled ages ago. But did I turn around? No. I kept on driving.

Because I wanted to see her face. I wanted to study her expression, her eyes, her mouth and see her for myself. Either I'd been blind to the lies. Or she was telling me the truth.

Regardless, I wasn't leaving Missoula without her last name.

The long drive did nothing but set me on edge. By the time I pulled into Missoula, I had so much nervous energy racing through my veins that I forced myself to stop at a gas station. I parked, went inside to take a piss, then took a walk around the lot as the truck was filling with gas.

I was calmer, barely, when I got behind the wheel again, then checked the location service on Nova's phone. She was still in the same place. I punched it into the GPS and followed the directions through town toward a neighborhood filled with new condos and overpriced homes. There was a place mid construction on Nova's street. I eased my truck in behind a white box trailer, using it as a shield.

Her condo was three down.

I waited. And I watched. The lights were on at her place.

About thirty minutes into my surveillance her neighbor's garage opened and a minivan backed out. A woman with a messy ponytail eased past me, reaching behind her to a toddler in the backseat.

It was quiet for another hour. My stomach began to rumble, I hadn't eaten in hours, but I stayed in my seat. Stuck.

Knocking on her door was out. I didn't want her to know how I'd found her. So I sat, regretting the impulse to drive here when I should have stayed home and done some damn research.

Leo texted twice, checking in. I texted a thumbs up but nothing more.

Then the upstairs light at Nova's place turned off. A minute later, her garage door opened and there she was, backing the Nova onto the street.

She headed in the opposite direction, away from my truck. She was dressed in a black leather jacket. Her hair was curled and her lips were painted red.

"So much for those sweats, huh, baby?"

I waited until her taillights disappeared around the corner before starting the truck and following. There was no need to get close, not with the location tracker. I hung back, letting the Saturday evening traffic swallow me up as we maneuvered downtown.

I hadn't spent a lot of time in Missoula. It was too far from Clifton Forge and I didn't particularly like big towns anyway. I took note of the restaurants and shops and shopping mall, just to get my bearings.

Nova parked in front of an upscale restaurant. I was at a stoplight two blocks away when she opened the door and stepped out.

Definitely not in sweats. What I hadn't been able to see earlier was that her jacket was cropped and beneath it was a tight black dress that hugged her hips and thighs. On her feet was a pair of sexy shoes I'd had on my bedroom floor more than once.

Anger surged because if she'd lied about her plans tonight, then what else had she lied about? Everything?

A young valet came over and she handed him her keys. Then she strutted to the restaurant as the kid climbed into the Nova and drove it away.

The light ahead turned green, but I hesitated long enough to earn a honk from the car behind me. I eased onto a side street, parking in the biggest spot I could find. Then I waited again.

I wanted to see who she was with tonight. In case they hadn't arrived yet, I gave them thirty minutes before setting off down the sidewalk.

The streetlamps were on though the sky was bright with the oranges and pinks of the sunset. The evening air would have been cold if not for the rage keeping me warm.

My bootsteps pounded on the sidewalk as I made my way to the restaurant, stopping outside its floor-to-ceiling windows. They were crystal clear, allowing a view to the entire restaurant.

I spotted her instantly.

She was sitting beside a man too old and too thick in the middle. The windows gave me the perfect view of her laughing at something he said.

They sat together, the table's corner the only thing separating them. The man's back was to me but he put his hand over hers. She smiled at him and leaned in to brush a kiss to his cheek.

I saw red. The color of her lipstick. The color of the soles of her goddamn shoes.

She was on a fucking date.

My hands fisted at my sides. I let out a growl. She couldn't have heard it but the sound might as well have been whispered in her ear. One minute she was smiling at her date, the next she was looking at me standing outside the restaurant.

That was when the color drained from her lying face.

CHAPTER SEVENTEEN

NOVA

Emmett.

My stomach dropped as he stared at me through the restaurant's front window.

"June?" Ira twisted to follow my gaze.

Emmett was gone before Ira had turned. Gone so fast that I wasn't sure if I'd imagined him there.

"Would you excuse me for a moment?" Ira didn't get the chance to answer because I was out of my chair and hustling away from our table.

I did my best not to run until I cleared the dining room, but the moment I hit the lobby, I was jogging toward the door. I shoved outside, the chill biting into my bare arms as I took in the sidewalk.

I looked left. Nothing. Right. Nothing. Emmett would have stood head and shoulders above the others milling about, but there was no sign of him anywhere.

Had I imagined it? He'd been so angry. So cold through the glass. Was it my imagination playing a trick on me?

I spun around once more, checking in all directions. The

street was busy tonight, many people downtown on a Saturday to enjoy the bars and restaurants.

A man bumped into me, his arms going out to make sure I didn't stumble. "Sorry."

I held up a hand and waved him off. "It's okay."

After one last check down the street, I shook my head and returned inside. Maybe I had imagined it. The sinking feeling in my stomach said otherwise.

If Emmett was here, he'd come to Missoula and found me on a date.

How had he found me? How had he known? I gulped and forced myself to return to my table.

Ira stood as soon as I reached his side. "Are you all right?"

"Yes, sorry. I thought I saw an old friend from college who I haven't seen in ages," I lied, resuming my seat. Then I reached into my purse and slid out my phone. The screen was blank.

"Did you?"

"Huh?" I looked to Ira. "Oh, my friend. No, it wasn't her. Whoops."

He gave me a pleasant smile, then lifted his glass of wine, waiting for me to do the same. Once I had mine lifted, he clinked the rims together. "Cheers. It's been too long."

I delivered yet another fake smile and took a long sip. God, what the hell had I been thinking? I couldn't do this. I couldn't pretend to date Ira and let him take me to his home. I couldn't slip anything into his drink and then kiss him until he passed out. I'd puke.

The only man's lips I wanted on mine were Emmett's.

I had to get out of here. Now.

The first thirty minutes of this dinner had been a disaster. Ira's voice was so nasal I'd almost begged our waiter for earplugs. When Ira had touched my hand, my skin had crawled.

It wasn't that he was a creep or that he'd done anything inappropriate. No, this sick feeling was all my doing because I was using him.

Apparently, that was who I'd become. A woman who used her face and body to trick men.

I didn't want to be this person.

When had I become this devious, jaded woman? Had I always been like this?

No. This wasn't me. I didn't want this to be me.

The only reason I'd called Ira was because I wanted so badly to unravel my mistakes. This wasn't the way. If seeing Emmett at the window had been my imagination, the contempt and fury and disgust in his expression were all too accurate.

If it really had been him, well . . . I'd earned that hostility.

My eyes flooded.

I wasn't this woman.

I didn't want to be this woman.

"June."

A tear slipped down my cheek and I didn't even bother wiping it away because numbers two and three followed close behind.

I wasn't June. I wasn't Nova.

Who was I?

"I'm sorry, Ira."

"Is everything okay?"

I met his concerned gaze and sniffled, blinking the tears

away. "No, it's not. Thank you for meeting me here tonight, but I need to go."

"Of course. Would you like me to drive you home? Or you can come to my place if you don't want to be alone."

Maybe it was an innocent offer, but this man was my father's attorney. I wasn't sure he understood the concept of innocence.

"No, thank you." I stood and grabbed my jacket, then bent for my purse and took out my wallet. "I'd like to pay for our wine. I insist."

Thank God we hadn't ordered yet. I would have felt compelled to stay.

"I couldn't possibly allow it." Ira stood too, taking my hand and pressing it between his own. Then he brought my knuckles to his lips and I forced myself not to rip my hand away. "We'll do this again."

No, we wouldn't. "Thank you for understanding."

He nodded and before he could say another word, I freed myself from his grasp and walked out of the room.

While the valet went to retrieve my car, I slipped on my coat and wrapped my arms around my waist, shifting from foot to foot. I looked up and down the sidewalk again, hoping to see Emmett, but there were only strange faces and a fading blue sky.

When the rumble of the Nova's engine reached me, I stepped off the sidewalk before the kid had a chance to put it in park. Then I was behind the wheel, racing home. Every minute was agony. Every three seconds I checked the rearview hoping to see a familiar Harley and its rider.

My street was quiet when I pulled into the garage. So was the condo.

I walked in, tossed my purse aside and shrugged off my

jacket. Then I stood in the living room, frozen, because the next step terrified me. The next step was the truth.

The truth.

Did I even know what the truth was? When had I become this pathological liar? When had I lost my way?

Maybe I'd never had it. My name was a lie. My family was a lie. My entire life was a lie.

Was that why Shelby never called herself Shelby? Was that why she didn't talk about our childhood or our father? Because she looked at her past and saw the lies? She'd made her future nothing but truths.

Oh, God. Emmett would never forgive me. When I told him the truth, he'd never forgive me, and I'd lose him.

I loved him. And I was going to lose him. Actually, I'd lost him the moment we'd met. This ending had only been a matter of time.

My soul ached and I couldn't breathe.

There had to be another way, right? There had to be a way to fix this tangled mess.

"I need a new plan," I whispered to the empty room.

A knock at the door made me jump and slam a hand to my racing heart. I knew before checking the peephole who stood on my stoop. I twisted the lock and there he was.

He'd found me.

I stepped back and opened the door to let Emmett inside.

He leveled me with that deep brown gaze but whatever anger and emotion I'd seen at the restaurant was gone. Instead he looked . . . blank. The look on his face gave me chills, and I shut the door, barely able to fill my lungs.

I wasn't sure who this man was. Whatever familiarity I'd seen in him before was gone.

He studied me like I was a stranger too.

I was a stranger.

"Ace, I . . ." I didn't know what to say.

His jaw, already clenched, turned to granite.

We stared at one another. Guilt crept over my skin like a rash.

He didn't move.

The silence was overpowering. I forced my body to stay still but the tension became so heavy that it pulled like a thousand pounds on my shoulders.

"Say something," I whispered. "Please."

He stayed quiet.

"How did you know where I was?" I wasn't foolish enough to think he'd come to Missoula to spend the weekend with me. He was here because he knew.

He had to know.

His laptops.

Shit. Maybe he'd found the receiver. Since Hacker's warning, I'd known this was a possibility. That was why I'd fled Clifton Forge. What exactly had I expected, Emmett to just let me walk away?

God, but I was a fool.

Did he know exactly who I was? Did he just suspect I'd been up to something? Had he come here to surprise me, only to find me on a date?

"The man at the restaurant . . . nothing happened." For some reason, explaining why I was on a date—or part of the reason—was the easiest truth to begin with. "I dated him for a while earlier this year. Dinner tonight was a mistake. I knew it the moment I sat down."

Emmett didn't so much as blink.

"Please . . . say something," I begged. *Anything.*

"What is your name?"

"Nova."

"Don't fucking lie to me."

I flinched at the volume of his demand. "It's the truth."

"What's your last name?"

Talbot. "Johnson."

He studied my face, searching for the lie. But again, it was the truth. Both names were part of the truth and part of the lie.

"I'm sorry," I whispered.

As my words echoed around us, disappointment washed over his face. It tore me in half.

He'd hate me. After tonight, he'd hate me.

But I was truly sorry.

Emmett shook his head, the pain in his expression like a knife to my heart. Everything was falling apart and all we could do was stand here and stare at one another.

Then he moved, not for the door, but for me. He shook his head as his hands came to my face. The pain there, the raw regret, caused my eyes to flood.

I deserved to cry. I deserved to hurt. For everything I'd done to this man, for everything I'd planned to do, I deserved every stab.

"I'm sorry," I whispered again. "I'm sorry."

It was all I could say. My only hope left was that when he walked away, he might believe it.

"Why?" he gritted out.

For my father. For my brother.

I opened my mouth to answer but the words never came.

He waited, studying my face. And when I didn't answer, a wall came down between us. He shut me out completely.

I braced, ready for him to storm out the door, but instead, he only held my face tighter.

His lip curled. Then his mouth slammed down on mine, shocking the hell out of me with a kiss that was nothing but agonizing punishment.

He licked my bottom lip and I opened for him. His tongue thrust inside and there was nothing sweet or affectionate about this kiss. He was angry and poured it down my throat. The nips of his teeth weren't playful. The way he sucked was intended to cause a sting.

I let him be angry. I let him empty that rage into my mouth because I knew this was the last kiss. This was the end and if all I could have of Emmett was his fury, I'd take it.

His arms moved from my face, sliding over my shoulders and down my spine. His hands moved much like his tongue, in fierce, bold movements. I wouldn't let tonight ruin the memory of his gentle caresses. The way a man so large could be so tender.

Emmett's hands dropped to my ass, molding to my curves. Then he squeezed so hard I felt the indents of his fingerprints through my dress. He pulled me into his body, slamming us together so I could feel his arousal against my hip.

Maybe a smarter woman would have pushed him away. But Emmett needed an angry, hard fuck, and there was no chance in hell I'd let him walk out this door and find it somewhere else.

My hands went to his shirt, shoving up beneath the hem and finding his washboard abs. I raked my nails over his skin, digging in to leave a mark.

His response was to stretch those long arms to the hem of

my skirt, grip it between his strong fists, and shred it up the seam.

I gasped as a rush of desire pooled between my legs.

If Emmett needed to tear the clothes from my body, so be it.

The tear went from my knees to the small of my back. His hands instantly found my skin, his grip bruising.

I moaned, the throb in my core almost unbearable as he kneaded and palmed my upper thighs. In one swift hoist, he had me up and walked me to the island, setting me on the cold granite counter.

Not once did he break his mouth from mine. He devoured and conquered and punished.

I fumbled with his shirt, doing my best to get it up and over his head. But he wouldn't let me. He kept his arms locked and no matter how high I lifted the cotton, he refused to take it off.

He was staying clothed.

I was not.

He yanked the zipper on my dress, the sound a whizz rather than the smooth clicks from when I'd put it on earlier. Fisting the ripped edges from the skirt, he jerked the entire garment over my head, leaving me in nothing but a bra and lace thong.

The panties were shredded in a quick snap. The bra was unclasped and torn off my arms, leaving me completely exposed and bare.

But that was the point of this, wasn't it?

Emmett tore his lips from mine and stared at me, our chests rising and falling in the same desperate heaves to suck in some oxygen.

His gaze bored into mine and in it, a plea.

Tell me.

All I could do was send my own plea back.

Forgive me.

I lifted a hand to cup his face, feeling the scratch of his beard. He leaned into my hand and for a brief second, I glimpsed the Emmett I loved.

Then, quicker than I could snap my fingers, it was gone. That wall was in place and he was here for a purpose.

Without a word, he unbuckled his belt, opened his fly and fisted his hard cock.

He inched forward, fitting the crown to my entrance. He didn't bother moving his jeans or boxer briefs down his thighs.

He knew I was a liar and this was a fuck to balance the scales.

Forgive me.

I widened my legs, holding on to his shoulders as he thrust inside, driving hard and deep. I moaned, the sound echoing in the kitchen as he moved, in and out. He didn't kiss or caress me, keeping his hands on the counter beside my hips. Other than where we were joined, he didn't so much as touch me.

And with every one of his strokes, it broke my heart.

I'd done this to us. *I'd* ruined us.

We'd been doomed from the start.

I held his gaze, the fury rising in those beautiful eyes. All I could hope was that he'd hear my plea and see the love and apology in mine.

Forgive me.

My body reacted to him the way it always did, with a blind and insatiable desire for more, more, more. Whether he wanted my touch or not, I clutched his shoulders and held on as long as I could before the pleasure became too much. I closed my eyes and pretended he wasn't hate fucking me in my kitchen.

I surrendered to him, coming on a cry, spasming and clenching around him so hard I worried I'd slip off the counter. He'd probably let me fall. But I managed to keep my seat until Emmett let out a groan of his own, squeezing his eyes shut as he poured into me.

The stars had barely cleared from my eyes as he pulled out. I forced my eyes open and hopped off the counter onto unsteady legs.

Emmett took two steps backward. He tucked himself back into his jeans, zipping himself up and refastening his belt. Then he stared, his hands on his hips, waiting for my confession.

My eyes flooded. No matter what I said tonight, it wouldn't be enough. "I'm sorry."

He hated me.

I saw it on his face. He hated me, and I didn't blame him.

Without a word, he marched to the door, flinging it open and slamming it behind him.

He left me standing in my kitchen, his come leaking down my thighs as the tears streamed over my face.

I listened for the sound of his bike but it never came. I waited, hoping against all hope, that he'd come back and I could find the words. That he'd calm down enough to hear them. But there was nothing. Only the sound of my ragged breaths and shattering heart.

I stood there until I began to shiver, then turned to pick up the tattered remains of my dress. As I took it to the garbage can and tossed it inside, my eyes landed on the stack of unopened mail on the island.

Each piece was addressed to June Johnson.

There'd been a utility bill on top. I kept meaning to opt into paperless billing from the power company but every month, I'd get the bill and smack my palm to my head for forgetting. As I'd gone through the stack, I'd set that bill on top, vowing to do it this time.

The bill was gone.

Emmett had taken it.

Because he'd known I was nothing but a lie.

I swept my bare arm across the counter, the stack of mail flying before the pieces landed on the floor. Then I dropped to my knees, no longer having the strength to stand.

It was over.

I'd lost him.

He was better off without me.

CHAPTER EIGHTEEN

EMMETT

I raised my fist to knock on Dash's door, but it swung open before I could touch the wooden face.

He waved me inside. "Hey."

"Hi." I stepped inside and toed off my boots so they wouldn't thud on the floor. It was five in the morning, and though Bryce and Dash were awake, the boys were likely in bed.

"Coffee?"

I nodded and followed him to the kitchen, where Bryce was standing against the counter with a steaming mug in her hands.

"Are you all right?" she asked.

I loved her for skipping the pleasantries and worrying about me above all else. "Yeah."

She opened a cupboard and pulled out a mug, filling it from the pot and bringing it over. "Liar."

I put an arm around her shoulders as she slid one behind my back for a sideways hug.

No, I wasn't all right.

Dash filled a mug of his own and then the three of us went to the living room.

I was too restless to sit so I walked to the fireplace, taking in the photos on the mantel. They'd changed over the years. The pictures of the boys were continually getting swapped out as they grew. But there were a few constants.

Bryce and Dash at their wedding, smashing cake into each other's faces. Dash and Nick standing beside two motorcycles, the brothers with their arms around each other's backs. Another of Draven working at the garage. And an older photo of Chrissy, Dash's mom, smiling so wide it lit up her face.

She'd been like an aunt to me. There had always been a group of mothers around the clubhouse, organizing family functions. Draven might have been the club's leader, but Chrissy had been the heart.

She, along with my mom, had done their best to keep Dash, me and the other kids out of trouble. She'd made the best chocolate chip cookies, and she'd been one of Mom's best friends. Dad had loved her like a sister—as I felt about Bryce—and would have done anything to protect her.

Another parent gone too early, murdered by a rival club.

This had to stop. Christ, I was tired of looking over my shoulder. My family couldn't take another loss. These women and men deserved to live in peace. To see their children grow.

Nova was a threat to that.

Fuck. I dragged a hand through my hair and turned away from the photos, setting my coffee mug aside to pull my hair out of my face and secure it with a tie from my wrist.

I was a goddamn mess. I'd been up all night, driving

home from Missoula and spending every hour since in my office.

Nova might have hacked my laptops in the office, but the important one I kept hidden away. I wasn't stupid enough to leave a machine that could land me in prison out in the open.

I had two locked safes at home, one obvious in the office. And another that I'd built into the bottom of my pool table. The only way to find it was to shimmy beneath the table and pull back a false panel.

Luckily, she hadn't stumbled upon it yet. Though I was sure that with enough time, she would have discovered all my secrets. Hell, given a year or two, I would have told her.

How could I have been so fucking gullible? How could I have let this happen? She'd slithered into my life like a viper, and I'd let her sink her poisonous fangs into my flesh.

There was no one to blame for this but me. I was the one who'd brought her into my bed. Into my home. Into my heart.

If something happened, it was on me.

Dash and Bryce didn't say a word as they sat side by side on the couch. They sipped their coffee and waited for me to pull my shit together.

I walked to a chair and sat on its edge, my coffee forgotten. I didn't need the caffeine. I'd spent all night digging into Nova, and adrenaline, rage and pain were fueling me at the moment.

"Did Leo talk to you?" I asked.

Dash nodded. "Yesterday."

"I met a woman."

"That's what he said."

"She fucking played me." God, I hated to admit this. I

hated to even say the words. The shame was nearly as brutal as Nova's betrayal. "It was casual."

Leo had probably already explained, but it felt important to say it again. To run it through from the beginning, not just for them but for me. Maybe I'd see where I'd gone wrong.

"We met at The Betsy. Hooked up. Was supposed to be unattached sex but . . ."

"But sometimes it gets more complicated." Bryce shared a look with Dash.

I dropped my elbows to my knees. My eyes felt like they'd been rubbed with sandpaper. My stomach felt like I'd been kicked with a steel-toed boot. My chest felt ripped to pieces from a gaping gunshot wound. "I fucked up."

"This isn't on you." Dash shook his head. "This is on her."

Her. "Nova. She told me her name was Nova."

And damn it, that name fit her. When she'd admitted it was her real name, there had been nothing but honesty in her voice. She was a Nova.

Except she wasn't. She was the best liar I'd ever met because her name was June Johnson.

Her license plates had been fake. But that utility bill I'd swiped from her counter was as real as they came.

The drive home I'd replayed each moment from her place. I wasn't sure why I'd fucked her. I wasn't sure why she'd let me. All I knew was that when I stared at her and there'd been nothing but guilt in her eyes, it had broken me. She'd shredded me to ribbons.

She'd fucking gutted me.

So I'd fucked her too.

"Her real name is June Johnson. She's a lawyer in Missoula."

"And you think she is affiliated with the Warriors," Dash said.

"She tampered with my laptops. Probably copied the hard drives and used my password to get past the encryption." Maybe she'd done it herself or maybe she'd had help. It didn't matter.

"Are you sure?" Bryce asked.

"I'm sure." I nodded. Almost every cell in my body wished that I was wrong, but after all I'd found last night, I was sure. "No one else has been in my house. My security system is tight. As tight as the one here."

I had video monitors inside and out. The only time they were off was when the system was disarmed. For that, you'd have to know the code.

Nova knew the code.

"You went to Missoula. Did she confess? Tell you anything?" Dash asked.

I shook my head. "No, but she didn't need to." There'd been no point in confronting Nova about it because the truth had been written on her beautiful face.

The guilt. The apology. She hadn't been able to hide it while I'd been inside of her.

I'm sorry.

How many times had she said it last night? *I'm sorry.*

She was fucking sorry.

"How is she connected to the Warriors?" Dash asked.

"I put a location tracker on her phone." I huffed. "I thought she might be in danger from the Warriors because she'd been spending so much time with me and I didn't want to risk it. After I noticed there was something wrong with my system yesterday, I drove to Missoula and tracked her to a restaurant. She was on a damn date. With Tucker Talbot's lawyer."

"Oh, fuck," Dash muttered.

"Pretty much." I rubbed my jaw, still dealing with the image of her sitting across from Ira Hug.

I hadn't recognized Ira at first because his back had been to me, but when Nova had spotted me through the window, Ira had turned enough for me to glimpse his face. I'd bolted before he could spot me because he'd know my face. And Dash's. And Leo's.

I sure as hell knew his.

Ira was a slimy motherfucker, though he'd have to be to represent the Warriors and Tucker Talbot. He preferred to represent criminals and had a talent for getting the guilty acquitted due to technicalities in the investigations. He was ruthless and cunning, much like his clientele.

Thankfully, the weasel hadn't been able to set Tucker free.

"You're sure it was him?" Dash asked.

"I'm sure." Ira, much like Tucker's family in South Carolina, was someone I kept a close watch on. Because if there was anyone relaying messages in and out of prison from Tucker, it would be Ira or a member of his team.

"Does she work for him?" Bryce asked.

"No." I sighed, standing to retrieve my coffee from the fireplace before sitting back down. "She does corporate legal work." Her photo had been on her firm's website. "Personal stuff like wills and prenups. She's not a criminal attorney so she's not connected to the Warriors through her firm."

"What about her family?" Dash asked.

"Still looking." I took a long pull from my coffee, trying to put the pieces I'd collected last night together. "I spent most of my time digging into Nova. I haven't gotten deep into the family yet. Haven't had enough time."

Just skimming the surface of her life had taken me most of the night. First, I'd started with Nova's credit cards. Maybe part of me had wanted to believe that it wasn't true, that Nova wasn't June Johnson. But then I'd seen the social media photos. The Louboutin purchases.

Next, I'd examined her family. A quick search had brought up a mother, a brother, a sister and a brother-in-law. There were probably a hundred friends to research too. Getting a holistic picture might take me close to a week.

Dash blew out a long breath. "There's got to be more of a connection to the Warriors beyond a relationship with a lawyer. That doesn't seem to be enough motive for her to come here, start something up with you and invade your life."

"Agreed."

"Then you keep digging."

"I don't want to," I whispered. "I don't want to keep digging."

Because the more I uncovered, the more I hated her.

The more I hated myself.

"Why?" Dash asked.

I didn't have to answer. The pity in Bryce's eyes said she knew exactly why. "You're in love with her."

I swallowed the lump in my throat. "I didn't even know her goddamn last name."

It had all been a lie.

That was what had driven me from my office this morning. Sure, I could have stayed at home and started looking into the family. I could have shown up at Dash's place with a hell of a lot more answers than I currently had.

But I'd had to get out. I'd had to be gone from those computers because information wasn't just useful, it was painful.

I loved Nova.

And Nova didn't exist.

"This is going to hurt," Dash said, his voice gentle and low.

"Yeah, it is."

But it wouldn't hurt as much as losing one of my family members. For them, I'd go through the pain.

"What can we do to help?" Bryce asked.

"Feel like pulling some news archives?" I asked. "See what comes up on her and any known family members."

"Absolutely." She nodded. "Would it help if I came to your place so we could work side by side?"

"No, but thanks." I needed to be alone, not only to concentrate, but to process whatever I came across. "You stay here with your family."

"You're family too."

I gave her a sad smile, then looked to Dash. "When is it going to get easier? When are sins from our past going to stop haunting us?"

"I don't know, brother." He shook his head. "Guess all we can do is our best. Pray it ends. Keep our kids out of it so they don't go through the same."

The next generation would have a chance at peace. Because they'd never know the Tin Gypsy life. I'd never been more grateful that we'd disbanded the club than in this moment.

Because while we might not spare ourselves, we might stand a chance at giving the kids a fair shot.

"I think we should leave Luke out of this for now," Dash said. "Give you a chance."

"I was thinking the same." As much as I liked my friend, he was a cop and bound by rules that didn't apply to me. While Dash and Leo were clean, I broke the law each time I hacked into someone's life. Luke knew what I did but that didn't mean he liked it. If I could keep him out of a compromising situation, keep from forcing him to turn a blind eye, then that was for the best.

"I'll get out of here." I stood from the chair, draining the rest of my mug before taking it to the kitchen sink.

Bryce and Dash met me by the door, watching with worried expressions as I tugged on my boots.

"I'll call you with whatever I find," Bryce said, her arms wrapping around me tight.

I hugged her back, then jerked my chin at Dash. "Brother."

"Brother."

They watched me from the doorway, standing together as I strode to my truck. When I backed out of the driveway, a little face poked between their legs.

Dash hoisted Zeke into his arms, then took his family inside.

I drove across town, yawning constantly. The lack of sleep from last night was catching up. I contemplated stopping by the coffee hut, but I'd hooked up with both baristas over the years and wasn't really in the mood to deflect any attention—positive or negative.

My eyes were heavy, and my limbs felt sluggish. I was spent. I'd given all my energy to Nova and she'd spent me like a roll of quarters at a slot machine in Vegas.

The house was dark and quiet when I walked inside.

The alarm panel beeped as I punched in the code—the new code I'd programmed last night. I trudged to my bedroom and slumped on the edge of the mattress.

She'd left her scent behind. A smell that was wholly Nova. The expensive floral perfume clung to the air. It clung to me. I couldn't bring myself to wash her off my body.

Though a shower and a nap were overdue, I shoved to my feet and walked the length of the house for the basement staircase. I crawled beneath the pool table, retrieving the laptop I'd stowed just this morning before heading to Dash's place.

With it under an arm, I carried it upstairs and to my office, settling into my chair. And even though I dreaded whatever I'd find, I got to work.

When an engine echoed outside, I jerked away from my monitors and checked the time. Three hours. Three hours had passed as if I'd barely blinked.

"Emmett," Leo called from the front door.

"Office," I called back.

His steps came down the hallway and I didn't bother getting up.

"Hey," he said, hovering at the threshold.

"Hey." I jerked up my chin.

"You're in the zone."

"Yep."

Without a word, he turned and retreated down the hallway. A second later, noise from the TV in the living room drifted my way.

He wouldn't hover but he wouldn't leave me alone. I was blessed with friends who understood me. And given that he hadn't asked any questions, Dash must have called and told him about our early-morning conversation.

He'd saved me the trouble of repeating it.

I went back to work and finished scouring Nova's sister's credit bureau report. I'd already gone through the mother's, the brother-in-law's and Nova's. *June's.* Reconciling them as the same person wasn't getting any easier, even as the hours passed.

"She doesn't have a father," I said, loud enough that Leo hit pause on whatever show he'd found on Netflix.

A minute later, he was at the door. "None?"

I shook my head and leaned back in my chair. "None listed on her birth certificate. Mother is January Johnson. Older sister is May. And she's June."

June Nova Johnson.

"Huh. All months."

"Except the younger brother."

"Who's the brother?" Leo came into the office and propped himself on the edge of my desk.

"TJ. And apparently it doesn't stand for anything. All I could find was TJ. Even on his death certificate."

"He's dead? How?"

"Accidental death was the cause. I texted Bryce about an hour ago to see what she could find in the Missoula newspaper archives. She emailed me the obituary about ten minutes ago and an article on his death. I haven't gone through it yet."

Bryce was more experienced with news archive systems, and I'd been busy gathering information that was not public record. Most of my time so far had been spent pulling raw data, which took time. Cracking someone's bank account and credit bureau report wasn't exactly speedy.

I'd learned over the years that the real secrets weren't kept on Instagram or Facebook for the world to see. The real secrets were always tied to money. If something suspicious was happening, nine out of ten times, the money trail was where you'd find it.

Soon I'd shift gears and start pulling photos and videos, the public information. I'd scour social media for the stuff people posted that they shouldn't. Combined with what I'd already collected, that would help paint the full picture.

My focus thus far had been on the living relatives for any chance that they'd also been in Clifton Forge. But the mother hadn't left Missoula in years. The sister and her husband had gone to Hawaii a year ago—and overpaid on their vacation rental—but otherwise, there was no indication they'd ever been to Clifton Forge.

Granted, they could drive here and back on a single tank of gas, but at the moment, they seemed like normal people living normal lives.

The same was true for Nova—June.

There was no reason she should have been in Clifton Forge. The only link so far was Ira Hug.

"Let's see how the brother died." Leo came to stand behind my chair, watching over my shoulder as I pulled up the attachments Bryce had sent over.

The article on the brother's death was first. It was fairly short, stating that TJ Johnson had been killed in a hunting accident at the age of eighteen and that alcohol was suspected to be involved.

"Eighteen," Leo said. "Damn."

"Jesus," I muttered as I kept reading. TJ's cause of death had been a gunshot wound in the leg. The bullet fired from a friend's gun.

I shouldn't feel pity for Nova. None. But it was there regardless, a pinch that she'd lost a brother too young.

I clicked the obituary. The first few lines included a list of now-familiar names as TJ's survivors.

"Emmett," Leo gasped.

"What?"

His jaw was clenched and the color drained from his face. He jerked his chin back to the screen.

While I'd been reading the top, he'd jumped to the bottom, where there was a smiling photo of TJ Johnson.

I blinked, narrowing my eyes and leaning closer.

It took me a moment to recognize the face in the grainy black and white photo, but then recognition dawned and my heart dropped. "That's . . ."

Fuck.

That face blasted me to the past, to an underground fight that had gotten way out of control. Leo had been there. So had Dad.

We hadn't known his name was TJ Johnson. All we'd known was that he'd worn the Arrowhead Warrior cut.

TJ Johnson had been a Warrior.

TJ Johnson wasn't dead because of a hunting accident.

TJ Johnson was dead because I'd killed him.

I'd shot Nova's brother.

CHAPTER NINETEEN

NOVA

"How are you?" I asked Dad.

His eyes dropped to his orange jumpsuit. "Fine."

Not fine.

I opened my briefcase, taking out the set of dummy papers I'd prepared last night before driving here this morning. Mom's latest letter was on page three.

My boss hadn't said a word about my last-minute request to take today off of work, other than an immediate approval. Probably because I'd worked nonstop over the past week, only stopping to sleep for a few hours before I'd wake, think of Emmett and dive back into work—in an effort to distract myself from thinking of Emmett.

So far those efforts had been in vain. Emmett was constantly on my mind.

I'd waited the entire week to see what he'd do. To see if he'd retaliate.

He'd taken that piece of mail, and by now, he had to know who I really was. Maybe not that my father was

Tucker Talbot, very few people in the world knew that, but Emmett would know my name wasn't Nova.

He'd know I'd lied.

Beyond that . . . it was a guess. I wouldn't put it past him to know about TJ.

For a week I'd waited for him to make his move, wondering if he'd contact me. If he'd come after me. If he'd show up at my condo and kill me. I didn't actually think he'd kill me, but Dad had promised the Tin Gypsies were murderers, so it wasn't completely out of the question.

But there had been no sign of Emmett and I couldn't tell if that was good or bad. Sitting idle, waiting for the other shoe to drop, had finally driven me insane.

Hence my visit to the prison today.

I needed to see Dad's face. I needed to hear his voice. I needed answers.

I needed to know who to believe.

Dad looked at the papers, his voice barely above a whisper. "What have you found?"

"Nothing," I answered. It was the truth. Because even though I had the flash drive, I still hadn't been able to open it. I hadn't had the courage to see what was there.

"Did my guy get ahold of you?"

Hacker. "Yes."

"And?" There was something in his tone. Expectation. He'd asked for results and I hadn't delivered, so he was growing impatient.

"Tell me about Stone."

His lashes lifted. "I already told you."

"Tell me again." I leveled my gaze to his and for the first time, I sent my father a look that wasn't adoring or affectionate.

He didn't like it. His jaw clenched.

Could he see how my insides were churning? Did he realize that my patience was gone? Maybe the irritation on his face was because I'd given him an order and no one ordered Tucker Talbot around.

Deal with it, Dad. I arched my eyebrows, waiting.

"Why?" He narrowed his eyes.

"Because I'm asking you to tell me."

"What's going on, Nova?"

"You'll just have to trust me that the reason I'm asking is important." The truth was important.

He pursed his lips and shifted, the movement to conceal a quick glance at the guarded door. "He killed your brother."

"At a fight."

Dad nodded once. "At a fight. The Tin Gypsies cheated. Those fuckers rigged the fight. Rigged the bets. When TJ called them on it, Stone shot him."

"Were you there?"

He shook his head.

So he didn't know exactly what had happened. Maybe he'd gotten it wrong.

"And Stone?" I asked. "What did you do?"

"I did what I had to do."

"I want specifics."

He shook his head but I wasn't wavering. He was in prison for three consecutive life sentences without the chance of parole. Sure, the FBI might be recording this conversation illegally, but it wasn't like a fourth life sentence would change anything.

Dad would die in this building.

And I wanted the truth.

"Nova," he warned.

"Tell me."

"I sent some men to Clifton Forge. Tracked Stone down at a bar." *The Betsy.* "They waited until he got up to take a piss and hauled him out the back door. Put a bullet between his eyes. For TJ."

"You did it. You pulled the trigger."

Dad didn't answer and the look on his face said he wasn't going to. I guess in the end, it didn't matter. That was the story Emmett had told me too.

No matter the voice speaking, it wasn't easy to hear. All I could see was the photo of Stone in Emmett's house. The one in the living room. His bald head. His long, braided beard. His large frame with an arm tossed around his son's shoulders. And a smile that was the same as Emmett's.

Stone had looked more like a Willie Nelson groupie than a kid killer.

So Dad's story matched Emmett's, and vice versa. Regardless, this was a sick cycle. Death and revenge and damn it, I was done. I was so fucking done.

This war of theirs would kill us all.

And silly me, I'd waltzed right into the middle.

Except it wasn't really a war, was it? Because the Tin Gypsies weren't fighting. They hadn't landed my father in this place. No, he'd done it himself. I'd known that fact all along, but I'd ignored it. Why?

I stared at Dad, his expression unreadable.

Did he love me? For so long, that was all I'd wanted. His love. But now . . . maybe Shelby was right. Maybe Dad was manipulating me for his own gain. Maybe the only thing Dad had ever loved was his club.

"Nova." His eyes softened because mine were on the verge of tears. "Whatever they told you is a lie. Trust me."

I nodded. "Of course."

"Good. I'm counting on you to finish this. For TJ."

For TJ? Or for him and his men? "I'd better go."

I waited, giving Dad a moment to flip to Mom's letter and read it. Then I pulled the papers away and returned them to my briefcase. The wig on my head was beginning to itch. The glasses on my nose pinched the bridge. The air in here was stifling, not because it was too warm, but because for every moment I lingered, my emotions choked me that much more.

Without another word, I walked to the door and knocked for the guard. He immediately opened, shot Dad a wary look, then escorted me to check out.

Pretending to be Nancy made my head spin. My heart ached as I went through the motions. I was being torn in two directions and whichever side I chose meant abandoning the other.

How many years had I wanted a relationship with Dad? Now I had the chance for one. Was there really another side to choose? For Dad, I'd lose Emmett. But I'd lost him on Saturday, hadn't I?

By the time I was led to the exit, I was numb. The exhaustion of not sleeping for a week had caught up with me. Without Emmett's arms to hold me, I tossed and turned. Without his warmth, even a pile of blankets couldn't keep the cold at bay.

My steps were so heavy through the prison's parking lot that my heels skidded rather than clicked on the asphalt. I was sluggish as I drove away from the prison and to my regular turnout spot. The second the Nova was parked, I tugged the wig from my head and the glasses from my face, stuffing them both in the briefcase. My blazer was suffocating so I stripped it off and tossed it into the backseat.

What am I doing? How do I fix this?

Visiting Dad should have made me feel better. I'd expected to feel better. Instead, my skin crawled, and my stomach twisted.

Dad's words ran on repeat.

Whatever they told you is a lie. Trust me.

Emmett had never told me to trust him. He hadn't needed to. Because he'd simply given me his own trust, expecting to earn mine in return through honesty. When people told the truth, they didn't need to order you to trust them.

How many times in my life had Dad said those words? *Trust me.*

A hundred. A thousand. I'd put my faith in my father, like my mother. Like my brother. And look where they were now. One would spend the rest of her life pining for a man she'd likely never see again. And the other was dead.

Trust me.

Trust was a dangerous concept.

Home was miles away, but I'd be there by dinner. Maybe if I drank a bottle of wine and ate an entire pizza, I'd be drunk and full enough to sleep through the night.

But as I put the Nova in drive and headed down the road, I didn't turn toward Missoula. Instead, I drove to Clifton Forge.

I wasn't even sure why. Just that I needed . . . more.

It was almost dark by the time I arrived. The sun was diving behind the mountains and the faint glow from the horizon cast the town in shades of black and gray.

There was a chance Emmett was home, but it was a

Friday night and before I drove all the way to his place, I figured I'd stop at The Betsy in case he'd come down after work. The stop paid off.

The orange and blue neon lights from the bar gleamed on the chrome of Emmett's motorcycle beside the door. I parked but didn't go inside. I waited, gathering the last of my strength. And then a calm washed over me.

On Saturday, after Emmett had walked out of my condo, I'd been upset and angry and hurt. Deep down, I'd known it hadn't been the end. But tonight was.

Tonight, this would finish.

I was ready for this to end.

Maybe I'd get the truth. Maybe I already had. But I wanted to know what had happened to my brother and for that, I needed the other side of the story. Emmett's side.

Country music greeted me when I pushed the car door open. A man in jeans and a flannel button-down was walking inside, the two of us converging at the entrance.

"Hey." He dipped his head as he opened the door for me. "How's it going?"

"Fine." I didn't so much as spare him a glance, though I felt his eyes track down my charcoal satin blouse and black fitted slacks.

"Are you meeting someone tonight? I'd love to buy you a dr—"

"Not interested."

There was only one man I'd be talking to tonight.

Once inside, I turned toward the pool tables. A group of men clustered around the rack of cues, each with a beer bottle in hand. But no Emmett. I took one step toward the bar, intending to find a seat, but froze when a pair of chocolate brown eyes snared mine.

Emmett sat on a stool at the bar.

And he was not alone.

A brunette was standing in between his open legs, his knees bracketing her hips. She wore a pair of jeans that fit her curves like a second skin. Her slinky tank top hugged her chest. Her hands were on his arms, roaming over his tattoos.

Those were my arms to touch. Those were my tattoos to explore.

He stared at me from over her shoulder, the woman short enough that even seated, he was taller.

She leaned in to whisper something in his ear.

He must have grunted a response because his chest rose and fell, then he lifted one of those hands and a beer bottle to his lips.

That had better be the only goddamn thing his lips touched tonight.

I had no claim on him. Not after what I'd done. But the surge of bitter envy through my veins was enough that I had to force myself to keep still. Otherwise, I'd walk over and rip that brunette's hair out from the roots.

If he'd fucked another woman . . .

My stomach churned. There was pain and then there was this, watching him watch me as another woman looped her arms around his neck.

He kept his eyes pinned to mine as she rose on her toes and brought her lips toward his ear.

For a moment, I was sure he'd turn and kiss her. That he'd let her take his lips while I watched.

I didn't look away.

This was my fault, not his, and I would bear the consequences.

I held my breath, my hands trembling at my sides, as she

pressed her body to his. Did he like the feel of her breasts on his chest? Did he like the scent of her perfume and the caress of her hands?

Oh, God. I was going to be sick.

I swallowed hard, a split second away from running out of the bar, when Emmett stood so abruptly that it forced the brunette away.

She stumbled and would have fallen if not for his quick grip, catching her by the elbow to right her on her feet. She stared up at him, shock etched on her pretty face.

He didn't give her an explanation. He simply walked past her and stalked my way.

I held my ground, my eyes never wavering from his. To keep them, I had to tilt my chin up the closer he came. Then he was towering above me. His scent filled my nose and I drew in a long breath, having missed it this past week.

"You let her touch you," I blurted. *Nice, Nova.* Maybe I should have led with something else.

His nostrils flared. "Who I fuck is none of your business. Not anymore."

"Did you?"

"Did I what?"

I gulped, hating myself for what I was about to ask, but I had to know. "Did you fuck her? Or anyone?"

He stared at me, his eyes so full of fury it was like seeing a different person. But he must have heard the desperation, the anguish in my voice, because he gave me a clipped, "No."

The air rushed from my lungs. "Ace."

"Emmett."

"Emmett," I whispered.

"What do you want, June?"

June.

Whatever composure I'd had shattered. He knew, of course he knew. I'd known for a week that he knew my real name. But I didn't want to be June, especially not with Emmett.

"It is June, right?" He leaned in closer.

"Yes."

He stood straight and crossed his arms over his chest. "What are you doing here?"

"I want the truth."

He scoffed. "I'm not the liar here. *Nova.*"

My shoulders sagged. "I . . . I'm—"

"Sorry? Yeah. I heard you last weekend." He shook his head, then pushed past me, walking for the door.

He left me behind. Again.

I sucked in one breath and when I looked up, the brunette was glaring at me from where Emmett had left her standing.

Could she make him happy? Could he love her? Could she give him a future? She was real. She didn't need to lie about her name or her family. Her biggest indiscretion was probably shoplifting lip gloss in high school.

She was everything I wasn't.

My father had probably murdered Emmett's father. His father had definitely murdered my brother.

There was no sick world where this would ever work between us. There was no redemption here, not for me, a woman who'd deceived him about everything for months.

Still, I clung to the hope that maybe . . .

There was no *maybe*. When was I going to get that into my head?

Going home was the answer. Starting my life over was

the next plan. My father would eventually work out his revenge on the Tin Gypsies, and they might deserve it.

But they might not.

And I had to know.

I unglued my feet and tore my eyes away from the brunette, turning and walking outside. I expected to see an empty space where Emmett's bike had been. I expected to drive to his house and pound on the door for hours until he let me in.

Instead, there he was, astride his Harley. Waiting.

He'd pulled on a jacket, the leather fitted to his bulky arms. Emmett jerked his chin, started his engine and roared out of the parking lot.

Much like our first night together, I climbed in my car.

And followed him home.

CHAPTER TWENTY

EMMETT

"Do you have a jacket?" I asked as Nova climbed out of her car. *Christ.* Did I really care if she got cold? *Yes.*

She blinked, looked to the house and then back to my face. "Um . . . yeah."

She went to the car's backseat and grabbed a blazer, quickly slipping it on.

I wasn't letting her inside the door, not just because I didn't trust her but because it was a goddamn wreck. After a week-long bender, my house was trashed. There were beer cans and liquor bottles scattered everywhere. My living room reeked of old pizza and my bedroom of dirty clothes.

I hadn't been on a tear like this since the club.

Ironically, I'd gone on a bender after shooting Nova's brother.

Leo had gotten me piss drunk last Saturday after I'd put it all together. He'd stayed the night, never leaving my side as I'd come to terms with this. Or tried.

I was still struggling.

And rather than deal with it, I'd spent most of my days in

the bottle. Hell, today was the first day all week I'd managed to sober up enough to head into work.

Dash had told everyone I'd gotten sick. He knew the truth. So did Leo. But TJ Johnson's death was club business, and even though I hated lying to Presley and Isaiah, it was better they didn't know.

I'd planned on drinking tonight away too and would have if Nova hadn't shown up. One look at her and it was amazing how quickly my buzz had disappeared.

She looked beautiful. Stunning, really. My fingers itched to dive into her hair. My mouth watered at the thought of fitting my lips over hers. Mostly, I wanted to pull her into my arms and pretend that this past week hadn't happened.

Instead I kept my distance, leading the way to the deck chairs we'd sat on countless times.

I took my usual seat.

Nova—*June*—whatever the fuck I was supposed to call her, took hers too. She placed her hands in her lap and looked out at the trees, her body tense.

I sat perfectly still, not trusting myself to keep from touching her. There'd been a split second at the bar, right after she'd walked in the door, that my heart had leapt out of my goddamn chest. I'd been so fucking happy to see her, but then it had all come crashing back.

The lies. The deception. She'd used me.

And now she was here because she wanted the truth.

I bit back a bitter laugh. *The truth?* We were months too late.

"I'm sorry, Emmett." She looked over and even in the dark I saw the tears swimming in her eyes.

It would be so easy to fall for those damn tears. To pick

her up, cradle her to my chest and promise her we'd figure this out. But it was too late.

"Was it all a lie?"

"No. Not all of it."

I stared at her, studying her face like I had at her condo last week. A face I thought I'd known so well and now . . . I didn't know shit. "What was true?"

"Most of it. More than you probably think. And when we were together, that was true."

I believed her. There was only so much she could fake. Her intentions here. Her name. But when our bodies had been connected, when I'd moved inside of her, there'd been no faking that.

She'd been mine.

And damn it, I would have kept her.

But I was a fool tricked into believing a string of lies. Tricked into thinking there was a woman out there for me. Tricked into falling in love with her.

"Why?" I knew the answer, but I asked it anyway. If she wanted the truth, she could blaze the trail.

"My brother was a Warrior." Her voice was so quiet it nearly got lost in the night. "You know that already, don't you?"

"Yes."

"He joined the club as soon as he turned eighteen. He didn't even finish high school. He wanted to be a Warrior and the second they'd let him prospect, he was knocking on their door."

It didn't sound all that much different than when I'd joined. The same was true with Dash. Granted, we'd graduated from high school. My parents wouldn't have allowed it any other way. But the moment I'd been able, all I'd wanted to do was ride a bike alongside my dad. To wear the cut and share in the pride of being a Tin Gypsy.

"When we were growing up, TJ was my best friend. That was his name. TJ. You probably know that too."

Again, I nodded.

"My older sister and I would fight a lot, but TJ and I were close. We'd spend our summers together playing outside. Mom would let us stay up late on Friday nights after school, so we'd camp out in the living room and he always let me pick the movies we watched. I helped him study algebra and would make him grilled peanut butter and jelly sandwiches whenever he flunked a test."

She'd loved him. Pure and simple. She'd loved her brother.

My insides twisted and chest pinched. I really should have had more to drink tonight. The guilt had been crippling this week but being here, listening to her . . .

There was no way she could know that I'd been the one to kill her brother.

Dad had insisted on taking responsibility. He'd made Leo and me swear that when we returned to the clubhouse after the shooting, we'd tell everyone Dad had pulled the trigger.

Technically, he had. But he'd been out of bullets, having used most of them earlier that day to sight in his new pistol. He hadn't reloaded his magazine.

My Glock had been loaded full.

I would have owned it, but the Gypsies had been at war with the Warriors for so long that a dead member was bound to cause another stir. Dad had wanted the retaliation aimed his way, not mine.

I'd wondered many times over the years if he'd known

just how the Warriors would strike back. If he'd known that by taking responsibility, he'd signed his own death certificate.

Dad had saved my life. He'd saved me so I could be here sitting beside Nova.

The only way she'd know was if I told her the truth.

She'd despise me.

Yes, she'd deceived me for months, but I wasn't sure I could stomach her hatred. She had every right. Just like I had every right to hate her.

Yet here we were, on my deck, sitting in chairs we'd sat in for months because I couldn't let her go.

"He was at a fight," she said, her voice hoarse. "Boxing or MMA or something. I don't know. But it was organized by your club."

"Boxing," I told her. "It was always boxing."

She nodded, tucking her hands between her legs. She was probably cold. The sun had disappeared behind the horizon and the temperature was plummeting.

"I don't know if TJ was a good boxer or not. I'd never seen him in a fight. He came home once from the Warrior clubhouse with cuts on his knuckles and a black eye. He didn't talk about what happened with the club. Not that he'd tell me anyway."

How had TJ even gotten hooked up with the Warriors? From the outside, the Johnsons were a normal family without any ties to a motorcycle club. They hadn't lived in Ashton, so it wasn't like TJ had been exposed to the Warriors on a regular basis. Was there a relative or some tie I'd missed? Maybe if I hadn't been in a drunken stupor this past week, I'd know the answer.

"He went to one of your fights." Nova's face hardened and she stared out into the distance. "You cheated him. I

270

don't know exactly what happened but the other Warriors who were there said that TJ got cheated out of his fight and his winnings. When he called you on it, he was killed. By your father."

There was rage in her voice. And that fury, right there, was the motivation for her charade. There was enough anger vibrating off her body to drive her to revenge.

Except TJ's death had been years and years ago. Maybe she hadn't known. Maybe the real story had only come out after the Warriors had all been arrested.

It was a fucking shame her story was wrong.

"That's what you think happened." I scoffed. "Figures."

"What figures?"

"It figures that the Warriors would come up with that bullshit story about how your brother was killed."

"It's the truth."

"Whose truth?"

She flinched.

"Do you want the truth or not?"

"How do I know you won't lie to me?"

I leveled her with my gaze. "One of us on this deck is a liar. It sure as hell isn't me."

Nova had the decency to look ashamed.

"I remember your brother."

She sucked in a short breath and even in the faint light, I saw the flush leave her cheeks.

"I remember that night." I never forgot those nights. The bad ones.

Those were the nights I questioned everything. The nights when I didn't want to wear the patch. The nights that stained my soul and no matter how many times I washed, the blood stayed on my hands.

"For the most part, we hosted our fights at the clubhouse," I said. "We'd have them in the basement. But every now and then, we'd organize something bigger. Something that would draw a larger crowd and more money. A lot more money."

The clubhouse fights had been an excuse to party. We'd fight and drink and mess around with women not afraid of some blood. When Draven had built the clubhouse at the far end of the lot at the garage, he'd made sure the basement was large and secure. It had been a bunker of sorts, a place where people could come in a disaster.

Most of the basement had been one large open room and that was where we'd had the fights. The basement's smaller rooms had been for other purposes. They'd seen far worse than some drunken fights. Which was why all the rooms, including the main room, had been built with a drain in the center to wash away blood and grime. Dad had once made the joke that the club should have bought stock in bleach for how much we'd poured down those drains.

TJ wouldn't have been allowed through the front door for a clubhouse fight.

But the bigger fights had required we loosen the restrictions on the guest list. We never would have invited a Warrior, but TJ and his fellow members had slipped in the door regardless.

"There was a rancher outside of town. He knew one of our brothers. They'd gone to school together. Somehow the topic of a fight came up and the rancher mentioned he had a large shop. He'd move out his equipment, let us come to his property and he'd look the other way while we hosted a fight. For a fee."

I ran into that rancher every now and again around town.

Sometimes at the hardware store. Others at the gas station. He'd been older than me and had known Dad better, but each time he saw me, he'd nod and wave.

I was recognized a lot around town. We all were. Small towns were like that. And people remembered who we were. The men we'd been. Dash, Leo and I had done our best to become upstanding citizens. Dash ran a successful business. I had my properties and investments. Leo made friends with just about everyone. But people remembered.

Those new to town would eventually hear rumors. There were women who'd always pull their kids behind them when they passed me on the sidewalk. Men who'd give me a sideways glance when I rode past on my bike.

We could pretend we'd been better men than the Warriors, but in the end, our clubs hadn't been all that different.

And here we were, still at war.

"We set up the fight," I told her. "Planned it for months. It wasn't like we sent out invitations, but it was an open event. If you knew the right people, you were in."

"How did TJ end up there? Why would you let a Warrior in?"

"Because he lied." I shot her a glance. "He came with three other guys. None of them wore their cuts so we didn't know they were Warriors."

There was no way I ever would have been without my patch, no matter the event. We wore them whenever we rode. It was a point of honor. Of pride. Apparently, getting into a fight and winning some money had been more important than club loyalty.

Maybe we should have asked more questions because TJ and his friends had come on bikes. But a lot of men, affiliated with a club or not, had rolled in on a Harley, a Victory or an Indian.

I'd been inside, getting the fights lined up, so I hadn't seen TJ or his fellow Warriors come inside. None of the Gypsies had recognized them either. We'd all known the Warrior leadership, but prospects? It was hard to keep track. TJ and his friends had shown up at the door, said the right names and been let inside.

"Each of them wanted to fight but we had a full schedule. Based on weight and size, we could only fit one of them in."

"My brother," she whispered.

We'd turned him down at first. He'd been young and cocky. He hadn't had the bulk of the grown men, but our smallest weight group hadn't had a lot of guys, so we'd agreed. Another fight meant more money. If I'd only known . . .

"I wish I had turned him away." And not just because she was here beside me. But because he'd just been a kid. An arrogant, reckless kid who'd gotten his ass handed to him in the second round.

"He fought in one of the first matches. He lost." I'd only caught a few glimpses of it, mostly toward the end. I'd been busy helping organize and also prep for my own fights. I hadn't given that kid a second thought after he'd cleared out of the ring.

Nova sat so still it was like she'd turned to stone, but she was listening. She blinked. Her chest rose and fell as I spoke. Her pain was tangible.

"Those fights went nearly all night. It was pitch black by the time we all started to clear out. Well past midnight and closer to sunrise than sunset. Most of the Gypsies stayed until the end. We'd planned to meet up at the clubhouse, have a party to celebrate. Three of us stayed back to lock up the rancher's shop. Me, my dad and my buddy Leo."

Back then, Leo was usually the first to race off for the afterparty, but he'd decided to hang with me and Dad that night. Make sure everything was secure. We'd cleaned up the shop. Shoved a fat envelope of cash in the top drawer of the rancher's toolbox, per our arrangement. Then headed out.

"We walked out of the shop, thinking everyone was long gone, and there were these kids. They started shouting at us that we'd cheated them. That we'd rigged the fights and stolen their money."

"Did you?"

I clenched my jaw. "No. There was no reason to cheat. You placed your bets right and you'd leave flush."

She must have believed me because her shoulders fell a fraction of an inch.

"It was dark but not enough to hide their cuts. They'd put them on, probably while waiting for us to be alone."

Leo probably would have died that night if not for them putting on their cuts. One glance and we'd gone on alert. We'd drawn weapons. If they'd shown up in hoodies, we wouldn't have thought to go for our guns.

"They fired first." At Leo. Then at Dad. Thank God it had been so dark that they'd missed. I'd been locking up the shop and had been a few steps behind. But because of where I'd stood, I'd had the best position. "Then . . ."

It had happened fast. Death rarely took its time when it came calling. There'd been bullets flying. Men shouting. Dad had fired the single shot he'd had left. Leo had shot twice and clipped a guy in the arm.

Maybe we could have talked it out. Maybe had we not drawn our guns, they would have listened. Maybe we could have paid them off.

It was easier to rewind now, to see where everything had gone wrong and think about *maybes*. But in the moment, I'd simply wanted to protect my dad and my friend from the men who'd been trying to kill them.

"Your brother took a hit to the leg." It must have hit the femoral artery because he bled out.

"From your dad."

I rubbed my hands over my face, not sure how to keep going. Dad had wanted to take this. To bear this burden. But it had never been his to own. It had always been mine and the time had come to pay the price.

"No. Not from my dad."

"W-what?" Nova's face whipped to my profile.

I turned, taking her in. If she'd wanted the truth, she found it on my face.

"It wasn't your dad." Her chin quivered and the pools in her eyes caught the starlight. "It was you. You killed my brother."

The heartbreak on her face was almost too much to witness. But she needed to know.

If she was coming after us for her brother's vengeance, then she should know the truth. She should know who deserved to be punished.

"It was me."

CHAPTER TWENTY-ONE

NOVA

Tears cascaded down my face. The Nova's tires screamed on the pavement, so I screamed too. I screamed and screamed and screamed.

Emmett had killed my brother. Not Stone, but Emmett. Dad must not know. TJ's friends who'd been with him that night must have gotten it wrong because if Dad had known . . . Emmett would be dead.

Except Emmett was alive. And I'd fallen in love with him.

I'd fallen in love with my brother's killer. The enemy. It was all too much for my heart, so I screamed.

The noise was raw and hoarse. The sobs shook my entire body and with each one came excruciating pain.

I wanted to go back, to erase the last hour. I wanted to forget that I'd asked for the truth and Emmett had given me just that. But there was no going back. There'd be no forgetting. And as my screams faded into the night, all that remained were the tears.

This had to end.

There were so many lies. So much hate. The devastation of this war between the Tin Gypsies and Warriors was horrific.

It had to stop before someone else suffered.

I had to stop it.

Part of me wanted to lash out and rage at Emmett. He'd admitted to killing TJ. He could have let that lie go on forever and no one would have been the wiser. But he'd confessed because he didn't lie to me.

God, how I wished he had lied.

I slapped a hand to my mouth as another sob escaped, my eyes so full of tears that the dark road ahead was nothing but a watery streak of black lit by my headlights.

"Why?" I whispered to the road.

It didn't answer.

"*Why?*" I screamed and pounded a fist on the steering wheel.

This was so fucked up.

This was so epically fucked up.

After Emmett had told me the truth, I'd run from his house. There'd been nothing to say.

It was me.

Another cry escaped my lips.

This had to end.

I swiped at my face, trying to clear my vision so I could see to drive. I swallowed hard, embracing the pain, then slammed my foot into the gas pedal. I aimed the Nova toward town and the Clifton Forge Garage. Toward the Tin Gypsy clubhouse and everything that it represented.

The Arrowhead Warriors had been destroyed. They were nothing but ash and smoldering coals. They were nothing. The Tin Gypsies should be nothing too. If there were no clubs and clubhouses, then there could be no more death.

The tears began to subside as I wound through town, my hands clutching the steering wheel, my knuckles white.

This had to end.

The garage came into view and the tall, chain-link fence that surrounded the property glowed from a nearby street-lamp. The front gate was secured with a chain and padlock, making it difficult to enter without a key.

I aimed the Nova dead center at the gates, illuminating them as I hit the accelerator. The car slammed into the fences, tearing them apart and busting the chain like a hot knife through butter. Motion lights flickered on as I raced past the shop, down the lot to the clubhouse.

My tires screeched as I slammed on the brake, sliding to a stop in front of the wide building. Another chain and another padlock wrapped around the handles of the club-house's door. Trees clustered around the dark-stained build-ing. Grasses brushed their trunks, the stalks overgrown and brittle from the change in season.

I shoved out of my car, not bothering to kill the engine. I wouldn't be in Clifton Forge for long. A slight breeze picked up a strand of my hair and blew it into my tear-streaked face.

Before me, the clubhouse loomed. The building swam in shadows. It sat abandoned and ominous.

"Fuck you," I said, my words swallowed up by the night. "Fuck you!"

Fuck the Tin Gypsies. Fuck the Arrowhead Warriors. I hated them both.

If the Tin Gypsies didn't exist, if their club was truly gone, then they didn't need this clubhouse, did they? I dove into the Nova and popped the trunk. Then I moved without hesitation, without regret or remorse but with an all-consuming purpose for my emergency supplies.

The butane lighter. The Glock. The gas can.

It was fitting that the fuel I'd kept for TJ would help me end this tonight.

I tucked my pistol into the waistband of my slacks. I hadn't touched it since my last practice session at a range in Missoula, before I'd ever set foot in Clifton Forge. Dad had insisted that both Shelby and I be proficient with a handgun. I doubted she'd touched a weapon in years. Not me. I'd always made it a point to practice regularly.

Then with my lighter in one hand and the gas can in another, I marched for the clubhouse, climbing the two wide steps to the concrete platform that extended down the length of the building. Above me was a small overhang. Its eaves were littered with silky white spiderwebs that glowed like strands of spun silver in the Nova's headlights.

The windows were filthy and behind their hazy glass panes were sheets of plywood. They'd boarded the building up from the inside, making it hard to break in.

Not that I had any intention of going inside.

This was a wooden building. The foundation was concrete and I was sure the basement was too, but this building was wood and wood burned.

I twisted open the plastic container of gas, the fumes wafting in my face as I took a step away from the door. Then I hefted the can to my hip, thrusting it forward so that a slosh of gasoline splattered on the door. Drops hit my shoes but I did it again until the door glistened with the liquid.

Setting the can aside, I took out my lighter and set the flame against the wood.

The gas caught with a whoosh, fire streaking up the

door's face and brightening the stoop. I stood there, watching it burn until the heat forced me back a step.

A hysterical laugh bubbled up my chest. I'd set the Tin Gypsy clubhouse on fire. Oh my God, I was crazy. Maybe I hadn't exactly expected it to burn. Maybe I was falling apart.

Definitely falling apart.

But the realization that I'd lost all control didn't stop me from swiping up my gas can and hurrying around the building to repeat the gasoline pour and ignition on each of the building's faces.

My shoes were covered in dirt and the heels caked by the time I made it around the clubhouse. The October darkness was no match for my fire and the parking lot shined with flickers of yellow.

The heat from the flames caught on the wind and carried the warmth to my face as I returned to the Nova.

I'd just committed arson. The last place I should be lingering was at the scene of the crime but I couldn't make myself move. I heaved the empty gas can toward the clubhouse, then clutched my lighter like a weapon and watched the clubhouse burn.

The flames danced against the midnight sky. The crackle and hiss drowned out all noise until a distant rumble caught my ear.

I tensed but didn't move. I knew they'd come. It was only a matter of time before Emmett found me. Probably the same way he'd tracked me down in Missoula, likely through my phone. Or maybe he'd gotten an alert when I'd broken through the garage's fence. Whatever the reason, I would stand here until he came.

This was my fire. He didn't get to take this from me. He didn't get to take this sliver of revenge.

This fire was all I had left.

The engine thundered into the parking lot and I glanced over my shoulder, surprised to see not one, but two headlights.

Emmett.

And Dash Slater.

I pulled the gun from my waistband and held it tight at my side.

"Nova!" Emmett yelled, leaping off his bike beside my car. He strode my way, his bootsteps loud. He reached for my elbow, tugging me toward him. "Get back."

I shook off his hold as Dash rushed to his side, his eyes fixed on the burning clubhouse.

"Fuck." Dash dragged a hand through his hair.

"What the fuck are you doing?" Emmett's eyes were wide, the flames reflecting in his brown gaze.

It was roaring now, its fingers stretching for the stars. Soon there'd be sirens. Soon there'd be questions.

"Get back." Emmett reached for my arm again, but I yanked it away. "Nova."

"No." I stepped back. "No."

His chest heaved. "What are you doing?"

"Taking this from you." I flung out a hand toward the building, the hand with my gun.

A familiar click sounded above the noise of the fire. Past Emmett's shoulder, Dash had pulled his own gun, both hands on the grip and the barrel pointed my way.

"Put the gun down," he ordered.

Emmett held up his hands, shooting Dash a look.

Dash ignored him. "Drop it."

"No." I raised my chin. "You can kill me first."

"No!" Emmett stepped between us, shielding me from Dash. "Baby, drop the gun."

"Don't," I barked, a fresh wash of tears coating my eyes. I wasn't his baby anymore. "You killed him."

"I didn't know," he said, his eyes so full of pain and remorse. "It was dark and—"

"Don't make excuses," I snapped, my hands and arms beginning to tremble. The gun practically rattled against my leg. "You killed him."

"I'm sorry."

"Are you?"

"For you, yes." He took a step closer.

"Liar." I raised the gun to his face, forcing his feet to stop. He held his arms up even higher.

"Emmett," Dash warned, shifting so that he could put his sights on me again.

"Back the fuck off, Dash," Emmett warned, his eyes never leaving mine. "Nova, please."

"You killed my brother." My voice cracked.

He only nodded.

"You sent my father to prison."

He opened his mouth, but then his body flinched. My words registered like I'd just slapped him in the face.

No more secrets.

This had to end.

"You ruined my family. You and your brothers." I flicked the barrel of my gun toward Dash.

"Your father." Emmett's arms dropped. "Who is your father?"

I stayed silent, holding his glare with my own. He'd put it together. I was in love with a very, very smart man.

"TJ." The realization clicked like pieces coming together. "Tucker Junior."

"You're Tucker Talbot's daughter?" Dash asked.

"Yes." For the first time in my life, I admitted it to someone who wasn't in my family. I was Tucker Talbot's daughter. I wasn't proud of it. I wasn't proud of him.

I was just so fucking sick of living this lie.

"No." Emmett shook his head. "Impossible."

I curled my lip. "Possible."

"You're not his daughter," he clipped. "I know who his daughters are. You're not one of them. You're fucking lying. Again. Tell me who you are. Who is your father?"

"Tucker. Talbot. I'm his daughter."

"No, you're not."

"I'm—" My argument died on my tongue.

I know who his daughters are.

The world tilted under my feet. Emmett's sentence sank deeper and deeper.

You're not one of them.

I was his daughter. Shelby was his daughter. If Emmett didn't know me then . . .

Who were the daughters Emmett knew?

"What the fuck?" Dash's eyes widened. "What is going on?"

My gaze flicked between the two, their profiles alight from the inferno raging at our sides. The blood rushing through my ears drowned out the noise.

Emmett reached for his side.

I raised the gun. "Stop."

"I'm just getting my phone, okay?" One hand dove into his jeans pocket while he held the other between us, palm open.

My entire arm trembled and the movement caused the gun to shake. But I held it to his face, watching as he flipped through his screen to open something up. Then he handed it over, the device extended like he knew what was on it was a bomb.

On the screen, he'd pulled up a picture of two women.

Sisters.

Sisters who looked exactly like *my* sister.

The strength left my arm and it dropped, the pistol slipping from my grip. It clattered to the ground beside my feet as I stared at Emmett's phone and the faces on the screen.

This had to be a lie. This couldn't be real, could it? Except they both looked so much like Shelby. Her nose. Her mouth.

A loud crash boomed.

Dash and Emmett both turned to the clubhouse as the building shifted. Maybe the roof was collapsing. Or a wall. I was too engrossed in the phone to pay it much attention.

"You're lying." I looked up to find Emmett's gaze waiting.

"I have never lied to you."

"You're lying!" Fresh tears streamed down my face, hot like the fire.

Emmett took one step forward. "You didn't look at what you took off my laptops, did you?"

I shook my head. Would I have found these photos? "These are . . ." My throat closed on the words. *His daughters.*

These women were his daughters.

Emmett, the Tin Gypsies, had known about them. Dad had daughters besides Shelby and me. He'd had a family.

And suddenly the reality of my life hit me like a tidal wave.

We hadn't lied to stay safe from his enemies. We hadn't hidden our names, our identities, to escape danger.

We'd lied to protect his lie.

We'd been his other family. The dirty secret.

"You didn't know," Emmett said.

"I don't know anything anymore," I whispered.

His phone slipped from my fingers, falling to the ground beside my gun. I took one step away from him, then another. I backed away until my knees hit the hood of the Nova, then I was gone.

I drove away from the fire. I drove away from Emmett. I drove until I got home.

The minute the Nova was parked in my garage, I plucked that flash drive from the ashtray and took it inside, not caring that I smelled like smoke and that my face was salty from crusted tears.

I sat at my own computer and loaded up the flash drive. It took me twenty minutes to find the file. First, I read the report from the private investigator. Then I started leafing through photos.

Dad standing beside a sweet, pretty brunette at a high school graduation. The next photo was of their whole family, when the girls—my half sisters—had been younger. They'd probably put it on a Christmas card. Because this was Dad's real family.

Everything else was a lie.

Including me.

CHAPTER TWENTY-TWO

EMMETT

"Heard from her?" Luke asked.

I shook my head and bent to pick up a piece of charred glass.

The clubhouse was nothing but rubble. The fire Nova had set two days ago had been devastating. The walls and roof had collapsed, then caved into the basement.

"I'm sorry." Luke sighed and walked closer, his own boots crunching on the debris.

He was wearing a Clifton Forge Police Department shirt, his gun holstered on his hip beside his badge. We'd been friends for years, long before he'd become the chief. The two of us would meet at The Betsy for a beer on a fairly regular basis. He'd take me fishing at the river. When we'd suspected that the former chief, Marcus Wagner, had been the one who'd set up Draven for murder, Luke had been the one I'd called to help take Marcus down.

That was before he'd married Scarlett. Now he was more than a friend. Now he was a part of us. Part of the family.

A different cop might have condemned us—*me*—for our

crimes. But Luke had a heart and I think he saw how hard we—*me*—were working to show the world the same.

"What do you want to do about this?" I asked, standing.

"I don't know." He sighed. "Tough for me to let this one go."

Luke was a good cop. A good man. Overlooking crimes went against his moral compass, but since he'd become tangled with the Tin Gypsies, he'd turned a blind eye when necessary.

But this was arson. Asking him to ignore this would be asking too much.

The fire department had shown up on Friday night just minutes after Nova had torn out of here. They'd done their best to extinguish the blaze but the damage had been done. The only wall still remaining was on the far side of the clubhouse. Once upon a time, I'd had a room along that wall.

"Talked to Dash this morning," Luke said. "He isn't going to submit this as an insurance claim, so they won't be requiring an investigation."

"And you?" I held my breath.

"I need to do something."

I let go of my breath. "Then say it was me. I got drunk. Came out here and was messing around. Started the fire on accident. Consider this my official confession."

"Hell, Emmett," Luke muttered.

Maybe I wasn't going to ask him to ignore this, but I was still going to ask for a favor. And if I had to play all my chips as his friend, then so be it.

"Is she worth it?"

"Yes." To save Nova this trouble, I'd take the fall.

"I'll have to fine you. Write up a report and all that."

"Do it."

He clapped a hand on my shoulder. "I'm sorry."

So am I.

I stayed rooted as he turned and walked to his truck, waiting for him to take off. Then when I was alone, I let my shoulders fall. I'd been standing tall for two days, but as I took in the wreckage, the exhaustion from the past few days settled so deep that even my bones felt tired.

Sleep had been nonexistent since Friday. It had taken until nearly sunrise for the fire to die down to a smolder. Dash and I had stayed here the entire time.

We'd each gotten the notification on the motion sensors at the garage when Nova had broken in. I'd pulled up the video feed, watched her bust through the gates and realized that after she'd left my deck, she'd come here. What I hadn't expected was to ride in and see the clubhouse in flames.

Dash hadn't spoken a word that night after Nova left. He'd just watched his father's legacy burn to the ground.

We'd both watched what was left of the Tin Gypsies turn to ash.

And the fucking crux of it was, seeing the clubhouse burn hadn't been as painful as knowing what Nova was going through. The devastation on her face, the utter heart-break and misery . . . I'd never get that look out of my mind.

Fuck.

Was she okay? I wanted to ask. I should ask. But I couldn't bring myself to contact her. And I doubted I'd ever see her again.

I swallowed the sting in my throat, either from the smoke or the emotion, then raked a hand through my hair. The hair tie I'd been wearing on Friday had disappeared at some point, and when I'd rushed home for a quick change of clothes, I hadn't thought to grab another.

It would probably be good to go home. Shower. Sleep. But home was the last place I wanted to be.

We'd gotten everyone together at Dash's place yesterday. And when all eyes had turned my way, I'd told them everything. How I'd met Nova. How we'd spent the last couple of months together. How I'd learned that she was actually June Johnson. How she was Tucker Talbot's daughter.

How she hadn't had a damn clue about Tucker Talbot's *other* daughters.

There was no way she could have faked that shock on Friday. Not a chance. I knew her face, I knew her expressions, I knew her eyes. Seeing that picture of Tucker's daughters on my phone had been the surprise of her life. And it had cut her to the core.

I wanted to slit Tucker Talbot's throat simply for the pain he'd caused her. That motherfucker had hidden a family. He'd hidden her.

Now that I knew what to look for, the ties were there. It made sense now why January Johnson had never held down a job. Maybe they'd passed it off as an inheritance, but the truth was that Tucker had funded their life and his secret family.

Most of the ties were from TJ to Tucker. Yesterday, after the meeting at Dash's place, I'd run home to get my laptop and change clothes. Then I'd gone to Leo's house, setting up at his dining room table, where I'd spent the afternoon, evening and night diving into TJ Johnson's life.

He'd been involved with the Warriors since high school, taking trips to Ashton. He'd purchased his first bike at sixteen. Tucker had likely been grooming him to join and eventually take over.

Until I'd killed him.

Did the other Warriors know that TJ was Tucker's son? Or had he hidden TJ's real identity from the club too? Maybe TJ had known about Tucker's real family, the other two daughters and the ex-wife. Maybe not.

For Nova's sake, I wanted answers.

Every cell in my body screamed to call her. To drive to Missoula and make sure she was okay. But I had no idea what to say.

She was Tucker Talbot's daughter. The man who'd killed Dad—or had ordered Dad's death—was her father. She'd come to Clifton Forge to exact his vengeance. On me. On Dash. On Leo.

Too much had happened. And fuck, I didn't know what to do.

I loved her. Entirely. But how could I trust her? How could I know if any of it had been real?

My Nova didn't exist.

Goddamn, I would miss her. Even though she was a lie, I would miss her. I would think of her for the rest of my days.

I forced myself away from the clubhouse ruins and walked to my bike. I'd been avoiding home. My house reminded me too much of Nova. My friends had been rocked by all of this too and they didn't need me at their doorsteps. So I rode to the one person who'd always been my guide.

My father.

The cemetery was bright under the October sun. Winter was coming, the threat of snow clinging to the air. But today the sky was a clear blue and hopefully the cold would numb the pain.

I'd expected the cemetery to be quiet on a Sunday morning, but as I rolled down the small looped drive, a familiar car was parked at the curb.

My boots crunched on the frozen grass as I walked to Dad's grave. My mother was bundled up in a coat, hat, scarf and gloves as she sat on the icy ground.

"Hi, Mom."

"Hi." She glanced over her shoulder and smiled. "Happy birthday."

"You told me yesterday." I'd called to tell her about the clubhouse. And that my party had been canceled. She'd invited me over for dinner, just the two of us, but I'd asked for a rain check. I'd needed time to do some research—and time to make sense of everything.

How could I explain to Mom that I'd fallen in love with the daughter of Dad's murderer? The past was too much. The betrayals were impossible to overcome. It was the harsh reality of the situation.

I'd come here to talk it out with Dad, see if I could make sense of it. Maybe if I told him, one day I'd find the words for Mom.

She shifted to the edge of her blanket, spreading it out to make a space for me.

"What are you doing here?" I asked, sitting at her side.

"Talking to your dad."

"About?"

"You." She gave me a sad smile. "We're both worried about you."

"Both of you, huh?"

"Of course." She nodded. "He's watching. Wherever he is, I can promise he's watching you."

Christ. I bit the inside of my cheek because damn it, I hadn't cried in years. Not fucking years. Not since the day we'd put Dad's body in his spot. But today, after the past weekend, I was on the verge.

Mom leaned her head on my shoulder.

I dropped my cheek to her hat. "Have you been going through more of his things?"

A good son would know the answer, but I'd been avoiding her and her house.

"Yes." Mom sighed. "I know you don't like it, but it's time. I never said goodbye. Sure, I went through the motions. The funeral. The grief. But I never really said goodbye to your dad."

Was that why she was here, talking to him? Maybe that was why we were both here. Neither of us had let him go.

"I don't want to say goodbye," she whispered. "I've been holding on to him for a long, long time. Holding on to the pain. I don't want to say goodbye, but your dad . . . he'd be so mad at me. If he could talk to me right now, he'd be so mad that I've wasted these years holding on to him."

The only thing Dad had wanted more than Mom's happiness had been her safety. That she live a long, happy life, even if that meant he wasn't a part of it.

"When the time comes, I don't want you to have to deal with both of our things," she said. "And because when I see your father again, I want to be able to tell him that I lived. That even though he wasn't with me, I lived. Holding on to a ghost isn't living."

"I don't want to say goodbye either."

"No one does. The true goodbyes are usually the most painful moments in our lives. But they're a part of it. We survive the goodbyes so when a hello comes along, we appreciate its beauty."

The sting in my nose was unbearable. A lump the size of

Montana had grown in my throat. My wise, incredible mother. We sat together with my father, a man who'd loved us both enough to trade his life for ours.

"I'll come over later and help you go through Dad's things," I said.

"You don't have to."

"I want to."

She sat up straight and when I met her gaze, her eyes were full of unshed tears. Mom looked older today. The creases around her eyes were deeper than I'd noticed lately. "I love you, Emmett."

"I love you, Mom."

She shifted, getting to her knees. Then she kissed my cheek and stood.

"What about your blanket?" I asked, shifting, but she waved me off.

"Bring it home when you're ready."

I nodded and watched as she walked back to her car. Then she was gone, leaving me alone with my old man.

What do I do?

Dad didn't answer. Maybe because there wasn't an answer here. Or maybe because the answer I knew was another goodbye.

I was in no hurry to leave, so I sat there, my arms draped over my knees, and let the sun warm my shoulders. I closed my eyes, drew in the clean air and hoped the answer would come if I stayed long enough.

Maybe I'd fallen asleep because I jerked at the sound of footsteps. Dash was walking over.

"Hey." He took Mom's place on the blanket.

"Hey. What are you doing here?"

"Same thing as you." He jerked his chin toward the other end of the cemetery. "Came to talk to my dad."

Probably to tell him that the clubhouse was gone.

"You all right?" I asked.

"No. You?"

"No."

I wasn't sure where we went from here. Tomorrow was a Monday, and I didn't know how I'd ride into the lot at the garage and not feel this gaping hole. Not from the clubhouse. There'd been times in the past when I'd hoped Dash would bulldoze the place to the ground. Because part of me had hoped that if it was gone, the sins we'd committed in that building would disappear too.

No, the hole was Nova.

How did I go back to my life and forget her? How did I move on from this?

How did I let her go?

The sound of an engine drifted over the grass. Both Dash and I turned to see Leo ride up and park behind my bike. Dash had driven his truck, which was probably why I hadn't heard him. That, or I'd been asleep.

As Leo crossed the grass, Dash and I shifted, making space for him on Mom's blanket.

He sat without a word.

We didn't need them.

This was what we were. Clubhouse or not. Tin Gypsy or not. We were brothers. We showed up for each other until the end.

Until we joined our fathers in this graveyard and said our own goodbyes.

"This couldn't be what they wanted," I said, breaking the

silence. "Dad. Draven. This couldn't have been where they wanted to end up."

Dash shook his head. "It should hurt, the clubhouse gone. All of it gone. It should hurt. But I just . . . I'm so fucking tired of it all."

"It has to stop," Leo said. "We can't keep living like this. In fear that someone will come after our wives and kids. We can't put that burden on our families. Teaching our kids to look over their shoulders. Making our wives go nowhere alone. How do we make it stop?"

If I had the answer, I'd move heaven and earth to see it happen. For them. For their women and children. "What a damn mess."

Dash hummed his agreement.

"What will you do about . . ." Leo trailed off before he could finish his question.

Not that he needed to. *Her.* What would I do about her?

"It's over." It had to be over. Nova and I had burned down just like Friday night's fire.

"I couldn't sleep last night," Dash said. "Just kept thinking about things. About the past. About all the things I wish I had done differently. What I wish I hadn't done, period."

Each of us sitting here was far from innocent. We were as guilty as the men we'd come to visit. The Tin Gypsies hadn't been good men. We'd killed. We'd inflicted pain. We'd ruined lives all in the name of the club and let violence blaze the trail. But because it had been in the name of the club, we'd given ourselves grace. Too much grace.

Then we'd quit the club, and in a way, disbanding had been our redemption.

A second chance we hadn't really deserved.

"There's no erasing it," Dash said. "None of it. All we can do is move forward. Do better than we did. And pray that when vengeance comes, it strikes swift. And it strikes true. That it leaves our wives, our children free. I won't have my sons tainted by this. If that means I sacrifice myself, the way Dad did for me and Genevieve and Nick, then so be it. I won't have my sons come home to find . . ."

Pain radiated off of Dash's body. He didn't need to finish speaking. We all knew that he was picturing Bryce at home, dead, left for her children to find.

This had to stop.

"I used to wonder . . . if Mom had asked Dad to quit, would he have done it?"

Dash nodded. "I wonder the same thing. But Mom never would have asked."

"Mine neither."

They'd loved their men, flaws and all. Much like Bryce and Cass.

"Last night, I told Cass everything." Leo blew out a long breath. "I don't know why. I didn't want to tell her anything. I didn't want her to look at me differently. We were talking about the clubhouse and it just . . . poured out. I thought she'd be disappointed or . . . I don't know. But she wasn't. She loves me for me, no matter my past sins."

"Bryce knows too," Dash said. "All of it. She's known for years. And I swear to God, she loves me more for it. Because she sees how hard I try to do better. She makes me want to be a better man. Every day."

"Maybe you need to talk to her," Leo said to me.

I shook my head. "I killed her brother. She's Tucker's daughter. It's just . . . it's too much to overcome."

"Life's short." Dash gestured to Dad's tombstone. "If our

fathers taught us anything, it should be to appreciate what you have because it can all disappear in a second."

"She came here for Tucker." I blew out a long breath. "We don't know what she was planning. To kill me. You. She came here for his revenge."

Leo nodded. "She did. But she didn't take it."

"I was there Friday night," Dash said. "She could have pulled the trigger, but she didn't."

No, instead she'd burned the clubhouse down. "Why are you telling me this? Shouldn't you be warning me away from her?"

"Probably." Dash chuckled. "She's Tucker Talbot's daughter. Bastard or not, she might be the only one to end this war. You pull her into our fold, he's got a reason to back off."

I laughed because of course Dash would see every angle to my love life. "Christ, you are a selfish prick."

"Yes, I am." He grinned. "That aside, I watched a woman's heart break that night. A woman you're in love with and a woman who I suspect is in love with you."

"I killed her brother," I repeated. "And as you so clearly just pointed out, she's Tucker's daughter."

"It's a lot to overcome." He nodded. "Maybe ten years ago, it would have been too much. But we've changed. We're not those men. And I, for one, wouldn't be who I am without Bryce. She changed my life."

Leo nodded. "And Cass changed mine."

What the hell? This was not the discussion I'd expected today. "She lied to me. About everything."

"Sounds like her entire life has been based on a lie. The truth has a way of changing your reality. A way of setting you free. There's a win, a win for everyone here. You and Nova included."

I dragged a hand over my face. "How do I trust her?"

Dash gave me a sad smile. What he didn't do was answer.

Because that wasn't his answer to find.

It was mine.

CHAPTER TWENTY-THREE

NOVA

There was serenity in my soul. Maybe serenity wasn't the correct word. I was calm. I was steady. I wasn't happy. I wasn't sad. Maybe it wasn't serenity so much as having completely detached from all emotion for the past week.

I was sitting in the same chair, in the same room, as my last visit to the prison. My hands rested on the file folder full of emails and photos I'd printed out this morning. Except this time, there was no blond wig. No glasses. No suit.

I'd come as myself this Monday morning, wearing jeans and my favorite heels. My turtleneck was thick and chunky since the weather had turned cold. It would be snowing for Halloween this week. My real name was etched on the check-in log. I'd handed over my actual driver's license for the guards to photocopy.

Technically, I was here as an attorney—not Dad's, but the prison staff had believed I was. It was the only lie I'd told in a week.

It was strange how I'd come to measure the time by my

lies. Hopefully I'd be able to go much, much longer than a week next time. Hopefully after this meeting.

I was unraveling the lies, one truth at a time.

It had taken me nearly the entire week to wrap my head around everything. To process it mentally and emotionally. I'd cried. I'd cried again. I'd had to take a few days off of work because I'd been so distraught that I hadn't been able to concentrate.

After the fire, I'd expected the police to show up at my doorstep and haul me to jail. But the only people who'd contacted me in the days immediately afterward had been my mom and sister. Mom had invited me to lunch. Shelby had asked me over for dinner.

I'd been so on edge, waiting for my arrest, I'd declined both. Finally, when four days had gone by, curiosity had won out, and I'd searched through the Clifton Forge newspaper for a story on the fire.

Bryce Slater herself had written the article. It stated that one of the garage employees had started the fire on accident. In the public police report, Emmett had been named that employee and that he'd be paying a fine.

He'd taken the blame.

He'd protected me.

Now it was my turn to repay that favor.

The door opened with a click and Dad shuffled inside, his hands cuffed. The guard at his side gave Dad a once-over, then took me in. He was the same guard who'd been here last time. Maybe he wondered why my face was on a brunette, not a blond.

Dad's expression flashed with surprise for a moment, then he scowled, a crease forming between his dark eyes as the guard left us alone. He took the chair across from mine. "Nova, what are you doing?"

"June." My voice was dull and flat. Serene. Numb. I'd bled all my feelings the night of the fire. "My name is June."

He stiffened. "What's going on?"

I flipped open the manila folder in front of me, pulling out the first photo on top. It was a family picture, one of Dad's real family.

He stood beside his ex-wife, their two daughters flanking them. He had his arm around the youngest. I knew their names, having memorized most of the report I'd found on the flash drive. But even though I knew their names, it was hard for me to think them, let alone say them aloud.

Emmett's PI in South Carolina was thorough. His report was comprehensive, with enough pictures to break my heart. And my trust.

I slid the photo across the metal table.

The moment Dad recognized it, his eyes darted to mine.

"All my life, I've trusted you. I think you were counting on that." He'd been counting on the fact that I wouldn't look into his personal life. Why would I? I *was* his personal life, or so I'd thought.

So many of our conversations had a different color now.

During my earlier prison visits, when he'd confided in me about the Warriors, he'd made me swear to stay away from the other members. That I could know about them but, even in prison, they must never know about me. He must have been worried that one of them would slip and mention his family.

After law school, I'd asked Dad if I should apply at his attorney's firm. He'd told me that was too dangerous. And it had been. For him.

I'd found Dad's divorce filing at the courthouse, done by Ira. I'd found his will, also prepared by Ira. If I had found Dad's file at Ira's, no doubt I would have stumbled onto his other daughters.

Except why would I have searched in the first place? I trusted my father.

I used to trust my father.

I was just another part of his game. Another piece on his board.

Not anymore. *I quit.*

"Nova—"

"June," I barked. "If you're going to make excuses, you can use my name."

He tensed, his eyes widening.

It would do him good to remember that I was in charge today. I was the one walking out of here. The rage I'd felt the night of the fire surged. So much for my serenity. I let the anger spread, warming me from head to toe. It burned beneath my skin but on the outside, I was ice.

"You will tell me the truth today."

He had the decency to look guilty as he gave me a short nod.

"I'm sure you can guess what papers and photos I have here." I tapped the folder.

His shoulders fell.

"Did they know about us?"

He shook his head. "No."

"Why?" Why would he go to such trouble to hide us?

"You would have been in danger. If anyone knew about you, they might have come after you."

"But your wife and other daughters wouldn't have been in danger?"

"That's different."

"How?"

"I was with them."

Right. He'd been there to protect them.

"The secret names. The random weekend visits. You hid us not from danger, but from them. From her." I pointed to his ex-wife's face in the photo. "You did this to hide Mom from her."

He looked up, his eyes searching, like he didn't recognize me. He should. This cold, calculating version of myself was entirely his making. "I loved my wife."

"Yet she left you anyway." There was a grim satisfaction in that. That even after all he'd done, she'd left him anyway. And, from what I'd gleaned from the PI's report, his daughters had disowned him.

Maybe that was why he'd kept us a secret. Not to hide us, but to hide himself so that we wouldn't see the criminal, the evil bastard he truly was.

"Does Mom know?"

"No." He swallowed hard and when he looked up, his eyes were full of misery. *Good.* "Please don't tell her."

"I won't tell her, but not for you. But because it would break her heart. She loves you. To know that you were *married*, that you have other children . . ." My hands balled into fists on the table.

My mother would be eviscerated to learn that she'd only ever been his side piece.

Just like we'd only ever been his side children.

"Did TJ know?"

He nodded. "Before he joined the club."

"But he never told us."

"It's club business."

"Oh, how I hate your fucking club." To the depths of my soul, I hated the Arrowhead Warriors.

"The Warriors are our legacy." His eyes narrowed, but he could glare all he wanted. It didn't surprise me in the least that he'd pick the club over his children.

"Your legacy?" I scoffed. "No, I am your legacy. May is your legacy. These half sisters of mine are your legacy. TJ was your legacy, and you and your club are the reason he is dead."

Dad pursed his lips, his own temper beginning to rise. "This is all coming from *them*."

The Tin Gypsies.

"No, this is coming from me. My eyes are wide open and I'm seeing you for who you really are. You've had your revenge for TJ. And that is where this will end. The reason you're in prison is because you're a liar. Because you cheated and stole and broke the law."

My statement went in one ear and out the other. "They will pay. For TJ. For my club." He motioned to the photo. "For feeding you this."

"For feeding me the truth?" *Unbelievable.* "Even now, you can't own this. You'll blame this on anyone else, just to avoid the fact that you are a liar. You are a cheater. You, a man I loved *so* much, are nothing."

He met my gaze, holding it without so much as a breath.

I stared back, unblinking. If he expected me to break, he'd learn quickly that it would take more than a glare. So I sat there, returning his dead gaze until he shifted in his seat under the scrutiny in my eyes.

"You're communicating with the other Warriors, in and out of prison, through Ira."

"How—"

I held up a hand. "Your attorney is a fool and all it will take is a single phone call from me to the FBI to alert them to your collusion. And to the death threats you've made to the Tin Gypsies." Maybe it would be admissible. Probably not. But it would certainly slow down the visits. If all I could do was make it harder for Dad to get his revenge, then so be it.

He opened his mouth. "I—"

"Quiet."

He clamped his mouth shut.

"You will not go after the Tin Gypsies."

"They put me in here."

"You put yourself in here."

"They committed just as many crimes as I did."

I lifted a shoulder. "They were smart enough to get out before they landed themselves with three consecutive life sentences."

His dark eyebrows narrowed and a lesser person would have cowered under his furious gaze. But he'd fucked up. And I wasn't scared in the least to call him on it. My father had no power over me, not anymore.

"It ends today," I said. "The revenge. The schemes. The lies. It all ends today."

He leaned back in his chair, staring at me like I was a stranger. "They'll come after you. Your mom. Your sister. You're a fool for trusting them."

"No more a fool than I am for trusting you, *Dad.*"

"They're playing you for a whore."

I didn't let myself flinch. "Maybe I have been a whore, but it was in your game, not theirs. But no more. So I'm making my final play. This ends now."

"Never."

"I love him." My statement wiped the arrogance off his face.

"No." He looked . . . panicked.

"You missed the big moments in my life. High school graduation. My prom. The father-daughter dances and the days when I came home and just needed my dad. You missed them all because you were with them." I pointed to his real daughters in the photo. "You missed my life. And when you needed me, when everyone but me abandoned you, I was here. You asked me if you could count on me, and I always said yes. I have never once asked you for anything. I have never once begged."

Dad didn't move as he listened, but with every one of my words, the anger drained from his eyes. In its place, the same pain I held in mine.

"I love him," I whispered, losing my fight with the tears.

Damn it, I didn't want to cry but I loved Emmett. And I'd lost him. I'd lost him because of my own father. Even if I never won Emmett back, I'd do what I could to protect him.

"You said you kept our identities a secret to protect us."

"I did."

"The Tin Gypsies won't hurt us. They have no reason to come after us. If. You. Stop."

He didn't move.

"If you hurt them, you hurt me. If I am truly your daughter, if you ever loved me, if I was ever more than just a kid you kept for the occasional weekend hug, then I am asking you now to stop. I am asking. I am begging. Will you stop this?"

He stared at me for a long moment, then gave me the slightest nod.

"Say it. Out loud. Show me that I'm more important

than your broken club. Show me that you'll give me this one gift and be the dad I always needed you to be. Leave them be. Please. Promise me."

He cleared his throat. The silence that followed was heartbreaking. Until he finally nodded again and said, "Promise."

"Thank you." I left the photo and the file on the table, standing and going to the door without a backward glance. It was done. And before I said more, before I let him see me break, I knocked for the guard and left my father in that small, gray room.

I managed not to cry as they checked me out. I managed not to fall apart when I stepped outside and into the cold air, knowing I'd never be back here again.

Knowing that I'd never see my dad again.

I didn't cry.

Until I started through the parking lot and saw a man leaning against the side of my car.

Emmett.

The tears came in quick succession, one after the other as I closed the distance between us. How many tears could a woman cry until she'd cried them all? A million? A billion? There was a decade of tears in my heart and not even crying a river would set them free.

I swiped at my face, pulling myself together, because whatever Emmett's reason for being here was, it probably wouldn't make my day better. I wasn't giving in to foolish hope.

He wore his signature faded jeans, the denim molded to his thighs and falling to his scuffed boots with frayed hems. Beneath his leather jacket was a gray hoodie, one I'd worn countless times.

I should have stolen that sweatshirt when I'd had the chance.

He stood tall, shoving off the car. When I was close enough, his hand stretched out like he was going to catch one of the tears, but he must have thought better of it because he pulled his hand away and shoved it into a jeans pocket.

"How did you know I was here?"

"How I've always known where you are." His eyes flicked to the purse tucked beneath my arm.

"My phone."

He nodded.

"Why?" Not that it bothered me. I didn't care that he'd followed me. But I asked because right now, I was running long on questions and short on answers. And I'd take whatever he'd give me.

"The Warriors," he said. "Thought they might come after you."

So he'd put a tracking device or software on my phone to find me.

"Why are you here?" I asked.

"Why are you?"

I turned and took in the prison for the last time. The tall walls and narrow windows. The unscalable fences and unbreakable doors. "I think I just said goodbye to my father."

And damn it, the tears just kept on coming.

I hated my father for keeping us a secret. For lying to me and Mom and May and TJ. I hated him for making me feel . . . less. I hated him for manipulating me.

I hated that I couldn't *hate* him the way I should hate him.

It wasn't fair.

The tears streamed, dropping to the pavement beside my

heels. One moment they were forming the start of my river, the next, they were falling into a soft gray hoodie.

Emmett's arms banded around me, pulling me close as I cried.

I buried my face in Emmett's chest, clinging to him as I let the regret and pain pour from my heart. I was crying too hard to speak but I hoped he could feel my sorrow for the misery I'd caused him.

He held me like no one ever would and when I finally reined in the tears, he still didn't let me go.

"You took the blame for the fire," I said, the words muffled against his body.

"Yeah."

"Why?"

"Because I should have burned it down a long, long time ago."

I squeezed my eyes shut, holding him tight as I wished for our reality to be different. I wished to rewind time. I wished to go back to the days when I sat on his kitchen counter while he cooked me dinner. When we talked and laughed and kissed and made love.

If there was a miracle to be had in my life, I wanted it to be him.

Emmett dropped his cheek to my hair, blowing out a long breath. "I can't do this."

There would be no miracles. No wishes granted.

The ache that spread through my bones and muscles nearly dropped me to my knees. It shouldn't have hurt as much as it did. I should have expected this from him because with all I'd done, I couldn't blame him.

I deserved this.

I unwound my hands from his waist and stepped away,

somehow managing to keep my feet. I wouldn't crumble in front of him either. He didn't deserve to bear any guilt for this when it was my fault.

"For what it's worth, I'm sorry. I'm so sorry, Emmett."

He stared at me like he wanted to say something. He stared at me with his feelings etched on his face. "Everything I know about you is a lie."

If he really thought that, then he hadn't been paying attention.

Yes, my name, my family, my motivation from the beginning had been a lie. But the moments together, our moments, those had been as real as anything in my life. The moments when we'd fallen in love.

I did love him.

He loved me too.

Those were words we would not voice. Could not voice.

He held my gaze, silently asking if I was okay.

I nodded and took one step away. Then two.

He didn't watch my third as he spun and strode for his bike parked beside the Nova. Then he was gone.

I stood there until the rumble from his motorcycle was a ghost on the wind. Then I pulled my sunglasses from my purse and I got in my car on shaking knees.

I loved him.

He loved me.

Words that would forever remain unspoken.

CHAPTER TWENTY-FOUR

NOVA

"I missed the snow."

It blanketed the world, made it a clean slate.

I needed a restart.

"It's pretty outside." My sister sank into the couch beside me, her gaze shifting out the front window to where the fat flakes drifted to the ground. We'd woken up this morning to a winter wonderland.

Jack had left for work already. Christian was on the floor, crashing toy cars together while a cartoon played in the background.

"Are you working today?" she asked.

"I should be." I sighed. It was Monday and by the time I went home and changed, I'd be hours late to the office. "But I might take the day."

I'd put in plenty of hours last week.

It had been a week since I'd gone to visit Dad. A week since I'd seen Emmett. I'd driven home from the prison and since home was not a place I wanted to be—alone with my thoughts was a dangerous place these days—I'd spent last weekend at the office.

It had been deserted except for one of the partners who'd come in briefly on Sunday afternoon. She'd said a quick hello and left me to my work.

Ira had called me twice and I'd declined each. Eventually, he'd get the message.

Otherwise, my blessedly boring, tedious work had been a salvation. I'd only gone home when absolutely necessary to change clothes and attempt a few fitful hours of sleep. Then Friday had come, and I'd left the office, but instead of going home, I'd come to Shelby's.

I'd found refuge with my sister.

She'd graciously let me stay the entire weekend. Saturday, I'd slept for fourteen hours. Yesterday, I'd lounged in a pair of borrowed sweats and played with Christian most of the day. And when I hadn't made any indication of leaving after dinner, Shelby had simply brought another pair of pajamas to the guest bedroom.

She hadn't asked why I was here. She knew something was wrong but hadn't pressed for an explanation. She'd just given me a safe haven until I was ready to talk.

"Thank you for letting me stay all weekend."

"You don't have to thank me."

I smiled at her and took a sip from my coffee, then went back to the window, mesmerized by the falling snow. It was only the first week of November. This storm would blow over and the snow would melt before winter really settled in for the season. But for today, I was grateful for the peace.

"I went to see Dad last week."

Shelby shifted on the couch, stretching for a remote to turn the volume down on the TV. "How'd that go?"

"Not great." I closed my eyes, took three heartbeats, then

opened my eyes and faced my sister. She deserved the truth too.

So I told her everything.

I told her every detail Dad had shared with me about the Warriors. If she was surprised, she didn't let on. She simply sat by my side and listened, taking small breaks to get Christian whatever he needed before coming back to the couch and letting me purge.

I told her what she didn't already know about Emmett. How TJ had really died. How he'd instigated the confrontation with the Gypsies and how Emmett had fired back in self-defense. How I'd fallen in love with the man who'd shot our brother. How that knowledge had sent me over the edge, and how I'd burned down the Tin Gypsy clubhouse.

God bless my sister for not looking at me like I should be in an asylum rather than her living room.

Then finally, I'd told her how I'd found out about Dad's real family. I'd told her that we'd been a secret and that we had two half sisters in South Carolina.

"Oh, I hate him." Tears glistened in her eyes by the time I was done. "I thought maybe he was done hurting us. After TJ died, I thought maybe he'd disappear. And when he went to prison, I was so glad. That's where he belongs. But this . . . I hate him for this."

I was furious at my father. Maybe the hate would come, maybe not. But it would take me years not to be angry. "I'm mad. I feel like a fool. Blindly believing him while he's lied to us our entire lives."

She scoffed. "This is a new low. Even for him. I mean . . . he hid us. How did we not know? How did Mom not know?"

"He kept us all at a distance. Even Mom."

"This would shatter her. All those years that she waited,

hoping he'd come to us. If she knew that he was married and had other kids, she'd be devastated."

"We can't tell her."

"I agree." Shelby nodded. "Did TJ know?"

"Yes."

"That little shit." The sadness was disappearing from her face, replaced by an anger I felt deep in my soul. "He was just like Dad. Cocky. Thought he could manipulate people. He knew about this and didn't turn his back on Dad. He chose Dad and that fucking club over us."

TJ's knowledge of Dad's secrets was the fact that hurt the worst. I was so . . . disappointed. He should have known better. He should have done better, for me and Mom and Shelby. We had been his family. We had been there for him every single day. But Shelby was absolutely correct.

TJ had made his choice and it hadn't been his family.

My brother had been young and rebellious. He'd been cocky and bold. He'd walked through life without a care, probably because whatever he'd needed, Dad had given him. All with the promise of being in that goddamn club.

And he'd died for it.

"Dad never should have brought him into that fucking club," she said. "But we should have stopped it."

"How?" TJ had been groomed his entire life to be a Warrior.

"I don't know." She looked to Christian on the floor.

He was mellow this morning, maybe because of the snow. Maybe because it was a quiet Monday morning. But he played and sent us his cute smiles whenever he tore his eyes away from his beloved cartoon.

"I love Mom," she whispered.

"I love her too."

"But we are more like Dad than her."

It was the truth. Our stubbornness. Our own bold personalities. Our strength. We'd inherited it from Dad.

"If I had been more like Mom, we probably never would have found out," I said. My own curiosity and drive had been what had uncovered the truth. "I wanted so badly to win him over. To have more from him. To finally win his attention."

"You've always wanted more from him. I've never understood it."

Maybe Shelby had known all along it was impossible. Unless I'd been born a boy and part of his club, I'd have always been second tier in Dad's life. Was that why she'd never tried hard to win Dad over? TJ hadn't had to try at all. He'd always been Dad's pride.

"I guess . . . because he counted on me," I said. "Like he always knew I'd be there and when the time came, I didn't want to let him down."

"He let us down."

Over and over and over again. "It hurts."

"It hurts," she whispered, her eyes on her son.

Christian would never know his grandfather. Shelby wouldn't allow it. She'd never take her child to a prison and I doubted there was a picture of Dad in the house.

"I'm sorry." I put my hand over hers. "For believing him. For bringing this all up."

"Never be sorry for the truth. I'm not sorry. It hurts, but I'm not sorry."

"Shel—" I stopped myself as I took in my sister's face. She wasn't Shelby. Like I wasn't Nova.

Her name was May. She'd always been May. Outside the walls of my childhood home, outside my own damn head, she'd always been May. The only person who called her Shelby was me.

I'd been so determined to prove myself to an unworthy father, to earn his love and loyalty, that I'd clung to *his* lies. To *his* names for us. Even Mom had no trouble calling us May and June.

It was me who'd kept that tie to the past.

"May." Her name was May. "I'm sorry for calling you Shelby."

She shrugged. "It's okay."

"No, it's not. You don't like it."

"Not especially."

"I don't like the name June," I admitted.

She laughed. "Then change it."

"Nova feels like Dad's. It feels like the lie. But . . ."

"Nova belongs to you." She squeezed my hand. "It always has. I was never Shelby. It was never who I wanted to be. But you're Nova, not because of him, but because it's who you are."

"Would that be weird to change my name?" How would I explain that to my coworkers? Or anyone, really? "Jack's going to think I'm crazy."

She gave me a soft look. A knowing look. And the realization hit.

"He knows," I breathed.

All these years I'd thought Jack didn't know about our father or our childhood. But he knew.

"Of course he knows." She nodded. "You give your truths to the man you love."

Jack knew about us. About our family. He'd always known. He called her May because that's what she wanted to be called, not because her identity was a secret. Because she'd given him her absolute trust.

"God, I screwed up with Emmett."

"Have you spoken to him?"

"No." What else was there to say? He'd made himself clear at the prison. I was a liar, and he didn't trust me. And I didn't blame him in the slightest.

"What are you going to do?" May asked.

"What is there to do?"

"You love him."

"I love him."

She shifted, leaning close to kiss my cheek. Then she got off the couch and picked up her son from the floor. "Should we go get dressed, buddy?"

He rambled something in his two-year-old speak to her as they started upstairs for his bedroom.

My coffee mug was empty. The snow had stopped falling outside and the sun was shining bright, the white nearly blinding. There was the slow drip coming from the gutters, the flakes already beginning to melt. As expected, it wouldn't last long and the roads were probably already plowed and clear.

I picked up my phone from the end table and shot off an email to my boss that was hours too late, explaining I wasn't feeling myself and wouldn't be in the office today. Then I climbed off the couch and hurried to the guest bedroom, stripping off my borrowed clothes for the outfit I'd been wearing when I'd come over on Friday night.

When my sister and Christian came downstairs, she didn't seem at all surprised to see me pulling on my coat with my car keys in hand.

"Drive safely." She smiled.

I pressed a shaking hand to my heart. "This is probably stupid."

"Probably."

"He'll probably slam the door in my face."

"But he might not."

He might not.

I hugged my sister goodbye and kissed my nephew, then drove home for a quick shower and change of clothes before getting on the interstate.

No trip had ever taken so long. The road stretched on endlessly and the miles passed at a glacial pace, even though I broke every speed limit. But finally, hours later, a familiar green sign welcomed me to Clifton Forge.

Driving through town again was like seeing it with a different pair of eyes. This had been enemy territory for so long that I hadn't really let myself appreciate it. I wanted to go to the diner downtown and sit at one of their booths instead of picking up takeout. I wanted to swing into the coffee shop for a latte and scone. I wanted to wander along Central and show my face to this community.

So far, I'd only viewed this town as a temporary guest. As an infiltrator. Now, I simply wanted to belong.

If Emmett would have me.

He was probably at work, which meant, unless I wanted to wait all day, I'd have to find him there. So I made my way along the familiar route toward the garage.

How could I drive into the lot? How did I show my face to his friends and coworkers? How could I look at the rubble that was the former clubhouse?

But I kept driving, swallowing my fear.

The storm had come to Clifton Forge today too, but in the warm early-afternoon sun, the roads were only wet.

Patches of brown grass were already poking through the melting snowbanks.

The Clifton Forge Garage came into view and my heart pounded so hard I felt it in my fingertips. I gripped the steering wheel tighter and eased the Nova into the parking lot.

The steel building was bright beneath the afternoon sun. The bay doors were open and as I parked, the sound of an air compressor hummed in the background.

Shit. What was I doing here? I should have waited but it was too late now. I'd have to face them eventually, right? I took one last fortifying breath, mentally bracing for the censure I most certainly deserved.

Don't look at the clubhouse. Don't look at the clubhouse. I didn't need to see its ruins, not today. It was bad enough that as I shoved my door open, I could scent the lingering smell of fire and ash on the breeze.

My heels had barely landed on the pavement when Leo came striding out of the garage. He had a red rag in one hand and a wrench in the other. There was no confusion on his handsome face, just cold scrutiny. He might not have met me before, but he knew exactly who I was.

I steeled my spine as he approached. *Here goes.*

Leo stopped before me and crossed his arms over his chest, the colorful tattoos on his forearms peeking out from beneath the long sleeves he'd shoved up to his elbows.

"Hi." By some miracle, my voice didn't crack. "Is Emmett here?"

He studied me, his pale gray-green eyes giving nothing away.

Another pair of footsteps sounded behind him. Dash

Slater walked my way. His face was impassive and his gaze as hard as the ground beneath my feet.

Dash came to stand beside Leo, matching his stance with his legs planted wide and arms crossed over his chest.

A blockade. A barrier. There was no way I'd get to Emmett unless they deemed me worthy to pass.

Maybe the version of me from months ago would have raised her chin. Would have demanded they let me pass or marched around them. Maybe then I would have shot them a glare as lethal as the ones they fired in my direction.

But there was little fight left in my bones, and I'd save it for another Tin Gypsy. I let down my guard. I showed them my vulnerability. And I said the words that were long overdue. "I'm sorry. For my actions. And for my father's."

Both men narrowed their gazes, their skepticism well earned.

"I don't think the Warriors will be a threat to you anymore," I said. "I can't promise anything, but my dad agreed to let this go."

"Except he's a fucking liar," Leo said.

"Yes, he is."

Only as I'd thought back on our final conversation, there'd been a truth there. Maybe the only reason I'd noticed was because it was so rare. Only time would tell, but I doubted these men had anything to fear from the Arrowhead Warriors.

Dash and Leo studied me long enough that I was beginning to think they'd never move. But then Dash finally shifted and looked to Leo. They shared a single nod, then Dash turned and walked away.

Leo gave me a devilish grin, like I'd passed some sort of

test. "Emmett's not here. He took today off. I suspect you'll find him at home."

"Oh. Um . . . thanks." *Hell.* I could have saved myself some stress, but this wasn't an entirely wasted trip. I waved goodbye, then returned to my car, reversing out of the lot.

In my rearview, Leo stayed rooted in place but that smile on his face never faltered.

My nerves returned tenfold as I drove to Emmett's. My hands trembled as I parked and shut off the Nova. He would probably slam the door in my face. I deserved that. But maybe not. And that maybe was enough to send me to the door to ring the bell.

My heart was in my throat as his footsteps approached beyond the door. Then there was a long pause, probably as he checked the peephole and saw my face. Then it opened and my fears just . . . melted away.

This was Emmett. My Ace. Even at his angriest, he wouldn't shut me out. That wasn't who he was.

He looked as breathtaking as ever. Insanely handsome with his hair up. He had on his jeans and a simple gray T-shirt. He'd trimmed his beard in the past week, the whiskers tight and clean to his strong jaw.

God, I wanted to kiss him. I wanted to sink into his arms and drown. But first, I had to give my truths to the man I loved.

"I hate shrimp."

He blinked.

"I like simple food too and I've made your tacos three times since the last night you made them for me. Your shower is the best shower in the world, and apparently, I can't sleep if it's not in your bed. The nights spent talking to you on your deck were the best nights of my life."

My words seemed to hurt him because he swallowed hard and dropped his gaze to the floor.

"My job is okay but I don't love it. Being a lawyer was my father's dream for me, and I've spent most of my life trying to prove myself to him. But I'm not going to do that anymore."

Emmett's face lifted and his eyes softened.

"I'm in love with a man I don't deserve." The lump in my throat began to choke me, but I pressed on. "I lied to you. I used you. And for that, I'm sorry. But I don't regret falling in love with you. I never will."

"Nova . . ." He caught himself on the false name.

But it wasn't false. It was who I was. I was his Nova. He was my Ace. "You said that everything about me was a lie. It wasn't. Not everything."

"How can I trust you?"

I didn't have that answer. I had no idea how he could trust me other than to try.

"I don't . . ." He ran a hand over his face. "I don't know. This is too much."

There it was. The inevitable slam of the door.

At least I could say I tried.

Before my tears could fall, before the break was severed clean, I moved in close, standing on my toes, and pressed a kiss to the corner of his mouth.

He dropped his forehead to mine.

I didn't linger. I dragged in a long inhale of his spicy scent, tucking it away in the corner of my heart, then I stepped back. "Goodbye, Ace."

He stepped back too. "Goodbye, Nova."

CHAPTER TWENTY-FIVE

EMMETT

Two months later . . .

"What do you want to do with his bike?" Mom asked.

"I don't know." I sat back in my chair, my plate empty on the dining room table.

Dad's bike was the piece in the garage that we'd both been avoiding. Going through his things hadn't been easy, but I'd been here every Sunday for the past two months to help Mom sort out his things. The process had been slow, intentionally so. Mom hadn't wanted to rush it, so the two of us would pick a handful of items, reminisce about each one, then decide on what to do with them.

Every box had been sorted. The books that Mom had wanted to read were on her office bookshelves. Others had come home with me. Most of Dad's clothes and housewares had been donated along with his old VHS collection of Westerns. I'd taken his hunting gear and fishing poles along with his tools and the dozen model cars he'd built over the years. They were on display on a new shelf in my basement.

Mom had been right about saying goodbye. It had been time. I thought of Dad every day, but the anger and the pain from his death that I'd been ignoring were finally beginning to ease.

Mom's garage was nearly empty now besides her own belongings. All that was left, parked in the far stall, was Dad's bike.

"What do you want to do with it?" I asked.

"We could sell it, then donate the proceeds to a charity in his name. Something for kids. He loved kids. He always thought kids going to trade schools needed more scholarships than were offered. Or . . . you can take it. He would have wanted you to have it."

My gut twisted at the idea of selling Dad's bike, even if it was for charity or a scholarship.

"I'll take his bike," I said. "Ride it this spring once the weather turns."

She gave me a sad smile. "He would have liked that."

Mom stood from the table, taking her plate. I did the same, following her to the kitchen, where I stepped to the sink and started on the dishes.

Today when I'd come over, there hadn't been anything to go through in the garage. We'd finished last week, but I'd come over anyway. Not just to spend the time with Mom but because there wasn't anything for me at home.

With nothing to sort in the garage, I'd shoveled the snow we'd gotten last night. Then I'd helped her hang a painting of Dad's in her bedroom. The faucet in the guest bathroom had a leak, so I'd fixed that. She'd found a documentary this week that she thought I'd enjoy so while she'd cooked us dinner, I'd watched the show.

I'd spent most of the day here because my mother's had

become a favorite hiding spot. Another was the garage. These days, I was the first to arrive and unlock the shop and was still the last to leave each evening. On Saturdays when we were closed, I had the place to myself, so I'd turn up the music and lose myself in whatever project we had going.

Anything to keep my thoughts from Nova.

It never worked.

She was always there, a constant. Thinking of her was as automatic as blinking or breathing.

Mostly I thought about the nights we'd spent together at my house, replaying them and sorting through the lies and truths. Other times, I'd think about us in bed and usually that would require a cold shower. Then there were the harder moments to relive. The fire. The last day she'd come to visit, when she'd told me she loved me. The day I'd followed her to the prison.

I'd thought for sure I'd find her there after gloating to her father that she'd burned down our clubhouse. Nope, she'd walked out of the prison heartbroken. She'd cut Tucker out.

She'd chosen me.

"You're not yourself today," Mom said, standing at the counter and watching as I loaded the dishwasher.

"What do you mean?" I knew exactly what she meant.

She shot me a knowing glare. "Let me rephrase. You haven't been yourself since the fire at the clubhouse."

"Yeah." I sighed.

Mom, like the rest of the world, thought I'd started that fire. The details had been in the newspaper—Bryce, like Luke, had gone along with the lie and printed that I'd started the fire on accident. The first Sunday I'd shown up here to help Mom, she'd met me at the door with a look of sheer disappointment.

The last time I'd received that look had been in high school after flunking a math test I shouldn't have flunked.

"Whatever happened with that woman you were seeing?" she asked.

"Didn't work out."

"Oh." Mom hadn't brought it up once. She also hadn't brought up Tera.

"She's moving." The words bubbled up before I could hold them in. I'd known for two days that Nova was moving but I hadn't told anyone.

Not that I talked about Nova.

The weekend after she'd come to town and we'd said goodbye at my front door, our crew had gathered together at Dash's place to talk about the Warriors. I'd told them that Nova had asked Tucker to leave us be and that she believed he'd honor his word. Then Leo had told me about Nova showing up at the garage.

The strength it must have taken her to go there and face them . . . Maybe if I'd known, I would have acted differently when she'd shown at the house.

Maybe not.

Regardless, that meeting was the last time I'd spoken of her to anyone.

"I'm sorry," Mom said.

"We had our goodbye." And it had ripped a hole in my chest.

Mom moved closer, reaching past me to shut off the water. Then she put her hand on my forearm. "You said it wasn't serious. I didn't realize that had changed."

Leave it to my mother to see past my subtleties. My damn friends were the same way. They might not have

327

brought Nova up in conversation, but I'd had my fair share of sympathetic looks in the past two months.

Through the window that overlooked the sink to the snow-covered yard, night was on its way. The light beside the back door cast a soft glow over the space and the fence that surrounded Mom's yard had tufts of snow on the wooden pickets.

"I love her, Mom. I've never been in love with a woman before."

Mom didn't speak. She just kept her gentle touch on my arm.

I'd told Nova that I couldn't trust her. But I did trust her. Even after so many lies, I saw the reason why. If I'd been in her position, I might have done the same damn thing. She'd been acting for her family, pushed to the extreme. Maybe I was a fool to think that the other pieces had been real but . . . fuck, they'd felt real.

"It's complicated," I said. "There are things in her past, in mine . . . I don't know if we can get over them."

"Emmett, if you're looking for your future over your shoulder, you're turned the wrong way."

Well . . . damn. She sure wasn't wrong.

"Does it have to do with the club?" she asked.

"Yeah."

"That fucking club."

I jerked my eyes away from the window to my sweet, loving mother, who rarely said the word fuck, or any of its variations, and who never spoke ill of the club. Even after Dad had died, she hadn't trashed the Tin Gypsies.

"I hate that club." Her nostrils flared. "I hate what it did to your father. To you. The day you burned down that clubhouse, I cried I was so happy."

328

My jaw dropped. "Mom, I . . . what?"

"I mean . . . I wasn't happy to see your name in the newspaper's police report. You know better than to get drunk and play with fire."

I shook my head, wondering if this was a dream and I'd fallen asleep watching TV.

"How did you think I felt about the club?"

"I don't know." For years I'd thought she'd loved the Gypsies. Respected the brotherhood. She'd never told Dad to quit. She'd let him divorce her to keep her safe. "Not like this."

"Your dad loved me but he'd been cheating on me for years."

"No."

"Oh, yes."

Never. Dad wouldn't have cheated on Mom. Hell, even after they'd divorced I hadn't seen him with another woman.

"I can see what you're thinking on your face. He cheated, but not with a woman. That club was his mistress. And he loved her. God, how he loved her. When he told me that we had to get divorced so that I'd be safe, I knew I'd never stand a chance. Because he'd tear our marriage apart before leaving that club. And I loved him enough not to ask him to leave it."

"You never told me not to join."

"Would it have done any good?"

"No," I admitted.

I would have joined the club no matter Mom's feelings. That had been my path and though I couldn't regret it, there were days when I wondered what life would have been like had I chosen a different trail.

"I understand you have a loyalty to the club," she said. "I

really do. And I respect that loyalty, even if I can't always relate, because I suspect it's similar to the loyalty I feel for you. But all of that aside, the reality is . . . that club came between me and your dad. We both let it. Don't repeat our mistakes. Don't let the club steal your future like it did your father's."

"There is no club."

And that was the answer.

There was no club.

Whatever had happened in the past with the Tin Gypsies and the Warriors didn't matter because there was no club.

I swiped up a towel from the counter and dried my hands. Then I pulled my mother into my arms for a hug before kissing her cheek. "Thanks, Mom."

"Bring her with you next Sunday. I'd like to meet this woman my son loves."

"Nova. Her name is Nova."

She smiled. "Nova."

"Bye." I rushed to the door, swiping my jacket from the coat rack, then stepped into the winter darkness.

The roads were quiet as I raced across town for the highway. I let out a sigh of relief that they'd plowed the roads as I hit the accelerator and headed toward Missoula.

Digging out my phone, I pulled up Nova's location. In these past two months, she hadn't taken the tracker off her phone. Maybe she hadn't known how, or maybe . . . maybe she knew that I checked on it at least ten times per day.

She went to work at the same time each morning. She was home most evenings by six, and when she wasn't, the little blue dot showed her at her mother's house or with her sister. Nova's life had been as unexciting as my own until two days ago, when I'd seen a check clear for a property in Oregon.

At first, I'd told myself that keeping tabs on her was simply because she was Tucker Talbot's daughter. We hadn't heard or seen anything from the Warriors, but we were just as diligent now as we had been for months. There was nothing to do but wait and watch.

So I'd watched Nova in the name of precaution. Really, I'd watched her because I couldn't let her go.

When I'd seen that check clear, it hadn't taken much to find the rental property details in Oregon. It also hadn't taken much to find the real estate listing for her condo. What I'd told Mom was the truth.

She was moving.

Maybe I'd already lost her. Maybe she'd send me home without so much as a word. But if there was a chance, it was worth taking. We owed that to each other, didn't we? Just to try?

There'd be no other woman for me. Nova had ruined me entirely and for the rest of my life, no one would take her place.

The hours on the road cleared my head but even with hundreds of miles, I wasn't sure exactly what to say. I still hadn't figured that out when I parked on her street and climbed out of my truck.

The TV was on inside her condo, its flashing colors illuminating her living room and giving me a view of the boxes stacked everywhere as I went to the front door. After sucking in a deep breath, I knocked, then let my heart race as the TV was muted.

She was nearly soundless as she came to the door, nothing but a whisper of her feet on the floor. Then there was no sound at all, like she'd frozen. I waited, my breath lodged in my throat, until finally the lock clicked opened.

And there she was.

Her hair was twisted in a knot on top of her head. She didn't have on any makeup. She wore a silk nightshirt that hit her midthigh. A thick cardigan billowed on her arms as she crossed them over her chest and stared at me with an expression that she'd purposefully blanked.

I didn't know what to say. Standing there, seeing her as breathtaking as ever, I had no idea how to start this conversation. The only words that came to mind were . . .

"I love you."

Her eyes widened but otherwise she didn't move.

"I don't know how to get to a place where we put this all behind us. Maybe we can't. But I'd like to try."

Nova stared at me, unblinking. And then her eyes flooded, and her arms fell to her sides. "I'd like that too."

I took one step forward and held out my hand. "Emmett Stone."

A smile pulled at her mouth as one tear dripped down her cheek. She swiped it away, then slipped her hand into mine. "June Johnson."

"Nice to meet you, June."

"Nova. June is my first name but everyone I love calls me by my middle name, Nova."

"Nova." I stepped inside, moving close enough to slide my palm against her cheek and catch another tear with my thumb.

Then I slammed my lips down on hers, swallowed a gasp before she threw her arms around my shoulders, holding on tight as I kicked the door closed behind me. Dragging my tongue across her lower lip, I savored the feel of her in my arms before I prodded her lips apart to sweep inside for a taste.

God, how I had missed her. How I'd craved her. If there were any doubts about this, they disappeared the moment her tongue tangled with mine and the world melted away.

The past melted away.

I kissed her until she was breathless, then pulled away to drown in those dark coffee eyes. "Hey, baby."

A smile stretched across her face. A smile I hoped to see every day for the rest of my life. "Hi, Ace."

CHAPTER TWENTY-SIX

NOVA

"They won't give me my deposit back." I set my phone on the counter in the bathroom. "But they're letting me out of the lease."

Emmett ran a comb through his hair, then dropped a kiss to my temple. "Fair enough."

While he'd been in the shower, I'd scrolled through the emails I'd avoided yesterday while we'd been unpacking. One had been from the property management company in Oregon who'd leased me a cottage on the beach near Manzanita. Considering how I'd backed out at the last moment, I was glad they hadn't pushed for me to pay rent.

When the dust had settled after the drama with Dad, a new town and a fresh start had seemed like the right next step. A little beach town where I could walk in the sand every morning had appealed, so I'd found the house to rent.

"It wasn't a small deposit." Three thousand dollars gone, and I hadn't even set foot through the cottage's front door. "That's enough for a new pair of heels."

He smirked, knowing exactly how much I'd paid.

I rolled my eyes.

Emmett had confessed to spying on my credit card and bank accounts, so he'd known that I'd planned to move to Oregon. I suspected now that we were living together, the spying would stop. Though he had asked me to leave the location tracker on my phone in case of an emergency.

If it gave Emmett peace of mind, then I didn't mind. Besides, I had a tracker on his phone now too, so we were equal. He hadn't argued at all when I'd brought it up, probably because I'd been on my knees and my tongue on his cock when I'd asked.

I leaned against the counter and caught a droplet of water as it skated down his bare chest. The towel wrapped around his flat waist, highlighting the perfect globes of his ass and doing little to hide the bulge beneath the V at his hips.

"It's just money," he said. "And I'll buy you all the shoes you want."

"I know." I sighed. I could make more money. Though first I'd need to find a job.

But I wasn't in a hurry to find a new career path. My condo in Missoula had gone under contract on Wednesday and since Emmett had refused to let me move anywhere but into his home, I'd have the equity from the condo's sale to keep me afloat.

My life looked much different than it had a week ago. And not at all like I'd planned.

"Do you think I'm crazy?" I asked.

"Yes."

I swatted at his chest and he chuckled, tossing his comb aside and shifting to pick me up and set me on the counter.

"No, you're not crazy."

"Do you think we're rushing this?"

"No, we're not rushing this."

I took a deep breath and asked the question I'd been avoiding all week. "Do you think we can move past it all?"

He framed my face with his hands, towering over me. "The future isn't behind us, baby."

No, it wasn't.

It might take us a while to get over all that had happened. It would take time to show Emmett that he could trust me, but I wasn't going anywhere.

I looped my arms around his shoulders, dropping my gaze to the hair that dusted his chest. "I hope your mom likes me."

He hooked a finger under my chin, forcing my gaze to his. "She will."

We were going to Cherie's tomorrow for Sunday dinner. I hadn't had a chance to be nervous about it yet. Between my last day of work on Monday, finishing packing on Tuesday and Wednesday, then Emmett and I hauling everything to Clifton Forge on Thursday, the week had passed in a whirlwind.

My furniture would stay with the condo and yesterday, the two of us had unpacked my things. I'd planned to do it over the weekend, to stretch it out since it wasn't like I had a job to dive into come Monday morning, but he'd insisted we unpack immediately. He wanted to make this our home.

"What should I tell her?" I asked.

"Whatever you're comfortable with. My mom was married to a Tin Gypsy for a long time. She knows what the club life is like. But if you don't want to tell her anything, she won't ask."

"Okay." I ran my fingertips through the hair beside his temple. My father's sins were my father's sins. I kept telling myself that, though I had plenty of my own to deal with. But Emmett and I had made an agreement last Sunday when he'd shown up at my door.

A clean slate. What had happened this summer was in the past. We were moving forward.

Together.

"I love you."

He bent down, brushing his lips over mine. "I love you."

My fingers went to the towel, loosening the fold that kept it around his hips. It dropped to the tiled floor with a muted *thump*.

Before I could take him in my grip, Emmett swept me off the counter and in a few long strides, we were in the bedroom and I was flying toward the mattress.

I bounced, laughing as he stripped off the sweatpants I'd pulled on this morning. They flew over his shoulder along with the T-shirt I'd worn to bed, one of his. It was gone with a whoosh before he came down on top of me.

He dove for my pussy, shoving my knees apart and without any teasing or delay, he dragged his tongue through my folds.

"Oh, God." My back arched off the bed as one of his hands snaked up my stomach to a breast.

He had my nipple pinched when his tongue stroked again. "You taste so fucking good."

I hummed and closed my eyes, the pleasure ripping through me as he feasted. My legs began to tremble by his ears and when he sucked on my clit, I cried out, twisting and writhing.

But he held me in place with that one strong arm, giving me one more suck until he was up and his mouth replaced his fingers on my nipple. Then the thick head of his cock was at my entrance.

"Ace, I need you." I tilted up my hips.

He released my nipple with a pop and shifted higher, locking his eyes with mine as his elbows bracketed my head. He was right. The future wasn't behind us. It was right here.

With one thrust he slid deep, my body stretching around him. "God, Nova. You feel . . ."

"Good. So good," I breathed, my inner walls already fluttering around him.

Then he pulled out only to slam inside again, hitting the spot that always made me shake.

Emmett planted a kiss on the underside of my jaw, trailing his lips up to my ear, then across my cheek as he started his rhythm, moving in and out until I writhed beneath him.

"Say it again."

"I love you," I panted.

"Again."

"I love you, Ace."

"Again."

"I love you, Emmett."

He let loose a groan and buried his face in my hair, dragging in a long breath before leaning up and reaching for my hand.

With our fingers laced together, he brought our hands between us to where we were connected. He held my fingertips over his slick shaft as he pulled out, then rocked inside, torturous inch by torturous inch. He kept me there, stroke after stroke, so I could feel us together.

"I love you, Nova."

I brought my free hand to his face, my thumb going to his bottom lip.

If there was a doubt that we'd be able to overcome everything, it vanished whenever we were together. Maybe that was why we'd been insatiable this week. In between the packing and moving, we were here, in bed or on the couch, our bodies linked.

Emmett lifted our hands, raising my arm above my head. Then he pinned it there in the pillows as he quickened his thrusts, increasing his pace until he was slamming into me and my orgasm came on a gasp, stars breaking behind my eyes.

I clenched around him, pulsing and squeezing as he lost himself to his own release and the two of us came together.

As the white spots cleared, I wrapped my legs around his hips, holding him to me. My hand clamped to his so he couldn't let me go. Then I took a moment to savor his weight on me, his heat enveloping me.

It was strange to think I'd been lost my entire life. That facing the man who should have been my enemy was what had brought me here.

I hadn't even known I was lost, yet here I was, found in Emmett's arms.

Emmett relaxed, twisting us so he wouldn't crush me, but he kept us connected. As soon as we were comfortable, I sighed, totally content to take a nap. He'd kept me up late last night and a lazy day in bed sounded like the perfect way to pass a Saturday.

But just as he was sinking into his pillow, his body tensed and he shoved up on an arm, his face whipping to the door.

"What?" I sat up, listening.

A grin stretched across his face and he kissed my lips, pulling out. "Better get dressed. We've got company."

My heart did a somersault. "What? Who?"

He winked and rolled out of bed, going for the closet. "Take your shower. I'll stall them."

"Them?"

He didn't answer. He disappeared into the closet as the sound of multiple doors closing echoed outside.

I rolled off the bed and hurried to the bathroom, jumping in the shower. I didn't bother washing my hair but did my best to put on some makeup with my hands shaking. The voices coming from the living room sounded like there were a hundred people in the house.

I dressed in a pair of jeans and a sweater. I stepped into my favorite four-inch Louboutins because I needed them to help me make it through today.

There was no need to ask who was here.

Whatever nerves I had for meeting Emmett's mother were tenfold when it came to meeting the greater Tin Gypsy family.

So much for easing into life here.

"I can do this." I closed my eyes in the closet and willed myself to be strong. Maybe they'd hate me. They had to think I was crazy. They were probably here to talk Emmett into rethinking this cohabitation idea because we were rushing this.

Going to the garage months ago had been one thing. I'd faced Dash and Leo. But this . . . there were many female voices drifting down the hallway, and meeting the women was going to be an entirely different experience.

Whatever the men might overlook, their wives would not.

I'd deceived Emmett for months. I'd used him and now I was living in his house. Did they think I was still using him? Did they think I was still in collusion with my father? At the moment, I was set on proving myself to Emmett. But his friends? How was I supposed to show his friends that I wasn't out to kill them or destroy their lives?

I'd burned down the clubhouse, for fuck's sake. Seriously, what was wrong with me? I was crazy. Officially, undeniably crazy.

"Hey." Two strong arms wrapped around me and my eyes whipped open. I was so stuck in my head that I hadn't heard Emmett walk into the closet in his bare feet.

"Maybe I should go."

"Go where? You live here."

I live here. That concept was a little flimsy at the moment. "A coffee shop."

He held me tighter. "They'll love you."

"How do you know?"

"Because I love you."

My body sagged into his. Mostly I wanted to avoid this forever, at least until Emmett and I had more time together. "How can you be so . . . sure?"

"They're my family."

"No, not sure of them." I twisted out of his arms and looked up to his face. "Of me. How can you be so sure of me? It's only been a week."

"Nova." His eyes softened and his hands came to my cheeks. "Don't doubt us."

I nodded and leaned into his touch.

Don't doubt us.

"Okay."

Today, I'd do my best. Tomorrow, those doubts would

come back, but for now, I'd borrow some of his confidence and face his friends knowing that *he* didn't doubt us.

"Come on." He laced our hands together and led me out of the closet and down the hallway into the chaos of conversation.

"Don't leave me," I whispered, hating the insecurity in my voice. But I needed him today.

"Never."

A little boy streaked across the mouth of the hallway, followed closely by another.

"Xander! Zeke!" a woman yelled. "If you want to play tag, go downstairs before you break something valuable."

They bolted in the other direction, disappearing as we emerged in the common area.

Conversation stopped. All eyes turned my way and I squeezed Emmett's hand tighter, raising my free hand to wave.

"Hi."

"Hi." A petite blond woman with short hair appeared at my side with a baby boy in her arms. She looked me up and down, wariness in her expression as she waved. "I'm Presley."

I knew them, of course. But I simply smiled. "I'm Nova."

A tall man appeared behind her and I did a double take. Shaw Valance.

It was one thing to know that Presley had married the famous Hollywood actor, but to see him standing here in Emmett's—no, *my* house was something entirely different.

"My sister has the biggest crush on you," I blurted, then cringed. *Smooth, Nova.*

Shaw chuckled. "Maybe we'll get to meet her someday. I'm Shaw."

I wiggled free of Emmett's grip and shook Shaw's hand. "Nova."

"Nice to meet you."

Was it? His wife smiled and though she didn't seem cold or rude, there was some hesitation there. Rightly so.

In the kitchen, there was another woman—a version of Presley with long hair braided over her shoulder. *Scarlett.* Presley's twin sister. Behind her stood Luke, the chief of police who had to know that I'd burned down a building in his community. Any minute now he'd probably haul out the handcuffs and drag me to jail.

Scarlett had to hate me. My father had kidnapped her. But the smile she gave me was a lot like her sister's. No hate. Just caution. Luke, on the other hand, grinned like he knew I was expecting the cuffs and he thought it was funny.

Emmett just gave me a wink.

The door opened and a beautiful redhead walked inside with a bouquet of balloons in one hand. "Hey. Sorry we're late."

Cassandra. The Warriors had kidnapped her too.

Leo came inside behind Cassandra with the most precious baby girl in his arms. Neither seemed fazed to see me. They came inside like they'd been here a hundred times. Cassandra handed over the balloons to Presley and then stopped before me to study my face.

There was pity in her gaze. It was worse than suspicion. I inched back, ready to retreat to the closet, when Cassandra's face softened and she pulled me into a hug.

She hugged me.

How did she know I'd needed one?

"I'm Cass."

"H-hi."

She let me go and glanced over her shoulder at Leo, then took their daughter from his arms before going to Emmett's side for a hug. "Happy birthday."

His birthday had been months ago.

"We postponed his party," Presley said at the confusion on my face.

"Postponed. Because . . . right." Because I'd burned down the clubhouse. My face flamed and even though I wanted to drop my chin, go back to bed and hide under the covers, I stayed strong and looked up at Leo.

He shrugged. "We've all wanted to burn that place down once or twice in our lives."

"True," Dash said, sliding off his stool at the island to join us. "Hey, Nova."

"Hi, Dash."

His beautiful wife appeared at his side, looping one arm around his waist and holding the other out to me. Her handshake was firm. Businesslike. This was a stretch for them all, but I'd give them credit for trying.

"I'm Bryce," she said. "Sorry we invaded your house but if we had asked, Emmett would have told us no. We're 'beg for forgiveness, not ask for permission' sort of people."

A nervous laugh bubbled free from my mouth. "I can relate."

She nodded for me to follow her into the kitchen, where I met Genevieve, Isaiah and their kids.

The party was actually nothing more than a Saturday barbeque except with balloons and cake. Whatever gifts they'd gotten for him he'd received on his actual birthday, which was nice because I didn't feel left out. And otherwise, it was surprisingly fun.

His friends pulled me into their circle. The day passed

without any discussion of the Tin Gypsies or the Arrowhead Warriors. When the party ended, hours later, I knew deep in my soul that there'd be no need to ask for their forgiveness. It would take some time to get to know each other. To trust. But forgiveness?

They'd given it before I'd even arrived in Clifton Forge.

It was dark by the time everyone began shuffling to their cars. They'd spent the entire day at our house, the guys watching a football game while I'd been encircled by their wives.

Genevieve was a lawyer and the two of us had chatted about her work. They'd all been interested to know what I'd be doing in town and if I'd open my own practice. *Maybe.*

Maybe I'd work as a freelance legal consultant. Maybe I'd find a job that had nothing to do with the law. My life was full of *maybes* at the moment.

Except Emmett.

He was my constant.

"Next week, our place," Leo said.

"Sounds good." Emmett nodded and handed over a sleeping Seraphina. She'd fallen asleep in Emmett's arms and he seemed reluctant to let her go.

Seeing Emmett with a baby brought up a lot of questions, ones I was desperate to ask, but I had held my tongue.

Did he want kids? Did he want marriage? Before I'd moved in, we probably should have talked about both, because it might crush my dreams if he didn't want a family. I'd take him anyway, but having his baby was an idea that had bloomed after seeing him with Seraphina.

"Let me know what we can bring," I told Cass, touching the soft skin on her daughter's cheek.

"I'll text you." She hugged me goodbye, then did the same with Emmett before sweeping outside with Leo.

"Well?" Emmett asked as he closed the door and took my hand, leading me to the bedroom.

"You were right." His friends had deserved every ounce of his faith.

He shot me a smirk and tucked me into his side. He didn't drag me to bed like I'd hoped. Instead, he brought me to the closet, where he took a hoodie from a hanger and tugged it over my head. Then he pulled on his own sweat-shirt, swiped my hand again and towed me to the deck.

Past the overhang, the railing was dusted with snow. The air was crisp and the night dark, the stars fighting to peek through the clouds that drifted by on the calm breeze.

Emmett sat in his chair, making room for me between his legs.

I settled into the seat, leaning against his chest.

There'd been a lot of good conversations here. Also some not so good. The last had been the night of the clubhouse.

We hadn't sat out here since, even after unpacking yesterday.

Proving he had a direct link to my brain, Emmett held me tighter. "Doesn't matter."

"We should talk about it."

"Someday," he whispered. "But not tonight."

"Okay." I relaxed into his chest, not wanting to ruin the night.

"How about right there?" He raised a hand and pointed to the small clearing in the tree line. It was beyond the boundary of his yard, not that you could see it with the snow, but I'd spent enough time here that I knew the yard like it was my own.

346

I guess . . . it was my own.

"Right there for what?"

He shifted us, pushing me so that I leaned against one arm while his hand dove into the pocket of his jeans.

I wasn't sure what I was expecting, maybe a key to the house or something, but a diamond ring was not it.

"How about we get married right there?"

My mouth fell open as he picked up my left hand and slid it onto my ring finger. The solitaire jewel caught the warm light streaming from inside. The platinum band was studded with smaller stones that sparkled as bright as the stars that chose that moment to shine through.

"Ace . . ."

"That a yes?"

I twisted to look at him, his handsome face blurring with tears. "Yes."

He flashed me a blinding smile that disappeared when his lips crashed on mine.

———

FIVE MONTHS LATER, when the forest was teeming with wildflowers and the smell of spring infused the air, we stood in that clearing.

Emmett made me his wife.

He became my husband.

And we stepped into the future, forging a life together, and leaving the past on the road behind us.

EPILOGUE
NOVA

F*ive years later . . .*
    "There are so many." I took in the sea of motorcycles crammed into the lot at the garage. More waited on the street.

"Over fifty." Emmett stood behind me, his arms wrapped around my chest as he took them all in.

"I'm proud of you for doing this."

He dropped his chin to the top of my head. "Dad would have loved it."

"He's watching. Draven too."

"Yeah. I think he is."

The door to the garage's office opened and Dash strode out with Bryce close behind. Both wore huge smiles and mirrored sunglasses for today's ride.

Presley came out next, walking to where Shaw sat on his own bike beside us. "Be safe."

"I will." He kissed her cheek, then laid his hands on her belly.

Pres was eight months pregnant with their third baby so

she'd be staying at the garage, taking charge of prep for the barbeque that would follow the ride.

Scarlett came out of the office last, walking over to say goodbye to Luke, who was riding Emmett's bike. Luke didn't ride much but it had meant a lot to Emmett that he'd come on today's trip. That his friend had volunteered to bring his bike so that Emmett and I could ride Stone's.

"Have fun." Presley cast a longing glance to the crowd. "I wish I could go too."

"Next year," I told her.

"Definitely." She nodded and rubbed her huge belly. "We'll be here when you all get back."

Genevieve and Isaiah emerged from the apartment above the garage's office and started down the metal staircase.

Their daughter, Amelia, came rushing out behind them. Next came Seraphina, and the girls giggled and whispered in each other's ears as they descended the stairs. Those two were inseparable. Not just friends, but best friends.

Our crew had grown over the years and with the kids so clustered together in age, there was always someone to play with. There was always a friend. Sure, there was the rare fight and as they became teenagers those would probably grow in frequency, but we were close and the arguments never lasted long.

Bryce, Genevieve, Presley, Scarlett and Cass were sisters of my heart. Like the men were all brothers. It had taken time to let go of the past, but we'd all put in the work. Now, this was our family.

And today was an important day for us all.

The kids would hang out at the garage today while the adults were on the ride. The apartment above the office was staged as kid central, with a TV and video games and board games and books and art supplies. The older kids had room to run and explore while the little ones had a place to crash.

"Where are Zeke and Xander?" Bryce scanned the crowd as she came to stand beside Dash's bike.

"I saw them disappear behind the shop with a football," I said.

"Sounds about right."

Asher, Genevieve and Isaiah's son, had been with them, along with Presley and Shaw's son Nico. Noah, their four-year-old, was in the apartment with his cousins Parker and Simon. Mary, Scarlett and Luke's oldest, would probably join the girls later, but it was no surprise that she'd rushed around the building to play football with the boys. Of all the kids, she loved sports the most.

Cass's red hair caught the sunlight, shining copper and orange as she came down the stairs with her and Leo's two-year-old, Farah. Behind her, Cherie emerged with Talulah holding on to one hand and Neal on the other.

The sight of my children put a smile on my face as they carefully moved down the stairs, coming to give us a sendoff.

Emmett let me go and bent as our four-year-old daughter spotted him, then sprinted into his arms. He tossed her giggling body into the air, her dark hair fanning out as he caught her. "Hi, princess. You be good for Grammy, okay?"

"Okay, Daddy."

"Mama." Neal toddled my way and I swept him up, kissing his cheek before settling him on a hip. He pointed wildly to all of the bikes. "Bike. Bike."

"Yes, those are bikes."

"Bike." He pointed them out, one by one. "Bike."

"Thanks, Mom." Emmett pulled Cherie into a sideways hug.

"Of course." She smiled and took in the crowd. "This sure is something."

There were happy tears in Cherie's eyes when she looked at me. As far as mothers-in-law went, I'd scored the jackpot. Not only was she an amazing grandmother to my kids, but she loved me like her own.

"All right." Dash clapped his hands and straddled his bike. "Should we do this?"

"Hell, yeah." Emmett set Talulah down and I passed Neal on to Cherie, waiting as they made their way to the office door and out of harm's way.

Dash glanced over his shoulder and smiled at his brother, Nick, and Nick's wife, Emmeline, who'd come to town for today's ride. Then Bryce climbed on the back of Dash's bike.

It was time to ride.

Dash started his engine first. The minute I was on the seat behind Emmett, he started his. The noise was a chain reaction, starting from the front of the group to those who'd parked back where the clubhouse had once been.

The roar of the engines was deafening under the July sunshine. The vibrations from the motorcycles behind us shook the earth.

"This is awesome!" Bryce shouted, her voice barely rising above the rumble. My friend looked as beautiful as ever as she turned her head to the blue sky and laughed.

Today was the first annual Clifton Forge Motorcycle Club charity ride.

Pride swelled in my chest as Emmett turned to Dash. The two friends—two brothers—shared a look that made it hard to breathe.

This ride was for their fathers. For Draven. For Stone.

Leo waited on Dash's other side with a hand pressed to his heart.

Dash gave Emmett a nod. Then another to Leo. Then he twisted to kiss his wife before holding one arm in the air.

The engines behind us revved and if the noise had been loud before, it was otherworldly now. It felt like Mother Earth herself was here with us, giving us her hum of approval.

Dash's hand dropped to a handlebar and he shot out of the parking lot, Bryce clinging to his waist as they started down the road.

"Ready, baby?" Emmett asked over his shoulder.

"Ready, Ace."

"I love you."

I kissed his cheek. "I love you too."

Then we were off, racing down the street.

Leo appeared at our side, keeping pace as we caught up to Dash and flanked his side. Cass smiled at me as she pressed her cheek to Leo's spine.

We'd all come to the garage early today to start setting up. While we'd been folding bandanas to give to today's riders, Cass and Leo had announced she was pregnant again with their third baby. She wanted a boy so badly that I prayed she got her wish.

Isaiah and Genevieve rode behind us. Genevieve's smile lit up her pretty face. Beside them rode Luke on Emmett's bike and Shaw on his own.

Emmett's hand dropped to my thigh, holding it there as we rolled through town toward the highway.

The plethora of riders behind us was nothing short of amazing.

At Christmas this year, we'd been sitting around at our house, letting the kids play with new toys, when the guys had started to reminisce about the good times they'd had with the club. Nearly every story had centered around a ride or trip and the fun they'd found along the road.

As the conversation had evolved, it had been Bryce who'd suggested they create a new club.

That day, the Clifton Forge Motorcycle Club had been reborn.

It was a tribute to Dash's grandfather, who'd started a club of the same name years and years ago, before it had turned into the Tin Gypsy Motorcycle Club.

There was no clubhouse. There were no meetings. This new club wore no patches.

We were all in our regular clothes today, though I'd swapped my heels for the pair of boots I wore on our longer rides. Emmett had tied a black bandana on his head, trapping his hair out of his face. My own was braided down my back to keep it from tangling.

We were simply riders today, joined by others from across the state to raise money for the Slater-Stone Memorial Foundation.

It was an organization that we'd started just months ago as the idea for this new club had started coming together. The money raised from this inaugural ride would go to kids in the area who wanted to go to trade school, to learn to be mechanics or welders or plumbers. The programs were endless and if it helped kids pay for their education, it would be money well spent.

I'd taken the lead in forming the foundation. My practice specialized in business law, so I'd happily volunteered to tackle the legal aspects.

After I'd moved to Clifton Forge, I'd taken six months off of work. I'd spent that time planning our wedding and reflecting. Healing.

Emmett and I had spent long hours talking about both the Tin Gypsies and the Arrowhead Warriors. He'd shared his stories and I'd shared what my father had told me. And after it had all come out, slowly and unhurried because each conversation came with an influx of pain, I'd discovered that most of what Dad had told me had been a lie.

Whatever his reason, whether to manipulate me or because those stories were Dad's warped version of events, it didn't matter. Too many lives had been lost, so I'd put it behind me.

We all had.

I'd decided to start my own practice, not wanting to completely forsake my education. Maybe law school hadn't been my idea but I'd worked my ass off to graduate and pass the bar. Maybe I didn't love my job, but it was a good job and since my practice was a practice of one—me—it allowed me to work from home. To stay close to my babies.

Because the job I truly loved with every fiber of my being was being a mother.

Three days a week, we had a nanny come over to watch the kids while Emmett and I worked. The other two days, Cherie insisted on babysitting. And because I was there, my office in the basement and just a floor away, I didn't feel like I was missing out on their lives.

Talulah and Neal were our priority and work simply a means to ensure they had a head start in life.

The sun shone down on us as we rode toward the highway. I breathed in the summer air, glad there wasn't a cloud in the sky. This ride would last a couple of hours, a big loop around the county until we came back to Clifton Forge for a barbeque.

The place where the clubhouse had been was now an enormous cement pad complete with an overhang. It was full of picnic tables and benches. The guys had built a firepit on the lot and put in a playground for our kids.

Tonight's barbeque was catered. There'd be a roast pig and kegs and live music. Dash, Emmett and Leo had insisted that we throw a party Draven and Stone would have been proud to attend.

But I knew, even if the only riders on the road had been the three of them, their fathers would have been proud.

"You good?" Emmett called over his shoulder as we followed Dash onto the highway.

I answered with a kiss to his shoulder. To the place where he'd put the tattoo of our children's names. Mine, he'd tattooed across his heart.

With a quick smile over his shoulder that told me we were about to take off, I held him tighter.

And then we flew.

Together.

We'd always been stronger together. Unbeatable.

In the five years since we'd been married, I hadn't heard from my father. There'd been nothing from any of the Warriors and as the years ticked by, I believed Dad's promise. He'd let go of his revenge.

For me. Because I'd asked him to.

I liked to think that he loved me in his own fucked-up way.

My sister and I had spent long hours debating if we should reach out to our half-sisters in South Carolina, but in the end, we'd decided not to. They didn't know about us, and no matter what relationship they had with our father, it would only bring pain.

Besides, we had each other. Though I didn't get to see May as often as I would like, we talked on the phone a few times a week. Her kids were growing as fast as my own and our annual summer trip to Missoula to spend a week with them was coming in August. Mom was already preparing her house for our invasion.

The countryside passed in a streak of green fields, blue mountains and blinding smiles. Dash and Bryce were in the lead, then behind us were Leo and Cass. We'd all formed a single line. A trail of riders behind them stretched for miles.

"I love you," I told Emmett, leaning close enough he could hear me over the whipping wind.

"I love you."

Then I kissed his shoulder once more, holding tight with my legs so I could let go with my arms and feel the wind, like I did on all of our rides. Like I'd done since the beginning when I had yet to realize that the man I'd been meant to ride through life with was Emmett.

He'd set me free.

We'd set each other free.

His queen. And my Ace.

BONUS EPILOGUE
EMMETT

This was goddamn terrifying.

Sitting in the passenger seat of a car that my daughter was attempting to drive was absolutely terrifying. Not only because she was an awful driver but because before too long, we'd set her loose. She'd be on the road alone and there was another level of fear knowing that she was growing up. That soon, she'd be out of my reach.

"Ease off the gas."

Talulah's fists strangled the wheel as her foot came completely off the pedal. I loved that my girl preferred the brake, and that she was arguably as scared as I was. Maybe that fear would keep her safe.

God, I hoped so.

She hit the blinker, signaling we were turning off the highway, and as she made a too-wide turn, then overcorrected, I sent up a silent prayer of thanks as the tires hit our private lane. Then I breathed for the first time in an hour.

"Good job, princess."

"Thanks, Daddy." Her smile was so wide that it twisted

my heart. She only called me Daddy when it was just the two of us. Otherwise, I was Dad.

She pulled the SUV we'd bought her into the driveway and parked. My heart dropped from my throat the minute the vehicle was off and my boots were on the ground.

Talulah gave me another smile as she ran for the front door, disappearing inside with her long brown hair streaming behind her as she ran.

I followed, taking a few deep breaths as the adrenaline rush ebbed. Goddamn. We had fifty-something hours left of driving practice. I wasn't sure my heart could stand the strain.

"It was so easy." My daughter's voice greeted me as I came inside and closed the door.

In the kitchen, she was telling Neal all about our excursion.

"I bet you're a bad driver." Tormenting his sister was a favorite pastime. "I bet you almost crashed."

"No, I didn't." She put her hands on her hips and shot him a glare. At fifteen, she was as tall as Nova.

Neal stood just an inch shorter than she did and it wouldn't be long before he towered over both his sister and his mother. "Dad, is she a bad driver?"

"No," I lied, going straight for the fridge for an overdue beer. "She just needs some practice."

"See?" Talulah smirked at her brother, then twirled out of the kitchen and vanished down the hallway, probably rushing to her bedroom to call or text her friends.

Nova had mentioned something about a potential boyfriend but I'd blocked out every word of that conversation. Talulah was only fifteen. I wasn't ready for a boyfriend yet.

"Dad, can I go to Parker's tonight?" Neal asked.

"You didn't mow the lawn."

"I was gonna do it right now."

Sure he was. "You mow the lawn and clean your room, then I'll drive you to Parker's."

"On it." He raced past me for the garage and not a minute later, I heard the engine to the mower start.

Luke had texted earlier and asked if Neal could spend the night. I'd already agreed but if I had told Neal that, I wouldn't have had the leverage to get him to mow and clean. I'd told Talulah this morning that I'd take her driving if she weeded her mother's flower beds before noon.

Motivating teenage kids was all about the leverage.

I took my beer to the deck, where a pair of long legs beckoned.

Nova was in her seat, a book in her lap, but she wasn't reading. Instead, her gaze was on the trees and the clearing where we'd gotten married.

"Hey, baby." I bent to kiss her head.

"Hi, Ace." She put her book aside, shoving her sunglasses into her hair. "How'd it go?"

I took a seat, then raised the beer bottle to my lips and gulped.

"That bad?"

"You'll find a dozen new gray hairs tonight. And you get to do the next lesson."

"Oh, no. Definitely not. You're in charge of driving practice."

"What?"

"I explained periods. And sex."

"So?"

"So we're dividing and conquering here. She's due for a

discussion on birth control. If I do driving practice, you have to tackle the pill."

"No." I grimaced. "I've got driving."

"Good." My wife reached over and snatched my beer, taking a long sip before handing it back. "How did the car work?"

"Fine." We'd bought Talulah a midsize SUV to drive. Neither of us wanted her in the Nova or maneuvering my massive truck, so we'd found her something safe that wasn't new in case she did crash it.

For Neal, we'd be buying a complete and total piece of shit because that kid was wild. If he drove a car the way he drove our riding lawn mower, God help the citizens of Clifton Forge.

He came whipping around the corner of the house, blazing a green trail in his wake. He had headphones in, his head bobbing to the music, and the mower was running at top speed. That kid took life as fast as he could go. In a way, he reminded me of Dash, who'd earned his nickname for the same reason.

"God, he scares me on that thing." Nova shook her head, her eyes glued to the yard.

"He'll be fine." One of these days, he'd slow down. It might take until he was thirty, but eventually, he'd take it easy.

"What do you want to do for dinner?" she asked.

"I was going to cook you tacos."

She smiled. "I was hoping you'd say that."

There wasn't much I wouldn't do to earn those smiles.

Never in my life had I expected to be this happy. But with my wife and my kids . . . this was the dream. I wished Dad were around to see it. To know my family.

"So . . . I walked down to the mailbox," she said, reaching for her book and pulling out a plain white envelope. "I got this."

"What is it?" I took it from her and froze at the return address.

The Montana State Penitentiary.

Tucker.

"What the fuck?"

In all our years together, we hadn't heard from him. Ever since the day Nova had walked out of the prison, he'd been nothing more than a ghost. And the Warriors had never bothered us again.

We had peace.

My wife—this beautiful, strong woman—had put an end to something that none of the men would have been able to. It had come at the cost of a father. She'd paid it and I'd forever be grateful.

It had taken years for Nova to come to terms with it all, to adjust to the truth and move past Tucker's lies. But she'd put it behind her.

And now that son of a bitch was writing her.

"Breathe, Ace. It's not bad."

I clenched my jaw. "You should have waited to read it until I was here."

"Probably." She stole my beer again and this time didn't give it back.

I pulled the paper out of the envelope and unfolded the sheet. There was only one sentence on the page and a scribbled signature at the bottom.

"That's it?" I read it again. Then a third time. Definitely not what I'd expected. Though . . . I hadn't given Tucker

Talbot a lot of thought over the years, so I guess I wasn't sure what to expect.

"Yup." Nova sipped her beer.

"He wants new pictures of the kids."

She nodded.

"New pictures. Meaning . . ."

"He has old ones."

"From who?"

"I'm guessing my mom must have sent him photos."

No surprise. January loved Tucker. She always would. And even though Tucker had told her not to contact him, even though her daughters had reiterated that message, January had done it anyway.

None of us would ever tell her that he was a lying motherfucker, because January was one of the sweetest, kindest women on the planet. She didn't deserve that sort of heartache. How she'd gotten mixed up with Tucker in the first place was something I'd never understand.

"Did your mom stop sending them to him or something?" I asked.

Nova shrugged. "Hell if I know. We've been so busy she hasn't seen the kids in a while."

And leveraging our teenagers into a family photo was no easy feat. Either Tucker was impatient, or this was his way of reengaging contact with Nova.

Later, I'd call Jack and find out if May had received the same sort of letter.

Nova kept her eyes on Neal as he continued to ride like he was in the lawn mower speed derby. No way she was letting that kid on a bike before he was eighteen. I wouldn't even argue. He could master four wheels before we gave him two.

"What do you want to do?" I folded up the letter.

"I want you to decide for me."

"Then I'll say yes."

Her face whipped to mine. "Seriously? I was sure you'd say no."

I stretched for my beer bottle, which was mostly empty. "He's left us alone all these years. If the asshole wants pictures of his grandkids to brighten the walls of his prison cell, so be it. If it means we keep the peace, so be it."

I would never forgive Tucker for the pain he'd caused me. Or the pain he'd caused Nova. But I loved my family more than I hated him. A few pictures to a man I'd never see again was worth it to ensure he stayed mollified in that goddamn cell.

"You okay?" I asked.

"No." Nova stood, coming to my chair.

I shifted and made room for her between my legs, then wrapped an arm around her to pull her close and kiss her hair. "I love you."

"I love you too." She relaxed into my embrace. "Now I'm okay."

This was how we'd dealt with the hard moments. Together. And usually on this deck. My life hadn't been the same since Nova had stormed in, a beautiful fury in six-inch heels.

She was the queen at my back, the most powerful player in the game.

I was her Ace up the sleeve.

And together we'd won every game.

ACKNOWLEDGMENTS

Thank you for reading *Tin Queen*! This series has been an amazing journey for me as a writer, and saying goodbye to these characters is bittersweet. The Clifton Forge crew will always hold a piece of my heart. When I introduced Dash in *The Clover Chapel*, I had no idea that years later, we'd be here. That I'd love the Tin Gypsy books so incredibly much. For everyone who's been with me to the end of this series, thank you!

Special thanks to my editing and proofreading team: Elizabeth, Julie, Karen and Judy. Thank you to Hang Le for the cover. Thanks to my agent, Kimberly, and the team at Brower Literary. And my publicist, Nina, and the team at Valentine PR. Thank you to the fantastic bloggers who read and promote my stories.

A massive thanks to the members of Perry and Nash. I love that you love the Tin Gypsies. I am so grateful for your daily encouragement and the joy you bring to my life.

To my friends and family, I am so blessed to have you all. Thank you for being the best support squad in the world.

ABOUT THE AUTHOR

Devney is a *USA Today* bestselling author who lives in Washington with her husband and two sons. Born and raised in Montana, she loves writing books set in her treasured home state. After working in the technology industry for nearly a decade, she abandoned conference calls and project schedules to enjoy a slower pace at home with her family. Writing one book, let alone many, was not something she ever expected to do. But now that she's discovered her true passion for writing romance, she has no plans to ever stop.

Don't miss out on Devney's latest book news.
Subscribe to her newsletter!
www.devneyperry.com